Robin Pilcher has worked as a f̶a̶... and PR consultant before beco̶... ...e writer. Son of bestselling novelist Rosamunde Pilcher, Robin is married with four children and lives near Dundee, his birthplace. He is the author of three other bestselling books, two of which, *A Risk Worth Taking* and *Starting Over*, are currently being made into films.

For more information about the author, visit his website at
www.robinpilcher.co.uk

Praise for *An Ocean Apart*

'Sensitive and compulsive'
Mail on Sunday

'[A] perfectly constructed fairytale of loss and recovery'
The Times

'A total tear-jerker'
Woman's Journal

'An ideal read for a lazy winter weekend'
Woman and Home

For *Starting Over*

'Compulsive, sensitive and at times quite funny; one
wonders why Pilcher didn't take up writing years ago'
Ireland on Sunday

For *A Risk Worth Taking*

'A beautiful and heart warming tale . . . written with
both style and sensitivity'
Scottish Daily Record

'An absorbing story'
Woman's Day

STARBURST

Robin Pilcher

SPHERE

First published in the United States of America by Thomas Dunne Books,
an imprint of St. Martin's Press
First published in Great Britain in 2007 by Sphere
This paperback edition published in 2008 by Sphere
Reprinted in 2008 (four times)

A CIP catalogue record for this book is available from the British Library.

ISBN 978-0-7515-3857-1

Typeset in Bembo by Palimpsest Book Production Limited,
Grangemouth, Stirlingshire
Printed and bound in Great Britain by Clays Ltd, St Ives plc

Papers used by Sphere are natural, renewable and recyclable
products made from wood grown in sustainable forests and certified
in accordance with the rules of the Forest Stewardship Council.

Sphere
An imprint of
Little, Brown Book Group
100 Victoria Embankment
London EC4Y 0DY

An Hachette Livre UK Company
www.hachettelivre.co.uk

www.littlebrown.co.uk

This book is dedicated to the memories of
two incandescent fireflies,

JOANNA and HENRIETTA MACRAE

Who held the Big Umbrella
While Rowena played her fiddle
On the castle esplanade

Acknowledgements

There are many aspects of this book that had never been covered by my own experiences, so I had to rely on quite lengthy research to make it seem as authentic as possible. I am therefore indebted to the following people:

Wilf Scott, MVO, Master Pyrotechnic, of Pyrovision
Owen O'Leary of the Edinburgh Festival Fringe
Susie Burnet of the Edinburgh International Festival
Alistair Rae of Hartlepool Borough Council
Christine Beroff of Le Conservatoire National Supérieur de
    Musique et de Danse de Paris
Harry Bell of Tern Television
Sergeant Wilson Gove of Tayside Police, Traffic Division
Roddie Urquhart of A& WM Urquhart, WS
Amanda Bower of the Sheraton Grand Hotel, Edinburgh
Sarah Rymer, concert violinist
Graham Nicholson for his knowledge of Edinburgh
Anna Wemyss for her knowledge of the Underbelly
Jamie and Sarah Jauncey for brainstorming Dessuin with me.

Also my daughter, Alice, who helped me work on the younger characters in the book, and my daughter-in-law, Abi, who gave me valuable assistance with the Edinburgh vernacular!

Walking around Edinburgh in late July, you'll likely feel the first vibrations of the earthquake that is festival time, which shakes the city throughout August and into September. You may hear reference to an 'Edinburgh Festival', but this is really an umbrella term for six separate festivals all taking place around the same time.

The best-known and oldest of these is the Edinburgh International Festival. The festival was founded in 1947, when Europe was recovering from World War II. Festival founders believed that some event was needed to draw the continent together and 'provide a platform for the flowering of the human spirit'.

In recent years, the festival has drawn as many as 400,000 people to Edinburgh, with acts by world-renowned music, opera, theatre, and dance performers, filling all the major venues in the city.

Edinburgh festival time can fill almost any artistic need . . . Edinburgh in August is an experience you are unlikely to forget!

– The New York Times

One

The confetti was a bit of a mystery. Two weeks after the wedding and the multicoloured flakes still kept appearing in every room of the flat. Sometimes they materialised in force under the new king-sized bed or piled up in small drifts behind the television in the sitting room; other times no more than a single fragment floated delicately on toaster thermals around the kitchen. At first, despite the need to vacuum every room on a daily basis, its presence had given Tess a warming sense of fulfilment, a constant reminder of everything that had happened on her Big Day. But now, as she pulled the polo-necked jersey from the top shelf of her wardrobe and a fresh flurry drifted down on to the polished floorboards of the bedroom, she felt it was all becoming a bit of an inconvenience and, like thawing snow, it had been around too long.

Tess had a sneaking suspicion that it was Allan who was to blame for it all. She had visions of him tiptoeing about the flat, sprinkling the tissue petals around like love dust so as to keep the spirit of their wedding day alive. But when she had broached the subject on the previous morning as he stood stark-naked shaving in front of the full-length bathroom mirror, he had rather disappointingly denied the whole idea. 'Nice thought, angel' – mouth to the left as he scraped away at the right cheek – 'but I'm afraid it's not been me' – chin pulled down for more scraping under nose – 'probably like sand after being on a beach,' – turns to look at newly wedded wife with perfectly formed shaving-foam goatee and gesticulates with razor in hand – 'you know, you find it between your toes and in your belly button and other places for days afterwards.'

That had been enough for Tess. The thought of 'other places' had cut any notion of romantic frivolity from her mind.

Seated on the edge of the bed, Tess pulled on her brown leather calf-length boots, wrestled the legs of her jeans over them, and then got up and walked over to open the wooden shutters on one of the room's tall sash-framed windows. Her spirits, which had been flying at Learjet height since the wedding, sank a little when she looked out on to another grey day in the Scottish capital. She could tell by the movement of the leafless trees just visible up by Heriot Row and by the way the pedestrians on the pavement below walked up Dundas Street clutching their coats closed at the neck, that the wind was coming from the north, sweeping cold and unguarded across the Firth of Forth. Spring is a season that's lost its reason, she thought to herself. The beginning of May and it could as well be February. An icy draught sought out a space at the side of the ancient window frame, surrounding her with a chill that made her shiver and clasp her hands under her armpits. It was about the one thing, being married, that she – regretted, having to leave her cosy little tenement block flat in West College Street and move here to Allan's great barn of a place, situated in the infinitely smarter New Town.

Tess picked up her mobile from the bedside table and thumbed a couple of buttons. She held it to her ear as she pulled on her woollen jacket and shouldered the strap of her laptop case. When Allan eventually answered, his greeting was unintelligible through a mouthful of food.

'It's me,' Tess said, picking up her keys from the table in the hallway.

She heard Allan swallow. 'I know. Your name came up. Sex Maniac.'

'It does not say that!'

'No, you're right. It says Mrs Goodwin.'

The name change was something else Tess was having diffi-culty getting used to. Back in her schooldays, her jotters had been covered with the test autographs of soon-to-be-famous Tess

Hartley, but now her pen found it impossible to flow from the *s* of Tess to the *G* of Goodwin, and her signature had taken on the appearance of that of an incompetent forger.

'That's nice,' she said with a smile, as she double-locked the door of the flat and began descending the stone steps, the clipping heels of her boots echoing up the chilly stairwell.

'So, where are you?'

'Sitting in a traffic jam on the M8, twenty miles from Glasgow.'

'What time did you leave this morning?'

'Six-thirty. I would have woken you but you were out for the count, so I just gazed hungrily at you and left. Are you still in bed?'

'No, I'm on my way out.'

'My word, that's a bit keen, isn't it? It's only just gone seven-thirty.'

'I know, but I've got to be up at the Hub early. Alasdair's calling in from Budapest at eight.'

'What's he doing there?'

'Sounding out some dance company he thinks might fill an empty slot in the programme.'

'What gives with Sarah then? I thought she liked hogging the morning phone calls with the great Sir Alasdair Dreyfuss.'

Tess smiled wryly as she pulled shut the heavy entrance door and walked the few steps down on to the pavement. Allan was right. Sarah Atkinson, the marketing director of the Edinburgh International Festival and her own immediate boss, liked to be the one who liaised with the director, especially when he was on one of his incessant scouting missions abroad.

'She's down in England, having a meeting with the Royal Shakespeare Company,' she replied, glancing down Dundas Street to see if there was a bus in sight. A double-decker, resplendently dull in the Edinburgh corporation colours of maroon and dirty-white, stood at the traffic lights. 'What time do you think you'll be home?'

'Sevenish.'

'Fancy something to eat out?'

3

'No, I fancy you.'

Tess felt a loved-up glow swell in her stomach. 'I know it. But that doesn't answer my question.'

'OK, we'll eat out. Hey, looks like the traffic's starting to move. Better get off the phone. See ya, angel.'

'OK, see you tonight.'

Tess slipped her mobile into the pocket of her jacket and boarded the bus, waiting for an elderly grey-faced gentleman dressed in a creased pinstriped suit and carrying a weary-looking leather briefcase to clear the stairs before she climbed to the upper deck and jolted into a seat, as the bus took off.

It hadn't been the best time to get married, what with Allan just getting a promotion and her working all hours at the International Festival office, but then again it had almost come down to a 'make or break' situation. If anyone were to ask her, she would say they'd been together for just over three years, but in truth that was a bit of a generalisation. Their relationship had always blown hot and cold, even to the extent that for a four-month period two years ago they had taken a complete break from each other. During that time, they slalomed into affairs and crashed out of them, coming back together to lick their wounds and begin to piece together the shaky confidence they had in each other. Those on-the-side flings were easy to forgive. The one Tess had the following year was not, yet even though it rocked their boat quite forcefully, it never succeeded in capsizing it. And that was the danger. It was Allan who said their relationship had become too comfortable, almost verging on the platonic, and that neither was doing the other any favours by continuing to live without any form of commitment. So he proposed to her, and Tess had agreed without even giving the question any thought. It seemed the most natural thing to do. It was just they'd never got round to doing anything about it.

In the same way that they'd never got round to organising a honeymoon. After the wedding, they'd both taken a couple of days off work to move her belongings into Allan's flat, but neither felt it the right time to head off on holiday. Maybe she would get on to the Internet this morning, if there was no urgent business to attend to once she'd spoken to the director, and see if she couldn't book a couple of weeks in September after the festival had finished. Right now, on this cold, raw day, she fancied somewhere sunny and warm, somewhere that sounded exotic, with white sandy beaches and palm trees and a blue sea that merged into the sky on the horizon. She smiled to herself and nodded decisively. Yes, somewhere like Barbados would just fit the bill nicely, thank you very much.

As the bus took the lights on Queen Street and edged its way slowly up the slope, Tess rubbed the sleeve of her jacket on the steamed-up window and gazed out at the sight of Edinburgh's citizens walking to work. Men and women dressed alike in formal, colourless clothes, adding to the general drabness of the day, but apt apparel for those who earned their daily crust in the city's many financial and legal institutions. It never ceased to amaze Tess that a city that seemed to wallow in a state of such stolid lugubriousness for most of the year should, for three weeks in August, suddenly behave as if its water supply had been spiked with amphetamine. But she knew only too well that this dichotomy had existed since the festival's inception in 1947, and even though it was now regarded as one of the foremost artistic and cultural gatherings in the world, it had only been in the past ten years that the opinion of the archetypal 'Edinburgh citizen' had really changed towards the event. Up until then, it had been viewed as a dreaded yearly inconvenience when taxis were impossible to find and restaurants were crowded out. Little was made of the cultural kudos the festival brought to the city, nor of the extra revenue generated for its businesses and householders by the thousands of visitors who came for those three late summer weeks every year. There was no doubt in the minds of everyone who worked in the International office that the favourable change of opinion was due, in no small part, to the present director, Sir Alasdair Dreyfuss, but he himself would be the first to deny it, being as reticent about promoting his own sizeable achievements as he was about using the 'handle' of his recently awarded knighthood.

Tess got off the bus and began to walk up Lawnmarket, the uppermost stretch of the Royal Mile. This was where she felt comfortable, the Old Town, with its small-windowed buildings of ancient, gnarled stone, its cobbled streets, its more youthful and exuberant inhabitants, its seedy but atmospheric public houses, its tacky tourist shops, selling everything from ghost tours to tartan ginger-wigged tammies, CDs of wailing Gaelic love songs, weaponry – the genuine article, of course – used by the Highland clans to fight the Jacobite cause in 1745; claymores so blunt that they would hardly give a clumsy sword dancer a bleeding toe, and studded-leather shields that bore not even the faintest scratch of a Redcoat bayonet. Every weekday morning, Tess made the journey from the New Town and it never ceased to give her a frisson of excitement to be back in her old stamping ground.

Crossing over the street, she entered the warm, aromatic interior of a Starbucks café, one of the few insurgent establishments in the street. As she took her place in the queue, two away from being served, the entrance door crashed shut behind her. Everyone in the chrome-strewn place looked up, clasping hands to rattling cups in saucers, deactivating jaws on half-eaten blueberry muffins to stare at the door, expecting the logo-ed glass pane to come crashing to the ground. When nothing happened, the stares were shifted to the young man with the frenzied mop of dark curly hair that spilled on to the shoulders of his far-too-large blue serge overcoat. He stood in front of the door breathing heavily, his hands held up as if surrendering, his eyes tightly closed and a pained expression on his face.

'Sorry . . . sorry . . . sorry.' He opened up one eye and surveyed his scornful audience. 'Sorry?'

Tess decided to help him out. 'That was some entrance, Lewis,' she said with a smile.

The young man took a couple of steps towards her. 'It was your fault, Tess,' he said quietly to her in a lilting Welsh accent.

'What d' you mean, *my* fault?'

'Well, I was just about to go into the Fringe office when I saw you get off the bus, so I've just had to run all the way up the High Street to catch you.'

Tess stared at him blankly for a few seconds, scanning through her memory files to work out if she'd forgotten an appointment or to make a telephone call. Lewis Jones was her direct contemporary in the marketing team of the Fringe, one of the seven independently organised festivals that were run under the conglomerate title of the Edinburgh Festival. Although their events were managed separately, each office still liaised closely on city issues and the general organisation of the Festival.

'What was so urgent?'

Lewis shrugged. 'Nothing, really. I just wanted to ask how married life was treating you. I haven't seen you since your big day.'

Maybe it *was* just the accent, but Tess was always aware of Lewis's disarming quality of being able to make people feel sorry for him. Right now, she felt like patting him on the head like a little boy and telling him not to get himself so worried – which was ridiculous, really. Not only did she know that Lewis was just shy of his thirtieth birthday – almost her twin, in fact – but also that he was a very shrewd operator, helping to co-ordinate in his laid-back-to-almost-horizontal way the logisitics for nearly two thousand performers during the three weeks of the Fringe.

'It's – very exciting,' Tess replied with a nod of affirmation. 'I strongly recommend it.'

Lewis sighed. 'No one on the horizon for me, I'm afraid.' He stepped in front of Tess when the girl behind the counter asked for the next order. 'Here, let me buy you a coffee and we can have a chat.'

'I can't, Lewis, sorry. I've got to be in the office in less than five minutes for a telephone call.' Tess turned to the girl behind the counter. 'A cappuccino to go, please.'

'Oh, well, never mind,' Lewis said sombrely. As soon as the girl had slapped the lid on the paper cup and put it on the counter, he picked it up and gave it to Tess. 'Here you are, this one's on me. You'd better get going up the road.'

Tess shot him a smile. 'Thanks, Lewis. See you around.'

If Lewis said anything in reply, she didn't hear it. She left the coffee house at speed, and with one hand clutching the cup and the other preventing the laptop case from thumping against her side, she ran as fast as her tottering boots would allow her up Lawnmarket, a Cinderella figure whose sole objective was to be at her desk before the bells of some nearby clock tower struck out its eighth peal.

The offices and headquarters of Edinburgh International Festival are housed in a converted church at the very top of the Royal Mile, the building having lost its ecclesiastical name along with its pews and pulpit and been 'rechristened' the Hub. Pushing her way through two sets of swing-glass doors, Tess hurried along the central passage, at one time the aisle of the church, with the Hub café behind a long glass partition to one side and the International Ticket Office on the other. She took the staircase two at a time, past the bright-red wall with its random shelves of sculptured figurines, and as she stopped momentarily on the upper landing to catch her breath, she heard the telephone ringing in her office. She ran in and reached across the desk for the receiver, simultaneously ridding herself of the coffee cup and allowing her laptop case to fall from her shoulder on to the ground with an ominous thump.

'International office, good morning.'

'Good morning, Tess. It's Alasdair.'

'Oh, morning, Alasdair.' Tess stretched out the telephone cable with her free hand and walked around the desk to her seat. 'I'm sorry, have you rung before?'

'No, I left it a little later just to give you the chance to get into the office.'

Tess couldn't tell from his tone whether he had said it with any seriousness, but nevertheless she felt her face pulse with nervous embarrassment. Her boss, Sarah Atkinson, was *never* late for her early morning telephone call with the director.

'So, how're things in Budapest?'

'All right. The dance company is good, but I don't think the choreography is up to scratch, so I'm not going to risk booking them for this year. I'll maybe see if I can't fix up some sort of collaboration with Hans Meyer for next year. He'll be coming to direct the Rombert at any rate.'

'Nothing you want me to do from this end, then?' Tess asked, tapping the point of a ballpoint pen expectantly on her desk pad.

'Not for this project,' the director replied, 'but listen, when I was flying out here, I noticed in the newspaper that Angélique Pascal is playing at the Barbican this Thursday. I know it's a bit early for publicity, but seeing she's going to be the International's star turn this year, try tracking her down and organising an interview, and then give Harry Wills a call at the *Sunday Times*. There's every probability you'll get stalled by Albert Dessuin, her manager, but give it a go.'

Tess jotted the names down on her pad, but it was only as a reminder. Both names, especially that of the young French violinist, were well known to her. 'Anything else?' she asked.

'Yes, I want you to ring up Jeff Banyon at the Scottish Chamber Orchestra and ask him if it's definitely Tchaikovsky they're going to be doing for the fireworks at the end of the festival. If not, then we'll have to change our theme to accommodate whatever they've chosen. Now, do you have anything else for me?'

Tess searched the top of her desk for any messages others might have left for the director. 'No, nothing at all.'

'All right. I'll be back in the office tomorrow late afternoon, if all goes well with Air Paperclip. When does Sarah get back?'

'This afternoon.'

'OK, let her know I'll speak to her first thing tomorrow morning. Bye, Tess.'

Tess replaced the receiver and whistled out a breath of relief. She really liked the director but had always felt quite in awe of him. He had an unsettling manner that could be taken as being ice cold if one did not understand the constant pressure he was under, and coming up to working at her third festival in the International office, she felt only now that he treated her as an integral part of the team. Yet the story could have been completely different if he'd ever discovered what had happened over the course of the previous two festivals.

Her affair with Peter Hansen had been clandestine, exciting, and fired by the creative energy that thrummed through the city at the time of the festival. Peter was one of Denmark's top artistic directors, brought in by Sir Alasdair Dreyfuss on a two-year contract to direct a number of theatrical productions, and it had been the director himself who had given Tess the job of chaperoning the man. In his mid-forties, Peter was famous, charismatic, and a practised seducer, and Tess, having just become involved in her first festival, had been flattered by his attentions, and soon accepted her energetic sessions in one of Edinburgh's five-star hotels as part of her duty. She and Allan had been going through one of their 'cool' periods, and even though they were still seeing each other quite regularly, there was never a question of him finding out about it. There was always the excuse of a reception or a dinner she had to attend, or a late-night tour of the city's nightclubs, entertaining the visiting classical performers. So, when the second year came round, both she and Peter took up where they had left off, and Tess knew at every moment of their affair that it was underhand and dangerous, not least because Peter Hansen just happened to be one of Sir Alasdair Dreyfuss's oldest friends, and that for the past five years their respective families had joined together for skiing holidays in Norway.

It had all come to an abrupt end a week before the end of the previous festival. She arrived at work one morning to find a note on her desk from Sarah Atkinson saying that Peter Hansen had rung to say he had no further need for her services and that he would be leaving for Copenhagen the following night, immediately after the final performance of the play he had been directing. Tess tried to contact him on his mobile phone, but he never answered. In time, she came to understand that her useful-ness to Peter had run its course and that he had simply been using her as a form of diversion, just as he had probably done with a plethora of stupid, gullible young girls in cities where he had been working throughout the world.

Sir Alasdair Dreyfuss never found out about the affair. If he had done so, there was no doubt in her mind that she would have been thrown out of the International office without her feet touching the ground. But Allan had found out. It was her own fault, really, walking around in a gloomy daze and bursting into tears for no apparent reason. So when he eventually asked her what was wrong, she told him everything. It could have all ended there. That's what she was expecting, but instead dear, sweet Allan simply pulled his snivelling wreck of a girl-friend close to him, heaved out a long, painful breath and said, 'We're going to have to stop doing this to each other, Tess. We can't sustain a relationship when we're constantly ignoring the basic rules of trust and fidelity between us.' And just when she thought her own selfish stupidity had cost her the love of the one person for whom she had really cared, he said, 'Our only chance of survival is to get married. What d'you think?'

And she'd accepted without hesitation.

Tess jerked her head to break away from her thoughts, realising she had been sitting staring at the telephone ever since she had finished her call with the director. She leaned over and picked up her discarded case from the floor, unzipped it and placed her laptop on the desk. As it was booting up, she glanced at her watch and decided it was too early to start trying to trace the where-abouts of Angélique Pascal and her manager. Consequently, she thought it as well to wait until nine o'clock before making any of her telephone calls.

Which gave her all of forty-five minutes to do a Google

11

search on 'Barbados Holidays' and look for a September booking for her much-delayed honeymoon.

Two

Due to an inadequacy of space in the rented industrial unit on the outskirts of Cheltenham, the offices and storage facilities of the Exploding Sky Company had recently been moved to a block of outmoded farm buildings deep in the rolling country-side of the Cotswold Hills. Even though it was a transaction that had stretched the relationship with his bank manager to near breaking point, Roger Dent, sole proprietor of the company, was extremely thankful at that particular moment that he had under-taken the move, if only for the soothing vista of sheep quietly grazing with their lambs in the verdant pastures outside his window. He sat slumped in a high-backed swivel chair at his desk, open-mouthed with jet lag, hardly aware of the fact that Cathy, his wife and personal assistant, had succeeded in turning the once dark and smelly piggery into the company's new stately office during the two weeks that he had been away. White-painted windows now replaced the cobwebbed jute sacks that had once flapped in the open frames, hardboard floors were laid and carpeted, and the walls, now lined with plasterboard and resplendently fresh in Dulux 'Magnolia', were hung with photo-graphs that displayed some of Roger's most triumphant moments: the darkened silhouette of Blenheim Palace lit by a blinding shower of green and silver cascading from its roof; the huge shimmering palm tree of illumination that arced above the barge on the River Thames, catching in its brilliant rays the frontal elevation of the Houses of Parliament and the stolid, square tower of Big Ben; and the largest of them all, an aerial shot that showed a night sky emblazoned with incandescent spirals and trailing meteors that fell earthwards in flames of red and gold on to the battlements of Edinburgh Castle. These, and the countless other photographs still packed away in removal boxes, were testament to his skills as a master pyrotechnic.

Roger was brought out of his soporific state by a coffee mug being placed with a clatter on the desk in front of him and a kiss being planted on the side of his bearded face. He closed his mouth and turned to watch with heavy eyes as his wife came to lean her denim-ed bottom on the desk beside him, her arms folded across the front of a faded blue cotton shirt and a concerned smile sliding her mouth to one side.

'You look all in.'

Roger stretched his legs out under the desk and ran a hand over the top of his thinning hair. Even though he was yet to reach his mid-forties, he no longer had the wherewithal for the ponytail that had, at one time, trailed down his back, covering the ESC logo on the back of his navy-blue sweatshirt, a garment which he wore, along with a pair of heavy-duty cotton chinos, as his constant uniform.

'I am,' he replied, mid-yawn. 'There was a problem with the plane in Shanghai, so we were four hours late in boarding.'

'What time did you get back here?'

'Six-thirty this morning. I didn't bother coming to bed. Thought I'd just disturb you.'

'That was very considerate of you,' Cathy said with a smile. 'So, tell me, how did the trip go?'

'All in all, really good. We . . . had a couple of "red tape" problems, which I suppose is the norm for China, but we did manage to visit the factories in Beihai and Hengyang and they got pretty excited about the new material we've ordered from them. We spent two days on the test ground with this new lad from the research department in Hengyang and I have to say that some of the new multishot batteries he'd come up with were just mind-blowing.' Roger took a hefty slurp of black coffee. 'Talking of which, have you seen Phil this morning? I have to remind him to send an e-mail off to that lad this morning.'

'He's with Danny in the storeroom, getting the gear ready for the weekend.'

Roger eyed Cathy for a moment, then leaned across his desk and opened his diary. 'Oh, for heaven's sakes, I'd forgotten about Cardiff. Looks like we'll have to be back on the road tomorrow to get that one set up.'

Cathy pushed herself away from the desk. 'Well, I'm afraid the best news I'm saving for last. Jeff Banyon from the Scottish Chamber Orchestra called this morning to find out how you were getting on with the Tchaikovsky piece for the festival.'

'What did you tell him?'

'I told him that you and Phil were working on it and that everything was going well.'

Roger snorted out a laugh. 'That'll be right. We haven't even made a start to it.'

Cathy gave her husband's hair a ruffle. 'Don't worry. You always say that some of your best displays are the ones you've left to the last moment.'

As she moved over to the door of the office it opened with force, and a short, well-built man with blond hair and eager blue eyes walked in. He encircled Cathy's waist with powerful forearms, picked her up off the ground and twirled her around.

'Hi there, Cathy. Good to see you, babe,' he bellowed out in a thick Australian accent. He dropped her with little care back to her feet, moved over to the desk and gave Roger a solid slap on the shoulder. 'How're you feeling this morning, Rog?'

Roger did not reply, but turned and fixed his right-hand man with a caustic glare.

'Not very well, actually,' Cathy replied for her husband, 'which makes me slightly wonder why *you*'re so chirpy?'

Phil Kenyon planted his sizeable backside on top of the desk, covering Roger's diary in the process. 'Oh, I never get jet lag,' he said cockily. 'Comes from all those years of flying back and forth to Oz.'

'Bully for you,' Roger mumbled quietly, giving his diary a sharp tug to free it from captivity.

Phil leaned over, his annoyingly fresh face only a foot away from Roger's scowling features. 'Not feeling our best today, are we, Rog, mate?'

'Don't bait him, Phil,' Cathy said warningly. 'It's not the best idea when he's in this kind of mood. In fact, I think I might just leave you both so that I don't have to clean the blood off the new carpet.'

'Oh, Rog wouldn't hurt me, would you, mate?'

The remark was met with a short disparaging laugh from Roger. 'I'd happily take you apart if we didn't have work to do.'

As Cathy closed the door behind her, Phil pushed himself upright and jumped off the desk with a purposeful clap of his hands. 'So what's on the cards today?'

'The Tchaikovsky piece for the Edinburgh Festival. We've got to start programming it.'

Phil's smile changed to a joyless grimace. 'Oh, man, that's a tall order.' He let out a heavy breath. 'Oh, well, we'd better give it a go, I suppose. Where d'you put the CD they sent us?'

Roger's energy levels were sufficient only for a finger to be pointed towards the row of filing cabinets against the wall. Phil walked over to them, selected a drawer and pulled it open. He retrieved the CD and returned to the desk, picking up a chair in passing and thumping it down next to Roger. He placed the disc in one of the CD players that were stacked to one side of the desk and sat down.

'Right,' he said, pulling forward a thick block of lined paper. 'Ready to make a start?'

Roger shook his head slowly. 'You know, Phil, I'm not really looking forward to trying to get this one programmed. With all those quiet passages, I just don't see how it's going to come together.'

Phil wrote, 'Tchaikovsky, Edinburgh' at the top of the page, and then dropped the pen on the desk and turned to his boss. 'I always seem to get an appalling attack of déjà vu when you say that kind of thing. Listen, mate, you've been doing the Fireworks Concert in Edinburgh for over twenty years now, and every year is more spectacular than the one before. I can't think of any reason why this one should be an exception to the rule.' He picked up the remote and pressed the 'play' button for the CD machine. 'So what d'you say we just chill out and get on with the job in hand?'

Roger laughed quietly. 'Were you born an optimist?'

'Na, mate, I was born in Wagga Wagga,' Phil replied, sticking his tongue in his cheek as the large floor speakers resounded with the opening bars of the classical piece.

Three

When the telephone rang, Lewis Jones made no immediate attempt to answer it. At this time of the year, it was almost certain to be some theatre company or comedy act leaving it to the last to book into the Fringe rather than anything to do with marketing. There were other people in the office whose jobs it was to handle such calls. However, when it continued on, he stopped reading through the gruesome forty-word description of Nick Cardean's forthcoming act, 'Four Weddings, Four Funerals and Four Acid Baths Somewhere-in-Between', got to his feet and looked over the partition that gave him a little privacy in the cluttered, open-plan space. There were eight others working in the Festival Fringe office at that time and each was engaged in a telephone call. So, with a resigned shrug, Lewis sat down again and picked up the receiver.

'Good morning, Fringe office.'

The man on the other end of the line spoke with a distinct North England twang, his words flowing out at a speed only matched in extreme by their inaudibility.

'All right, let's just go through one thing at a time,' Lewis interjected as the man avalanched him with information. 'What was the name of the performer again?'

The noise in the office was only a low hum of voices, but

nevertheless Lewis had to push a finger into his uncovered ear to be able to hear what the man was saying.

'So it's Rene Brownlow, is it? . . . No, I don't need to know what kind of act it . . . oh, it's comedy, is it? . . . Yes, I'm sure she's very funny – look, could you just hang on a mo' and I'll see if I can find her name on the database.'

Someone in the office had nicked Lewis's mouse mat, so he had to slew the mouse halfway across the slippery surface of his desk before he got the arrow on the icon at the top of his computer screen. He typed in the name, thumped on a key and the name appeared.

'Right, I've got Rene Brownlow, care of Andersons Westbourne Social Club, Hartlepool. That's the one, is it? . . . OK then . . . Well, it looks like you've paid the registration fee of twelve pounds, but nothing else.'

That set the man off like a train on a downhill stretch, his explanation gradually picking up speed until it was both unstoppable and incomprehensible. Lewis, however, managed to ascertain from it all that a venue had been booked in West Richmond Street (cheap, he thought to himself, but a comedian's graveyard down there), that money was coming from different sources and that it had all been very complicated to coordinate.

'I can understand all that,' Lewis cut in loudly, hoping that volume might scare the man silent, 'but in the monthly bulletins we sent out to you, it does say that to secure your place and get your name in the programme you have to pay three hundred quid before the end of April – and now it's two weeks into May.'

The man stuttered out some lightning-fast excuses, and then careered off sideways into a non sequitur about someone being 'very hard done by' and 'life dealing her a cruel blow'.

'Could you just hold it a moment?' Lewis asked, holding up a hand, a pointless and ineffectual action when trying to halt such a barrage of unseen verbosity. Hearing the man still speaking when he pressed the 'hold' button, Lewis got to his feet and once more peered over the partition. Everyone was still engaged in telephone calls, so he plumped on interrupting Gail at the next desk, waving a hand semaphore-like to try to attract her attention. She didn't see it.

'Gail, give us a help here, will you?' he whispered loudly to her.

Gail swung round in her chair to face Lewis. She asked her caller to hold the line before clamping her hand over the mouthpiece. 'What is it?'

'I've got some fellow from Hartlepool here who hasn't paid up the three hundred pounds yet.'

'Has he got a venue?' Gail asked.

'Seems so.'

'And has he got the money?'

'Apparently.'

'Well, just tell him to get it here by tomorrow latest, along with his act description. We won't be finalising the programme for another two weeks.'

Lewis gave Gail a solid thumbs-up, sat down at his desk and put the receiver to his ear. 'Hullo? Right, the story is this. If you get a cheque and an act description to us by tomorrow, then you'll be all right . . . yes, better to do "next day delivery" . . . Not at all, glad to be of help . . . no, I'm not Indian, I'm Welsh . . . that's all right, don't give it another thought . . . goodbye.'

Standing at the bar in Andersons Westbourne Social Club, known in all parts of Hartlepool as Andy's, Stan Morris replaced the receiver on the payphone and shovelled the remainder of the change off the dog-eared telephone directory into his cupped hand. He let it cascade with a jangle into his trouser pocket, and then turned to smile at the four men that eyed him expectantly.

'Well?' the smallest of them asked, his face wrinkled up to stop his bottle glasses from falling off the end of his snub nose. 'What did she say?'

'It was an *'e*,' Stan replied importantly, clearing a path for himself through the eager band by holding the palms of his hands together like an old-fashioned diver. Everyone fell into step behind him as he headed back to the table in the corner of the sparsely furnished bar, where seven pints of beer in varying stages of consumption and a scattered set of dominoes awaited them. Wooden chairs were shifted back noisily on the linoleum floor as they resumed their seats. 'I thought 'e was Indian,' said Stan, taking a sip from his glass, then carefully wiping his mouth with a folded handkerchief he kept stored in the breast pocket of his tweed jacket, 'but 'e was Welsh.'

'Bugger 'is nationality,' exclaimed the little man with the glasses, taking a pinch of Golden Virginia tobacco from a greasy leather pouch and dexterously rolling himself a twig of a cigarette, 'what did 'e say about Rene?'

Stan shot a haughty look at the man. 'I was merely telling ye that, Skittle, as a point of interest.' A universal groan went round the table. 'All right, the man said we were still in time as long as we got a cheque in the post tonight and sent it "next day delivery".'

A murmur of relief greeted the news.

'For a moment, I thought ye'd blown it,' said Derek Marsham, whose long face, sunken cheekbones and down-turned mouth gave the impression that he suffered constant and immeasurable unhappiness.

'I beg your pardon, Derek,' Stan retorted. 'What d'ye mean by that?'

'Well, ye prattle on so, ye do. It was a bloody wonder the man understood one word of what ye were saying to 'im.'

Stan puffed out his cheeks and pulled himself upright in his chair. 'I'll have ye know, Derek my friend, that at one time I was an accomplished after-dinner speaker. Sought after the length and breadth of Yorkshire, I was, and never before 'as the allegation been made that—'

'Come on, lads, this is getting us no place.' The voice abruptly stopped Stan's protest, and four faces turned to look at the man sporting the short denim jacket with the turned-up collar.

Even though Terry Crosland, in his mid-fifties, would have been younger than his companions by at least ten years, his long dark sideburns and Teddy-boy quiff seemed to put him in a distant and bygone era, while the others, who kept what was left of their hair barber-short and garbed themselves in cloth caps, mufflers and belted raincoats, were timelessly fashioned as their fathers and grandfathers would have been before them.

Stan Morris composed himself once more, but not before he had given Derek a sharp look of contempt. 'I quite agree with ye, Terry. Well spoken, that man.'

Terry rubbed his hands nervously on the legs of his jeans. 'What I think we should be discussing is . . . OK, so we've got the money together, but don't you think it's time we told Rene what we've been planning?' The suggestion brought about a rumble of agreement. 'Also, there's another three months before the festival, so 'ow's about we put the motion before the committee that we keep raising the money for 'er, because we can't send 'er off up to Edinburgh flat broke.'

Norman Brown cleared his throat and leaned forward to enter the circle of discussion for the first time. 'That's a good point,' he said, clutching a hand to his arm to stop the shake of developing Parkinson's. 'Our Maisie lives up Clavering way and 'er kids go to the same primary school as the Brownlow kids, and she says that the Brownlows took out a mortgage on one of those newbuilds just before Gary Brownlow lost 'is job with Daiwong Electrics, so they're just about skint . . .'

Norman tailed off, silenced by the hardened stare on Stan Morris's face. 'Thank ye, Norman,' he said, a condescending smile twitching his cheeks momentarily. 'I think we know that, otherwise we wouldn't be bothering to do all this for Rene.'

'Oh,' said Norman Brown quietly and shrank back out of the circle.

'I don't mind going up to see Rene and telling 'er what's been planned.' It was Terry who spoke, just after he had shot a wink at disheartened Norman to give his fragile confidence a bit of a boost. 'I 'ave to 'ead up toward Clavering any road this evening to do a paint job, so it won't be that much out me way.'

Stan Morris, who sensed that his commanding action in dealing with Norman's stupidity had brought proceedings back under his control, knocked a fist on the table. 'I think that's a very good idea. Much better to break the news to 'er in the comfort of 'er own home, rather than when she's all caught up pulling pints behind the bar 'ere. Everybody in agreement that Terry should take this on?'

The assembled company nodded their approval.

'Right, then,' Stan sang out, taking a ballpoint pen and a notebook from the inside pocket of his jacket. 'So what we 'ave to do now is come up with a forty-word description of Rene's act.'

Skittle squinted at Stan through his glasses, a quizzical expression on his face. ''Ow the 'ell can we do that when we don't know what she's going to be saying?'

'We have to use our imagination then, don't we, Skittle,' Stan replied in a schoolmasterly voice. He flicked a thumb over his shoulder. 'We've all heard 'er up there on that stage every Thursday night for the past six months, so we have a fair inkling of what 'er act's going to be about.' He creased open his notebook with the side of his hand. 'Right, then, I'll start the creative ball rolling. What about "'Ilarious comedienne from 'Artlepool"?'

'That's only four words,' droned sombre Derek Marsham.

Raising a long-suffering eyebrow, Stan threw the pen down on the table and crossed his arms. 'Ooh, I can tell this is going to be a long afternoon.'

Four

In the small sub-office of the *Sunday Times* in Edinburgh, Harry Wills opened the top drawer of his desk, took out a square of Nicorette chewing gum, unwrapped it with one hand and popped it in his mouth. At the same time, with the receiver jammed in against chin and shoulder, he continued to write his own form of shorthand on the spiralled notepad, sometimes interspersing the text with longhand words for which, in his thirty-odd years in journalism, he had never worked out abbreviations.

He clicked the top of the ballpoint pen and dropped it on the desk. 'Thank you, Monsieur Dessuin, for your time. I think that's all I need to ask. You said you were going to be at the Tower Hotel until tomorrow, is that right? . . . just in case there's anything else I need to know . . . good . . . well, thank you again . . . goodbye.'

Harry thumped the receiver down on its cradle in frustration and then briefly read through his spidery jottings before lobbing the notebook on to the desk and, with an angry groan, leaning his considerable bulk back in the old wooden armchair with force enough to make it creak violently in protest. There wasn't a story there at all. Not that it really surprised him that much. He had been trying to get a personal interview with Angélique Pascal for two years now, ever since she had become the 'great new discovery' after winning the coveted Prix du Concours Long-Tibaud at the Conservatoire in Paris, but never had he been able to get further than speaking to her manager and mentor, Albert Dessuin. He laughed quietly to himself and shook his head resignedly. Well, at least he knew he wasn't alone in his failure. It was a well-known fact amongst all his journalistic colleagues that Dessuin kept the young French violinist under such a tight rein that her existence could at best be described as reclusive.

Heaving himself out of the chair, Harry walked over to the window and gazed down on to the sun-striped lawns of Princes Street Gardens. This year, he thought to himself, right here in Edinburgh. With Pascal being located in the city for more than a week when she performed at the festival, there would never be a better chance to get that interview.

On the fifteenth floor of the Tower Hotel in London, Albert Dessuin also stood gazing out of the window, his picture-postcard

22

view being no less spectacular than that of Harry Wills in the northern capital city. Small cutters and sightseeing barges plied the murky waters of the River Thames, appearing and disappearing under the majestic span of Tower Bridge. His mind, however, was not focused on the view. He stood with an elbow resting in one hand, the other playing with the collar of his cashmere polo-neck sweater. His thin lips were pursed and his eyes twitched rhythmically behind the gold-framed spectacles that were seated firmly on his long, thin nose. He was listening intently to the strains of the violin that drifted in through the closed door of the adjoining room, as it played through the first movement of Sibelius's Violin Concerto in D Minor. With every downbeat, he jerked his head, making the high cockscomb of jet-black hair pulse as if powered by an electrical current. Then, in an instant, he threw up his hands, simultaneously clicking his fingers, and strode over to the door and pulled it forcefully open.

'Angélique, what are you doing?'

The girl stopped playing instantly. She turned to look at him, her large brown eyes beneath the straight fringe of short dark hair eyeing him with uncertainty. She dropped the violin from her shoulder and began twisting the bow back and forth in her fingers.

'What do you mean?' she asked hesitantly.

'I can tell from through here in my room that you are not concentrating. You are missing so many beats.'

The girl's full mouth broadened into a wide smile. 'I know. I was looking out of the window. It is so beautiful out there with the sun glinting on the river. Have you seen all the boats?'

'Yes, I have,' replied Dessuin with little enthusiasm.

'Oh, Albert, I love London. It is such a wonderful place. I am going to come to live here one day.'

'Pfoo! Why would you want to live here?' Dessuin snapped. 'Paris is so much more superior. It has better shops, better restaurants, nicer people.' He moved across the room to the girl and dismissed the idea with a light backhanded brush to her shoulder. 'You are mad to even think about it.'

A sparkle of excitement glinted in her eyes. 'Maybe one has to do mad things at some time or other.'

'Of course, but not at *this* time. You are twenty-one years old and you are very fortunate that together we are being able to cut out an excellent career for you, and that is what you should be concentrating on right now' – he put a hand under her violin and guided it back under her chin – 'starting with you getting those downbeats right.'

Angélique lifted her bow to the strings and with a gentle dip to her head, closed her eyes and began to play. After the opening three bars, she stopped abruptly.

'I heard you talking on the telephone. Who was it?'

Dessuin shrugged his shoulders. 'Some *journaliste* from Scotland. Now keep playing.'

Angélique bit at the side of her mouth and tapped her bow on the strings of the violin. 'Why don't you allow me to talk to the press? I'm quite capable of doing so.'

Dessuin narrowed his eyes at the girl before fixing her with an insincere smile. He draped an arm around the shoulders of his protégée. 'Of course you are, but it is so much better for you to do what you are best at, and I will do likewise.' It may have been his imagination, but as he planted a protective kiss on the side of her head, he felt pressure on his hand as if she were drawing herself away from him.

'Your mother has been on the telephone,' she said quietly.

Dessuin dropped his arm from her shoulder. 'When was this?'

'About an hour ago.'

'Why did you not tell me?'

'Because you were away from your room at the time.'

Dessuin nodded slowly. 'And what did she say?'

Angélique played a merry trill on her violin. 'She thinks she is suffering from flu again,' she said lightly. 'She wants you to call her.'

Dessuin turned and strutted over to the door of his bedroom. He opened it, and then turned to glare angrily at Angélique. 'You know, my mother has been very good to you. You should

24

have more respect for her and not be so mean about her *fragilité*.' His rebuke was met with a blank stare from the young violinist. 'I think you are a very cold person sometimes, Angélique. I am going to call her now, and then I am going out to get some fresh air.'

'Oh, can I come too, Albert?' Angélique asked breathlessly. She hurriedly placed the violin and bow down on her bed and moved towards him. 'I know I should not have been so *flippante* about your mother. I am sorry. Please, when you speak to her, tell her I was asking after her.'

Dessuin huffily shrugged his shoulders. 'I suppose you could come, but are you sure you are ready for the concert tonight?'

'Albert, you know I can play Sibelius with one hand tied behind my back.'

'Five minutes ago, it sounded to me that you were.'

'You don't mean that.'

'Most certainly I do, and if you play it like that tonight, you will make yourself a laughing stock.'

Dessuin could tell from the look on Angélique's face that he had succeeded in casting doubt in her mind. He decided to push her a little further. 'And what about Mozart in two days' time? Your reputation would be shot down in flames if you screwed up in Vienna.'

The enthusiasm that Angélique had displayed visibly drained from her being. 'Maybe I should stay and do a bit more practice.'

He smiled at her. 'A good idea. Anyway, it's cold outside. We don't want *you* getting a chill like my mother, now, do we?'

Angélique stood watching as Dessuin closed the door behind him, then turned and picked up the violin from the bed. She closed her arms around it, holding it hard to her chest, feeling its shape press against her small firm breasts. It was her comforter, her friend these days, almost her only friend. Since leaving the Conservatoire two years ago, she had hardly seen any of her old acquaintances, and certainly she had not had the time to make any new ones. The routine had been constant. One hotel room after another, one concert hall after another. Of course, she understood what Albert was always telling her, that she had been blessed with a supreme gift of music and that it was her duty to share that gift with all the people of the world who did not possess it. But the pressure was becoming intense. She wanted a break from it all. She wanted to go out once more to the cinemas and to the bars in Paris with her friends from the Conservatoire, and she wanted to go home to Clermont Ferrand to visit her family and spend time with dear Madame Lafitte. Oh, how she missed that wonderful woman!

Without relinquishing her hold on the violin, Angélique sat down on the edge of the bed and blew out a long breath to steady the wave of nausea that flooded up from her stomach. She knew only too well, however, that the cause of this was not the onset of such an illness from which the dreaded Madame Dessuin constantly claimed she was suffering. This was worse, and had begun to take place more frequently over the past two months. It was brought on by the unthinkable realisation that she, Angélique Pascal, was beginning to feel bored of playing this wonderful instrument. How could she ever entertain such an idea when there were those who clamoured at the box offices of the great concert halls to hear her play? How could she tell such a thing to Albert Dessuin, the man who had nurtured her through her days at the Conservatoire de Paris and who had given up everything to become her manager and counsellor? And what would she ever be able to say to Madame Lafitte?

Angélique kicked off her shoes and lay down on the bed, pulling her legs up so that her ankles rested against the curve of her narrow-hipped bottom. As she nestled her head deep into the pillow, a tear slowly trickled down her cheek and was immediately absorbed by the white linen pillowcase.

'Hullo?' The voice on the telephone sounded weak and quavering.

'Hullo, Maman. It's Albert.'

'Oh, Albert, *mon cher,* why have you not called me before

now? Where have you been?' A pathetic cough followed.

'I am sorry, Maman. I did not know you *had* called until a moment ago.'

'Do you mean the girl never gave you the message?' Suddenly there seemed to be strength in the voice.

Dessuin rested an elbow on the dark-stained desk and rubbed the palm of his hand against his forehead. For eight years, Angélique had been living with him and his mother in their capacious apartment in the *quinzième* district of Paris, and still she could hardly bring herself to call her son's young protégée by name. 'I have been away from my room, Maman, and Angélique has been practising for the concert tonight. It was not her fault.'

'I am not feeling at all well, Albert.' The voice changed for the worse once more.

'So I understand. Have you called the doctor?'

'Pah! The doctor knows nothing. Anyway, he is too busy even to visit a sick old woman.'

'In that case, you must send Simone round to the *farmacie* for some paracetamol.'

'Albert, it is Tuesday. Simone only comes for two hours on a Tuesday. She has left already.' Another feeble cough sounded down the line. 'When are you coming home, Albert?'

'I cannot be back in Paris before Friday, Maman.'

'Ah, *mon Dieu,* Friday! I may very well be on my deathbed by then, if I have not gone before.'

'Maman, that is ridiculous,' Dessuin said irritably. 'You are as strong as an ox.'

'How would you know how I am feeling?' Again the strength in the voice returned. 'You have never considered how I am feeling. If that had been so, you would never have left your teaching job at the Conservatoire to fly around the world with that girl.'

'Maman, I have talked to you countless times about this.'

'You were never able to make the grade, were you, Albert? You are only doing this because you see in her the talent that you lacked. Don't forget that if it had not been for my contacts, you would never have got that job at the Conservatoire.'

'That is most unfair, Maman.'

'Pah! What age are you now? Thirty-seven years old? And you are going to be content to follow this girl around the world like a lapdog for the rest of your life?'

Dessuin did not reply, but leaned back in his chair and wound the telephone cord tightly around his fingers. He let out a short silent laugh. 'Isn't it strange how you always seem to sound so much better when you get angry?'

There was a moment's silence.

'Albert,' the suffering in the voice had returned, 'I am sorry to say such things to you. It must be the fever. I do feel quite delirious.'

'Well, I suggest you take yourself to bed with a cup of hot lemon and a shot of cognac, and if you are feeling no better by Friday, I will take you to see the doctor.'

'You are a good boy, Albert. I know that. *Mon seul fils, et je t'aime beaucoup.*'

'*Et je t'aime aussi, Maman.* I must go now. I have things to do. I will call you tonight.'

Dessuin replaced the receiver and sat for a moment focused on the letterheading of the Tower Hotel, stacked neatly with its matching envelopes in the leather stand at the back of the desk. He then leaned slowly forward and clenched his hair with both hands, squeezing tighter and tighter until the pain brought tears to his eyes. Why was it so much part of her very nature to belittle those who were closest to her? She had acted exactly the same with his father as well, so much so that the man had often been driven to vent all his pent-up emotions in an irrational rage that had left neither Albert nor his mother physically untouched. He had too vivid memories of his puny young arms braced against his bedroom door, jarring like shock absorbers against the power of his father's shoulder as he tried to gain entry, desperately reaching out a foot to hook round a chair so that he could jam it under the handle. And when his father would eventually calm down and Albert could hear him muttering to himself as he stolidly descended the stairs, Albert would then lay himself down carefully on his bed, fold his aching arms across his chest and feel the comforting coolness of the linen pillowcase against his throbbing, bruised face.

He knew it had never been his father's fault, but when, in his last year at school, he returned home one day to find an ambulance and two police cars outside the house and was then told by a gruff police inspector that Guillaume Dessuin had locked himself in the attic bedroom and had subsequently taken his own life with the revolver he kept as a souvenir from the last war, Albert's desolation was tempered by an overwhelming sense of relief. He had now escaped the violent reach of the unfortunate man.

Yet as the months went by thereafter and his mother's silent chagrin finally lifted from her sad, embittered being, Albert found himself becoming the new and unwitting target for her verbal abuse, now more vitriolic than ever before. And it soon came to him that Guillaume Dessuin, through his actions, had inflicted on his only son a wound more permanent than any received during those regular beatings. He had succeeded in doing something at which Albert himself was forever destined to fail, and that was to rid himself of the very cause of so much misery in his life.

Abruptly, Albert stood up and strode over to the minibar, the memory of his troubled youth and the matriarchal ball and chain he dragged through his adulthood being too prevalent in his mind. He took out two small bottles of whisky, poured their contents into a glass and drained it in two gulps, feeling his body give out an involuntary shiver at the immediate impact the alcohol had on both his throat and his brain. In that moment, he became aware that no sound was coming from the next-door room. He moved across to the adjoining door and opened it quietly.

Angélique was lying fast asleep on the bed, her stockinged feet curled up under her bottom and her violin clutched like a comforting teddy bear in her arms. It was a sight that made Albert smile despite his melancholy mood. He had watched that girl grow up, becoming more attached to her than she would ever know, and he knew only too well what that particular instrument meant to her. It was her childhood, her passion, her fairy-tale world to which she used to escape from the impecunious and uncultured lifestyle of her family in Clermont Ferrand. And, over the years he had witnessed it gently coaxing from her one of the most truly remarkable talents he had ever had the pleasure of hearing. Oh, how easy life would be, he thought to himself, if one needed only to take one's solace from a shapely piece of veneered wood with a few steel strings attached to it.

Dessuin soundlessly pulled the door closed and turned once more to raid the minibar of its anaesthetising contents.

Five

The shutters in the drawing room of the house in Clermont Ferrand were always kept closed during the summer months to protect the antique furniture from the sun, especially the lacquered top of the grand piano, which stood at an angle in the large bow window, squatting like a giant toad on its turned-out legs. It was covered with a white lace cloth upon which sat a weighty stack of music scores and the large blue Limoges terrine in which Madame Lafitte always kept an abundant supply of Nestlé's plain chocolate secreted under its patterned lid.

So efficient were the shutters that it was always impossible to see anything in that room, even at ten o'clock on a summer's morning when the sun was high enough to clear the trees that lined the rue Blatin and hit the front of the house full-on. But if one entered quietly when nobody else was about and took care not to bump into anything, it was actually possible to *smell* one's way around the room, which turned out to be so much more exciting than actually being able to see it. Starting on an anti-clockwise course, the fireplace came first with its acrid reek of cold, unswept chimney; next the long bookshelves, which gave off a heady whiff of leather; round past the grand piano, which was always sweet with beeswax; feel one's way to one side of Dr Lafitte's high-sided armchair with the rich aroma of hair oil on its linen head cloth; then along the smooth-fronted sideboard, which gave off first the obnoxious tang of spent pipe tobacco, followed by the fading bouquet of potpourri; and then, finally, journey's end came by the small Louis XV chair nestling beside the door, which ponged of Madame Lafitte's two elderly Pekineses.

It was during one of these unsighted sojourns, when the perpetrator had decided to widen the search for new discoveries behind the grand piano, that a foot came into contact with some form of solid object, causing it to sound off a muffled reverberation in protest. After a moment of thumping heartbeat, during which ears were sharply attuned to the possible approach of footsteps, small hands were used to explore the shape of the object. First curvaceous around its base, then into a narrow waist, then some smaller curves before its lines ran parallel to the top. Imagination could not help in any way to understand what the box contained, and that was not to be of any satisfaction to one so curious. Accordingly, ten little fingers sought to break the sacrosanct spell of darkness, gripping hard at the edge of one of the tall shutters and pulling it open to allow the narrowest sliver of light to fall upon the box and upon nothing else. The little girl in the shapeless cotton dress and dirty plimsolls, who now revealed herself for the first time to her inanimate acquaintances in the room, knelt down in front of the box and slowly undid the three spring catches on the lid, and then carefully, oh, so carefully, she opened it up.

She did not touch its contents. She just gazed at them, so mesmerised by what she saw that, after an unknown quantity of time, she felt no discomfort from kneeling on the hard parquet floor, nor was she aware of the commotion that had started outside the room.

'You try upstairs, Marie. I will look for her down here.'

A door on the opposite side of the hallway groaned open on unoiled hinges before being closed immediately with an echoing bang, and then the door to the drawing room was opened and a light turned on.

'Angélique? Are you in here?'

As she stood by the door, the woman, who, despite her advanced age, was tall and upright and elegantly turned out, her grey hair pinned in a circular plait to the back of her head, was puzzled by the crack of light that showed through the shutters. She walked over to the window and let out a cry of surprise when she came across the little girl huddled on her knees behind the piano.

'Oh, Angélique, what a fright you gave me,' she said, clutching a hand to her white-bloused heart. 'What are you doing in here, little one?'

The little girl looked up at the old lady, her face radiant with delight. 'What is this?' she asked, pointing at her discovery.

The lady was so warmed by the child's expression that any thought of reprimand quickly melted from her mind. 'That, Angélique, is a violin.'

'Is it very special?'

The old lady smiled. 'That one is, yes.' She held a finger up to the little girl. 'You wait right there. I must tell your mother I found you.' She walked over to the door and called out, 'Marie?' into the hallway.

'I have not yet found her, Madame Lafitte,' a panicked voice sounded out from some distant point on the upper landing.

'She is down here in the drawing room, Marie, so calm yourself.'

Madame Lafitte walked back to the bay window, placing her long, graceful hands on the back of a low armchair and pushing it on squeaky castors to where Angélique remained as instructed, her face no more than ten inches away from the instrument.

The old lady sat, tucking in her grey worsted skirt under her legs and shifting her knees demurely to one side. She reached down and lightly moved a thumb over the strings. The tone of the violin was muted by the thick green baize that lined its box.

'It was given to me by my father many years ago,' Madame Lafitte said, as if beginning the telling of a fairy tale. 'He was a very kind and generous man. I had not long started playing the violin when he came home with it one evening. "Lillian," he said to me, "if you want to be a really excellent violinist, you need the assistance of more than just a good teacher." So he gave me that case, and I, like you, opened it up and just stared at it in wonderment.' She reached down and pulled the violin case towards her. 'Of course, it is only a small one because I was very young at the time.'

'How old were you?' the little girl asked, briefly taking her eyes off the violin to look up at Madame's kindly wrinkled face.

Madame Lafitte laughed. 'Oh, now that is difficult. Not as young as you, at any rate. What are you now? Six? Seven?'

'Six and a half.'

'Well, I think I was probably about ten, and—'

Madame Lafitte was interrupted by the arrival of a heavy tread and the sound of an unhealthy wheezing in the room. In the doorway stood a large woman with a wild tangle of brown curls adorning the top of a very red and very round face. Her figure, which resembled that of an all-in wrestler, was encased in a sleeveless floral overall that looked large enough to double as a two-man tent and under which, judging from the expanse of bosom revealed, she wore little other than an overloaded, flesh-coloured brassiere, the straps of which were almost lost in the pudginess of her shoulders. Below the bivouac, her thick legs were sheathed in black calf-length stockings that ran amok with ladders, while her considerable weight was borne by a pair of battered, woollen bedroom slippers.

'Oh, Madame,' she gasped, as she rocked her way over to the piano. 'I am so sorry. I cannot understand what she was thinking of. She knows this room is *interdite*.' She placed her fists on her

33

wide hips and frowned angrily down at her daughter. 'Angélique,' she boomed, her voice suddenly taking on the force and volume of a Marseillaise fishwife, 'you come out from behind that piano and apologise immediately to Madame.'

Seeing the fear on the little girl's face as she got to her feet and quickly backed away as far as the bay window would allow, Madame Lafitte held up a hand. 'It's all right, Marie,' she said in a calming voice, 'no harm has been done. It is good for little girls to be so inquisitive.'

'But not here in your house, Madame. That is unforgivable. She can be as inquisitive as she likes in her own home, but not here at my work.'

'And how much more work do you have to do this morning?' Madame Lafitte asked, trying to steer matters away from Angélique's trivial misdemeanor.

'I have yet to finish off the polishing in Dr Lafitte's study, Madame, and then if I might leave the dining room until tomorrow, I would be very grateful. I have to be home to make lunch for all my family.'

'What?' Madame Lafitte asked quizzically, knowing that the three Pascal sons and elder daughter laboured alongside their father in a furniture factory on the outskirts of the city. Marie Pascal had been working in the house for nearly eight years, and consequently Madame Lafitte knew that Angélique's birth had been a bizarre mistake, remembering well the woman's surprise and shock on discovering that she was pregnant fourteen years after her previous confinement. 'Why would they be home on a Wednesday? Do they not all have lunch in the canteen?'

Angélique's mother flicked back her head. 'Of course, that is usually the case, Madame, but today, they are all on strike.'

Madame Lafitte clicked her tongue. 'Oh, not another strike. How long is this one going to last?'

The housekeeper threw out her hands. '*Je ne sais pas*, Madame. I hope a very short time, otherwise there will be no food in the house for me to cook for them.'

'Well, Marie, you get yourself off home when you have finished the study, and while you are doing that, I shall keep Angélique here with me so that she does not feel the need to carry out any more of her explorations.'

'Oh, you need not trouble yourself. Angélique will come to sit quietly at the kitchen table and wait for me to finish my work. She has been—'

'Marie,' Madame Lafitte cut in sharply, 'I am very happy to have Angélique with me here. We are going to have a little talk about the violin.'

Marie frowned. 'The violin, Madame? Angélique would not know what such a thing is.'

'In that case, I would like to explain it to her.'

With a shake of her head and a low muttering to herself, Angélique's mother turned and headed towards the door, running a yellow duster she had taken from the front pocket of her overall along the full length of the sideboard before departing the room.

Madame Lafitte smiled conspiratorially at the little girl, who had waited for her mother to leave before sinking to her knees in front of the violin once more. Angélique watched with wide eyes as the violin was taken from its case and the bow unclipped from the lid. Madame Lafitte placed the violin under her chin and plucked at each of the strings, turning the small wooden pegs at the end of the fingerboard to tune the instrument.

'Oh, my word, it has been so long since I have played. My fingers are not so nimble nowadays and also the violin is quite small for me, so you must be ready to excuse a great many mistakes, Angélique.'

The little girl watched as the old lady straightened her back, held the bow lightly against the strings, and then began to play. Immediately the dark, soulless room was warmed by the sweetest sound that Angélique had ever heard. She stared open-mouthed at the hand that moved effortlessly over the strings, at the fingers that quivered to make every note resound more beautifully, and at Madame Lafitte's face, which suddenly seemed to have become so much younger than before. Oh, it's like magic, Angélique thought to herself; this is the most special thing I have ever discovered.

When Madame Lafitte eventually finished playing, she laid the violin and bow across her knees and smiled at Angélique. 'Well, that wasn't so bad, was it? Not so many mistakes after all.'

'Do you always have to pretend you're sleeping when you play?' Angélique asked.

Madame Lafitte laughed. 'No, my dear, I close my eyes to concentrate. One has to try to become part of the music, and if you are not looking at other things, like the piano there, or even at you, then you are not distracted.'

'If I closed my eyes, would I be able to play?'

'I don't know. Would you like to have a try?'

With a gasp of amazement, Angélique jumped to her feet. 'Am I allowed to?'

'Of course you are. The violin might still be *un peu grand* for you, but let's see if we can't play a note or two. Come here and stand beside me.'

When the violin was placed under the little girl's chin, her face was at such an angle that she had to peer sideways to look at the strings. Madame Lafitte bit at her lip pensively. 'Now, that does not look very comfortable.'

'Oh, it's very comfortable,' exclaimed the little girl, terrified the old lady would take the violin away from her.

'All right, then.' She put the bow in Angélique's free hand and raised the girl's arm so that the bow rested on the fourth string of the violin. 'We are only going to use this string, so that is the one the fingers of your other hand need to press, *tu comprends?*'

'*Oui.*'

'*Bon.* So let us start with that finger, which we call your fourth finger, and now gently move the bow across the string.'

Angélique did what she was told and the violin emitted an ear-piercing screech. The girl let out a shrill laugh. 'That sounds like the noise our cat makes when Papa stands on its tail by mistake!'

Madame Lafitte smiled. 'In that case, we must immediately stop the suffering of your poor cat! Come on, we shall try *encore une fois*.'

The note, this time, came out almost perfect.

'That was wonderful, Angélique. Well done, you. Now what I want—'

But Angélique had already begun to play again, this time with her eyes screwed tightly closed, and when she repeated the note, she mirrored the technique of the quivering finger that she had seen Madame Lafitte use. It resounded exactly as the old lady's had done. So Angélique pressed her third finger to the string and pulled the bow back across it, and again the lower note came out as pure as the last. And then she moved to the second finger, and after an initial screech, she readjusted her little wrist and the note once more came out perfect.

The old lady did not try to stop her, but watched the girl's tenacity with fascination. 'All right, now let's try the next string over. The same thing again.'

The bow and the fingers moved together to the next string, and following one false start, three perfect notes were sounded, the playing hand arched just as it should be to avoid coming into contact with the fourth string, and then, without prompting, Angélique moved back to that string and played the three original notes again.

'Do you want to try the second string now?'

Angélique did not reply, nor did she open her eyes, her fingers feeling instinctively for the next string. Madame Lafitte could tell from the expression on the girl's face that this was indeed an effort with fingers as short as hers. She managed almost immediately one clear note before the moment was broken by the sound of the drawing-room door being forcefully opened. Angélique's mother entered the room, pulling on an enormous raincoat.

'That's the study finished, Madame. Again, I am sorry about my daughter's behaviour and I can assure you that it will not happen a second time.'

Madame Lafitte did not give her a reply, but with a gentle smile took the violin from the little girl. She could tell, in that second, that a spell had been shattered, and she saw the longing in Angélique's eyes as the violin was replaced in its case.

'Marie, why is Angélique here today? Why is she not at school?'

'There was a holiday today, Madame. Oh, I cannot tell you how sorry I am that I brought her. In future, I will—'

'I would like you to bring her here at any time that you possibly can, schooldays or not.' She turned and looked at the housekeeper. 'Would you be able to do that?'

Angélique's mother was perplexed by the request.

'Madame? 'I'm not sure what you—'

'It's very simple to understand, Marie. Would somebody be able to bring Angélique to my house every day and then fetch her later?'

'May I ask why?'

'Because I want to teach her the violin.'

The housekeeper let out a short laugh. 'The violin? Ah, Madame, it is very kind of you, but you don't want to bother yourself trying to teach my daughter—'

'Marie, what I do in my own time is my affair. So, the question still stands. Can someone bring Angélique to my house every day and then collect her at a later time?'

Angélique's mother shrugged her huge shoulders. 'There are six of us in the house. I suppose someone can walk her round, but it would depend on the shifts that the others work.'

'It doesn't matter. Anytime. I am always here.'

'Very well, Madame.'

Madame Lafitte put her arms around Angélique, who had come to stand enthralled beside her. The old lady planted a kiss on the side of her short dark hair, before whispering in her ear, 'I think, Angélique, my dear, that one day you will become an exceptional violinist.'

And so it was that Madame Lafitte became the most important person in Angélique Pascal's young life. It was she who gave

Angélique her lessons until the ability of the ten-year-old outshone her own; it was she who arranged and paid for the teacher who continued to nurture her extraordinary talent, and together with whom Madame Lafitte put out a search for a full-size violin that had the same resonance and playing style as the one Angélique had been using, eventually tracking one down in a backstreet shop in Munich that held a scant but exceptional stock of stringed instruments, and subsequently purchasing it with little regard to its enormous price tag; it was Madame Lafitte who set up the interview and audition for the thirteen-year-old at Le Conservatoire National Supérieur de Musique et de Danse de Paris; and it was she who mollified the stupid prejudices of the Pascal family and made them understand that her attendance there would have no detrimental impact on their lowly finances, and that Angélique's future promised much more than working in a furniture factory in Clermont Ferrand.

It was Madame Lafitte also who accompanied Angélique to Paris for the first time, the girl holding tight to her hand as they rode below the streets of the city on the Métro before emerging at La Porte de Pantin station in front of the inspirational white structure of the Conservatoire. Then, having watched Angélique being taken off for her audition, carrying the new, but equally treasured violin, the old lady had sat alone in the echoing foyer, drinking a cup of coffee whilst keeping the fingers of her free hand tightly crossed, watching the music students struggle along the corridors with bulky instrument cases and the leotarded dance students who sat in the chairs around her, chatting to their friends as they effortlessly stretched their legs into positions that would be unachievable for mere mortals.

It was a full hour and a half before Angélique eventually returned to the foyer, accompanied this time not by the young public relations woman but by a tall bespectacled young man wearing a dark-green corduroy suit. When they reached the perimeter of the seating area, he put a hand on Angélique's shoulders and spoke to her. The girl smiled at Madame Lafitte and pointed a finger in her direction. Settling Angélique in a chair, the man bought her a bottle of orange juice from an illuminated dispenser next to the wall, gave it to her along with a reassuring smile and approached the old lady.

'Madame Lafitte?'

'*Oui, c'est moi,*' she replied, struggling to raise herself out of the awkwardly shaped chair.

'Oh, please, don't get up,' he said, reaching down to her an elegantly shaped hand that bore the hallmark of a musician. 'I am sorry that we have taken so long with Angélique. My name is Albert Dessuin and I am a teacher of the violin here at the Conservatoire.'

Madame Lafitte shook the hand and watched as the young man lowered himself into a chair on the opposite side of the table. She could not bear to wait for news of the audition.

'Monsiuer Dessuin, can I ask how Angélique got on?'

Dessuin leaned forward in the chair, resting his elbows on his knees and linking his hands together in front of his chin. 'Madame Lafitte, all I can say is thank you for bringing Angélique to the Conservatoire.'

The old lady felt her heart give a huge thump, and tears immediately sprang to her eyes. She opened up the blue leather handbag on her knees and extracted a white linen handkerchief. 'Oh, I am so pleased you said that. She has a wonderful talent, *n'est-pas?*'

'I certainly believe it, and that is why we felt the need to discuss at length her future here.' The young man dropped his hands from his chin. 'Madame, I have had a word with the *directeur* of the department and asked if he would allow me to take Angélique under my wing. I truly feel that I can make something wonderful out of this talent.'

The old lady shook her head slowly. 'I have always believed this,' she said quietly, almost to herself, 'from the first moment that I allowed her to lay hands upon that violin.'

'Oh, it is *your* violin. I wondered, because it is certainly a most beautiful instrument.'

'No, Monsieur Dessuin, I was talking about a small one given

40

to me by my father many years ago. I shall always have that one in my house as a keepsake. The violin she is using now I bought for her.'

Dessuin smiled at the old lady. 'Then, what a wonderful gift you have made to her.' His face became serious. 'Now, Madame Lafitte, what I want to say about Angélique is that I feel that one so young, and one who has – how can I put this? – has not had a great deal of experience of the outside world, should not be put into the system of staying by herself in a students' residence.'

Madame Lafitte nodded. 'This has been one of my great worries, also.'

'Good, so I hope that the suggestion that I am going to make, which has been approved wholeheartedly by the *directeur,* will be acceptable to yourself as well. Madame, I live with my mother in a very large apartment here in the *quinzième* district, and we have customarily lodged some of the younger students from the Conservatoire. The girl who is with us at present is now of an age to move into the students' residence, which means that Angélique could take over her room. It would be a most beneficial arrangement for her because it would facilitate my supervision of both her music tuition and the educational studies that she will receive here at the Conservatoire.'

'Monsieur Dessuin, that would seem the most perfect idea, and would certainly take a weight off my mind. Of course, I will be the one to recompense you and Madame Dessuin for this.'

Dessuin held up a hand. 'Well, let us see what I can first arrange. For a girl from Angélique's background, I am sure that there are grants available to cover such costs.'

Madame Lafitte tilted her head to the side. 'Whatever you think, but if you cannot succeed in that, then I shall certainly meet all her costs. My husband and I were never fortunate enough to be blessed with children, Monsieur. Circumstances and *la guerre* put pay to that. Maybe it was then the plan of some greater being that I should wait until my eighties before being called upon to nurture a child as I now do Angélique. She need never worry about money, *comprenez-vouz?*'

41

'Of course, Madame. I can assure you that I will keep in close contact with you regarding all financial matters relating to Angélique.'

'I am very grateful, Monsieur Dessuin.' She tucked her handkerchief back in her handbag. 'So when are you thinking that she might start?'

'Next month, in September. Is that reasonable?'

Madame Lafitte nodded thoughtfully. 'I cannot give you a definite answer now, Monsieur Dessuin, because I must first talk to Angélique's parents. However, I am sure I will be able to persuade them by then.'

'Well, that is the start of the year at the Conservatoire, and I can tell you, Madame, that for once, I am very happy that it is starting so soon!'

Madame Lafitte glanced over to where Angélique sat, watching intently the comings and goings of the students around her. In her arms, she held the violin case as if protecting it.

Madame Lafitte smiled. 'Now, I think, would be a good time to give her the news.'

Every week for the next six years, Madame Lafitte received a letter from Angélique, telling her everything about the particular piece of music she was playing, about the friends she had made, and about the walks along the banks of the river Seine and the visits to museums and art galleries she had made with Albert Dessuin. In turn, Madame Lafitte would read these aloud to Angélique's mother, whom she knew had never received such a letter. Happiness seemed to radiate from these dispatches, so much so that it never occurred to Madame Lafitte that, not once, had Angélique mentioned her home life with Albert Dessuin and his mother. If she had but known about the tirades, the selfish hypochondria and the cold unfriendliness of the dreadful woman, the heavy clinking of bottle against glass that sounded from Dessuin's bedroom as Angélique passed by late at night to go to the bathroom, then Madame Lafitte would have taken the first train to Paris to make other arrangements. But Angélique never included a word of this in any of her letters, frightened that such a disclosure might end her time at the Conservatoire.

It was two days before her eighty-eighth birthday that Madame Lafitte received the news from Angélique that she had won the Prix du Concours Long-Tibaud. In another letter from Albert Dessuin, which arrived on the same day, he announced to Angélique's guardian that he had decided to give up his position at the Conservatoire and continue to teach Angélique and manage her affairs, as already she was being inundated with requests from concert halls around Europe to hear her play, and Dessuin felt that there was no way she could cope alone with such a pressure.

Madame Lafitte did not open, nor did she read, either of the letters herself. That was left to a young male nurse who sat on a chair close to the stroke victim's bedside in hospital. When he had finished, he looked closely at her face and nodded. Good news, he thought to himself, for both her and for the doctors. The smile was the first sign of understanding she had given since being brought there.

Six

The battered Transit van with the blown exhaust drove slowly through the confusion of streets, every one of them lined with identical stark-fronted, drab-harled houses, before coming to a halt at the entrance to a wide cul-de-sac. Terry Crosland rolled down the window and studied the street sign, just being able to make out the letters of Bolingbroke Close beneath a swirl of black graffiti. He swung the nose of the van around and reversed down the street to a point where he wouldn't interrupt the game of three-aside football that was in progress. As he opened the door, a deafening bang resounded around the tinny confines of the van and he saw the football dribble past him on the pavement. Thumping the door closed, he went over to the ball, pulled it towards him with his foot and deftly flicked it up into his hands.

A young boy came running down the street towards him. 'Sorry 'bout that, mister.'

'No 'arm done, lad,' Terry smiled at the boy and lobbed him the ball. 'Any idea which is the Brownlows' 'ouse?'

'Number seventeen, over there,' the boy replied, pointing to a house that seemed to have aged worse than others in the ten or so years of its life. 'That's Robbie Brownlow playing in goal for the opposition.'

Terry cast an eye towards the small figure that stood in front of the goal-chalked wall at the far end of the cul-de-sac. He was gazing up into the sky, seemingly more interested in the vapour trail of a plane flying overhead than he was in getting on with the game of football.

'Good, is he?' Terry asked.

'Nah,' the boy replied disparagingly. 'That's why we put 'im against the wall. We'd keep losing the ball if 'e was at this end.'

Terry watched the boy kick the ball back into play, and then walked across the road and entered the Brownlow property through a wrought-iron gate that a spare five minutes and a lick of black paint would have improved considerably. The pathway to the front door was blocked by a pile of large stones with weeds growing amongst them, a planned rockery never fulfilled, so Terry walked down the narrow passage with the high slatted fence that divided the twelve-foot gap to the adjacent house.

A quick glance at the back garden was more than enough evidence for Terry to realise that Gary Brownlow wasn't in the habit of frequenting the gardening department of the local DIY store. He went up to the back door and knocked twice, and then turned away to smooth back his greased hair and give his quiff a quick remodel. By the time the door opened, he was standing with his hands pushed into the pockets of his jeans, the collar of his denim jacket turned up.

The woman who stood at the door was short and dumpy, her streaked hair shaped in a pageboy cut. She was wearing black leggings with a pair of scuffed white trainers, her large hips and big bottom well hidden beneath the tails of a blue cotton man's shirt. Her face, however, was smooth-skinned, her cheeks healthily rosy, and the shape of her mouth and the slant in her eyes radiated humour.

'Well, if it isn't Elvis 'imself,' she said with a laugh, and then began to move her fat little body in the twist, whilst singing the refrain of "Return to Sender" in a deep, sexy voice. When she stopped she stretched her hand up the side of the door, pouting her unmade-up lips provocatively. 'If I'd known ye were coming round, I'd 'ave put on me see-through negligee.'

Terry smiled. 'I take it that Gary's not home, then.'

Crossing her arms beneath her huge bosom, Rene Brownlow raised her eyebrows. ' 'E's where 'e normally is. In the sitting room, watching telly. I doubt 'e'd notice if we had a *bonk* in front of 'im.' She dropped her hand from the side of the door. 'Nor would 'e probably mind, come to that.'

Terry cleared his throat uncomfortably. He liked Rene, but he was, in nature, a shy man and could never quite cope with her totally up-front frankness. But that was why she had the reputation of being probably the best comedienne on the Hartlepool circuit, and consequently the heroine of the members of Andy's Social Club, where she worked part-time behind the bar. Terry also knew from the general gossip in the club that her domestic relationship had been under a strain since her husband lost his job, but he certainly hadn't come round to get mixed up in all that. Rene sensed his unease and heaved out a sigh. 'So what can I do for ye, Terry me lad?'

'I need to 'ave a word.'

Rene leaned her back against the open door. 'In that case, ye'd better come in.'

Terry walked past her into a tight-spaced kitchen, still cluttered with dirty pans and dishes from the evening meal. Rene squeezed herself between Terry and the small kitchen table.

' 'Ere, let me clear ye some room,' she said, quickly stacking up some plates and moving them to the sink. ''Ave a seat there.' She pointed to a small plastic-covered stool. 'Like a cuppa?'

'Aye, that would be grand.'

Rene gave the water level in the electric kettle a cursory check by swishing it around. ''Ow d'ye take it?' she asked, flicking on the switch.

'Milk and two sugars, please.'

Rene let out a low growl. 'Ooh, I like a man with a sweet tooth.' She shot Terry a smile, but it went unreciprocated. She shook her head. 'I'm only joking, ye know, Terry. I can't 'elp it. It's the way God made me.'

Terry nodded. 'I know.'

Rene plopped a tea bag into a mug. 'And bloody 'ell, it's 'ard enough trying to keep joking round 'ere at this very moment in time.'

'Aye, probably,' Terry replied.

Rene pulled a stool away from the table with her foot and sat down. Instinctively, Terry shot a look at its thin wooden legs and wondered if it was going to be able to take the strain. He turned his eyes away before Rene had a chance to notice and, as a form of diversion, pulled a pepper pot across the table and began spinning it around in his fingers.

Rene leaned over and took it from him and pushed it to the far end of the table. 'Ye're worse than the kids, y'are. Always find something to fiddle with when they're going to tell me something . . . bad.'

Rene emphasised the last word and watched closely for Terry's reaction.

'No, it ain't bad, Rene. Far from it . . . I think.'

'In that case, let's be 'aving ye, then,' she said, getting up from the stool and pouring hot water into the mug.

Terry rubbed his hands on the legs of his jeans, as he always did to settle himself to talk. 'Well, it's like this, lass. The lads down at the club 'ave been 'aving a whip-round for ye.'

Rene frowned questioningly at him as she slowly stirred sugar into the tea. She placed the mug in front of him and resumed her seat. 'For what reason?'

'We've arranged for ye to go up to Edinburgh in August.'

'Edinburgh? Why on earth would I want to go up to Edinburgh? Are you and the lads trying to tell me the act's that bad, ye want to banish me to Scotland?'

'No. Listen, Rene, it's for the Edinburgh Festival – or for the Fringe, to be exact.'

'The Fringe?' Rene shook her head. 'I'm sorry, Terry, ye've lost me, lad. I don't understand what ye're saying 'ere.'

''Ave ye 'eard of the Fringe?'

'If we're talking about 'aircuts and the neat finishing on candlewick bedspreads, then I 'ave. If not, then ye'll 'ave to enlighten me.'

Terry scratched at the side of his face. This was not going as easily as he had hoped. 'The Fringe, Rene, is part of the Edinburgh Festival. It's the name for a whole load of different acts put on in different venues all round the city. There are all sorts of plays and reviews and things – and also comedy shows.'

'So what are ye saying?' Rene asked quietly.

'We think ye should go up there and put on a show.'

Rene let out a short laugh and stared incredulously at Terry. 'Ye're joking!'

'No, far from it.' He leaned forward on the table. 'Listen, Rene, ye're a bloody wonderful comedienne, but ye're never going to get anywhere just staying 'ere in 'Artlepool. The lads down at Andy's think ye could make it big, and the Fringe is known for being a really good launching pad for people like you.'

'People like me?' Rene exclaimed. 'You and the lads 'ave lost the plot, you 'ave, Terry.' She got up and began to slide dishes with a clatter into the sink. 'People like me don't do that kind of thing. We live in 'ouses with unemployed 'usbands. We go to the supermarket and 'ang around the shelves where all the stuff that's past its sell-by date is stacked. We take the kids on a Sunday to Ward-Jackson Park to feed the ducks with stale bread because we can't afford to go to the cinema complex down at the Lanyard. We don't even entertain the idea of leaving 'Artlepool. I mean, a 'oliday for me would be spending a weekend with the "codheads" round on the 'Eadland!' She threw a washing-up cloth with force into the sink. 'We can't afford to have pipe dreams, Terry, about making it big and getting our names up in lights. It just don't work that way.'

'Who says it don't? What about people like Jim Davidson and Jimmy Tarbuck and the like?'

'Oh, yeah? They made it big "on the Fringe", did they?' she asked sarcastically.

'I'm not sure of *that*, exactly, but they both came from pretty 'umble rootings as well.'

'I know that, Terry, but they are them and I am me.' She sat down heavily on the stool. 'Ye know, I'm really touched you and the lads 'ave done all this for me, but go back and tell them to spend their money on something more worth-while' – she laughed quietly – 'like getting something better than an 'ole in the ground for the ladies' toilet in the club, for a start!'

Terry shook his head. 'No, it's you going to Edinburgh or nowt.'

'Why's that?'

'Because we've paid the money and booked the venue.'

'Ye never 'ave!'

'So if you don't go, we'll all be out of pocket.'

'But why the 'ell did ye pay before telling me about it?'

Terry simply smiled at her, a knowing look on his face. Rene flicked back her head, understanding everything.

'You knew there wasn't a chance of me considering it other-wise, isn't that right?'

'Something like that,' Terry replied quietly.

Rene leaned her elbows on the table and rested her forehead in the palms of her hands. ''Ow long's it for? A couple of nights or summat?'

'Three weeks.'

Rene shot upright. 'Three weeks! Terry, I can't go up to Edinburgh for three weeks. For a kick-off, I couldn't afford it!'

'That's all been taken care of.'

'Oh, bloody 'ell, Terry! This has not been thought through at all! I mean, I couldn't just 'ead off and leave the kids to fend for themselves, could I?'

'What about Gary? 'E's not working.' Rene had her mouth open, ready to set off again with another stream of reasons-why-not, but was cut short by Terry's raised hand. 'Rene, don't find excuses for this one. We can work around it. You 'ave a real gift, lass, for making people laugh. Doesn't matter who they are or where they come from, ye could make anyone laugh. Why keep it for 'Artlepool when ye could make yerself some decent money elsewhere? It's only three weeks out of yer life, and if it doesn't work out, well then, ye 'aven't lost out on anything, 'ave ye?'

Rene did not reply, but sat biting at her bottom lip.

'But,' Terry continued, 'if you let this chance slip, ye could go regretting it for the rest of your life.'

The door leading from the kitchen into the front of the house opened and a tall skinny man, dressed in baggy jeans and a checked lumberjack's shirt, open to reveal a grubby white T-shirt, leaned his shoulder against the door pillar. 'What's going on in 'ere, then?' he asked, taking a long drag on his cigarette and exhaling the smoke through his hawk-like nose.

Rene smiled at the man. 'Ye know Terry, don't ye, Gary? Ye've met him at Andy's.'

The man nodded his head briefly in greeting. 'Terry.'

'Nice seeing ye, Gary.'

Gary walked over to the sink, ran water on to the stub of his cigarette and threw it into the bin. He turned around and leaned his bottom against the kitchen sink and folded his arms. 'So what gives 'ere? Voices were raised that much, I could 'ardly 'ear the telly.'

'Nowt, really,' Rene replied, narrowing her eyes at Terry in a bid to stop him from even starting on an explanation. Terry chose to ignore it. He had come this far and he needed an answer before he went off to do his paint job.

'What d'ye think of Rene as a comedienne, Gary?'

'She's damned good,' Gary replied with a flick of his head. 'Makes us all laugh, any road.'

Terry shot a look at Rene. 'Aye, that's what I was telling 'er.'

Gary snorted out a laugh. 'So that's what ye've come round to tell 'er, is it? That she's a funny person?'

'No, not exactly.'

'So, what's yer explanation for being 'ere, then?'

'Gary!' Rene reproached him tentatively, detecting the edge of hostility in his voice. She took in a deep breath. 'Right, then. I'll do the explaining. Some of the lads down at the club 'ave put money in a kitty to send me up to Edinburgh in August to do me act at something called the Fringe.'

'Oh, aye?' Gary said, taking a cigarette packet from the breast pocket of his shirt. 'And what 'ave ye said?'

Rene glanced at Terry. 'I've told 'im that I can't make a decision right now.'

Gary put a cigarette in his mouth and lit it. He took a deep drag. 'What would ye 'ave to do?'

'Just do me act.'

Gary shrugged. 'Why not, then? Ye could take the train up and get back next day.'

Rene looked at her husband. 'It would be for three weeks, Gary.'

'Three weeks? No way, then! Ye can't go off and abandon yer family for three weeks, especially not in August! That's when Robbie and Karen'll be getting ready to go back to school. Who's going to manage all that?' Gary took another long drag from his cigarette and shook his head. 'A nice thought, Terry, but it wouldn't work out at all.'

'Excuse me,' Rene exclaimed, her voice rising in volume, 'but is there any good reason why you shouldn't look after Robbie and Karen? After all, ye're not doing owt else at the moment.'

Gary leaned over, inches away from Rene's face, his eyes pierced with anger. 'It's not my bloody fault I don't 'ave a job. And anyway, what would 'appen if I got a job while ye were away? Who'd look after the kids then?'

'*I* don't know, Gary. I haven't given it that much thought yet!'

'Well, forgive if I'm wrong, lass, but it sounds as if ye've thought about it good and proper!'

Terry got slowly to his feet and pushed the stool under the table. 'Look, I'd better get off and leave you two alone to talk about it.' He eased his way between them, and then, with another pensive scratch to his cheek, he turned back and smiled at Rene's husband. 'Listen, Gary, I know it's 'ard for ye right now. I appreciate it all, mate. I got laid off at the shipyard back in '92, and it took me an age to get back on me feet after that blow. But you 'ave a wife with an amazing talent, and to 'ave that locked away here in 'Artlepool is a real waste. I mean, she could make a whole load of money doing what she does.'

'And are ye trying to tell me that I'm not capable of making the money then, is that it?' Gary replied irately, taking a step towards Terry.

Terry held up his hands defensively. 'No, I never meant that, mate.'

'I'm the one who's been bringing all the money into this family up until now, Terry, my friend. I wasn't to know that the bloody Koreans were going to pull the rug out from under our feet because of some sodding "global restructuring" plan.'

'I know, Gary,' Terry said quietly. 'I'm sorry, it was never meant to sound that way, 'onest, lad.' He gave Rene a sad smile. 'I'll let meself out.' He opened the door and closed it behind him, and as he stood on the step he blew out a long breath of both regret and relief. He walked around the side of the house, past the weed-ridden rubble and out through the paint-starved gate. The game of football had ceased in the road. No doubt a case of 'bad light, stop play', he thought to himself. He walked over to the van, jerked open the ill-fitting door and got in, cranking up the engine with a roar from the broken exhaust. He was just about to pull away from the kerb when again he was made to jump at the sound of something heavy hitting the side of his van. He glanced in his wing mirror only to find Rene standing beside him on the pavement. He rolled down the window.

'All right, lass?' he asked concernedly.

She nodded. 'Aye, I'm fine.'

He flicked his thumb over his shoulder. 'Sorry about that in there. I didn't—'

'I'll do it.'

'What's that, lass?'

'I'll do it. I'll go to Edinburgh for the whole bloody three weeks.'

'What about Gary?'

'For once in me life, Terry, I'm not even going to think about Gary. This is *my* chance, and I want to give it a go. Ye're right, it'll never come round again.'

'Ye can still think about it, if ye like.'

'I don't 'ave to. I've made up me mind this is exactly what I want to do.'

Terry gave her a wink. 'And, by God, you'll show 'em, lass.'

He rolled up the window and took off up the cul-de-sac, and as he drew out into the street he couldn't resist giving three long blasts on his feeble horn, even though he could hardly hear them above the noise from the broken exhaust.

Seven

Roger let out a long groan and pressed the 'pause' button on the remote with force. He leaned back in his chair and slapped both hands to his forehead. 'Dammit, we should have started on this before now. I just don't see how on earth we're going to make it work.'

Phil Kenyon drummed his pencil on the desk as he studied the two pages of roughly drawn diagrams, his supreme confidence at their being able to programme the piece beginning to wane. 'I reckon we're all right for the first fifty-nine seconds. The timings seem to be spot on.'

'Yes, but that section has the whole orchestra involved. Now we dive into these three quiet passages, followed by two crescendos before we get the volume back again. If we just sequence in a load of flares and fountains, the audience will either end up bored rigid or fall fast asleep by the time we reach that point in the music.'

Phil stuck the pencil behind his ear and pushed himself out of his seat. 'We'd better have more coffee,' he said, clamping together the two empty mugs on the desk with his fingers, 'otherwise we'll be in danger of doing the same.'

Roger glanced at his watch. It was only ten past five in the afternoon, but having only managed four hours' fitful sleep in the past thirty-six hours, all he really felt like doing was crawling into bed and flaking out for an eternity. He pressed the 'start' button on the remote and once again listened through the muted string section of the Tchaikovsky piece.

'OK,' he said, as Phil placed a cup of black coffee on the desk in front of him. 'Let's work first on the crescendos. We don't want them to overrun, so we'll use some of those short-timed items we're getting from Hengyang and then when the volume hits in again, we'll catch it with a battery of four-inch flash mines. How does that sound?'

Phil took the remote from Roger and scrolled back through the music. As he listened again to the piece, he thumped his fist on the desk, out of time with the music but knowing intuitively each moment of firing. He pressed the remote at the end of the section.

'Yeah, I reckon that would work. We'll have to back-time the mines by at least two bars, otherwise we'll lose synchronisation when the whole orchestra comes in again.'

'Shall we risk it?' Roger asked, feeling too tired to make a decision on it for himself.

'I don't see why not,' Phil replied, reaching over to the CD machine and switching it off, 'but my suggestion is that we don't make a decision right now and go sleep on it.'

Roger rubbed both hands at the side of his bearded face. 'That's about the best idea you've come up with all day.'

Eight

Rene Brownlow stood watching long after the van had pulled out of sight, its one-time presence in the cul-de-sac still marked by the lingering smell of exhaust fumes. Well, that's it, then, she thought to herself, ye've gone and done it, 'aven't ye? In the last fifteen minutes, ye've made a decision that's going to change the course of yer life. All right, let's be practical about it, everything could go belly-up and ye might well end up back here in 'Artlepool with yer tail between yer legs. But so bloody what! An opportunity 'as opened up to get away from this dreary little 'ouse in Clavering, to break into a new world outside of this cold, windy town teetering on the edge of Britain. Not that 'Artlepool is a bad place to live, but twenty-five years is a long time to be stuck in one place. Ye may have spent the first ten years of yer life twenty miles away on the North Yorkshire moors, but now ye're a real West Docker, through and through.

She turned and walked slowly back to the house, and as she reached the gate she stopped and looked back to the end of the street, her face thoughtful as something clicked in her mind. 'You'll show 'em, lass,' that's what Terry had said. And he'd said it once before, hadn't he? Rene kicked the gate shut with her foot and then walked along the narrow passage to the back of the house. Aye, it was quite fitting that it was Terry who should break the news. If it hadn't have been for him in the first place, this whole thing would never have come about.

Saturday night at Andersons Westbourne Social Club was always busy, but on that particular occasion, there was hardly room to move, due to the impending and much publicised visit of

Danielle Vine, a young singer who had recently been a finalist on the television show *Stars in your Eyes*, thanks to her superb - yet not quite superb enough to win - impersonation of Celine Dion. Consequently, Harold Prendergast, manager and licensee of the establishment, decided to come out front for a spell so that he could watch with eagle eyes as the money flowed in and out of the three cash tills that were spaced evenly along the shelf at the back of the long bar. He felt this was a necessary precaution, seeing that two weeks before, he'd had to sack one of his eight bar staff for having 'light fingers'. Not that he knew for certain it was that particular girl who was the culprit, but losing money in such a way ate into his profits, and he thought it necessary to show the rest of the staff that he would not tolerate such practice. OK, truth be told, he'd had to pay her off just to keep her mouth shut about what happened, or more to the point, what *hadn't* happened behind the closed doors of his office, but he'd always considered it a perk of the job, having a bit of fun with the girls, and he wasn't used to having his advances spurned in quite such a forceful manner.

He leaned against the bottle shelf at the back of the bar and crossed his arms as he eyed the new girl at work. This one wasn't so much of a looker as the last, her size certainly outweighed her beauty, but there was something definitely sexy about her. It was his theory that a girl could be as pretty as paint, but still exude as much sexual attraction as a cross-eyed donkey. Talking of which, he thought to himself, as he glanced over to the permanently reserved table next to the stage where his wife sat, chatting away primly with her set of friends from Thursday-night bingo. With a shake of his head, he turned away from the sight that, over the years, had come to offer him little attraction and found a space between the spirit-dispensing racks to look himself over in the mirror that backed the full length of the bar. He adjusted the striped bow tie, which drooped a fraction to the left, picked at a loose thread on his white double-breasted tuxedo jacket, and with forefinger and thumb smoothed his well-trimmed moustache from centre outwards. Out of the side of his eye he caught sight of the reflection of the new girl, wrestling to control the size of head on a pint of Guinness. He turned, shot a look over to where his wife was seated, before gliding over to the girl and putting his hand on top of hers on the tap.

'Come on, Rene, lass,' he said kindly, 'ye've been working 'ere two weeks now. Ye should really 'ave mastered the Guinness tap by now.'

Rene looked round and smiled. 'Sorry, Mr Prendergast. I think it's because Joe's just changed the barrel.'

'Never mind, we'll do this one together. Just pour the head off into the waste tray and we'll try it again.' He pushed up the tap and then eased it down, taking the opportunity to move his hand gently against Rene's. 'There, that's going wonderfully.' He took another brief glance towards the stage before leaning closer to Rene's ear. 'I think ye'll manage that now, won't ye?'

'I think so. Thanks for the help, Mr Prendergast,' Rene replied.

'That's what I'm here for,' he said soothingly, putting a hand on her shoulder and giving it a tight squeeze. He started to move away, then turned back and put a pensive finger to his lips. 'Actually, Rene, maybe ye could spare me a moment in me office after ye've finished that round of drinks. Just a few things I need to say.'

Rene looked anxiously at him. 'I can do them most times, Mr Prendergast. It was just the new—'

'No, no,' he cut in with a smile and a shake of his head. 'Nothing serious, lass. Just a couple of encouraging words.'

Five minutes later Harold was seated behind his desk watching the close-circuit television that relayed front-of-house proceedings to his office, when there was a knock on the door. Getting up from his mock-leather executive swivel chair, he ran a hand either side of his parted hair before moving over to the door and opening it.

'Come in, Rene.' He stood aside and ushered her in. 'Take a seat over there,' he said, indicating with outstretched hand the chair in front of his desk. Rene smoothed her black skirt over her large bottom and sat down. Harold scrutinised her actions, and then opened up the two doors of an ornate-fronted cabinet that hung on the wall next to a large black-and-white photograph of himself and Bernard Manning, the bear-like comedian, shaking hands with each other onstage.

'I think we could do with a little freshener,' he said, inspecting the bottles in the cupboard. 'What would yours be, Rene?'

'Nowt for me, thanks, Mr Prendergast. I've never been a great one for taking a drink.'

'An admirable quality,' he said, unscrewing the top from a bottle of Glendurnich malt whisky and pouring a large shot into a crystal tumbler, 'especially when ye work behind a bar. In my book, that's the kind of thing that can earn a girl like you pretty fast promotion.'

He took a sip from his glass before seating himself on the edge of the desk beside Rene. 'So, tell me, how are ye finding the work?'

Rene shrugged. 'Fine, I suppose.'

'Not too much of a strain?'

'No.' She snorted out a laugh. 'Not when the heaviest thing you have to lift is a pint of beer.'

Harold threw back his head in mirth. 'That's not what I meant, lass, but it's very funny.' His face became serious. 'No, what I really wanted to say to ye, Rene, is that if ever there comes a time when ye *do* feel stressed or ye find that things are beginning to get on top of ye, then ye must know that the door of my office is always open to ye.'

'That's very kind of ye, Mr Prendergast.'

'Not at all, Rene,' he said, putting his glass down on the desk and moving around behind her, 'because, ye see, I know all about tension, Rene. It just happens to be my speciality.' He placed his hands on Rene's shoulders and began to knead the back of her neck slowly and rhythmically with his thumbs. He leaned over close and whispered in her right ear. 'For I am a man, lass, who has been gifted with 'ealing 'ands.'

57

'Oh? That's summat, in't it?' Rene replied brightly, darting her eyes from side to side in an attempt to work out why he was doing all this. Surely Mr Prendergast wasn't trying to come on to her? No, that's a really stupid thing to think. He wouldn't pick on a dumpy girl like her, especially tonight of all nights, when the place was jam-packed with punters. And what's more, he knows there's a husband kicking about someplace, because she'd told him about Gary losing his job at the interview. No, Rene, you stupid twit, you're barking up the wrong tree here. Mr Prendergast is just trying to be kind.

Nevertheless, she wanted it to stop right there and then. She jumped to her feet and circled her arms, easing out her shoulders. 'Ooh, that was lovely, Mr Prendergast. Just set me up right for the rest of the night.' She turned to him and smiled, pointing to the door. 'I think I should be getting back now. Work to be done, and all that.'

'No, no, there's no hurry, lass,' he sang out, taking her by the arm and trying to guide her back to the chair. 'That's only the beginning. I've got to work on the full length of yer spine yet.'

Rene pulled her arm away from his grip. Keep smiling at him, she thought to herself. Don't make it look as if you're rebuffing him. 'No, let's make it another time, Mr Prendergast. We shouldn't really keep the punters waiting, should we?'

Rene saw the hand moving back towards her, but then a knock on the door made the manager retract it immediately and he moved swiftly round the back of his desk and sat down, his face masked in composure.

'Come in,' he called out.

Joe, the assistant manager, put his head round the corner of the door. He gave a brief smile to Rene before looking towards the manager. 'We've got a no-show, Harold.'

Harold sat bolt upright in his executive chair. 'What d'ye mean?'

'Danielle Vine's mother has just turned up and said her daughter's come down with tonsillitis.'

Harold slapped a hand to his forehead. 'Oh, bloody 'ell! That's all I need. Can't she do nowt at all?'

'I doubt it. Seemingly, her throat's all closed up and it's gone the colour of a ripe tomato.'

'Please, spare us the details. What about our reserve act, then?'

'Eddie's away in York doing a show tonight. He told you about it last week.'

Harold scratched the fingers of both hands hard at the back of his head. 'Right, then, ye'd better leave me, you two. I've got some bloody thinking to do to come up with an act in the next 'alf an 'our.'

With relief, Rene followed Joe out of the office and closed the door behind her. She took in a deep breath and let it out slowly to compose herself before walking along the passage and out into the bar. Most of the customers were sitting at tables, waiting expectantly for the act that Rene knew wasn't going to happen. The rest of the staff stood in a huddle at the other end of the bar, chatting amongst themselves.

'Be a lass, Rene, and give us a pint of ale.'

Rene turned to see Terry Crosland smiling over the bar at her. She hadn't been working in Andy's long enough to put a name to all the regulars, but she knew Terry because there had been a couple of quiet nights when he'd come in by himself and they'd both had a chinwag together. He always struck her as a bit of a loner, but there was something, she liked about his quiet and friendly manner.

'Coming up,' she replied quietly, still distracted by what had just happened in the office. Without saying a word, she drew the pint, put it on the bar, took his money and rang it up on the till. She placed his change in front of him and turned away.

'What's the matter with you tonight, lass? Cat got yer tongue?'

Rene smiled at the man. 'No. Sorry, Terry, I'm just feeling a bit . . . strange right now.'

Terry raised his eyebrows. 'Right. Well, that were a tenner I gave ye just then,' he said, knocking a finger on the bar next to his change, 'so ye owe me another fiver.'

'Oh, I'm sorry, lad.' She opened up the till and found the ten-pound note slid into the compartment that held the fivers. She moved it over, then took out Terry's additional change and shut the drawer. 'There y'are,' she said, placing the note on the bar. 'Sorry about that.'

'So what's wrong?'

Rene shook her head. 'Nowt, really.'

'Well, there must be summat up, because ye haven't come out with any of yer jokes yet.'

'I can't tell ye, Terry. Anyway, it's probably just my imagination, but the thing is I really do need this job, what with Gary being out of work an' all.'

Terry slowly nodded, his eyes narrowed as he began to understand the situation. 'Ye've just been in the office with 'Arold Prendergast, haven't ye?'

Rene stared at him. 'What d'ye mean?'

''E's tried to come on to ye, 'asn't he?'

Rene leaned forward on the bar, relieved that someone else had knowledge of her predicament. ''Ow d'ye know that?' she asked secretively. 'I mean, 'as 'e done it before?'

'Not that anyone would suspect, lass, but aye, 'e's done it before . . . countless times.'

'Who knows about it, then?'

'You, me, and the other girls who have had to leave because they told 'im to get lost!'

''Ow come you know?'

'Because I found out about it from the first girl that it 'appened to. Met 'er outside in tears just after she'd been given the sack. She was still 'olding the money in 'er 'and that 'e'd given her to keep 'er mouth shut.'

'And ye've done nowt about it?'

Terry shook his head. 'I know, it doesn't sound right, does it? The man's definitely got it coming to 'im, but the opportunity's never come up.'

Rene looked at him questioningly. 'I don't understand.'

Terry turned round, his eyes looking towards the table by the stage. 'You see that group of women over there?'

'Aye.'

'Third one from the left is 'Arold's wife.'

Rene stared with wide eyes in the direction of the stage. 'I don't believe it. D'you mean to say 'e'd try it on with . . . with 'is *wife* here?'

'That's the kind of man 'e is.'

Rene let out a long puff of breath. 'What a bloody *scumbag*!'

'Exactly,' said Terry, turning back to face her. 'So that's what I mean about the opportunity not coming up yet, but it soon will, Rene my girl, you mark my words.'

Rene did not say anything for a moment, but stood biting her lip and eyeing the stage, her eyes deep-set with hostility.

'I think, Terry, old fruit, that our opportunity has just presented itself.'

'Oh? Why d'ye think that?'

'There's a no-show tonight.'

'What?'

'Danielle What's-'er-face has got tonsillitis, and the reserve act's 'eaded off to York.'

'Oh, bugger me!' Terry exclaimed, looking open-mouthed at the hundreds of people in the packed club. He let out a high-pitched chuckle. 'Oh, my word, 'Arold's for the 'igh-jump!'

With that, the lights on the stage were brought up to full power and Harold Prendergast came out of the side wing, squinting blindly into the room. He was greeted by a thunderous hand clap and deafening wolf whistles, the audience expecting this to be the preamble to a wonderful night's entertainment of songs made famous by the French-Canadian diva. Harold approached the microphone too fast, making it screech with feedback. He took a step back and cleared his throat. 'Ladies and gentlemen, I'm afraid that I 'ave some quite bad news for ye.' This brought about an immediate and complete silence, which did nothing to help Harold's nerves. He now let out a couple of hacking coughs. 'I'm sorry to inform ye that our star performer, Danielle Vine, 'as been taken unexpectedly ill . . .' He got no further. The audience erupted with angry jeers and loud whistles, and a chorus of 'We want our money back!' soon took hold and boomed around the club. Harold held up his hands in an attempt to pacify them, but soon realised the battle was lost and reversed away sheepishly to the sanctuary of the side wing.

'Right, go up and introduce me, Terry,' Rene shouted above the noise.

Terry turned and stared at her. 'What?'

'Go up and introduce me,' she yelled louder.

'I 'eard you the first time. I can't go up there.'

'Terry, I know ye're a shy man, but this is our opportunity. All ye've got to say is something about the club being lucky enough to have some in-house entertainment tonight.'

'And what are *you* going to say?'

Rene burst out laughing. 'I don't know yet.'

Terry shook his head. 'Ye're mad, ye are.'

Rene nodded. 'Probably, but do it. Go on.'

Terry reluctantly left the bar and made his way slowly through the tables. Nobody noticed him until he jumped up on to the stage and walked over to the microphone. The noise abated to a questioning hum before there was silence.

'Ladies and gentlemen, we might not be able to 'ave what we came for tonight . . .' A voice yelled out: 'Too bloody right, we're not,' but others in the audience hushed the protester. Terry smiled and held up his hand in thanks. 'But I know this girl who is funnier than anyone *I've* ever seen up on this stage, and what's more, she works right 'ere in Andy's. So I ask ye now, ladies and gentlemen, to welcome 'er up 'ere by giving our own Rene Brownlow a big round of applause.'

There was a smatter of clapping and all eyes turned to watch Rene duck under the bar lid and make her way towards the stage. As she passed Terry, she reached out and gave his hand a squeeze. He leaned over and whispered 'Break a leg!' in her ear.

The first laugh came before Rene had even got on to the

stage. There being no steps at the front, Rene tried to get up by swinging one leg first and then the other before turning turned round and pulling two well-built lads out of their chairs to give her a heave-up. They carried out their task with such power that Rene's feet hardly made contact with the ground until she was centre stage and she had to grab hold of the back-drop curtain to stop her from falling flat on her face. She walked forward to the microphone. 'Thanks, lads,' she said, smiling down at the two men. 'I'll take your numbers later in case I ever want to get shot into space!' The remark brought some chuckles and she watched as the two guys had their backs slapped hard by those around them.

'Right. First I'd like to thank Elvis for that kind intro-duction.' More laughter as people turned to look at Terry, who reacted by running both hands over his quiffed hair. 'Not every girl who gets her act announced by the King himself.' That continued the laugh for a moment or two, sufficient time for Rene to work out what the hell she was going to say next. 'OK, my name's Rene Brownlow. I'm the short fat one who works over there.' She pointed towards the bar. 'Of course, anyone who's the same 'eight as me 'as probably never clapped eyes on me before. Either that, or ye've thought I was just a disembodied 'ead rolling backwards and forwards along the bar.'

That gave her another thirty seconds to get her train of thought going. Her eye was caught by a shadowy figure standing in the side wing. It was Harold Prendergast. She smiled to herself and moved forward to the microphone once more. 'Of course,' she said, moving her wide hips provocatively from side to side, 'I'm no Marilyn Monroe, but I'm extremely 'appy in me skin, and I'll 'ave ye know there are some who find me *most attractive*!' There was a loud cry of agreement that Rene didn't allow to end. 'OK, 'ands up, all you sexy gentlemen out there,' she yelled above the noise, 'who finds me outrageously attractive?'

It was working. She looked out on to a sea of hands, laughed and then turned towards the side wing. ''Ang on a moment!' she said, putting her hands on her hips and frowning theatrically. 'There just 'appens to be a man over 'ere who 'asn't put 'is 'and up.' She saw Harold begin to slide away, so she moved quickly over to the side wing and grabbed his arm. 'Oh, no, no, no, sunshine, you come right out 'ere.'

'What the *'ell* are ye playing at?' Harold Prendergast hissed angrily at her. 'Don't ye realise my *wife's* out there?'

Rene turned back to the audience. 'Oh, he says 'is *wife's* out 'ere. Where is she, 'Arold? Stop hiding yerself in there and come and point 'er out to us all.'

The laughter in the club was growing louder, but it was never as strong as the chorus of 'Come out, 'Ar-old!'

With a sneer of fury, Harold allowed Rene to drag him on to the stage and the audience applauded his arrival for at least half a minute. Rene held up her hand and there was immediate silence, and in that briefest of moments she knew she had the audience totally with her.

'So, go on, 'Arold, tell us all where yer good wife is sitting.'

Harold pointed down to the table in front of the stage and flashed an uneasy smile at his wife.

'That's no use, 'Arold,' Rene exclaimed, shaking her head from side to side in time with her words. 'I can see at least eight beautiful ladies sitting at that table.' She took hold of his arm and pulled him to the front of the stage. This time there was no resistance and he followed on after her like a lamb to slaughter. 'Which one is she, 'Arold?'

'That one,' Harold said quietly, pointing again to his wife.

Rene shielded her eyes against the glare of the lights as she made a show of appraising the manager's wife. 'Wow, 'Arold, you've got a real stunner there! Tell me, 'ow long 'ave you two been married?'

There was a look of intense concentration on Harold Prendergast's face as he carried out a quick bit of mental arithmetic. 'Twenty-four years,' he replied meekly.

Rene drilled a finger into her left ear. 'I'm sorry, 'Arold, my 'earing doesn't seem to be too good tonight. 'Ow long did you say?'

'Twenty-four years,' he repeated, only a fraction louder than the first time.

'Twenty-four years!' Rene exclaimed, jamming the microphone under her armpit as she joined in with the audience's applause. 'Well, that is what I call a wonderful achievement!' She moved close to Harold and leaned her head against his chest, anguish written all over her face. 'I can see now why ye never put yer 'and up. How could I *ever* compare with someone as beautiful as that?'

There was a cry from the back of the hall. 'Put yer bloody 'and up, ye tosser!'

Others began to join in the refrain and Rene saw with glee that even Mrs Prendergast's companions at the front table were calling out their disdain, their own hands shooting up into the air.

Very slowly, Harold Prendergast raised his hand, and Rene Brownlow began to smile serenely, as if she were Sleeping Beauty just aroused from her sleep by the handsome prince. She pulled Harold Prendergast's face down towards her and planted a lingering kiss on his cheek, and the club was filled with the hammering of feet and the beating of pint glasses on the tables.

Rene felt the manager's hand grip tightly to the back of her blouse and he leaned over towards her, as he continued to look out at the audience with a smile fixed on his face. Rene knew what was coming. As he made to speak, she leaned her hand against his right shoulder. He was so distracted with anger and humiliation that he did not realise that that was the hand in which she held the microphone.

'I want to see you in my office immediately afterwards, d'ye understand?'

He had meant it to be a whisper, but his words rang with instant betrayal around the club. There was no need for Rene to say anything, but she couldn't resist turning towards her audience with a knowing grin on her face and giving a slow continuous nod. To begin with, the audience burst out laughing, but then, as four hundred eyes focused on Mrs Prendergast to witness her reaction, the volume faded away to an uneasy silence. Even in the dim light of the auditorium it was possible to see her cheeks redden with embarrassment at the sudden and improper attention that her husband's remark had brought upon her. Glaring with hostility at his drooping form onstage, she got quickly to her feet, grabbed her jacket from the back of the chair, shouldered her handbag and, with her head bowed, started to make her way towards the exit. And as she ran the gauntlet, the only sound that emanated from the crowd was the uneasy clearing of throats and the creaking of chairs as her progress was followed across the hall.

By the time the door had closed behind her, Harold had disappeared from the stage, quickly making for the fire door in order to catch up with his wife and start to make immediate amends. Having captured her audience's attention once more with a quick-fire remark, Rene kept them engrossed for the next hour, never giving Harold Prendergast another thought nor mention. After the show, she went to his office as he had asked, even though she was not sure whether he would be there, and entered when a weak voice answered to her forceful knock. Ten minutes later she reappeared, clenching her fist in triumph as she closed the door behind her. She literally bounced back along the corridor and out behind the bar.

Business was going so well that the bar staff were having a hard time keeping up with the orders. For a while, Rene could do nothing to help out, as those who thronged the bar greeted her with loud cries of congratulations and thrust out hands for her to shake. Rene smiled and said her thanks while scanning the bar for Terry. She eventually caught sight of him over in the corner, leaning on the bar lid and watching her every move. She walked along to the end, ducked under the bar lid, and hardly had the chance to straighten up before she found herself enveloped in a tight hug in his arms.

'You were bloody fantastic, lass. That was absolutely spot-on.'

'D'ye think so?'

Terry pushed her away and eyed her suspiciously. 'Ye know fine well it was, don't ye?'

Rene smiled and nodded. 'Aye, I suppose I do, really.'

'I don't think ye've left 'Arold Prendergast much of an 'eart to try out his old tricks again, that's for sure.'

'No, I reckon 'e'll be well occupied trying to seduce one particular lady for the foreseeable future.'

'So, did ye go to his office to see him?'

'Aye, I did.'

'What 'appened?'

Rene shrugged her shoulders. 'We threw insults back and forth across his desk for five minutes, and then we negotiated.'

'Right,' said Terry, wanting to hear everything immediately. 'So what did ye come away with?'

Rene's face broke into an excited grin and she reached up and grabbed hold of the lapels of Terry's denim jacket. 'A bloody raise and an 'alf-'our comedy spot up on that stage every Thursday night!'

'Ye never 'ave!'

'I 'ave!'

Terry grabbed her by the shoulders and gave her a shake. 'That's just the best bloody news I've 'eard for a long time. Ye'll show 'em 'ow it's done, lass, ye'll damn well show 'em.'

Nine

Having shown the affluent-looking man into her pristine front sitting room, the small elderly woman politely excused herself from his company, closed the door and walked past the dark-varnished staircase to the kitchen. She filled the kettle from the tap, put it on to boil, then slid open one of the double-glazed doors that led out into the small garden at the rear of the house, allowing immediately the thundering noise of the traffic on the Kingston bypass to fill the room. With one hand on the door handle to steady herself, she stepped down on to the concrete-slabbed patio and walked out of the shadow of the house to the edge of the immaculately kept lawn, feeling the warmth of the mid-morning sun permeate through her woollen cardigan.

'Leonard,' she called out, 'are you there?'

There was no reply. She walked out on to the grass and made her way around the curved herbaceous flower bed where she found her husband kneeling on a black plastic sheet, carefully digging around the stubborn roots of a dandelion with a hand fork.

'Leonard?'

Leonard Hartson pushed himself upright and turned to look at her, shielding his eyes against the sun with an earthy glove. 'Hullo, Gracie. Coffee time, is it?'

'No, dear. It's Nick Springer. You remember, he called you two nights ago and said he was going to pop in today.'

'Oh, goodness gracious!' her husband exclaimed, getting laboriously to his feet. He took off his cap and pulled the back of his gloved hand across his glistening forehead, leaving behind a streak of dirt. 'I totally forgot he was coming. You should have reminded me, Gracie.'

'I did, dear, this morning at breakfast.'

'Oh, bother me, did you?' he said, pulling off his gardening gloves. 'How forgetful of me.' He cast an eye over his earth-smudged corduroys and ragged home-knit jersey. 'Do you think I should change my clothes before I see him? I do look rather scruffy.'

'I don't think he'll mind. He seems very nice.'

Leonard smiled at his wife. 'That sounds like Nick. He always was a charmer with the ladies.'

Putting a hand on her elbow, he guided her back towards the house, not relinquishing his hold until she had negotiated the step back in the kitchen. 'Where is he, then?'

'In the front room,' she replied, licking her thumb and rubbing away the streak of dirt from his forehead. She caringly ran her hand either side of his straggling grey hair to make him look slightly more presentable. 'You go through and see him, but take a raincoat or something from the coat stand in the hall and put it on the chair before you sit down. I've just had those loose covers dry-cleaned and I don't want you making them all dirty again. I'll bring through coffee and biscuits in a moment.'

Using the aluminium ledge of the sliding door to pull off the rubber gardening shoes, Leonard then pushed his feet into a pair of bedroom slippers that lay in wait for him and shuffled through to the hall, unhooking a sleeveless quilted jacket off the coat stand as he passed by. He opened the door of the sitting room and entered. Nick Springer turned from the mantelpiece where he had been studying the photographs spread along its length.

'Leonard!' he shouted out enthusiastically, approaching the elderly man with his hand outstretched. 'How wonderful to see you!'

Leonard winced a smile as he felt the grip send an arthritic jolt up his arm. 'Nice to see you too, Nick. What a real surprise.' He walked over to the sofa and spread out the jacket on the pale-blue loose cover. 'You'll have to forgive my appearance. I'm afraid it had completely slipped my mind that you were coming, hence the reason you find me in my gardening clothes.'

'I hope this hasn't inconvenienced you, then.'

'Not at all,' Leonard replied, waving a hand towards an armchair as an indication for Nick to take a seat before he lowered himself slowly on to the sofa. 'It's very rare that I see anyone from the old days in the film industry.'

Nick gave a sharp pull at the creases of his navy-blue suit trousers before sitting down in the armchair. 'It's been a long time. I was just working it out while I was driving down here, and I reckon it's all of twenty-eight years.'

'Really? That long?' Leonard shook his head slowly. 'Oh, well, time stops for no man, as they say.' He observed the younger man as he brushed a hand across his thick dark hair, noticing now that there were traces of grey showing above each ear. His recollection of Nick was that he had been one of his better camera assistants, a quick learner with a good sense of humour, an essential when one had to spend so much time in each other's company, both travelling and on location. However, he had always felt that Nick had an arrogant streak in him, and it seemed to show now more with age in the narrow set of his eyes, the determined jaw and the slide of his mouth when he talked. Whatever he had done with his life, Leonard could tell that he had accomplished it with some success. 'So, are you still behind the camera?' he asked.

Nick shook his head. 'No, I run my own production company now. I did operate camera for a time with Gerry Mansell. You'll remember him, of course?'

'Most certainly I do. We joined Pathé News together many moons ago. Gerry became a particularly gifted lighting cameraman and he and the director Doug Standing formed a most successful partnership. I remember on the film *The Man From Syracuse,* he shot a number of scenes with very little use of a key light. It was both a brave and brilliant concept and the effect was quite staggering.' Leonard chuckled. 'I tried it out myself once, but I'm afraid it all ended up a bit of a disaster.'

Nick smiled at him. 'The only reason I got the job with Gerry was that he knew I'd worked with you. He was equally complimentary about your work.'

'Really? Well, that makes a certain amount of pride course through these old veins of mine.'

The door handle of the sitting room rattled, but it did not open. Jumping up from the chair, Nick was there in two strides, opening the door with force and taking the tray from Grace Hartson's hands before she had even the chance to enter the room.

'Where would you like me to put it?' he asked, swinging the tray from side to side in a way that made Grace fear for the safety of her precious Royal Doulton coffee set. She scuttled around the back of the sofa and spread out Leonard's *Guardian* newspaper on the low stool in front of the electric fire. 'Here, I think, would suit you both,' she said, smiling nervously at the man. 'Thank you for your assistance.'

'Nick, you've met my wife, Grace, haven't you?' Leonard asked, making an effort to push himself to his feet, then deciding not to bother.

'Of course. I was reminding Mrs Hartson that we met many years ago, when I picked you up here once on the way down to Portsmouth for a shoot.'

Grace shot her husband a worried look. 'I'm afraid I had to tell Nick that you had so many assistants over the years, I couldn't quite remember—'

'No reason why you should, Mrs Hartson,' Nick interjected with a laugh. 'I was just saying to Leonard that it was all of twenty-eight years ago.'

'My word,' she said quietly, already making her way towards the door. 'Well, I'll leave you two to have your chat in peace.' She opened the door and closed it soundlessly behind her.

'Shall I do the honours?' Nick asked, squatting down on his haunches and picking up the coffee pot from the tray. 'How d'you like it?'

'Just milk, please.'

'What? No sugar, Leonard? I remember when we used to stop in transport cafés on our way around the country, you put so much sugar in your coffee that you could practically stand a spoon up in it.'

Leonard laughed. 'Goodness, you do have a good memory, don't you? I'm afraid I can't get away with that any more.' He patted his heart. 'Doctor's orders, you know.'

'Really?' Nick handed Leonard the cup of coffee and then sat back down in the armchair, precariously balancing his own cup on the arm.

Leonard pointed to it. 'You'd better not put that there. Just in case . . . you know.'

Nick grimaced. 'Sorry. Is it all right on the carpet, then?'

'Safer there, I think.'

Taking a sip from his cup before placing it and the saucer on the floor, Nick leaned back in the armchair. 'So, is that the reason you gave up work?'

'What?'

'The heart. Was that the reason?'

Leonard shook his head. 'Oh, no. That's only been a slight problem for the past five years.'

'So why did you give up? It really took everyone in the industry by surprise.'

'Now, I know you're overexaggerating on that account, Nick. I never did quite make *that* kind of a mark.'

Nick pushed himself forward in his chair. 'You always were a bit of a self-deprecating devil, Leonard. That is simply not true. I went up to Sammie's on Cricklewood Broadway to pick up some hire equipment about three months after you retired, and I was reliably informed that they'd received endless correspondence from the likes of David Watkin asking why you'd retired.'

'You're not being serious.'

'I certainly am. Come on, Leonard, you were at the top of your professional career and I know for a fact that you were only a stone's throw from being made a member of the British Society of Cinematographers. So, why did you choose that particular moment to give it all up?'

Leonard took a sip from his coffee cup, placed it back on the saucer and let out a long sigh. 'There were a number of reasons, Nick, but overall it was because I was becoming disillusioned with all the changes taking place within the industry at that time. The ACTT union had become far too powerful and was hindering a lot of new blood entering, and I really had no time for all the new video technology being introduced. I hated the lack of refinement in the way that one was supposed to just blast a set with lights. There was no delicacy any more in the technique of lighting, no artistry. Everything was just too immediate. I used to love those nail-biting twenty-four hours when one had to wait for the rushes to come back from the lab, and then see the results up on the screen in the viewing theatre. I really thought it to be the death knell of the industry as I had known it. I even believed that features would eventually end up being shot on video.'

'But they haven't.'

'No, that's true, but you have to remember I was working more and more in documentaries, using sixteen mill, and that was the part of the industry hit hardest by the surge in popularity of video. It was much cheaper, less of a risk, and, to my mind, it all seemed to be becoming so . . . amateurish.'

'The quality of video production has really improved in leaps and bounds, you know, especially now with the introduction of High Def Digital.'

Leonard laughed. 'I'm afraid you've lost me on that one, which really only goes to confirm my belief that if I'd stayed on I would have just become a bit of an old dinosaur.'

'So what did you do after you left? You could only have been in your mid-forties.'

Leonard let out a short laugh. 'It was a difficult one. I had no training to do anything else. I'd left school at the age of sixteen with no qualifications and went straight to work at Ealing Studios as a general dogsbody. I'm close on seventy-three now, so yes, you're right, I would have been in my mid-forties, and prospects for further employment at that age were not very bright. I did do a brief spell in financial services but found it appallingly dull, so I gave that up and became a taxi driver.'

Nick started with amazement. 'What? A London cabbie?'

'No, just a private hire company here in Kingston. Actually, I found it quite a relief. I'd spent so much time away from home and from Grace, I really enjoyed getting back to my own house every night . . . or in the morning, if I was working night shift.'

Nick picked up the cup and saucer from the floor, drained his coffee, then leaned forward and placed them on the tray. 'Do you have any regrets now?'

'What about?'

'Leaving the film industry.'

Leonard pulled at his earlobe thoughtfully. 'I would say that

73

I *did* have regrets, but they have faded with time. You have to understand, Nick, that film-making was in my soul, and I never quite came to terms with the fact that, in my mind, I had never accomplished what I would have considered to be my definitive film. There were just so many different facets of lighting that I wanted to try, being able to push the film stock to the limit, but the type of jobs I was getting didn't allow me to try them out. I'm an old man now, Nick, and I'm quite happy pottering around in my garden, but if you really want to know the truth, I did harbour a very deep frustration for a number of years after I'd given everything up.'

Nick nodded slowly. 'Do you still remember much about how you worked?'

Leonard smiled. 'You don't forget how to ride a bicycle, do you?' He knocked a finger at the side of his head. 'It's all still up here. I don't know what I'd be like at operating a camera now. My hands may be a bit shaky, but no doubt equipment will have improved and someone will have invented a tripod that's even superior to the great Miller fluid head. And I'm sure film stock will have changed for the better too. I would have thought a much finer grain to it.' He let out a quiet, nostalgic laugh. 'My word, you've got me harking back, haven't you?'

Nick had not sat back in the armchair, but rested his arms on his knees, his hands clutched together. 'Do you remember a job we did at the Royal Ballet?'

'Of course I do. We shot it all on 7242 Ektachrome with available light. All pretty grainy, but it turned out to be quite effective.' He pointed a finger at Nick in recollection. 'You operated on that job. First one I ever allowed you to do.'

Nick laughed. 'Now whose memory is working overtime! I don't even remember that.'

'You did a damned good job of it too. It was after that one I was convinced you were going to make the grade.' He let out a sigh. 'But you gave it up too and went into production, right?'

'Yes,' Nick's face became serious, 'and that's really the reason I've come down here to talk to you today.' He rubbed his hands together as he gathered his thoughts. 'Leonard, I'll get straight to the point. Would you ever consider coming out of retirement?'

Leonard observed the man for a moment, his eyes and forehead creased in question. 'Did I just hear you correctly?'

Nick laughed. 'Yes, you did.'

'To do what?'

'A job for me. I want you to film a Japanese dance company at the Edinburgh Festival in August.'

Leonard continued to stare at Nick, and then, with a slow, disbelieving shake of his head, he turned and fixed his eyes in silence on the electric fire.

'Look, Leonard, let me explain the situation,' Nick said, leaning so far forward with intent that his bottom was only just in contact with the edge of the armchair. 'I received a telephone call last week from an old friend of mine, Alasdair Dreyfuss. I used to play tennis with him on a regular basis at Queen's Club before he moved north to become director of the Edinburgh Festival. He told me one of the big Japanese conglomerates is sponsoring this traditional dance company at the festival this year, and consequently one of the broadcast companies from Tokyo has been in contact with me, asking if I could arrange the filming of the event. There are, however, certain stipulations, or a better word might be "complications" attached, in that the commissioner has given express instructions it should be shot on film rather than on video, so that, in his words, "the essence of the dance can be captured in its purest and most natural form".'

Nick was becoming uneasy at Leonard's total lack of response to his proposal, but he decided to continue with his explanation.

'Now to be quite honest, Leonard, my line of work is strictly corporate, and we have always centred our business on video production, but the moment that Alasdair told me about this particular project, my mind was taken back to that job we did with the Royal Ballet—'

'That was all of thirty years ago, Nick,' Leonard cut in quietly.

'I know it was, but you said yourself that the knowledge is still there.'

'Maybe so, but that doesn't mean I could suddenly take on a job like this. For heaven's sakes, I'm seventy-two years old, Nick!'

'So? There are plenty of DOPs still working at your age, and if I'm not very much mistaken, the great Freddie Young was still making films way into his nineties! I'd get you a full working crew, Leonard. You wouldn't have to lift a finger other than just light the set and shoot it.'

Leonard slowly shook his head. 'My word, Nick, what an extraordinary proposal.'

'Three weeks of shooting in August, Leonard. That's all it would be. I'm not asking you to head off for four months to shoot a feature. Three weeks and you just make your own time. The dance company knows it's to be part of the sponsorship agreement to have the show filmed and therefore the director of the company will go out of his way to help you.'

Leonard bit at the corner of his mouth. 'You said I would have to light the set. Surely the company would be performing in a theatre with fixed lighting.'

'I'm going to send a location scout up to Edinburgh to see if he can't find an unused warehouse with a three-phase supply, just in case you want to use heavy lighting. I would suggest that some you shoot under theatre light during the perform- ance to get the atmosphere and the rest you shoot in the ware- house.'

'How would that edit?' Leonard's eyebrows arched with worry. 'And what about film stock? For goodness' sakes, Nick, I'm so out of touch, I wouldn't have the first idea what to use!'

'We have three months before the festival, Leonard, and by the time it comes around, I'll make sure you know as much about the equipment and the film stock and the lighting as you did thirty years ago. It would be as if you'd never left the industry.'

Leonard rubbed at his forehead with splayed fingers, as if kneading away a headache. 'I really don't understand why you are suggesting all this to me, Nick.'

'Well, truth be told, I did have someone else lined up to do the job, but he asked if I could let him off the hook so he could go shoot a big-money documentary in Canada.' He clicked his fingers. 'And then you just happened to spring to mind, Leonard, because word still has it in the world of cinematography that no one has ever come close to being able to film the medium of dance as well as you.'

Leonard thought to rebuff the remark, but then felt such a sudden and long-lost feeling of pride and achievement well in his being that he realised he had no wish to suppress the compliment.

'This could turn out to be your definitive film, you know,' Nick said quietly, taking the retired cameraman's silence as need for further encouragement. 'Why not take the chance to achieve it?'

'I would have to speak to Grace about it,' Leonard replied eventually.

'Of course,' Nick said, shifting back in the armchair with relief, knowing now he had managed to sow the seed of acceptance. 'I'll give you a call in the next couple of days and you can let me know your answer. And if it's yes, then we'll start the ball rolling.' He pushed back the cuff-linked sleeve of his shirt and glanced at the Rolex watch on his wrist. 'I must be on my way. I have a lunch meeting in the West End at one.' He sprang to his feet and stood as Leonard raised himself stiffly from the sofa.

He moved slowly to the door, opened it and ushered Nick out into the hall.

'It was very good of you to remember me, Nick,' Leonard said, undoing the Yale lock on the front door. He held out a hand and when Nick grasped it with his own, Leonard wrapped his other hand over it and gave it an affectionate squeeze. 'I'll have an answer for you when you call.'

'I do hope you take the job, my friend. I feel I'd be repaying a great debt to humankind if I managed to persuade the great Leonard Hartson to get himself back behind the camera.'

Leonard followed the tall man out on to the gravelled path and stood watching as he opened and closed the gate and then slid himself into the dark-green Jaguar parked by the pavement. As the car sped away, he turned to find Grace leaning over a sad-looking azalea bush, plucking away some of its withered leaves.

'Hullo there, Gracie,' he said absently.

'This doesn't seem to be doing very well here, Leonard. I think we should move it to the back garden.' She straightened up and turned her gaze to the Jaguar as it turned out onto the main road and vanished out of sight. 'What a nice man that is.'

'Yes, he is,' Leonard replied quietly as he watched his wife.

'He has a very loud voice, though. Do you think that's requisite for being successful in business nowadays?' She turned to look at her husband and her face broke into a broad grin when she witnessed a sparkle in his eyes she knew had been absent for so many years.

'What?' he asked, perplexed by this sudden burst of humour.

Taking a step towards him, Grace put her hands on his shoulders and planted a long kiss on the side of his cheek. 'Are you going to do it, then?' she asked.

He pushed himself away from her, taking hold of both her hands and giving them a squeeze. 'I don't know. The idea of it all fills me with fear, but at the same time I am honoured he should have asked me. What do you think, Gracie?'

His wife was silent for a moment before replying. 'I could give many reasons why you should *not* do it, my dear,' she said. 'I would worry about you, about your health and about your physical ability to take on a project such as this. But this is not about me, Leonard. You have been given a challenge and an opportunity to counter all those lost years away from the industry that you so dearly loved.' She gave his hands a solid shake. 'So

78

I would suggest you go for it, give yourself this chance, and I am sure no one will be disappointed in what you achieve, least of all yourself.'

Ten

Fred Brownlow gave himself the once-over in the mirror that hung in the narrow hallway of the terraced council house in Wilson Street, Hartlepool. Taking hold of the lapels of his blazer, he gave them a sharp tug, adjusting the fit across his broad shoulders, before giving the sleeves a brisk smooth-down with his hands and turning slightly so that the shaded ceiling light shone on the gold-threaded emblem on his breast pocket. He stood to attention, admiring his turnout just as he had done three decades before when serving as a company sergeant major with the Durham Light Infantry.

'Is that you ready to go?'

He turned to see his wife come along the passage from the kitchen. She was wearing her 'indoors' attire, a floral housecoat with woolly bedroom slippers, and those sparkling eyes that had attracted his attention almost forty-two years ago were made brighter still by the blue frames of her spectacles.

'Aye, Agnes me luv,' he said, taking the white cap down from the hook on the hallstand and fitting it snugly on to his head. 'Ready for action.'

Agnes approached him and began to scrutinise the front of the white V-necked sweater he wore under his blazer. 'That stain came out nicely, didn't it? You make sure to use a paper napkin now when ye 'ave yer tea after the match. No more chocolate down yer front.'

Fred laughed. 'I'll be a good lad, Mother,' he said, giving her a kiss on the forehead. He took a bunch of keys from the stand and put them in the pocket of his light-grey slacks, and then scooped up the bag that contained his bowls from the floor. 'I'll not be late the night. I said I'd give Bert 'and at his allotment tomorrow.'

'Right. Well, play well and don't get all moody if ye get beaten.'

Fred flicked back his head at such a notion. 'As if I ever do,' he scoffed.

And as he left the house, Agnes gave a shake of her head. Although to anyone else her husband's answer may have sounded ambiguous, she knew from experience that one followed the other more often than he cared to admit.

Fred closed the latch on the iron gate, giving a proud glance at the tidiness of his cobbled front patio, and began to walk up Wilson Street. As he hit his stride, he caught sight of the man with the two children walking towards him, seemingly unaware of his presence. He quickly sidestepped off the pavement and crouched down in front of a parked car, but he had hardly time to complete his act of concealment before two high-pitched yells rang out and the slap-slapping of feet came running up the pavement towards him.

'We know ye're there, Grandpa!' he heard the voice of his grandson call out. 'We saw you 'iding!'

Fred stood up just as Robbie came to stand beside the car, a beaming smile on his face. 'Rats! I thought I'd managed to outsmart ye that time,' he said, giving the boy's hair a rough tousle. He turned just as Karen reached him and launched herself into his arms.

'Oh, my word!' he cried out, dropping his bowling bag with a clatter to the ground and catching her up and swinging her around in a full circle. 'Ye're almost getting too big for that kind of thing, lass. Nearly had your old grandpa off his feet.' He put her down and gave his son a welcoming nod as he approached. ''Ow ye're doin', Gary? All well?'

'Aye, good enough,' Gary replied sullenly, dropping his cigarette butt to the ground and grinding it out underfoot.

'Come to pay us a visit, 'ave ye?'

'That was the idea, but looks like ye're on the way out.'

'Aye, I've got a bowling match on. Semi-finals of the district league.' He cocked his head back towards the house. 'Yer mother's in, though. Go pay her a visit. She'd like to see the kids.'

'Ah'll do that.'

'No luck yet, then, with the job-'unting?'

Gary shook his head. 'Bugger all. There's nowt much doing.'

Fred gave his son's arm an encouraging squeeze. 'Ah, well, summat'll turn up, lad. Keep yer spirits up.' He picked up his bag. 'Best be off, then. Can't keep the boys waiting.'

'See and play well,' Gary replied, raising a hand in farewell as he turned to follow the children, who had already disappeared into the house.

The television in the front room was on at full volume when Gary shut the front door behind him. He glanced into the room in passing and saw Robbie and Karen squeezed together into one of the maroon velour armchairs, their eyes transfixed on the screen.

'What d'ye think ye're doing?' Gary asked heatedly as he entered the room. 'Ye're here to see yer nan.'

'She said we could,' Robbie replied, turning to him with a plaintive look on his face.

'Aye, I did that,' Agnes said as she came in carrying two glasses of orange juice. She placed them down on the lace mat she had arranged on the small occasional table next to the children's armchair. 'Fancy a cup of tea, luv?' she asked, giving her son's arm a loving rub.

'Aye, that would be grand.'

'We'll go through to the kitchen, then, and leave these two to their programme.'

Gary followed the small figure with her neat grey curls along the narrow passage to the kitchen. He pulled out a stool at the end of the Formica-topped table and sat down, instinctively putting his hand to the breast pocket of his shirt for a cigarette. He stopped, remembering that his mother had banned smoking in the house since the day her husband had stalwartly kicked the habit six months before.

'Rene working today?' Agnes asked, freshening up the brew in the china teapot with boiling water.

'Aye, she was asked to do the afternoon shift down at Andy's.' Gary drummed his fingers agitatedly on the table. He really could do with a cigarette. 'Probably just as well. She's not in the best mood with me.'

"Ow's that, luv?' Agnes asked concernedly as she poured out two mugs of tea.

Gary sighed. 'This lad from Andy's came round the other day, said that they'd been raising money to send Rene off to Scotland for this Edinburgh Festival thing, you know, to do her comedy turn, and she wants to do it – only I've sort of put a dampener on the whole idea.'

'Oh? Why's that, then?' Agnes asked, concentrating on carrying the brimming mugs over to the table.

'Because it was for three weeks, Mum, that's why! She can't go off for that length of time. Anyway, it's just when the kids will be getting ready to go back to school.'

Agnes sat down opposite her son. 'And that makes a difference, does it?'

'Of course it makes a difference!'

'Why?'

'Well, because . . .' Gary hesitated, his eyes flashing around the small orange-walled room. "Ere, I thought you'd support my point of view on this one.'

'Oh, luv, I am supportive of you, and the lads at Andy's must be pretty supportive of Rene as well if they're willing to pool their 'ard-earned cash to send 'er all the way up to Scotland to do 'er comedy bit. They must think she's really good.'

'Oh, she is. There's no question about that,' Gary replied with enthusiasm. 'It's just that . . .' He paused and Agnes noticed his shoulders slump with dejection.

'Just what, luv?'

'I was 'oping I might 'ave found meself a job by then.'

Agnes reached across the table and patted her son's hand. 'And I'm sure ye will, Gary, but even when that happens, we can all still manage. I can do my bit with the kids and so can yer dad. It's a pleasure for us, ye know.' She gave a thoughtful shake of her head. 'She's a real brave one, is our Rene.'

''Ow d'ye mean?'

'Well, she's considering taking off from 'Artlepool, a place she's 'ardly left in her life, and spending three weeks away from 'er family in a place where she'll know absolutely nobody. That's not a decision to be made by the faint-hearted. She must really feel she can make a success of 'erself at this festival.'

Gary bit at his lip as he watched his mother smiling encouragingly at him. 'All right, I get yer point.'

'In that case, why not just get right behind 'er and give 'er the encouragement she needs? After all, ye never know what might come of all this.'

Gary nodded slowly. 'Ye reckon she should go then.'

'Absolutely, and if ye want to show how much ye love her, which I know ye do, then ye'll be waving her off up to Scotland with flags unfurled.'

At that moment, Karen sidled into the kitchen and came over to sit on her father's knee. 'Dad, I'm feeling hungry,' she said, looping an arm around his neck.

'Are ye, my luv?' Agnes said, pushing herself to her feet. 'In that case, what d'ye say to yer nan making us all a nice big plate of bangers and mash?'

Gary laughed and gave his daughter a tight squeeze. 'I think we'd all say that's a really good idea, Nan, wouldn't we, darlin'.'

Eleven

On a warm, cloudless morning at the beginning of August, Jeff Banyon strode along Princes Street at a brisk pace, feeling a bead of sweat break out from under the collar of his shirt and trickle slowly down his back. There was still one week to go before the Fringe started in earnest and two weeks before the

International, but already there was an increase of tourists on the street. He body-swerved a tall blonde probably Scandinavian couple, heavily laden with haversacks, who had suddenly stopped to consult a street map, then almost stumbled over a young Japanese photographer who was squatting down on his haunches trying to work out the best angle to capture the line of sail-like pennants that hung on every lamp post from the Scott Monument to the junction with Lothian Road, heralding the forthcoming festival.

When his mobile rang, Jeff had to juggle with his briefcase and jacket, which he carried forefinger through hanging loop and slung over his shoulder, to free up a hand to answer the call. As he walked, listening more than he was speaking, he looked down over Princes Street Gardens to where the railway track broadened out before entering Waverley Station to see if the eleven-o'clock train to London was yet in sight. He quickened his pace to a loping run as he turned down Waverley Bridge, seeing the slanted front of the dark-blue-and-red GNER engine appearing from the tunnel below the castle. It was a natural reaction, but then, on glancing at his watch, he realised he still had a good ten minutes before its scheduled departure, so he slowed once again to a fast walk, not wanting to be soaked with perspiration by the time he boarded the train.

As he made his way into the station he ended the call and slipped his mobile into the breast pocket of his jacket, letting out a sigh of relief. It was his fourth season working with the Scottish Chamber Orchestra and dealing with the organisation of the Fireworks Concert, yet time and experience did not seem to make it come any easier. Over the last three months he had managed to speak with Roger Dent, the owner of the Exploding Sky Company, on just four occasions, and it was only now that it had been confirmed to him they had finally succeeded in scoring the Tchaikovsky piece and had already begun to stock-pile the required equipment and hardware needed for the show.

Dealing with Roger had always been one long run of high-octane stress. The man was a law unto himself, totally unorthodox in the way he conducted his business, but at the end of the day he never failed to come up with the goods, always producing a display that left the audience open-mouthed in awe, something his company had succeeded in doing for the past twenty-odd years. However, Jeff knew that Roger Dent would never be aware of the amount of bluffing and downright lying he himself had to solicit on the part of the pyrotechnic to appease the demands and enquiries of both the sponsors of the Fireworks Concert and Sir Alasdair Dreyfuss, the director of the International Festival.

He flashed his ticket to the stern-faced official at the barrier and made his way down the long platform towards the front of the train. Thank goodness he had known well in advance about today's meeting in Newcastle. It had resulted in his acquiring a first-class ticket off the Internet at a much-reduced rate. That gave him at least an hour and a half of comfort and tranquillity to gather his thoughts before meeting with Sir Raymond Garston, the man charged with conducting the Scottish Chamber Orchestra when it accompanied the Fireworks Display on the final Saturday night of the festival.

At the rear section of the train, Leonard Hartson eventually managed to squeeze his suitcase into a luggage rack, half a carriage away from where he had his reserved seat. He edged his way back along the central aisle, his path hindered by children who stood staring in blank fascination at other passengers, and old ladies who were hoping to rely on the goodwill of others to help them put their bags and coats up onto the overhead racks. Eventually, he found his seat and excused himself past his travelling companion, a man of stocky build and unshaven face wearing a woollen plaid shirt and jeans tucked into rigger boots. As Leonard squeezed past him he noted from the reservation ticket on the man's seat he had boarded the train at Aberdeen and already there were several empty cans of McEwans Export on the table in front of him. Leonard smiled briefly at the beery-breathed man before sitting down in his seat with a puff of relief and turning to look out of the window at a young family on the platform who were mouthing words of farewell to an elderly lady seated in the row in front of him.

Despite Gracie's encouragement, he had taken his time over his decision to agree to Nick Springer's request. In the cold light of day after the producer's visit, Leonard began to doubt his ability to take on the Edinburgh job and to question Nick's judgement in not using a cameraman who had both age and technical knowledge on his side. Nick, however, was not to be swayed and arranged for Leonard to study the work of a young freelance cameraman for a week, saying that Leonard could give him an answer after that period.

It turned out the cameraman knew well of Leonard's reputation and appeared more agitated and nervous at the prospect of working with the cinematographer than Leonard was of starting from scratch. Leonard had stood aside as the young man set his lights, watching in fascination as he positioned the small 1K redheads to illuminate an area that would have required at least two 5Ks as 'fillers' in his day. Leonard politely questioned the man about the speed of his film stock, doubting whether he had enough lights to shoot the scene without the need to 'bump it up' a stop or two during processing in the laboratory. The cameraman had told him there had been a huge improvement in both the quality and speed of Eastman Colour over the years, and then, knowing the reason for Leonard's question, he had cast a look at his lighting set and said with a smile that he thought he would probably get away with it. Leonard continued to study the young man's technique as fine adjustments were made, and as his own knowledge came flooding back, he found himself having to bite his tongue at times to stop himself from suggesting the use of a piece of diffuser scrim here or the partial closing of a 'barn door' there. But then later, when he had walked around amidst the nostalgic blaze of lights with his old leather-cased Weston light meter held out in front of him, Leonard was very glad that he had held back any form of criticism. The set was not lit for any great effect, but it was certainly perfectly balanced.

However, it wasn't until Leonard touched the redesigned body of the Arriflex 16SR3 camera that he suddenly felt back where he belonged. His hands moved instinctively around the grainy cast of the apparatus, accustoming himself to the new positioning of handles and buttons and focus lugs. With a steadying hand on the rear-mounted film magazine, he levelled the tripod head, unlocked the tilt and pan levers and with his eye pressed to the foam eyepiece on the adjustable viewfinder, he swung the camera through a smooth figure of eight, exactly the same movement he had practised so many years ago with the old two-wheeled mechanical Moy head on the studio floor at Ealing. The young cameraman watched his action closely, and then changed the static lens for a Canon 10:1 zoom, inviting him to try it out. Leonard pressed the button on the automatic zoom, marvelling at its smooth action and thinking that long gone were the days when a jerky movement on the manual lever would have resulted in a scene reshoot. With the zoom tight in, he focused on a book that lay on a table in the centre of the set, and then returning to wide angle, he once again went through the figure of eight, ending up close in on the book, perfectly focused. When he had finished, he locked off the tripod and stood back from the camera and smiled. Nothing had changed, and he knew from that moment on he still had the knowledge and the ability to accept Nick's commission.

And now, having carried out his recce in Edinburgh, and having seen the warehouse the location scout had found, Leonard knew exactly what he required. He had made out the list the night before in his hotel bedroom and faxed it to Nick's production manager. In two weeks' time, he would be back here in Edinburgh to meet up with his assistant cameraman and two electricians who would be bringing the equipment up from London, ready to start the job.

The train eased off slowly on its journey south, and Leonard watched as the young family waved frantic goodbyes to the woman in the train, moving quicker along the platform in an attempt to keep up with the carriage as it accelerated away. Then, just before they were out of sight, Leonard witnessed the effects of a sudden gust of wind blowing at the woman's cotton dress, making her push it down between her knees, her mouth oval with embarrassment.

Three miles to the north of Waverley Station, over the genteel crescents and ordered rows of the New Town, that same surge of wind blew hard through the weathered concrete five-storey blocks of council flats on Pilton Mains before losing its force somewhere out over the expanse of the Firth of Forth. It billowed out the lines of faded washing that hung on the small railed balconies, a flash of green breaking the grey starkness of the scene as a Hibernian football strip fluttered earthwards from a washing line on the top floor. It landed noiselessly beside a young boy with a shaven head and a silver stud in his ear who had been ambling across the bare swathe of litter-strewn grass. Darting his eyes around the buildings to make sure no one was looking, he quickly picked it up and bundled it into the folds of his zipped jacket, before walking on with practised nonchalance.

In Thomas Keene's bedroom, situated on the third floor at the end of one of the blocks, an empty Tesco baked beans tin, positioned on the extreme edge of the broken-backed chair by his bed, also fell victim to the gust that blew in through the uncurtained window. It clattered to the ground and rolled noisily across the bare floorboards, leaving in its wake a trail of ash and self-rolled cigarette butts, adding little to the detritus already covering every square inch of the room. The figure on the bed stirred under the crumpled, uncovered duvet and a leg shot out in a long juddering stretch, revealing a dirty green undersheet that was too short for the grubby, swirl-patterned mattress. After a moment of complete stillness, the duvet was thrown back and Thomas Keene, known to those few friends he had in the locality as T.K., greeted the brightness of the new day with a rub at his stinging eyes, a long and successful sniff, and a string of expletives.

Swinging his legs over the side of the bed, T.K. sat for a moment in his T-shirt and shorts, scratching his head and dragging fingers with difficulty through his thin tangle of greasy brown hair. He stood up and pulled on a pair of jeans that had lain in wait since he had removed them the night before, and then, progressing a step further, he pushed his bare feet into a pair of dirty trainers, their laces already tied, and kicked them on as he walked over to the bedroom door. Pulling a hooded sweatshirt off the bare screw in the wall that had at one time supported a shelf, he opened the door and walked into the sitting room, where his father slumped low in a battered armchair, smoke curling from the cigarette he held cupped in his hand, as he eyed vacantly the chatty banter of the presenters on the television.

'Whit's there tae eat?' T.K. asked, pulling the sweatshirt on over his head. He stood rubbing a hand down the soft, unshaven stubble on his pockmarked cheek, his mouth hanging open as if the weight of his flabby bottom lip were too much for his narrow jaw to bear.

His father answered with a negative flick of his head.

'Could ye gie's some money, then?'

'Awa' tae hell,' his father replied, without taking his eyes off the television. 'D'yae think ah'm daft or summat?'

'It's fi food.'

'Oh, aye?'

T.K. shook his head slowly at his father's mistrust. 'Ah'm clean, you know. Ah havnae touched the stuff fi twa months. Gie's some credit fi tha'.'

Putting the cigarette in his mouth, Thomas Keene senior turned, a sneer on his face, and began to slow-handclap his son in strong, aggressive beats, the action making the long ash fall from the cigarette on to his mountainous belly. He scattered it with a flick of a finger and turned back to the television. 'Try getting yersel' a joab then, if yuv stopped fryin' yer brains.'

'Ah cannie.'

'How no?'

'There's naine aboot.'

'Well then, dae wha ye did last year. Awa' an' tak' photies of a' thae tourists aw aboot the toon.'

'Ah cannie,' T.K. replied morosely.

'How?'

'Ah've flogged the camera.'

His father turned and glared at him 'Fi a fix?'

'Na, fi cash!' T.K. replied angrily. 'Ah told ya before, ah'm clean!'

His father shook his head and leaned forward to stub out his cigarette in the overflowing ashtray on the table in front of the television. 'Mon then, get yersel' uptoon and see wha gives.'

'I've nae change fi the bus.'

His father let out a long sigh. 'God gae ye legs, lad. Awa' an' use 'em.'

T.K. shambled over to the door of the flat and opened it with force. He turned and gave his father a middle-finger salute before slamming the door behind him.

He always used the stairs, because the lift never worked, and if it did, there was more likelihood of being roughed up inside it. Nevertheless, he was now in the habit of sticking his head around every turn in the staircase as he descended, just in case there was a dealer hanging about or someone waiting for the chance to dish out a bit of GBH. He took the concrete steps two at a time, his hand sliding down the graffitied wall, trying to hold his breath for as long as possible so he didn't have to take in the mixed odour of disinfectant and urine that came at every turn. He burst out into the sunlight at the bottom, heaved in a gulp of fresh air and made his way across the estate to the cul-de-sac where the dustbins were kept, the entrance to the shortcut uptown.

As he turned into the cul-de-sac, he stopped and quickly pulled back against the wall. He edged his head around the corner of the building and eyed the two policemen who were walking around the dark-blue Ford Mondeo. One was talking in a low monotone while the other was writing details down in his notebook. The police car was drawn up alongside the stolen vehicle, its blue light flashing, but T.K. could hardly make it out in the glare of the sun.

He had no option now other than to go the long way round. If he was seen anywhere near a stolen car, he knew he'd be roped in for it. No doubt within the hour his father would be getting a visit from the two policemen, asking of his son's where-abouts last night. But this time it hadn't been him. He hadn't nicked a car for the past few months, ever since he had given up on the hard stuff. It had been hard graft trying to break both habits, but he owed it to his solicitor, Mr Anderson, for somehow getting him a two-month probationary order with compulsory rehab instead of the expected spell in borstal. 'I can't help you any more, Thomas,' Mr Anderson had said to him afterwards outside the juvenile court. 'One more offence like this and you'll have me looking a real fool and you'll be facing lock-up for at least two years.'

T.K. ran out to the front of the estate and turned eastwards on to the main road that headed towards Leith Docks. Not that he didn't miss it, though. The joy-riding, that is, not the drugs. He still took the 'script', the prescribed methadone, but he was determined not to go back on the hard stuff, not after suffering those interminable days of gut-wrench and vomit and shivering and hallucination.

But the joy-riding was a different matter. First time he'd done it was when he was fourteen years old. It was a Ford Fiesta, parked up for the night in Northumberland Street Lane. The boy he was with got into the car and hot-wired it within one hundred seconds, and with a heavy burn of rubber they'd headed off on an exhilaration trip that took them up on to Queen Street, down Leith Walk and then back along Ferry Road, even-tually ending the evening triumphantly by abandoning the car with its front wheels on the top step of the war memorial in the centre of the gravel sweep at Fettes College. As they made their escape across the playing fields back towards Ferry Road, the boy had panted out proudly that on their journey they had come across ten sets of traffic lights showing red and he'd never stopped at one of them.

After that, T.K. had been hooked, and in the two years that followed he took off no fewer than fifty cars. He became an artist at his craft, being able to break into the most sophisticated German car, disabling its alarm, hot-wiring its supposedly fool-proof ignition system, all within the space of two and a half minutes. He did get caught once in his early years, and that's when he'd first met Mr Anderson, who managed to get him off on the grounds of his age and it being his first-time offence. T.K. hadn't asked for the seven cars he had stolen previously to be taken into account.

And then he had done the contract theft of the BMW for the man in Craigmillar and he suddenly found himself with two hundred pounds in his pocket. He didn't go looking for the drug dealer. Word just got around the estate that Thomas Keene junior had money and the man came knocking on the door of the flat. And after that, he never again had the concentration nor the ability to carry out his craft. He had tried on a number of occasions, but his brain lacked any degree of coordination and his hands shook so much that he would set the car alarm off before he had even the door unlocked. And so he had come to rely on petty theft to feed his habit, hanging around the bus stops and coffee shops uptown, watching out for an open handbag or a jacket or coat slung casually across the back of a chair.

Then three months ago, impulse had made him jump into the Vauxhall Vectra left outside the newsagent on West Granton Road with its engine running, the owner having rushed in to buy something like cigarettes or a newspaper. T.K. had been pretty loaded up at the time and only managed to drive it for a mile before sideswiping a parked car at speed. The impact slewed him across the road, and although somehow he managed to thread an unscathed path through the oncoming traffic, the car ended up with the driver's door caved in against a tree. His brain had been so completely rat-arsed that it never occurred to him to make his escape through the passenger door. He just waited patiently until the police came to free him. And it was following the resultant court case that T.K. decided to take Mr. Anderson's advice to heart.

After an hour and a half's walk, T.K. found himself heading with aching legs up Broughton Street towards the top of Leith Walk. He stopped for a rest, leaning his shoulder against a lamp post, and glanced across the street at a small coffee shop, its stone surround painted in pastel green with the words 'The Grainstore' written in looping purple italics above the door. Even at that distance, T.K. could still smell the rich aroma of ground coffee beans and warm bread drifting out through the open door, and his stomach began to ache with hunger, not having had anything since his paltry meal of a slice of pizza and half a can of baked beans the evening before. Pushing himself away from the lamp post, he shambled across the street and peered in through the plate-glass window at the coffee shop's busy interior. Customers were talking or reading newspapers, some seated at the small round tables, other perched on high stools, their coffee cups resting on the narrow wooden ledge by the window, while a long but orderly queue snaked along the full length of the display counter. He let out a resigned sigh and ambled into the establishment. Ignoring the queue, he approached the girl with the short blonde hair and black hairband who was operating the till at the far end of the counter.

'If you want something, you'll have to join the queue,' she said, not looking up at him as she counted out change in her hand.

'Nuh,' replied T.K. abruptly.

'I'm sorry?' the girl asked, now giving him a quizzical frown.

'Ah mean, ah'm no' aifter some' in' tae eat or drink. Ah'm aifter a joab.'

The girl let out a short laugh of disbelief. 'Oh, you are, are you?'

'Yeah, ah'll dae onythin'. Waash dishes, whativver ye waant.'

The girl's humour disintegrated from her face and she turned to catch the eye of a tall thin man wearing a red-striped butcher's apron, who was in the process of laying succulent strips of rare roast beef on to a baguette with disposable-gloved hands. She beckoned him over with a flick of her head.

'Can I help you?' the man asked, his brow creased questioningly as he took in T.K.'s dishevelled state.

'Ah've just said tae the girl here that ah'm needing a joab,' TK repeated.

'I'm afraid we're fully staffed,' the man said curtly, an uncertain smile flickering across his mouth. 'Now, if you want to buy something, please join the queue. Otherwise, I must ask you to leave.'

T.K. shrugged his shoulders. 'Aye, cheers onyway, mate.'

He turned and made his way over to the door. The queue had now grown to such a length that it stretched out on to the pavement, causing a bottleneck in the entrance with those who were trying to leave the coffee shop. As T.K. joined the throng, he was pushed hard against the back of a chair, and he shot an apologetic smile at its elderly occupant, who turned around enough for T.K. to spy the small American flag stuck into the lapel of her cotton jersey. And then he saw the open bag slung over the back of the chair and the silver glint of the camera inside. It was so close he could make it out quite clearly to be one of the new compact JVC digital video cameras. He scratched at an imaginary itch on the side of his leg, judging the camera would be no more than nine inches from his outstretched hand once he was upright. A feigned stumble would be all it would take.

During the next ten seconds, T.K.'s mind went into turmoil as images of right and wrong flashed in his brain. His father's words of 'Awa' an' tak' phanies of the tourists' spun around his head, merging with Mr. Anderson's 'I can't help you any more, T.K.' He looked back at the counter and saw that both the girl and the man were too preoccupied in serving customers to bother looking in his direction. And then the crush of the bottle-neck started again, and T.K. felt a dunt on his shoulder from behind, powerful enough to make him nearly lose his balance, and he was pushed along with the crowd and out on to the street.

T.K. turned left down Broughton Street, walking swiftly until he had cleared the corner of the coffee shop, and then, tucking the camera into the front pocket of his sweatshirt, he pulled up the hood and took off as fast as his tired legs would carry him. Even though he heard no cries of alarm behind him, he was still convinced that some silent fleet-footed coffee drinker was giving chase, and there was no lessening in his pace as he raced around the corner into London Street. At that point, he felt he had to look back to see if there was need for him to jettison the camera and make a break for it. He did not see the lad walking towards him with the two paint cans in his hands, moving from side to side in an attempt to avoid a col-lision. As T.K. turned again with relief, he veered to the same side of the pavement as the paint carrier. Their shoulders came into heavy contact, sending the two cans clattering to the ground.

T.K. heard a yell of anger behind him, but he didn't turn round nor did he stop running until he came to Dundas Street, at which point he thought he would be safe enough from any pursuit.

Twelve

Jamie Stratton stood rubbing a hand at his throbbing shoulder and watched with annoyance as the hooded figure with the sagging jeans disappeared at speed around the corner.

'Effing junkie,' he said quietly and then walked across to the edge of the pavement and stepped down into the gutter where the two paint cans had come to rest. Both bore large dents but somehow they were still intact. He picked them up and held them out at arm's length, just to make sure there were no leaks, then, switching them to one hand, he took the bunch of keys from the pocket of his paint-spattered jeans, walked up the wide stone steps and opened the heavy black entrance door.

He had got into the habit of taking the stairs to his third-floor flat at a run, two at a time, as it helped to keep his leg muscles toned for rugby, both in and out of season. He let himself in, stooped down to pick up the mail and then walked into the large kitchen, depositing the keys, the paint cans and the pile of mail on the table. He moved across to the sink and removed a couple of dirty saucepans so that there was sufficient space to fill the kettle. He put it on its base, flicked the switch, and then, folding his arms, he leaned back against the Formica worktop and listened to the eerie, unnatural silence in the place.

He had bought the high-roomed Georgian flat at the beginning of his second year at Edinburgh University, his father being the instigator of the purchase. He had lent Jamie the deposit for the mortgage, saying that it would be a good investment and that he could pay off the monthly instalments by renting out the three other bedrooms to fellow students. Having bought the flat at a knock-down price because of its appalling condition, Jamie had cajoled four friends to help him to gut the place during the summer holidays with the promise of a party-to-end-all-parties on completion. They stripped the walls of several layers of ingrown wallpaper, filled the cracks and buffed them down to their original state. They teetered precariously on makeshift scaffolding to fit new roses for the lights and clean and paint the endless cornicing, then sanded acres of dark stain from the pine floorboards. They defied gravity when stretching from stepladders to replace the broken cords on the tall sash windows, and retched with disgust as they pulled rubber-gloved handfuls of human hair from the shower outlets and delved into the mechanics of the lavatory Saniflo to clear blocks caused by certain unsavoury items. Then, having painted the place from top to bottom, they sought out auction rooms within a radius of thirty miles of Edinburgh and spent hours chatting up traffic wardens to allow them to park the Land Rover and Ifor Williams livestock trailer, lent to them by Jamie's father, on the single yellow line outside the flat while they unloaded the furniture. And when they had finished their two-month slog, they had the party-to-end-all-parties. The problem was Jamie had then set the precedent by it and over the next three years the place had endlessly thumped with the sound of music and laughter, to such an extent that he was more than relieved at the end of his university career, two months before, to walk away with a 2:2 Honours degree.

And now it had all come to an end. His three flatmates had left, two to start jobs in Newcastle and Manchester and the other to travel the world, while he had been offered a September placement with a publishing company in London. He had discussed the future of the flat with his father, being reluctant to let it go, but his father had persuaded him it was time to move on and better to sell the place and roll his capital over into a small property in London. So, with heavy heart, Jamie had decided to heed his advice. The plan was made for the flat to go on the market in mid-September and that Jamie would ready it for sale over the summer months, eradicating all signs of the four years' worth of hell-raising (a job which the two cans of paint would finish off completely), and covering the intervening mortgage payments by renting out the three empty bedrooms during the three hectic weeks of the festival.

Jamie sighed nostalgically and turned to shake a heavy dollop of Nescafé into a mug before pouring in the now-boiling water from the kettle. He walked back to the table and sifted through the mail, lobbing the circulars and catalogues directly into the bin by the cooker. He kept in his hand the two letters that remained, one a heavy, buff-coloured A4 envelope from the *Edinburgh Fringe Review* and the other from the accommodation agency that was to be renting out his flat. He tore open the envelope from the newspaper and emptied its contents on to the table. It enclosed a Fringe programme, a heap of flyers on the forthcoming acts and the treasured yellow ticket that would allow him free passage into any of the shows. He read quickly through the accompanying letter, confirming they were pleased he would once again be joining their team of reviewers and setting out the conditions of use of the ticket and the deadlines for the submission of articles. The job generated little money, but it did mean that he could see as many of the Fringe shows as he wished as well as keeping his writing skills honed before joining the London firm in September.

Jamie spun the letter on to the table and set to opening the smaller envelope. He unfolded the crisp parchment paper and glanced through its short message.

'*Shit!*' he yelled out, whacking the letter ineffectually on the side of the table. He gritted his teeth and closed his eyes tight in exasperation before reading through the letter once more.

'What the *hell* do I do now?' he said with a shake of his head, as he refolded the letter and repeatedly creased its edges so hard that it would have become three separate pieces with no more than a flick of a finger. Tossing it on to the table, he ran his hands over his thick blond hair as he tried to work out what options were now open to him. With a further loud expletive, he strode out of the kitchen into the hallway, extracting a battered Moleskin notebook from his back pocket, and walked over to the dark mahogany sideboard upon which sat the telephone. He pulled the elastic band off the notebook, opened it at the back page, and then picked up the receiver and dialled a number.

'Good afternoon, R. and J.L. Mackintosh, Solicitors,' a female voice sang out in a refined Edinburgh accent.

'Yeah, can I speak to Gavin Mackintosh, please?'

'May I ask who's calling?'

'Jamie Stratton.'

'Just hold the line, please, and I'll see if he's in his office.'

The line went on to hold and Jamie drummed his fingers irascibly on the top of the sideboard.

'Hello, Jamie, Gavin here.' The solicitor spoke in a slow, deep, methodical voice, one that Jamie had always found strangely comforting, as if Gavin Mackintosh had the ability to sort out any problem, regardless of its complexity.

'Hi, Gavin.'

'How's that father of yours keeping? Still chasing sheep over the Lammermuirs, is he?'

'Nothing changes,' Jamie replied with a chuckle. His father and Gavin Mackintosh had been friends since their time together at Loretto School, and consequently Gavin had become his father's solicitor almost from the moment he joined the family firm, hotfoot from university. He and his father still played fierce rounds of golf against each other at Muirfield and the two families always came together for the international rugby matches at Murrayfield.

'So you've finished with university. Did you get what you wanted?'

'Yeah, a drinking degree.'

'A what?'

Jamie laughed. 'A 2:2. I was hoping to squeeze a 2:1, but what the hell, I've still managed to get a job with a publishing company in London, starting September.'

'Good for you. And what about the rugby? Are you going to keep that up?'

'Yeah, I'll try. I'll go and see if either Rosslyn Park or London Scottish have any need for a stand-off who moves like a dead turtle.'

'Don't think so little of yourself, lad. Scotland has dire need of a player with your skills.'

Jamie scoffed. 'I'm afraid that's wishful thinking, Gavin. There are about three or four lads from the Border clubs who'll get a trial before me.'

'I'm not so sure. You played for the under-21 team, so it should be a natural progression. Anyway, let's get ourselves down to business. How can I be of help?'

'I just wanted a bit of advice about the sale of the London Street flat.'

'Right. So just remind me, it was September, was it not, when we were going to be putting it on the market?'

'Yeah, but the thing is I had the flat rented out for the festival through an agency and they've just written to say the theatre company involved has cancelled. Trouble is I really need the money to cover my last mortgage payments, and the agency won't be able to get anyone else so close to the start.'

'Oh, what a blessed nuisance for you!'

'It's more than that. I'm not sure what to do now. Maybe we should think about bringing the date of the sale forward? I've practically finished doing the place up, and if I sold it off quick-like, then I'd get some money to pay off the mortgage.'

Jamie heard Gavin hum thoughtfully on the other end of the line.

'My first instinct, Jamie, would be that you wouldn't benefit much by doing that. We could certainly put it on the market now, but I would advise you against going for the quick sale. You might well find yourself undervaluing the property if you hurry it along, and anyway, conveyancing can be a long, drawn-out affair. Even if you sold it immediately, I wouldn't think you could expect payment for a good couple of months, which really doesn't help your predicament, does it?'

'Not really,' Jamie replied despondently. 'So what d'you suggest I do?'

'Take one step at a time would be my best advice. I know the festival is only a week away, but there are still quite a number of notices in shops and newsagents all over the place advertising rooms to let, so why don't you do the same? I can't believe there aren't people out there still desperately looking for somewhere to stay for the duration.'

'Yeah, that's not such a bad idea. Certainly worth a shot.'

'And while you're doing your rounds, drop a couple of flyers into the Fringe office. That might be a good bet as well.'

Jamie twisted his fingers around the telephone cord. 'But if nothing comes of all that, how the hell am I going to pay the mortgage?'

'We'll get you fixed up with a short-term bank loan to cover the payments. You'll have to pay a bit of interest, but you'll no doubt recoup it by allowing the flat to be on the market for a good competitive period.'

'D'you reckon I'd get the loan, though? I'm pretty near being flat broke.'

'Don't worry about that, Jamie. That flat of yours will have appreciated in value by a fair amount over the past few years.' He laughed. 'I'm sure you'll find the banks falling over themselves to get your business.'

'Well, that's good news. Cheers for that, Gavin.'

'Not at all, Jamie. Keep in touch and let me know how you get on.'

'Will do. Bye.'

Jamie replaced the receiver and blew out a long breath of relief. 'Thank God for that,' he said out loud, his voice carrying around the high ceilings of the empty flat. He went back into the kitchen, picked up a random spoon from the sideboard and set about opening up one of the tins of paint.

Thirteen

Gavin Mackintosh made a quick longhand note of his telephone call with Jamie Stratton on a pad of lined paper, ripped off the page and floated it into the wire tray at the corner of the large leather-inlaid desk. He carelessly discarded his reading spectacles, picked up the cup of now-lukewarm coffee and sat back in his chair, swinging it round so he was facing the tall window that looked out across Heriot Row on to the tranquil shrub-lined paths of Queen Street Gardens. He watched as an elderly woman with two small dogs, straining on a joint lead, stopped beside one of the cast-iron benches that bordered the paths. Sitting down, she leaned over to free the dogs, and as they darted off in different directions, she took a magazine from her bag and settled herself to read.

Gavin hadn't really given much thought to the fact that it was festival time again until that moment when he had spoken with Jamie. It always posed a bit of a quandary for him, because although every year he had great intentions of going out and enjoying some of the events, unfailingly his workload seemed to increase at that time and the whole three weeks came and went without him hardly noticing anything out of the ordinary had ever taken place. His wife, however, persevered regardless, booking tickets for concerts and operas, but she usually ended up having to take a friend or prising one of their two daughters away from their ever-increasing young families to accompany her. The previous year, one small window of opportunity had arisen and he had managed to counter the growing exasperation of his wife by attending a production of De Rojas's *Celestina,* but his mobile phone had vibrated in his breast pocket just before the end of the first act and he had had to leave, shrouded in a black cloud of unpopularity, to answer a call from the police station in Portobello and interview a young man who had been caught in the act of breaking and entering.

Pushing himself out his chair, Gavin walked over to the stack of brown cardboard folders on the long refectory table beside the door, selected one and returned to his desk. Maybe this year would be different, he thought to himself. There was one particular event he did especially want to attend, a welcoming reception for the young French violinist Angélique Pascal, in the Sheraton Grand Hotel. He had been more than surprised when he had come across the stiff-backed invitation sitting on the drawing-room mantelpiece at his house in Ravelston Road. Despite constant badgering from friends, he had always been pretty sceptical about how much additional fee income could be generated from sponsoring an event at the festival, and consequently he and his wife had never made it on to the 'preferred' list of guests. However, this time he was going to make every effort possible to attend the party, even though it might lead to a barrage of requests for financial support. It would be worth it just to get a glimpse of the extremely talented and extremely attractive young musician.

Opening the folder, Gavin pulled his chair in close to the desk and put on his spectacles, and began reading through the Last Will and Testament of Mrs Annie Dalgety, a long-time client of the firm who had just failed to reach her one hundredth birthday by a mere six weeks. It was destined to be a lengthy wrangle, as she had always been a crusty old soul, constantly falling out with her three sons in turn and changing her will to benefit the one who happened to be in favour at the time. It was further complicated by the fact that her lineage stretched to three generations below her, and there were no fewer than thirty descendants all looking for a share in the carve-up of her estate. This included a three-storey town house in Royal Crescent, one of the remaining few not to have been divided up into flats, and a substantial share portfolio built up over many years by her late, but in his time very shrewd, stockbroker husband.

Gavin had just begun to note down a few diplomatic observations on his pad, readying himself for the second, and no doubt confrontational, meeting scheduled for four o'clock that afternoon in the partners' room, when there was a loud knock on the door. He put down his pen, took off his spectacles and called out for the person to enter. John Anderson, one of the firm's junior partners, stuck his head round the door.

'Have you got a moment, Gavin?'

'Certainly, John.' He indicated the chair at the other side of his desk. 'Come in and have a seat.'

The lean, bespectacled solicitor moved in an ungainly lope across the room, placing the large pile of folders he had been carrying under his arm on the desk in front of him. He positioned himself in the chair as if about to answer Mastermind questions.

Gavin eyed the folders suspiciously. 'What have we got here, John?'

John Anderson clenched his teeth. 'Ah, I *thought* you might have forgotten,' he murmured.

Gavin leaned back in his chair, an expression fixed on his face that would indicate his lack of recall was about to cause him a considerable amount of physical pain.

'OK, let me have it.'

John rubbed his hands together apprehensively. 'I'm off on holiday for two weeks on Monday.'

'Och, jeezy-peeps!' Gavin exclaimed, hitting the palm of his hand hard against his forehead. 'Of course you are. It had completely slipped my mind.'

'I'm sorry. Maybe I should have reminded you earlier.'

Gavin waved a dismissive hand at him. 'No, it's my fault entirely. It's been in my diary for at least three months, and what's more, I should know by now. This is about the third year I've been covering for you on the Legal Aid cases, is it not?'

'Fourth, actually,' John replied with an apologetic smile.

Gavin let out a rueful laugh and shook his head. 'Funnily enough, I was just thinking about how I never seemed to find enough time to go to any of the festival events. Now I remember it's *you* I've got to blame for that.'

John leaned forward in his chair uneasily. 'Listen, Gavin, if you want, I'll see if I can get someone else to—'

'No, no, I was only joking,' Gavin interjected. 'Of course I'll handle them for you.' He pointed at the pile of folders on the desk. 'Are those your ongoing cases?'

'Yes, but I promise it's not as bad as it looks. Three of them are appeals that probably won't be called to court until I get back.'

'And the others?'

'Five pleas of guilty and two of not guilty. I'm due to be in the magistrates' court for the next couple of days and hope to clear up two of them, so I won't be leaving you with too much.'

'Depends what comes up when you're away, though, doesn't it?'

'Yes, I suppose it does,' John replied quietly.

Gavin slapped his hands down on the desk. 'Never mind. You

go away and enjoy yourself, John, and come back refreshed and raring to go. Where are you off to this year?'

John got to his feet and picked up the pile of folders. 'Majorca again,' he replied, his tone much lighter now that he had accomplished his mission. 'It suits the kids. They get to go to the night-club while Deborah and I can just crash out on the beach.'

'Sounds a good arrangement. You have a good time, then.'

'I will, and thanks for taking this on yet again, Gavin.' The solicitor made his way towards the door and opened it. 'I'll leave those cases I haven't cleared with your secretary on Friday after-noon, if that's OK with you?'

'That'll be fine, John. I'll read them up sometime over the weekend.'

As the door closed, Gavin screwed up his eyes and rubbed his fingers hard on top of his balding pate. Oh, well, he thought to himself, looks like another few weeks of uncultured bliss. No doubt you'll hear the boom of the fireworks from the house and realise it's all over for another year. One thing for certain, though, you'll be getting yourself to that reception in the Sheraton Grand come hell or high water, even if it does mean leaving some young whippersnapper in the clink overnight.

Slipping on his spectacles, he picked up his pen and resumed his quest to sort out the estate of the indomitable Mrs Dalgety.

Fourteen

Phil Kenyon carefully lowered the heavy silver fireproof case to the floor, his knees bent to avoid giving his suspect back a twinge. He straightened up, letting out a puff of effort, and turned to look over to the far end of the old grain shed as one of the large double doors was slid open. Roger Dent entered and heaved the metal door closed with an echoing clang. He walked towards his Australian colleague, pushing a folded piece of paper into the pocket of his chinos.

'Did you speak with Jeff Banyon, then?' Phil asked as his boss approached.

'Yup, all went well,' Roger replied, giving a thumbs-up. 'I think I came out with all the right things to appease him.' He sat down on the case that Phil had just been handling and crossed his arms. 'He's on his way down to Newcastle to meet up with the fellow who's going to be conducting the orchestra on the night.'

'Have we worked with him before?'

'No, so we'll just have to hope he doesn't go apeshit, knowing he's got the eyes of about a quarter of a million people glaring down on him. If he rushes his way through this one, our timings are certain to go all up the creek.'

Phil raised his eyebrows. 'And what about the score reader? Have they got that fixed up yet?'

'Yes, it's the same girl we had last year from the BBC Scottish Symphony Orchestra.'

Phil bit at his lip. 'Ah, Helen,' he said quietly.

Roger smiled knowingly. 'Of course, I'd forgotten you'd had a bit of a fling with her.'

'Could be a bit awkward,' Phil murmured.

Roger got to his feet and gave his sidekick a hard slap on the shoulder. 'I'm sure you'll cope with the situation quite manfully, Phil.' Taking the piece of paper from his pocket, he unfolded it and quickly scanned through the handwritten list. 'How're you doing with the trucks for Edinburgh? Have you booked them yet?'

'Yeah, they'll be here on the Friday night.'

Roger nodded. 'OK, so let's just stick to the same game plan as we had last year. We'll aim to get up there on the Sunday before the final night, and that'll give us the full week to get set up.' He folded the piece of paper and stuck it back in his pocket. 'I'll go up in the first truck with the workshop equipment, and then you and the crew can stop off in Birmingham en route and pick up all the hardware from the store there.'

'No worries. We've got four weeks in hand, so that's time aplenty for getting it all ready and putting the final touches to the programme.'

Roger fixed the stocky Australian with a humorous look of subterfuge. 'If you ever happen to pick up the telephone in the office and find yourself speaking to Jeff Banyon, please, whatever you do, don't tell him that.'

'Why? What did you say to him?' Phil asked with a conspiring twinkle in his eye.

Roger shrugged his shoulders. 'That the programme was complete and we had most of the gear stockpiled.'

Phil laughed. 'Oh, well, you've got to lie a little to live a little.'

'Exactly my sentiments, mate,' Roger replied as he turned and threaded his way through the equipment back towards the entrance doors, 'especially seeing we've got four more displays to get through before we head up to Edinburgh.'

Fifteen

''Ere, Robbie, quit doing that and come over and stand by me!'

Rene Brownlow's yell was barely audible above the cacophony of noise on Darlington Station, dominated at the precise moment of her reprimand by a crackling announcement on the tannoy system heralding the imminent arrival of the Intercity service to Edinburgh. Robbie pushed the luggage trolley at speed along the platform towards his mother, giving it a final spin to extract one more squeal of delight from his sister, who clutched hard to the handle, her feet splayed out across its bars.

'They're doing no 'arm,' Gary Brownlow said quietly.

'What d'ye mean? They could quite easily go right over the edge and under the train.'

Gary smiled at his wife. ''Ow're ye feeling? A bit nervous?'

Rene blew out a shivering breath. 'Only as much as I'd be

feeling if I was 'eading off to me own execution. Before now, an excursion to Darlington for me was about as rare as a mule with offspring, and 'ere am I going even further off the beaten track.'

Gary laughed and put his arm around his wife's shoulder and gave it a reassuring squeeze. 'You'll be fine, girl, I know it.'

Rene gazed up at her husband. 'Are ye sure ye're all right about me doing this, Gary? We don't seem to have spoken much about it recently, what with one thing and another, but I can't 'elp remembering yer first reaction when Terry—'

'Oh, forget that, lass,' Gary cut in with a wave of his hand. 'That was me just voicing me own frustration. I should've kept me big mouth shut. What I want you to do is get yerself up to Edinburgh and knock 'em all dead.'

Rene smiled fondly at her husband. 'It'll turn out all right for ye, Gary. I know it will. But listen, if something comes up while I'm away or ye find ye can't cope with the kids—'

'Don't worry yer 'ead about that,' Gary interjected again. 'Between me and me parents, we'll cope.'

'Aye, I reckon ye will.' Rene turned her head and looked past Gary. 'I feel like the bloody Queen,' she said out of the side of her mouth.

''Ow d'ye mean?'

She glanced sideways. 'My entourage.'

Gary glanced round at the five committee members of Andersons Westbourne Social Club, who stood smiling at them from a distance of twenty-five feet.

'D'ye think we could get a photo now, Rene, seeing that the train's approaching?' Stan Morris asked, taking Gary's look as an opportune moment to cut in on the couple's farewell.

Rene laughed. 'Aye, why not, Stan?' she called over to him.

As the committee chairman slipped the camera out of the leather case he had dangling from his neck, the other members rushed forward and gathered themselves around the Brownlow family. Putting arms around shoulders, they grinned inanely in the direction of the camera.

Stan squinted through the eyepiece. 'Right, all squeeze in a bit. That's better. Skittle, I can't see ye, so get in front beside the kids. No, Norman, not you! You stay where y'are! OK.' He took the camera away from his eye, just to give a final check that it was loaded with film. 'Right, one, two, three . . . oh, 'ang on a minute, the train's pulling in.' There was a universal groan from the assembled group. 'All right! All right!' Stan said shirtily, 'I'm an experienced photographer, I'll 'ave ye know, and it wouldn't do to 'ave the background go all blurry.'

'Well, stop yakking and get yer skates on, then,' said sombre Derek Marsham. 'We've only got the minibus booked until two o'clock.'

Derek's remark produced the laughs that were to be captured for posterity on film. The group broke up as the first of the carriage doors started opening.

'Ye're in the one down 'ere, Rene,' Terry Crosland said as he scooped up her suitcase and hurried off down the platform, the farewell committee following on his heel like ducklings. Rene ambled along, holding hard to Gary's hand. 'I'll call ye every night.'

Gary nodded. 'Aye, you do that.'

Reaching up, she pulled his head down towards her and gave him a long kiss on the lips. 'I'll miss ye, lad. I wish ye were coming too,' she whispered into his ear.

'Ye'll do fine on your own,' he said, putting his arms around her ample body and giving her bottom a tight squeeze.

Rene broke away and gave each of her children a kiss and a hug. 'Ye look after yer dad now, you two, and don't be giving 'im any bother.'

Robbie and Karen both replied with a nod before breaking away from their mother's loving hold, eager to head off once again on their trolley.

'Come on,' Gary said, grasping her arm. 'Let's get ye on board.'

Leaning out of the window as the train pulled out of the station, Rene watched the cluster of waving hands until they bend in the train hid them from sight. She pushed up the window and let out a long nervous breath. Well, that's it, lass, she thought to herself, ye're on your own now.

Thomas Keene junior had worked up quite a tidy little business for himself over the week. Having discovered how to take digital stills with the video camera, he had set himself up on the junction of Princes and Hanover streets and started waylaying tourists as they passed, offering to take their photograph with Edinburgh Castle as the backdrop. It was a success from the start. Once he had at least ten different customers on record, he would whip out the memory card, take it up to the Kwikflick shop halfway up Hanover Street, put it in for a half-hour service and have the prints back on Princes Street within the hour, catching the punters on their return. Of course, at the outset there had been a few problems to sort out. Having not one bean to his name, T.K. had had to persuade an elderly Dutch couple to pay him upfront and then get them to stand outside the shop for the time it took for the photographs to be printed. Then the woman in the shop started complaining about his ever-increasing appearances, so he ended up agreeing to pay her the full hourly rate. He was pretty sure the extra money was going straight into her pocket, but it didn't really bother him that much. At the end of the day, he always had enough money to get himself a double cheeseburger and large Coke from McDonald's on Princes Street and then catch a bus back home afterwards.

That day, however, had not been the best for trade. T.K. didn't really know the reason, but he thought maybe it was because the street theatre had already started up on the Royal Mile, seeing as the Fringe shows were due to begin the following day. He waited until the Kwikflick shop had closed, then pulled his meagre takings from his pocket. It was a toss-up between the meal and the bus. Seeing it was a warm, cloudless evening and he was in no great hurry to get home, he opted for food and headed along the street to get himself a burger.

The cardboard cup and polystyrene container were discarded

over the railings of a basement flat at the bottom of Dundas Street, just before T.K. started out on one of the many complicated short cuts he knew to get back home. He zigzagged through narrow cobbled alleys, climbed walls, squeezed his narrow frame through loose wooden fence panels and swung himself over arrow-tipped railings by grabbing the branches of overhanging trees. He jumped up on to the precipitous wall that ran above Glenogle Road and walked along its length until he came to the point where he knew a number of near imperceptible footholds existed. Lowering himself over the parapet, he eased his way down the wall, jumping the last six feet to the ground. He crossed the road and began to make his way past the many narrow cul-de-sacs that made up the rabbit warren of two-storey terraced houses known as the Stockbridge Colonies.

As he turned the corner to cut down the last street, he stopped and drew himself back against the end gable of the row of houses. He peered around the corner and watched the two boys who ambled slowly along the road towards him. One was positioned on the pavement, nonchalantly looking about him, studying the windows of the houses and occasionally casting a glance down to each end of the street, while the other walked parallel to him on the street, looking for the nod from his mate before glancing quickly in through the driver's-side windows of the row of parked cars.

T.K. drew back behind the wall and laughed to himself. He knew exactly what they were doing, but what he found so ridiculous was they were about to attempt a car theft in broad daylight. Six o'clock in the evening during the winter months maybe, but not at the height of summer. He put his head around the corner once more and noticed them spending time over one particular car. Good choice, lads, he thought to himself, an old Ford, easy to get into, easy to start and plenty of room to make a quick getaway.

It was at that moment T.K. remembered the video camera. He pulled it out of the front pocket of his sweatshirt and switched on the power. Right, he thought, let's see how fast you two can pull this off. Clicking the camera on to 'standby', he stuck the lens around the corner of the building, adjusting the viewing screen so that he could see what was going on. His timing was perfect. He started the camera running the moment the boy on the street ducked below the level of the roof. He straightened up, took one last cursory look around him, and then wrenched the door open and got in, leaning over to pull up the lock of the passenger door. The accomplice jumped into the car, and there followed a moment when T.K. could hardly stop the camera from shaking, as he watched a silent, yet obviously desperate shouting match develop while the driver struggled to hot-wire the car. Then suddenly the engine roared to life, and with a squeal of tyres the car shot out of the parking space and sped down the street towards him. Without stopping at the T-junction, the car veered right out on to the main road and headed away.

He kept the camera rolling until the car disappeared at the end of the street. Putting his hand over the screen to shield it from the glare of the evening sunlight, he read the length of the recorded scene on the time code. Four minutes twenty seconds. He laughed out loud. That is effin' lousy, lads, he thought to himself. If you go on like that, you may as well just *drive* yourself to the juvenile court.

Closing up the screen, T.K. stuck the camera back in his sweat-shirt pocket and swaggered off down the street in the proud knowledge that he, Thomas Keene junior, just coming up nineteen years old and without a driving lesson to his name, was not only a veteran of the game, but also still one of the unbeaten artists at the job.

Sixteen

When Rene Brownlow arrived the following evening at the Corinthian Bar in West Richmond Street, half an hour early for her first show, the last thing she felt like doing was standing up on a stage and being funny for an hour. The first wave of apprehension and homesickness had engulfed her the moment she got off the train on to the crowded platform at Edinburgh, and thereafter events conspired to reduce her fragile confidence to rubble. Not wanting to waste her scanty finances on a taxi, she had dragged the heavy Samsonite suitcase, bought for her by Terry Crosland at a car-boot sale, to her digs in Morningside, not realising beforehand the two-mile distance nor the orienteering nature of her journey. The first part seemed to be interminably uphill from the station until she reached George IV Bridge, where there was eventual but momentary respite from the incline. Despite consulting the map that had been included in the package from the Fringe office, wrong turnings were frequent, and even though the streets were swarming with people, the majority of those from whom she breathlessly asked directions also turned out to be visitors to the city.

The woman who eventually responded to the third knock on the front door of the unspectacular little bungalow in Greendykes Terrace eyed suspiciously the plump figure with the bright-red face that sat wheezing on the suitcase at the bottom of the stone steps.

'You'll be Rene Brownlow, then,' she stated, folding her arms defensively across her fawn-jerseyed bosom.

Rene had simply nodded, not having the essential breath left in her body to answer her.

'Right, I'm Mrs Learmonth, your landlady. You'd better get yourself inside, and I'll show you to your room.' Ignoring Rene's load, the woman turned and walked back into the house.

As Rene used her last ounce of energy to carry the heavy suitcase double-handed up the steep staircase, Mrs Learmonth stood on the top landing watching her ascend and lambasted her with the endless rules of the house. Only one shower to be taken every day, and that between half past seven and eight o'clock in the morning; breakfast at nine o'clock on the dot; no visitors; no use of the house telephone, but she would give directions to the nearest call box; keep the noise down at all times; and the room should be vacated between the hours of eleven o'clock in the morning and three o'clock in the afternoon to allow for cleaning. When Rene cast a spirit-sapping eye around the small, sparsely furnished bedroom that had been built into the low sloping roof of the bungalow, she couldn't quite work out why the tight-mouthed Mrs Learmonth needed five hours to clean such a minute area. However, she was too exhausted to pass comment either on that or any of the other conditions, just wanting the woman to leave her alone so that she could rest her weary body on the low wooden-framed bed that looked more suited to the dimensions and weight of an undernourished pixie. Later on that evening, after she had picked at a near inedible meal of overcooked stew and boiled vegetables in Mrs Learmonth's dingy little dining room, with only the scraping of cutlery on willow-patterned plate to keep her company, Rene had stood in the littered telephone box three hundred yards from the house desperately trying to maintain her self-control when Gary's quiet, laid-back voice had sounded at the other end of the line.

At precisely eleven o'clock that day, Rene had left the house, eager to spend as little time there as possible, even though it meant facing the prospect of killing time in a strange city with little money. She sat for two hours on a bench at the top of the Meadows, watching the joggers and the people walking their dogs and the golfers practising their swings; she walked all the way back to the High Street to locate the Fringe office and then tagged on to a small gathering which had formed around a brightly dressed young man who was shaping a dog out of balloons for a young toddler in a pushchair while she washed a tasteless ham sandwich down with a can of Coke; and when the sky clouded over and a bitter wind picked up, she sought out the warmth of a crowded pub where she sat alone at a corner table, trying to eke out the last inch of her half pint of shandy for as long as possible whilst reviewing her act in her head.

But it was to no avail. All day long, she had only been able to think of what Gary and the kids would be doing, picturing their weathered little house with its untidy garden in Bolingbroke Close. She thought of Stan Morris and his cronies sitting round their usual table in Andy's, snapping down their dominoes and talking excitedly about what she, Rene, would be doing at that precise moment. She thought about what food she should be buying that week from the discount shelves in Morrison's supermarket, and then her imagination took her across Marina Way and down to the end of Jacksons Landing, where the seagulls glided lazily on the wind, the riggings clinked against the tall masts of the yachts and the water lapped lazily against their sleek bows. And then she wished above all other wishes that, right there and then, she could somehow transport herself away from this alien city back to the familiar, warm-hearted surroundings of her own Hartlepool.

Taking in a deep steadying breath, Rene pushed open the heavy glass door of her venue and entered. The Corinthian Bar was obviously a new establishment, equipped from top to bottom with all things chrome. The tables, chairs, handrails, footrests below the bar all sparkled, reflecting myriad small low-voltage lights that were suspended from wires cobwebbing the ceiling. To the right of where she stood there was a small ticket booth with racks of coloured leaflets on its counter, advertising the forthcoming shows; and to the left, a flight of stairs that led down to the toilets and, as indicated by a temporary sign, to the theatre. The whole wall at the back of the stairs was covered with posters, all larger versions of the front covers of the leaflets. Rene took one of her own from a rack on the counter and glanced through it as she walked along the wide ceramic-tiled passage to the bar.

Whilst every other eating and drinking establishment Rene had passed that day seemed to be filled to capacity, the Corinthian Bar had barely any business at all. There were only about ten people in the place, two couples eating at tables, while the rest sat on stools or stood leaning on the dark granite surface of the bar. As Rene approached it, a young barman with gelled spiky hair came over to her, greeting her with a flick of his head.

'Hi there, what can I get ye?'

'Oh, nothing, thanks,' Rene replied. 'I'm actually here to do a show.'

'Oh, right. Just hang on a minute then.' He scanned the floor before catching sight of a girl coming up the stairs. 'Hey, Andrea!' he called over to her. 'This is the woman who's doing the show tonight.'

Rene felt immediately downhearted by the boy's introduction. He didn't call her a 'comedienne', or even by her name. Just 'the woman'. She turned to watch Andrea approach, a sleek blonde who dressed to accentuate her elegant contours in a pair of black tight-fitting jeans and polo-neck jersey.

'Hi, you must be Rene,' she said, offering out a hand that gushed blood-red nails. She spoke in a twanging English voice with no softening trace of a regional accent.

'That's right,' Rene replied with a smile, conscious of the podginess of her own hand when clasped in Andrea's talon.

'Good. Well, look, I think the best thing is for me to take you straight downstairs and show you where everything is.' She turned on the stilettoed heels of her boots and Rene followed on behind her as she headed back along the passage and clipped her way down the stairs.

The grandly named 'theatre' turned out to be nothing more than the pub cellar, hastily converted by way of a black backdrop being strung across the width of its combed ceiling. About ten plastic tables with matching chairs, two apiece, were crammed into the small auditorium, some sloping at weird angles because of the uneven flagstoned floor. The place was dingy, damp and stank of stale beer, and Rene was only thankful that it was brightly lit by two spotlights positioned on stands against the back wall, their beams focused on the microphone that stood in the centre of the backdrop.

''Ow many people d'ye expect will be coming?' Rene asked flatly as she stood with her handbag hanging limply at her side and casting an eye over the paltry seating area.

Andrea crossed her arms over her neat little bosom. 'It

depends, really. We're a bit off the beaten track here, but if the word gets round there's a good show going on, then it can really fill up. Believe it or not, we've had as many as thirty people in here.'

The girl shot her such a bright, enthusiastic smile that Rene felt she had to muster up some sort of jovial response. 'Oh my, that's summat, in't it?' she said, with the thought going through her mind that any wild hope of her 'making it big' in Edinburgh had just suffered the worst form of spontaneously combusted.

'Of course,' Andrea continued, 'it also depends on how well you've been able to publicise the show yourself.'

Rene looked at the girl questioningly. ''Ow am I meant to do that?'

Andrea's smile faded away. 'Have you not been handing out leaflets?'

'What d'ye mean?'

'Leaflets, like the one you have there. You should have been handing them out all day up on the High Street.'

Rene glanced at the leaflet in her hand. 'I didn't know that.'

Andrea raised her eyebrows. 'How else do you expect anyone to come? That's where all the punters are during the day. You've got to go up there and attract them.'

'Oh,' Rene replied quietly.

'Otherwise you could find yourself well out of pocket when the show comes to an end.'

Rene swallowed hard, feeling her cheeks suddenly glow with apprehension. ''Ow's that, then?'

Andrea let out a sigh that gave off little sympathy. 'Don't you know about the conditions?'

'No, I don't,' Rene replied quite forcefully, becoming irked by the girl's attitude. 'I didn't arrange this 'ole thing. It was done for me.'

'All right,' Andrea countered defensively, holding up a hand to steady Rene's mood. 'I'll explain then. We rent out the theatre to you for a fixed sum over the three weeks. If you don't manage to cover that figure through box office takings, then you are liable for the shortfall.'

'And 'ow much does the theatre cost?'

'Seventeen hundred pounds.'

Rene stared at the girl with her mouth open. 'Bloody Aunt Ada,' she exclaimed, as the figure flashed in her mind like a neon warning light. 'That means . . .' She looked around the room, counting the seats, trying to calculate what chance she might have of bringing in that amount of money. Twenty times, say five quid a ticket, gives a hundred quid a night; times twenty-one nights equals . . . just over two thousand pounds! And that was with a bum on every seat! 'Oh, bloody Aunt Ada,' she said again, rubbing a hand at her forehead. 'That's damned near impossible! I don't suppose there's a chance I could do an afternoon performance as well?'

Andrea shook her head, her eyes almost managing to register kindly concern. ''Fraid not. The theatre is booked morning, noon and night.' Her look brightened in encouragement. 'But it does mean you'll have the whole day to hand out leaflets and woo your audience. And then, of course, you might get a brilliant review in one of the papers and find yourself playing to a packed house every night.'

'I s'pose,' Rene replied unhopefully.

The voice of the barman rang down the stairs. 'Andrea, there's a couple of people waitin' here tae buy tickets.'

Andrea glanced at her wristwatch and walked over to the door. 'On my way!' She turned back to Rene. 'If you could be ready to start in about ten minutes . . .' She nodded her head towards the backdrop. 'I'm afraid it's a bit cramped behind there, but you'll find a small table with a mirror if you want to get yourself made up or whatever.' She cast a look at Rene's handbag. 'I don't suppose you use your own props or anything.'

Rene shook her head. 'No. What ye see is what ye get.'

Andrea shrugged her shoulders as if signifying there was nothing further she could do to help Rene. 'All right. I hope it goes well, then. Billy will be down shortly to make sure the sound system is working properly.' And she swung round on her sharp-heeled boots and left the comedienne to her fate.

Rene's first show was played to a grand audience of five, and despite the glaring spotlights she could tell from the moment she took up her position at the microphone that at least three of them were foreigners. From their reaction to her first joke, which had never before failed to produce a roar of hilarity, it was also quite apparent that what ability they had to understand the English language did not stretch to the complexities of a North Yorkshire accent. During her performance Rene struggled to raise one good laugh, finding herself having to fill in the dreadful silence between jokes with feeble ad libs that fell on her own ears like an appalling speech impediment. As she watched two of her audience noisily scrape back their chairs and make their way towards the door halfway through her act, it took every ounce of concentration to keep talking and not to silently gawp at them as they departed. After forty-five long minutes, during every second of which she wished the greasy flagstone floor would open up and devour her hopelessly unfunny self, she called an end to her suffering fifteen minutes early. She waited behind the backdrop until her remaining audience quickly made their exit, and then came out and sat down at one of the tables in the deserted theatre. Covering her face with her hands, she relived every cringe-making moment of the show and wondered to herself how on earth she was going to be able to take another three weeks of similar disasters.

'How did it go?'

Rene dropped her hands to the table and turned to see Andrea's smiling face pop round the side of the door. Rene bit at her lip and slowly shook her head.

'Don't worry,' Andrea said as she flicked off the switch of one of the spotlights. 'First one's always the worst. Once you've got used to the intimacy of the theatre here, you'll find it much easier.'

'Maybe,' Rene replied solemnly, wondering how Andrea had the ability to distort her marketing jargon to such an extent as to describe this subterranean torture chamber as being 'intimate'. Picking up her handbag from the table, she got slowly to her feet and made her way towards the door.

'It's a bit of a pity, though,' Andrea said, turning off the other light and plunging the place into coal-mine darkness.

Rene stopped at the bottom of the stairs. 'What's a pity?' she asked.

'That you felt it didn't go too well tonight,' Andrea said brightly as she pulled the door to the theatre closed. She edged her way past Rene and began climbing the stairs. 'There was a reviewer from Radio Scotland in the audience.' She turned and gave Rene a thin smile. 'Never mind, he might not bother saying anything about it at all.'

Rene kept staring up the stairwell long after Andrea's tight little bottom had disappeared from view, and then, putting a steadying hand on the chrome banister rail, she lowered herself slowly on to the bottom step, clutched her handbag to her chest, and burst into tears.

Seventeen

Harry Wills sat at a small metal table in front of the Costa coffee stall in Edinburgh Airport, toying with a small cup of espresso, as he kept an eye on the two photographers who stood chatting together at the entrance through which the recent arrivals on the British Airways flight from London flooded into the baggage reclaim area. He saw them separate, their movements suddenly becoming more animated, and when a series of blinding flashes went off, Harry got to his feet, draining his coffee, and began to make his way towards them. The two photographers were now moving backwards away from the entrance, focusing their lenses on a tall bespectacled man in a navy-blue raincoat who accompanied a young dark-haired girl with a violin case in her hand. The man paid little attention to the photographers as he approached the cluster of uniformed drivers. He spoke to one, who immediately lowered the sign he had been holding up, and guided them with outstretched hand over to the luggage carousel that had just begun to move.

As the two photographers hurried away towards the terminal exit, their assignments successfully completed, Harry pushed his bulky figure through the mass of people gathering around the carousel and approached the man from behind.

'Monsieur Dessuin, Mademoiselle Pascal, welcome to Edinburgh.'

The man turned round, a questioning frown creasing his high angular forehead, and slowly put out a hand to the one that Harry offered in greeting. 'I'm sorry, I'm not sure if we have—'

'Harry Wills, the *Sunday Times Scotland*.'

'Ah, of course,' Albert Dessuin murmured, giving Harry's hand a single shake, his face registering no sign of pleasure at meeting the journalist.

'I thought I'd come along today just to introduce myself in person. We've spoken often enough with each other on the telephone.' Harry switched his attention to the young girl who stood watching the luggage go past on the carousel. 'However, I haven't had the pleasure of speaking to you before, mademoiselle.'

'Mr Wills,' Albert Dessuin cut in, 'we arrived early this morning in London after an all-night flight from New York, and after a long delay at Heathrow we have now made it here to Edinburgh. Tonight we have to attend a reception that will no doubt drain us of all our energies, and tomorrow Mademoiselle Pascal will have to have recovered sufficiently to start rehearsing for a concert the following evening in your Usher Hall. I would suggest, therefore, that this is the wrong time and the wrong place to try for an interview.'

'Of course, I understand that. I was just hoping to fix—'

'I seem to remember also, Mr Wills,' Dessuin continued, clicking his fingers at the driver and pointing to a large brown suitcase on the carousel, 'that it was only a few months ago that I gave over a great deal of time for an interview with you. I would not think, so soon afterwards, there would be much I could add to that.'

Harry Wills took in a deep breath before clearing his throat noisily in an attempt to cover for the anger he felt at the man's measured hostility. Then, on an impulse, he decided to go for broke. 'Monsieur Dessuin, what I really want to do is to write a story from Mademoiselle Pascal's point of view. I want to write about her influences, about her background, about her interests . . . and about being Angélique Pascal. She is becoming one of the most famous violinists in the world and everyone, including the young people, want to know about her.' Harry turned to Angélique, who, having just pointed out another suitcase to the driver, now stood watching the journalist with a look of silent intent. 'Mademoiselle Pascal, would there be any time over this next week when you would be willing to do an interview with me?'

'Mr Wills,' Albert Dessuin exclaimed irately as he grabbed the full luggage trolley from the driver, 'over the years you have continually tried my patience and now I will not take it any more.' He put a hand against Angélique's back. 'From now on, I will not consider one further interview with you, and please remember in future that it was your own dogged stupidity that led to this.'

Harry Wills stood watching as the driver hurriedly escorted his charges towards the terminal exit, Albert Dessuin guiding Angélique Pascal almost forcefully with a hand on her arm. Letting out a derisory grunt, Harry scratched hard at the back of his head and then ambled off to get his car.

As the Renault Espace came on to the Western Approach Road, Angélique broke the silence that had existed since leaving the airport twenty minutes before. 'Albert?' she said, as she stared out of the window at the traffic that sped past.

'*Oui*?' Dessuin replied, without looking up from his copy of *Le Monde*.

'I want to ask you something.'

'What?'

'Tonight at the reception, I want you to allow me a little space.'

Dessuin glanced across at her. 'What do you mean by that?'

'Just let me move around by myself.'

'Do I not always allow you to do that?'

Angélique let out a quiet laugh. 'No, Albert, you do not.' She turned and fixed him with a smile. 'I know you have my best interests at heart, but sometimes you can be quite . . . suffocating.'

Dessuin shrugged his shoulders. 'It may seem that way to you at times, but it is my job to protect you and I know that Madame Lafitte would—'

'Please, Albert,' Angélique interjected, 'don't bring Madame Laffite into this. You are always using her name like . . . some kind of blackmail.'

Dessuin shook his head, and with a huffy expression on his face turned back to read his newspaper.

Angélique leaned across to him. 'So will you give me a bit of freedom tonight? I'm not going to run away from you.'

Dessuin lifted a hand dismissively. 'Do as you please, but no talking to *journalistes, tu comprends?*'

'*Oui, bien sûr.*'

In the office of the International Festival, Tess Goodwin ended her telephone call and once more ran through her checklist for the reception scheduled that night in the Sheraton Grand. The hotel's events manager had confirmed that the function room had been set up as Tess had requested, and all arrangements for the finger buffet and wine had been put in place. The public relations agency who were helping her out during the festival had already hung the two large photographic posters of the Italian baritone, Guiseppe Montarino, and the young French violinist, Angélique Pascal, in whose joint honours the reception was being held. Now all that was left for her to do was to make a few courtesy calls to those sponsors of International events who had been remiss in replying to the invitation. As she stretched out a hand for the telephone, she saw the director's intercom light flash a split second before it began to ring. She picked up the receiver, noticing the outside call he kept on hold.

'Yes, Alasdair?'

'Are we all set for tonight, Tess?'

'Yes, everything's ready. I'm just about to call up some of those sponsors.'

'OK, but before you do that, I've got an old friend of yours on the line. He wants to have a word with you.'

'Who is it?' But the director had already put down his receiver and Tess addressed the question to the person who wished to speak to her.

'What do you mean, "who is it"?' a male voice replied with a laugh. 'Did your boss not tell you?'

Tess felt her face flush with panic, recognising immediately the smooth voice with its precise foreign accent. It was one she had hoped never to hear again.

'Is that you, Peter?'

'Of course it's me. I'm sure you did not really need to ask.'

'Why are you wanting to speak to me?'

'Why not? Alasdair is not the only one in the International office with whom I share some pretty wonderful memories.'

Tess closed her eyes tight, feeling the skin on her back tingle with nervous apprehension. 'Listen, Peter, I think—'

'So, how is everything going? I wondered if you would still be working in the office?'

'Why shouldn't I be?'

'No reason.' Tess heard Peter Hansen sigh. 'Listen, I thought it would be a good time to make amends for the way I behaved towards you at the end of the festival last year. It was just that things got a little bit difficult back in Copenhagen. I thought if we could meet up—'

'What do you mean? Where are you?'

'Here in Edinburgh. I came over for the festival . . . and to see you, of course.'

Tess gave a short cry of disbelief. '*What?* Are you being serious?'

'Never more so.'

Tess shook her head at the sheer gall of the man. 'Peter, I really am too busy to meet up. For a start, I've got a reception tonight, and anyway, the last thing I really want—'

'In that case, I could be round in your office in five minutes. It would be good to see Alasdair as well.'

'You will do no such thing,' Tess exclaimed, knowing only too well the director's intuitive nature would pick up on her uneasy vibes.

'Then where shall we meet?'

Tess pressed a hand to her forehead. 'I really do have a lot of work to do, Peter.'

'OK, then. Why not invite me to the reception tonight?'

'No!' She bit hard on her bottom lip, realising he was leaving her with little alternative other than to meet up with him there and then. 'Right, where are you?'

'About two hundred yards away. There is a church on the right-hand side of the High Street. I am standing on the steps.'

'Give me five minutes then, but I warn you, I haven't got long.'

'I'll be looking out for you – and, Tess?'

'What?'

'I'm longing to seeing you again.'

By the time Tess had made arrangements to cover for her short absence from the office fifteen minutes had elapsed before she reached the small paved square where the church was situated. Peter Hansen was instantly recognisable in the crowd. Tall, lean, with a shock of Viking-blond hair that curled against the collar of his dark-green jacket, he possessed an almost visible aura of self-admiration about himself. As soon as he caught sight of her, he lifted his hand in a brief wave, pushing himself away from the stone pillar against which he had been leaning at the entrance to the church. He descended the steps and threaded his way through the mêlée of pedestrians and street entertainers towards her, and as he approached he held out his arms, enveloping her in a hug and planting a kiss on the top of her head.

'Tess, it is so good to see you.' He pushed her away from him, resting his hands on her shoulders. 'My word, you look fantastic. Life is good for you, yes?'

Tess gave him a brief smile. 'Yes, it is. Never been better.'

He put an arm around her shoulders. 'Come on, let's go and get a cup of coffee.'

Tess pulled herself away from his hold. 'I said five minutes, Peter, and that's all I'm going to give you.'

'I think we can down a cup of coffee in that time,' he said, already starting to make his way across the High Street to a small café outside which a few metal tables and chairs took up half the width of the pavement. Tess stood her ground for a moment, and then, with a resigned shake of head, followed on after him.

Having ordered up a cappuccino for Tess and a herbal tea for himself, Peter leaned his elbows on the table and smiled affectionately at her, accentuating his annoyingly good looks, although Tess was pleased to see that a few age lines now creased his tanned face. When she met his gaze with an ice-cold stare, he reached across the table to place his hand on hers, but she avoided the contact by sitting back in her chair and folding her arms.

'I think you are still very angry with me,' he said with a quiet laugh.

'I was, but I really haven't dwelt on it too much.'

He nodded his head slowly. 'Listen, it was wrong of me to leave last year without talking to you. I had to get back to Copenhagen pretty urgently.'

'So your note said.'

'It was just that my wife . . . well . . . she had not been in very good spirits . . .'

'I hope she's better now.'

Peter paused for a moment, eyeing Tess, unsettled by her quick-fire remarks. 'Yes, thank you, she is. But what I really wanted to—'

'Why was it you never answered your phone?' Tess asked,

126

leaning forward on the table and glaring at him with intensity. 'I called enough times.'

Peter held out his hands apologetically. 'I had no alternative, believe me. My wife is very . . . untrusting of me . . .'

'With every reason, too,' Tess interjected sharply.

Peter twisted his mouth to the side. 'My word, you are being quite sharp today.'

'What are you doing back here, Peter?'

The question once more disarmed him momentarily. 'I have come for the festival, but more to see you. I cannot tell you how much I have missed you. I don't think a day has passed when I have not thought of you.'

Tess nodded. 'Right, so let me get this straight. You just want to take up where we left off.'

'Of course not. That would be asking a great deal of you, but maybe I thought we could meet for dinner and remember the good times . . . because they were good times, Tess. You know it as well as me.'

Tess choked back a laugh. 'To be quite honest, I hadn't given them another thought. And I'll tell you why, Peter. You see, I'm not free now, for you or anyone else, because I'm married.'

Peter shrugged. 'I know all that. Alasdair told me on the telephone. You married Allan, didn't you?'

'Yes, I did.'

'And if I remember right, you had been going out with him ever since we first became . . . involved.'

Tess bit at the side of her mouth. 'So?'

'So, if that is the case, nothing really has changed. A very innocent dinner, that is all I am asking. What difference would that make to your relationship with him?'

'Every difference.'

'But there's no reason for him ever to know. You could simply treat it as part of your routine entertainment at the festival.' He paused to take a sip of his tea. 'To make it legitimate, maybe I could speak with Alasdair.'

Tess swallowed hard. 'No, I don't want you to do that.'

Peter raised his eyebrows. 'Ah, yes, of course. We certainly don't want the director to find out about our little affair. That could make your life very difficult.'

'And yours too.'

'Not really. Alasdair knows the way I am, but maybe he would think it rather unprofessional of you.'

'Are you saying you would tell him?'

Peter laughed. 'Of course not. It's just that if I have to take more formal action to arrange a simple dinner date with you, well then, it might put you in a bit of a predicament, don't you think?'

Tess stared at him for a moment. 'That's as good as blackmail.'

Peter frowned. 'Oh, I hope nothing so serious as that, surely, but I think it does prove how much I want to see you again.'

Needing time to consider her options, Tess turned her head and fixed her eyes on a young female street performer who was juggling with three blazing torches whilst standing on the shoulders of two worried-looking young men she had obviously pulled out of the crowd. God, Tess thought, the girl's not the only one playing with fire here. She had been right in saying that Peter's proposal was as good as blackmail, but then again, she had brought it upon herself. There was really only one option open to her. Have dinner with the man and finish it for good, and then neither Allan nor Sir Alasdair Dreyfuss need ever be the wiser.

She turned back to Peter. 'All right, we'll have dinner.'

Peter's face registered victory. 'I'm so glad to hear it. When shall it be, then?'

Tess took her diary from her handbag and flipped through the pages. She shook her head. 'This week's out. It'll have to be either next Tuesday or Wednesday.'

Peter nodded. 'OK, I'll call you.'

'No, I'll do the calling.'

'You still have my number?'

'If you haven't changed it.'

Peter shot her a knowing wink. 'No, it's exactly the same.'

Tess glanced at her watch. 'Dammit, this is ridiculous. I'm so late.' She drained her coffee, pushed back her chair and stood up, slinging her bag on to her shoulder. Peter got to his feet at the same time. She made a move to walk back up the High Street before turning back to glare with hostility at her ex-lover. 'The dinner next week will be the last, Peter.'

'In that case, we will have to celebrate it in style.' He came round the table, hoping to bid her an affectionate farewell, but she had already gone.

As soon as Angélique Pascal entered the vast function room of the Sheraton Grand that evening, she was sure she would not be wanting to leave Albert Dessuin's side during the course of the event. As she descended the wide carpeted steps to the crowded floor, she felt three hundred pairs of enquiring eyes turn to look at her and reacted to it by putting out a hand to grasp her manager's arm for reassurance. She shyly returned the smiles that were beamed her way as Albert led her through the parting crowd to a small group gathered by the window. A thin, studious man with black-rimmed spectacles and wearing a dark-blue suit that looked decidedly crumpled detached himself from the group and came towards Albert and Angélique with his hand outstretched.

'Albert, I am sorry. I didn't see you enter. Welcome to Edinburgh.' He shook Albert's hand, and then turned to his charge. 'Angélique, what a pleasure it is to meet you at last. I'm Alasdair Dreyfuss, director of the International Festival.' He gave her a light kiss on the cheek and she turned her head, expecting the second, but the man was already walking back towards the group. 'Come on over and I'll introduce you to some of my colleagues, and then I'll organise some drinks for you. Right, this is our marketing director, Sarah Atkinson . . .'

Angélique listened to the introductions, but she did not catch any of them, as the man spoke English too fast, a trend that seemed to be set thereafter. Whenever a question was asked of her, she turned to Albert and he answered on her behalf, turning to smile at her every time as if to say, 'So who thought she could manage without me, then?' It made her determined to try to understand so that she could answer at least one question for herself, but the noise in the room was deafening, and no matter how hard she concentrated, she could not pick up the gist of one single conversation. After three quarters of an hour of listening to unintelligible words being spoken to her, she suddenly felt very tired, realising now Albert had been right in saying to the journalist at the airport that they would be drained of all energy by the time the reception was finished. She looked around the function room and noticed a small recess over by the huge floor-to-ceiling windows. Squeezing Albert's arm and gesturing with a finger for him to lean over, she whispered in his ear that she was going to look out of the window for a few minutes. He nodded his approval and she moved quickly over to the recess, her head down, in case someone else should take the opportunity of engaging her in yet another incomprehensible discourse.

The recess was luckily much deeper than she had imagined, a twenty-foot carpeted passage that ended at a wall on which a large gilt-framed mirror was hung. Finding herself completely hidden from those in the function room, Angélique crossed her arms and leaned against the window, looking down on to the bustling crowds and the slow-moving traffic in the street below. As she then turned her gaze to the huge dark-stoned castle sitting high above the city, she let out a long, lingering yawn.

'You must be exhausted,' a female voice said.

Angélique turned to see a girl approach her tentatively along the passage. She was carrying two glasses of champagne in her hands.

'I saw you didn't have anything to drink,' she said, handing Angélique a glass.

'Thank you,' she said, smiling at the girl. She had noticed her before at the back of the group when Albert had greeted the festival director, and it had occurred to Angélique at the time that they must have been about the youngest two people in the room. Although the girl was a few years older than herself, Angélique had immediately liked the way the she looked. Her close-cropped brown hair framed an honest, happy face, and she was dressed quite informally in comparison with the other women at the reception, in a light red wrap-around dress over a black polo-neck sweater and blue jeans.

'I'm sorry, we weren't introduced,' the girl said, offering a small light-skinned hand. 'I'm Tess Goodwin. I work in the International office.'

'I am pleased to meet you, Tess,' Angélique said, shaking her hand.

'You speak English very well. I'm afraid my French is almost non-existent. Languages were never my strong point at school.'

'Oh, my English is not so good, and I find it very difficult when there are many people in a room,' Angélique said, casting her eyes along the corridor from where the noise of the reception boomed. 'I cannot concentrate enough.' She took a sip from her glass and looked out of the window. 'Edinburgh is a very beautiful city, I think. Do you come from here?'

'No, I'm originally from Aberdeen, which is much further north, but I live and work here now.' Tess stepped closer to the window, her eyes searching above the roofs of the buildings to one side of the large square in front of the hotel. She pointed a finger. 'Do you see the church spire there?'

Angélique nodded.

Tess smiled at her. 'I was married there five months ago.'

'How wonderful for you!' Angélique exclaimed with genuine excitement. 'I think you must be a very happy person, then.'

Tess laughed. 'Yes, I suppose I am.'

'What is your husband's name?'

'Allan.'

'I like the name *Alain*,' Angélique remarked decisively, giving the name its French pronunciation. 'It is very strong, very . . . er . . . the French word is *sûr*.'

Tess grimaced embarrassedly. 'I can only guess at something like "dependable"?'

'Yes,' Angélique replied with a confirming nod of her head. 'That is exactly right. Does *Alain* work in Edinburgh, too?'

Tess studied the interest in Angélique's face. She was really beginning to warm to the open friendliness of this young celebrity whom she had only seen before on television, hiding her face from the cameras. 'Yes, here and in Glasgow. He's just recently been promoted in his company, so he's having to work very long hours.' She gazed out of the window, her mind caught up with the clandestine arrangement she had made with Peter Hansen only hours before. 'We don't see much of each other at the moment.'

Angélique screwed up her nose. 'That is very hard for you both, *n'est-ce pas*?'

Tess turned and smiled at the girl. 'Very. We didn't actually even have time to go on honeymoon for that very reason.'

'*Oh, ça c'est triste!* But you will go eventually, will you not?'

'Yes, once the festival is over and done with. We're going to Barbados for two weeks.'

'Ah, I believe it a very beautiful place. It is one place I have never been.'

'It must be one of the *only* places you've never been.'

Angélique gave a short, hollow laugh. 'You are right, but unfortunately, my life means I am never in one place long enough to enjoy it or to learn about it.'

'I can understand that. I'm sure constant jetting around the world isn't as glamorous as it sounds.' Tess put down her glass on the low windowsill and opened the zip on her small suede shoulder bag. 'Listen,' she said, taking out a business card and handing it to Angélique, 'maybe you'd like to come out one night with Allan and me? We would both love to show you around Edinburgh.'

Tess noticed sadness glaze over the violinist's eyes as she studied the card. 'That is very kind of you, Tess. I'm afraid I don't think I will have the time, but I am very happy you have asked me this.'

Tess shrugged her shoulders. 'Well, keep the card anyway. If you do find you have a spare moment, or even if you just want to have a chat, you can always contact me at any time on my mobile phone.'

Angélique's eyes never lifted from the card. 'Thank you very much, Tess. I would like to do that.'

'Excuse me, I hope I'm not breaking into a private conversation here.'

Both girls turned to look at the balding middle-aged man who stood peering around the corner of the recess at them. He was smartly dressed in a dark-grey pinstriped suit with a striped shirt and yellow silk tie, but his most striking feature was the kindly smile that he beamed in their direction.

'I just wanted to have the opportunity of saying to Mademoiselle Pascal how much I enjoyed her playing,' the man said as he came along the passage towards them.

Tess turned to Angélique. 'I'll leave you with your fan,' she said with a quiet laugh.

The young violinist came forward and gave Tess a kiss on both cheeks. 'I have enjoyed meeting you, Tess.'

'Me too,' Tess replied, making her way along the corridor past the man. He watched her until she had disappeared back into the reception.

'I'm sorry, I didn't mean to cut in like that,' the man said, seemingly quite flustered about having invaded Angélique's privacy, 'but I really did not want to leave tonight without saying to you in person how marvellous it is that you are here in Edinburgh. I have greatly admired your playing over the past few years.'

'Thank you very much,' Angélique replied, accepting the compliment with a small bow of her head. 'That is a nice thing to say.'

The man put out a hand to her. 'My name is Gavin Mackintosh, Mademoiselle Pascal, and I am most honoured to meet you.'

'And it is also an honour to meet you, too, Mr Mackintosh,' Angélique replied with a laugh as she took his hand.

'Please, you must call me Gavin.'

'And you must call me Angélique.'

'I would like that,' Gavin said, suddenly realising he was holding a hand that must be insured for millions. He quickly relinquished his grip. 'So, I'm right in saying this is your first time here in Edinburgh?'

'Yes, it is.'

'And how do you like it?'

Angélique turned to look out of the window. 'This is all I have seen of Edinburgh. It appears very beautiful from here.'

'So you've just arrived?'

'Yes. I was in New York last night.'

Gavin sighed. 'I don't know how you have the stamina. You must be extremely tired.'

Angélique shrugged her shoulders. 'I get accustomed to it.'

'And how long are you going to be here?'

'I think seven nights. I am rehearsing tomorrow and then I will be playing in concerts the following two evenings in the . . . how do you say? . . . Ush . . .'

'Usher Hall.' Gavin pointed to the large round ornate stone building on the opposite side of the road. 'That's it over there.'

'Ah,' Angélique said, moving her head slightly so she could see the building. 'Not far to walk, then.'

Gavin laughed. 'No, not far. And for the rest of the week?'

'I think there are also some late-night concerts when I am to be playing some of the Bach violin sonatas.'

'And then you head off again?'

Angélique gave him an uncomprehending look. 'I'm sorry?'

'And then you travel to another place.'

'Ah, yes. To Singapore.'

Gavin shook his head. 'I don't know how you do it.'

Angélique laughed. 'It is sometimes quite hard. Do you also live here in Edinburgh?'

'Yes, I do, and have done all my life. I went to school here, and then university, and now I work here.'

'What is your job?'

134

'I am a solicitor.'

'I'm afraid I don't know that word. What would it be in French?'

Gavin burst out laughing. 'Don't ask me! I have no idea. It's all to do with law, anyway.'

'Oh, I understand. And do you have a family?'

'I do. I have a wife, who is somewhere next door probably trying to find me, two daughters and four grandchildren.'

'Four grandchildren! That is wonderful. But you do not look old enough for that.'

Gavin slowly nodded. 'You know, that's probably the nicest thing anyone has ever said to me.'

'*Mais, c'est vrai!*'

'And that's even nicer.'

Angélique pushed herself away from the window. 'I think maybe I have been hiding in here too long,' she said, threading her hand through his arm. 'Please, will you take me to meet your wife, Gavin? I would very much like that.'

Gavin placed his hand on hers and gave it a light squeeze, totally captivated by the charm of the young violinist. 'Nothing would give me greater pleasure.'

They had taken no more than a couple of steps towards the function room when Albert Dessuin suddenly appeared and looked along the short corridor towards them. Gavin could see his eyes focus on the hand that was nestled under his arm. 'Angélique? What are you doing? Why have you been in here so long? There were so many people whom you should have met, but they have left already.' He spoke his French very fast as if to ensure that Gavin, if he had any knowledge of the language, could not understand what was being said.

'Albert, I have been speaking to Tess and Gavin, who are both new friends of mine,' Angélique replied in English, 'and I am now going to be introduced to Gavin's wife.'

Gavin felt Dessuin's glare of distrust almost burning into him. 'I am sorry, but there is no time,' he replied, this time in English. 'Our plans have changed. We are now having dinner with Sir

135

Alasdair Dreyfuss in a restaurant and already he has left. We are to follow immediately in a taxi.'

'Oh, Albert, can I not please first meet Gavin's wife?'

Gavin noticed her tone had suddenly changed to that of a little girl pleading for a favour.

Dessuin came over and took hold of her free arm. 'I am sorry, but we have wasted enough time.' He looked at Gavin, his mouth creasing into a smile that displayed not one ounce of friendship. 'I apologise, monsieur. It will have to wait until another time.'

'Of course,' Gavin replied, knowing full well the occasion would never present itself again. Unfolding her hand from his arm, he bent down and gave her a kiss on either cheek. 'It's been my pleasure, Angélique.'

The young violinist looked up at him with a smile. 'I hope I might meet your wife another time, Gavin.'

'Please, Angélique, we must go now,' Dessuin said sharply, hustling her away long the corridor.

Gavin watched them as they walked away, his mind filled with two conflicting emotions – how much he liked her, and how much he disliked him. He put his hands into the pockets of his suit jacket and began to walk slowly back to the function room. Just at that point, Angélique appeared again.

'Two tickets for the concert.' She turned away. '*Albert, j'arrive!*' She looked back at Gavin. 'I shall leave them at the concierge desk. Please come.' She blew him a kiss and disappeared.

As Angélique followed Albert Dessuin across the hotel foyer, she stopped momentarily to put down her handbag on the floor and shrug on her jacket. She watched Dessuin forcefully push the heavy glass door open, nearly knocking off balance a small elderly man who was about to enter. She let out a gasp at Albert's total lack of manners and ran towards the door just as the man entered, looking visibly shaken.

'I am so sorry,' she said, putting a hand on his arm. 'Are you all right?'

'Yes, thank you very much,' the man replied with a nod, but

Angélique could tell from his ashen face the incident had given him a tremendous shock. He smiled distractedly at her and hurried off towards the concierge desk.

Angélique pushed open the door and ran down the steps to where Albert was standing, hands on hips, on the pavement. 'Albert, why did you do that just then?' she said fiercely. 'You could have seriously injured that old man.'

'Oh, never mind about him. Look at this problem we have now!' he exclaimed, throwing up his hands in frustration. The taxi that had been waiting for them was completely hemmed in by two large white vans, one of which had the name 'CinElectrics' emblazoned on its side.

Dessuin stepped off the pavement in front of the taxi and hammered his fist on the window of one of the vans. The young driver, who was speaking on a mobile phone, slowly lowered the window.

'What's up, friend?' he asked.

'Could you please move your van? You are blocking in our taxi.'

'Hang on a minute,' the driver said, holding up his hand to stop Dessuin's protest. 'OK, so that's final, is it?' he said into the mobile. 'You definitely want us to head back to London tomorrow with all the gear . . . all right, if that's the order.' He jabbed angrily at the button on the phone to end the call. 'Bugger this for a larf.' He tossed the phone on to the dashboard and turned to Dessuin. 'Sorry about that, mate. We'll get out your way now.'

Eighteen

Having been watching the departure from the hotel of the famous violinist Angélique Pascal, the young female receptionist had also witnessed the incident at the entrance door. She made a move to go around the front desk to check on the well-being of the elderly man, but then stayed where she was when she realised he was fast approaching her.

'Are you all right, sir?' she asked concernedly, seeing his obvious agitation.

'Yes, I'm quite well, thank you,' the man replied, casting an eye around the hotel lobby. 'I wonder if you could tell me where I might find a telephone.'

'Certainly, sir, there's a payphone in the corner over there,' she replied, pointing to a glass door beside the lifts, 'or might I ask if you are staying in the hotel?'

'Yes, I am. Hartson, room 215.'

'Ah, Mr Hartson, a gentleman has been trying to contact you quite urgently.' She turned and took an envelope from one of the cubbyholes at the back of the desk. 'No message was left, but he asked that you ring this number as soon as you returned to the hotel. I was going to suggest you might like to use the telephone in the seating area over there and I'll just add it to your bill.'

'Yes, that would be the best idea,' Leonard Hartson replied absently as he moved away from the desk without acknowledging the girl's kindly aid. He made his way across the lobby to the seating area and pulled the chair away from the small telephone desk. Taking a spectacle case from the pocket of his tweed jacket, he placed it on the desk along with the envelope and sat down, and once he had fussed over both for a moment, he drew the telephone towards him and dialled the number.

'Good evening, Springtime Productions,' a female voice replied immediately.

'I would like to speak to Nick Springer, please.'

'Who's calling, please?'

'Leonard Hartson.'

'Oh, Mr Hartson, we've been trying to get in touch with you all day. Hold the line and I'll put you straight through to Nick.'

Leonard took off his spectacles, folded them in one hand and put them back in the case.

'Hullo, Leonard?' It was Nick's voice.

Leonard sat forward in his chair. 'Nick, there seems to be a great deal of confusion up here. Have you any idea what's going on?'

'I'm sorry, Leonard, I have tried to get in touch. It's a pity you don't have a mobile phone.'

'Well, I don't because I've never had need of one, so please tell me now what's happening.'

'This is all very difficult, Leonard. I know how much of a disappointment it's going to be to you.'

Leonard slumped back in the chair and pressed his thumb and forefinger into the corners of his eyes. 'So it's true, then. You are recalling all the equipment.'

'I'm afraid so.'

'For what reasons, Nick?'

'I had an e-mail today from the Japanese broadcast company that commissioned the film. It was pretty abrupt, to be quite honest, but the gist of it was that they're presently shedding jobs like crazy and a freeze has been put on all recently commissioned works, and, unfortunately, your job just happens to be one of them.'

'Oh, my word,' Leonard said, pressing a hand to his brow. 'Is there nothing we can do?'

'The dance company will obviously still be performing at the festival, but I'd never be able to find another broadcast company to take on the commission at such short notice. That's really why we've got to cut our losses now and get the equipment back to London as soon as possible.'

'Nothing more to be done, then,' Leonard murmured despondently.

'I'm afraid not. I really am sorry about this, Leonard. I know how much you were looking forward to doing this job.'

'Not your fault, Nick.'

'Listen, the boys are heading back tomorrow with the vans, but there's no reason for you to return straightaway. Why not stay up there for a day or two and go to some concerts or whatever, and I'll foot your hotel bill? That's the least I can do.'

'No. I think I'll just catch the train tomorrow morning and get back home.'

'All right. I quite understand.'

'It would have been a wonderful film to make, Nick, and I can't thank you enough for entrusting it to me.'

'Believe me, if there was anything I could do at this stage to continue with the project, then I would, but I really can't think of anything.'

'I know, and I appreciate that.'

'Keep in touch, and I promise I'll call in to see you next time I'm on my way down the A3.'

'You do that, Nick. Look after yourself.'

'And you do likewise, Leonard.'

The old cameraman reached forward and put down the telephone. He sat for a moment staring at the wall in front of him, and then, with a tired sigh, he pushed himself to his feet and made his way slowly back to the reception desk.

'All right, sir?' the young receptionist asked him with a smile. 'Did you manage to contact the gentleman?'

'Yes, thank you, I did. I'm afraid I'm going to be booking out of the hotel tomorrow.'

'Oh, I'm sorry to hear that, sir.' She looked down at her computer monitor and typed quickly on the keyboard. 'Your bill is going directly to Springtime Productions, so there'll be no need to settle up on anything in the morning.'

'Right, well, thank you for all your help, and I'm sorry if I appeared a bit distracted before.'

The girl laughed. 'It's a pretty crazy time for us all right now in Edinburgh, so there's absolutely no need to apologise. We all get caught up a little in the excitement of the occasion.'

'I suppose so,' Leonard replied resignedly. 'Well, I'm off to my room now, so I'll bid you good night.'

'Good night, sir, and I hope we have the pleasure of having you to stay with us again very soon.'

Leonard emptied out the pockets of his tweed jacket and placed everything on the dressing table alongside the key card to his bedroom. He shrugged off the jacket, slipped it on to a hanger and put it in the wardrobe, and as he made his way across to the bed, he loosened the knot on his woollen tie and undid the top button of his Viyella shirt. He sat down on the edge of the bed and eyed the telephone, wondering how on earth he was going to break the news to Gracie. He himself felt aged with disappointment, so he couldn't imagine how she, being the one who had encouraged him almost to the point of vehemence to take the job, would react to the news.

He reached out a hand for the telephone, held it hovering above the receiver for a moment as he gathered his thoughts, and then picked it up and dialled the number.

'Hullo?' Grace answered. Even in that one word, Leonard could sense an air of excited expectancy in her voice.

'Gracie, dear, it's Leonard,' he replied, trying to force light-heartedness into his own voice.

'Oh, I've been longing to hear from you, my love. How's everything going?'

'All right.'

'And has all the equipment arrived safely?'

'Yes, about an hour ago.'

'Oh, how exciting! So when do you think you will start shooting?'

Leonard did not answer, but closed his eyes tight and clenched his fist, banging it up and down repeatedly on his knee.

'Leonard?' Gracie asked quietly, her voice filled with concern. 'Is everything all right, dear?'

'We're not going to be shooting, Gracie,' Leonard replied, his voice suddenly weak with emotion. He cleared his throat to control it. 'I've just spoken to Nick. The job's fallen through.'

'What? But why?'

'The funding's been withdrawn, and he says there's no time to find it elsewhere.'

'Oh, Leonard, I can't believe this. Is there nothing that can be done? It all seems such a dreadful waste of time and effort.'

'I know. I had such wonderful ideas as well, about how I was

141

going to film it. With all this new equipment, I was going to take risks I'd never dared to try before. I really do believe, Gracie, that I could have done a wonderful job here.'

'Your definitive film,' Gracie replied in a voice heavy with chagrin.

'Yes, I think it might well have been.'

There was a silence before Grace spoke again. 'So what happens now?'

'We're all returning tomorrow. I should be back home sometime tomorrow evening.'

'And what will happen to us, Leonard?'

'Nothing will happen to us, my dear. We will just continue with our lives in gentle retirement, just as we have done for the past seven years.'

'With nothing to look forward to except our eventual demise.'

Leonard laughed. 'I don't think we need to be considering that *just* yet, Gracie.'

'Well, then why don't you and I take some risks? You were going to do it in the making of the film. Why don't we do it together?'

'How do you mean?'

'Leonard, we have no children nor grandchildren to bless with an inheritance. We just have each other, and time is running out for both of us.'

'What are you saying?'

'Have you any idea what the budget for this film was?'

'No. Nick never told me, and I would have no idea what the costs are nowadays.'

'More than three hundred thousand pounds?'

'I wouldn't have thought it would be *that* much. I remember reading about a low-cost feature being made recently for a quarter of a million pounds. This film was only to be a forty-minute documentary, so probably around a hundred thousand.'

'In that case, I think you and I should fund it ourselves.'

'*What?*'

'Leonard, my dear, when we thought about moving to a smaller house two years ago, the estate agent valued this one at two hundred and seventy thousand pounds. It must now be worth much nearer three hundred thousand. We don't have a mortgage, so why don't we just use it as collateral against a loan for the film? If, in the worst scenario, we don't make any money from it and we lose a hundred thousand pounds, well, then that's the time we move to a smaller house.'

Leonard held the receiver away from his ear for a moment, staring at it in disbelief at what Gracie had just suggested. He put the receiver back to his ear. 'Gracie, my dear, have you gone quite bonkers?'

'No, I have never been more serious in my life, neither have I ever come up with such a sound idea. Leonard, you know yourself that you have rued the very day you gave up work in the film industry, and you were heading into the twilight days of your life feeling dissatisfied and unfulfilled. Living with you over the past few months has been an exhilaration, a complete joy for me. I have seen you returned to me as the man I knew thirty years ago, and I love it, and I love you. If you came back now, everything would change, and with nothing to look forward to, I doubt much time would pass before one of us would just fade away. Leonard, we are only talking about a third of the capital value of the house, but in all honesty I would rather risk losing everything we own than to lose you, the way you are right now.'

Grace's impassioned monologue brought tears to Leonard's eyes and he dug into the pocket of his trousers for a handkerchief and gave them a wipe. 'Gracie, you truly are a remarkable woman, you know.'

'Shall we do it, then? Shall you and I take the risk?'

'We've always been so careful with our finances, Gracie. We've never done anything quite so foolhardy in all our lives.'

'Yes, but how rejuvenating for us both it would be.'

Leonard laughed. 'Well, in that case, why not? Let's just cast our fates to the wind.'

'Good, and no regrets, my dear, whatever the outcome. No regrets.'

Leonard pushed the handkerchief back in his pocket. 'I'll give Nick a call now.'

'You do that, and first thing tomorrow morning I'll go down to the bank and organise the loan.'

'No, don't do that just yet, Gracie. Let me first find out from Nick how much the film was going to cost and then I'll see if I can't work out a way of shaving a bit off the budget. I'll give you a call tomorrow night.'

'All right, my darling. You get a good night's sleep now and don't go mulling it over in your mind. We've made the decision, and you will be needing all your energies over the next few weeks for making the most wonderful film.'

'Goodnight, Gracie. I love you, my girl.'

'I know you do.'

Having sat there motionless for five minutes, taking in what he and Gracie had just agreed and trying to work out some of the more immediate logistics, Leonard got to his feet and sought out Nick Springer's mobile number. He stood, apprehensive, as he dialled it up.

'Hullo, Nick Springer.'

'Nick, it's Leonard Hartson.'

'Oh, hullo, Leonard. Just give me a moment while I pull the car over.' Leonard heard the rev of an engine and then quiet. 'Still there?'

'Yes, I am.'

'Are you all right?'

'Yes, fine. Nick, I wonder if you might be able to tell me what the approximate budget for the film was?'

'Why do you ask?'

'I just wanted to know.'

'Well, off the top of my head, I think it was about one hundred and fifty thousand pounds, perhaps a bit less.'

'Right. Nick, could you do something for me immediately?'

'Certainly, what?'

'Could you call up both the camera-hire company and CinElectrics and cancel the return of the equipment?'

'What are you saying, Leonard?'

'Gracie and I have decided we're going to fund the film ourselves.'

'*What?*'

'We're going to take out a loan against the value of our house and make the film ourselves. We've decided.'

'No, I can't allow you to do that. You mustn't.'

'Is there any reason why not?'

'Because . . . you and Grace can't put your security at risk like that, Leonard.'

'Yes, we can. Anyway, if you say the full budget is between a hundred and a hundred and fifty thousand pounds, then we would only have to take out a loan on about half the value of the house, and I have a few ideas already on how to reduce the costs still further.'

'By doing what?'

'By sending the electricians and the assistant cameraman back to London. I'll find someone local to give me a hand. I'll move out of this hotel, of course, and look for somewhere a little cheaper.'

'Leonard, are you really being serious about all this?'

'Never more so in my life.'

'Then I have to come in on the deal.'

'Nick, you don't need to—'

'No, I insist. I feel totally responsible for having brought you both to this decision and I simply cannot allow you to take on such a financial risk alone. I shall put up a figure of fifty thousands pounds and you, Grace and I will produce it as equal partners under the umbrella of Springtime Productions. I'll give you backup for whatever you need and arrange for all processing and post-production work to be done here in London.'

'Are you sure, Nick?'

'In your words, Leonard, never more so in my life. I'm just so delighted you're still going to be able to make the film. Dammit, if I wasn't so busy, I'd come up and assist you myself!'

Leonard laughed. 'Now, that would make it just like old times.'

'Yes, but I'm afraid an idea that's totally unviable. Are you sure you're going to be able to find someone to help you? I haven't got one single contact in Edinburgh.'

'Don't worry. I have a couple of days in hand to get myself sorted. I'll put the word around at the theatre where the dance group are performing, and I've also met the man who owns the warehouse where we're doing the shooting. He appears to have his fingers in enough pies.'

'Well, don't go doing anything rash, Leonard.'

'In what way?'

'You won't try going it alone, will you? It really is not worth the cost cutting. You have to remember you're not as young as you were, and you have to consider your health.'

'Nick, I know my limitations.'

'I sincerely hope so. Have you been in touch with the dance company yet?'

'Yes, I'd just got back from their hotel when the equipment arrived. They have a young Scottish girl acting as an interpreter, and together we spoke with Mr Kayamoto, who is the director. A very nice and courteous man. He didn't mention any changes to the schedule, so I doubt he knew at that time. I'll give the girl a call now and arrange another meeting for tomorrow. I'm sure Mr Kayamoto will be willing to continue as planned.'

'One problem has just occurred to me, Leonard.'

'What might that be?'

'You have two van-loads of equipment up there. How are you going to manage to drive both? And what will you do with all the equipment overnight?'

Leonard pondered on this for a moment before replying. 'I think, Nick, having seen the warehouse, that I can afford to get rid of some of the equipment, so I'll just keep hold of one of the vans and get the boys to drive the other back to London with what I don't need. And you don't have to worry about security. I can lock the van and the equipment in the warehouse.'

'That's good, then, and listen, my contribution to this venture is accessible now, so if you're in need of any money short-term, you must just get in touch. Is that understood?'

'Thank you, Nick . . . for everything. I can't tell you how happy I am this is going to go ahead after all.'

'Not half as happy as I am now that we've managed to come up with this solution. My heart has felt like concrete ever since ending that last call with you. But now we're into exciting times, Leonard, exciting times!'

Leonard chuckled. 'Yes, we are, aren't we, if not a little precarious.'

Nineteen

The following morning, Leonard left the hotel after an early breakfast and took a taxi over to the lodgings where the rest of the crew were staying. He found them in a gruff mood, having had the night to mull over the fact that they had lost out on three weeks' work, but Leonard managed to mollify their anger by telling them that he would ask Nick to seek some form of compensation for them from the Japanese company. This news seemed to have a visible effect on their spirits, and by the time they set off back to London in the spare van, having helped Leonard to sort through the equipment at the warehouse, any ill feeling had dissipated and they left with hands waving from the windows and cries of well-wishes.

The day, however, did not continue in such a positive vein. Having booked himself out of the Sheraton Grand the previous evening, he spent the lunch hour and the early part of the afternoon on the telephone in the hotel lobby, with local newspapers and magazines scattered on the table in front of him, vainly trying to track down somewhere to stay. At three o'clock, he realised that it was all to no avail. With little alternative open to him, he approached the reception desk to ask if he might have his room back for one more night, only to be told that it had been taken almost the moment he had handed in his keys. In desperation, he explained his circumstances to the receptionist, who had little to suggest other than he should try going to the offices of the International to see if they could be of any assistance to him.

The taxi took Leonard the short distance up past the castle and dropped him off outside the old church at the top of the Lawnmarket. He entered the building towing his suitcase behind him, and made his way along the passageway to the ticket office. He approached a young man wearing a festival logo-ed sweatshirt, who sat in one of the booths.

'Can I help you, sir?' the young man asked with a cheery grin.

'Yes, I wonder if it would be possible to speak to someone in the International office?'

'Do you have an appointment?'

'No, I'm afraid I don't, but my name is Leonard Hartson, and I'm up here to film the Japanese dance company that's performing this year.'

'Ah, right.' He picked up the receiver on the telephone and pressed an intercom button. 'Hullo, Tess, there's a Mr Hartson here in the ticket office who's needing to speak to someone . . . no, he doesn't, but he's filming the Japanese dance company . . . All right, I'll tell him.' The young man put down the receiver. 'Mr Hartson, Tess Goodwin will be down to see you in about five minutes. If you go across to the Hub café on the other side of the corridor, Tess will meet you there.'

'Thank you very much,' Leonard said with an acknowledging smile and walked the few steps across the corridor and pushed open the glass entrance door of the coffee shop.

Ten minutes later, as he drained the last drops of his now-lukewarm coffee, the door of the café swung open and a young woman came in, dressed in a pair of jeans and a brightly coloured shirt and holding in her hand a spiral notepad. She scanned the tables before catching sight of Leonard, who had risen to his feet on her entrance.

She came over to his table. 'Mr Hartson?'

'Yes, that's right.'

'Tess Goodwin,' the young woman said, offering out a hand to Leonard. 'I work in the International marketing department.'

'Miss Goodwin . . .' Leonard began, shaking her hand.

'Tess, please.'

Leonard nodded. 'Tess, thank you for sparing time to meet me. I know you must be very busy right now.'

'Up to the eyeballs, actually.' She pulled out a chair for herself. 'But never mind, let's sit down and you can tell me how I can be of help.'

Leonard resumed his seat once she had slipped a mobile phone from her back pocket, put it on the table beside her notebook and made herself comfortable. She opened up the notebook to a fresh page and hovered her pencil expectantly above it.

Leonard took this as a sign that she did indeed have little time to spare for him, so he started his explanation immediately. 'Tess, this might not be part of your remit at all, but I'm afraid I didn't quite know who else I should ask. The fact is that, for reasons that I won't bore you with, I have to find other lodgings for the duration of the festival, and so far I've had absolutely no joy.'

'Where are you staying at the moment?'

'At the Sheraton Grand, but there have been unforeseen changes to the budget of the film, and I can't afford to stay there any longer.'

Tess bit at her lip thoughtfully. 'You're right. This is not usually my remit. We have an artiste liaison team which handles everything to do with the International performers, and they're usually booked into the more expensive hotels in Edinburgh.' She tapped the end of her pencil on the notepad. 'I can't promise you anything,' she said, picking up her mobile, 'but I'll try the Fringe office. They have many more performers than we do, so they might have something available.' She dialled a number and held the mobile to her ear. 'Hullo, can I speak to Lewis Jones, please? It's Tess Goodwin at International.' She smiled reassuringly at Leonard as she waited to be connected. 'Lewis, good afternoon, it's Tess . . . absolutely hectic . . . no, you're right, no time to enjoy married bliss at all. Listen, Lewis, I am with a Mr Hartson who is in

Edinburgh to film one of our events and he needs to change his accommodation arrangements . . . Yes, he's staying in the Sheraton Grand right now, but he's looking for somewhere a bit cheaper. You don't know of anything available, do you? . . . No, I understand that.' Tess looked across at Leonard. 'He says the whole of Edinburgh is chock-a-block.' She listened once more to the man on the line. 'Oh, right. Yes, I can hold.' She took the mobile away from her ear. 'He says someone came in a couple of weeks ago who had rooms to let, due to a cancellation. He's just trying to find the piece of paper now.' A voice sounded down her mobile and she listened once more. She raised her eyebrows hopefully at Leonard as she picked up her pencil and began writing. 'Jamie Stratton . . . OK . . . was that number seven London Street? . . . Right, and telephone number? . . . that's brilliant, thanks, Lewis . . . Yes, a drink would be good, if I can find the time . . . bye.' She punched the 'end' button on the mobile. 'Well, that sounds hopeful. Let's give this Mr. Stratton a call.'

'If you would prefer, I could—'

'No, let's see if he has anything available first,' she cut in, dialling the number written down on her notepad. She bit at a fingernail as she listened for the telephone to be answered. 'Hullo, Mr Stratton? . . . yes, this is Tess Goodwin at the International office. I believe you had some rooms to let . . . you still do . . . oh, that's wonderful . . . just the one, it's for a Mr Hartson . . . Right, and are you going to be in this morning? . . . Good, so Mr Hartson could come round anytime . . . Many thanks indeed . . . bye.'

'You're in luck,' she said with a smile as she ended the call and laid the mobile down on the table. She tore off the sheet from her notepad and handed it to Leonard. 'London Street is quite central, so you should be able to find it easily enough. You can make your move whenever you want.'

'I can't thank you enough, Tess,' Leonard said, folding the piece of paper and tucking it into the top pocket of his tweed jacket.

'I'm glad we managed to sort something out for you,' Tess said, rising from her chair and picking up her notepad and mobile.

'Now, if you'll excuse me, I must really dash.' Giving him a brief wave, she turned and hurried away towards the glass door.

Walking out on to the Lawnmarket, Leonard crossed over the cobbled street, feeling the late afternoon sun warming his back, and began walking down towards the High Street where the street theatre was in full swing. People thronged the closed-off thoroughfare and gathered around the acts in progress. There was first a jazz band, and then a juggling stilt walker, and further on an escapologist, naked to the waist, his face crossed in the blue and white of the Scottish saltire, who appeared to be hanging himself from a lamp post. His attention being captured by this alarming form of entertainment, Leonard never noticed the small dumpy woman who kept abreast with him on the other side of the street, trying to keep the large Samsonite suitcase that she dragged behind her from keeling over on the uneven paving slabs.

Rene Brownlow bumped the suitcase uncaringly up the two stone steps and pushed open the door to the Fringe office. She towed the suitcase into a corner where it wouldn't be in anyone's way and, puffing out a breath of exhaustion, she approached the long counter that was piled high with flyers and leaflets. A girl, dressed similarly to the appalling Andrea from the Corinthian Bar, left her computer screen behind the counter and approached her.

'Can I help you?'

'Yes. My name's Rene Brownlow. I've been doing a show in the Corinthian Bar, but I want to—' She didn't get any further, feeling the lump rise in her throat and the tears bubble in her eyes, just as they had done endlessly for the past twelve hours.

The girl smiled at her. 'Don't worry. I know exactly who you need to talk to.'

She went back to her desk and picked up the telephone. 'Lewis,' Rene heard her say, 'you have another tortured soul to deal with.'

The girl put down the receiver and came round from behind

the desk and put a hand on Rene's shoulder. 'Come on, I'm going to take you to see Lewis Jones. He'll sort everything out.'

These were about the first kindly words that had been spoken to Rene since she had arrived in Edinburgh a week and a half before, so by the time that she took her seat at the desk in front of the young man with the unruly mop of dark curly hair, she was snivelling uncontrollably. Lewis leaned forward on the desk, spinning a pencil about in his fingers, a huge grin spread across his stubbly face.

'Come on, things surely can't be going that badly, can they?' he said in a lilting Welsh voice. He took a handful of tissues from a large box of Kleenex at the side of the desk and passed them over.

Rene nodded as she peeled one off the pile and blew her nose with force. 'They couldn't go any worse,' she sobbed. 'I've 'ardly had anyone come to the show, and no one understands me 'umour and I'm never going to be able to cover the theatre cost. I just want to go 'ome now.'

Lewis leaned back in his chair, the grin still fixed on his face. 'Rene, would you believe you are the fifth person I've had in today, saying exactly the same thing?'

Rene wiped at her eyes, her sobs slowing down as his words sank in. 'Really?'

'Yes, really. You're not the only one in the boat, you know.'

'But I'll never be able to cover the—'

'Look, it's early days,' Lewis said, leaning forward on his desk once more. 'Quite a number of the performers get a bit despondent about this time. That's why I get a rash of visits about now. My advice to you is to stick it out, because you're sure to regret it if you don't.'

At that point a dark-haired girl put her head over the partition that separated Lewis's desk from the rest of the office. 'Lewis?'

Lewis watched Rene turn her head away to stop the girl from seeing she was crying. He looked up at the girl. 'Not now, Gail, I'm busy.'

'I know, but is that Rene Brownlow you've got with you?'

'Yes. Why?'

'I thought you might like to see this.' She handed him over a folded copy of a newspaper before disappearing once more behind the partition. Lewis scanned through the piece that Gail had highlighted in fluorescent yellow.

'There you are, you see,' he said, turning the newspaper round to face Rene. 'You are being a bit hasty, aren't you? That's in the *Scotsman*. Everybody reads that in Edinburgh.'

Rene picked up the paper and stared at the black-and-white photograph of herself. She glanced quickly through the words written underneath. 'Rene Brownlow . . . an original wit . . . splitting my sides at her characterisation of the members of Andersons Westbourne Social Club in her home town of Hartlepool . . . this act is definitely worth a visit.' Rene placed the newspaper back on the desk and let out a short laugh that was caught up in the last of her sobs.

'Not bad, eh?' Lewis said.

'No,' she replied quietly.

'I wish I could have produced reviews like that for the other four people who came to see me today.'

Rene smiled at him. 'I'd better get on with it then.'

'I think that would be the best idea. You wait until tonight. I bet you'll find the place packed.'

Rene lowered her head and pulled another handkerchief from the pile and once again began wiping at her eyes.

'What's up now?' Lewis asked in a baffled voice.

'I don't want to go on living where I am right now,' Rene said with a renewed sob. 'I'm in this 'orrible 'ouse with this dreadful woman, and I 'ave to be out every day at eleven o'clock and I just 'ave to walk the streets all day.'

Lewis puffed out his cheeks in disbelief. 'Oh, that's all a bit violent, isn't it? It sounds like that particular lady deserves to lose your custom.' He sucked in air through his teeth as he gave Rene's predicament some thought. 'Hang on a minute.' He began sifting through the piles of paper that littered his desk. 'Now where the hell did I put that address?' He shifted his attention to a wire tray, going through its contents. 'I only had it in my bloody hands about ten minutes ago.' He ducked out of sight for two seconds and came up brandishing a scrumpled piece of paper. 'Here it is. Under my foot, it was.' He put it on his desk and smoothed it out with a hand before picking up the telephone and dialling a number. 'Let's just keep our fingers crossed,' he said, shooting a wink at Rene.

'Hullo, is that Jamie Stratton? . . . Right, well, this is Lewis Jones at the Fringe office. I've just given your name to a colleague of mine . . . yes, that's right . . . ah, so do you have any more rooms available? . . . oh, you do. Well, in that case, I've got someone here who would like to take one of them . . . Yes, her name is Rene Brownlow . . . Yes, how do you know that? . . . ah, well, there you go then. I've just given it to her to read . . . Right, so she can come round any time, then? . . . Good, thank you, Jamie.'

Lewis smiled at Rene. 'There you are, you're famous already. Your new landlord has just read your review.' He quickly copied out the address on to a notepad, tore it off, then pushing himself out of his chair, he came round the side of his desk and handed it to Rene. 'You're going to be in London Street, which is just down the road a bit from the top of Leith Walk, so it's a good place to stay. He says you can go round anytime you want.'

Getting to her feet, Rene reached up and threw her arms around the lanky Welshman's neck. 'Lewis, you're a real star. Thanks for being in the right place at the right time.' She gave him a big kiss on the cheek. 'And sorry about all that blubbing.'

Lewis laughed. 'That's what I'm here for. That's why they call me Jones the Sponge.'

Twenty

Putting down the receiver, Jamie Stratton punched the air and let out a loud whoop of relief. Thank God things were looking up at last. One month had passed without any income coming into the flat, and his bank balance was just about at its limit. Now, in the space of twenty minutes, he had managed to rent out two of the rooms. He glanced at his watch, working out that he probably had enough time before anyone arrived to head round the corner and get a celebratory cup of coffee from The Grainstore. He scooped up his keys from the hall table and left the flat at speed, descending the three flights two at a time.

Jamie bought more cups of coffee per day at The Grainstore than was probably good for him, but he had an ulterior motive for his visits. It was his considered opinion that, underneath her red-striped apron, Martha had a body to die for, an uncommon asset for a girl who edged him in height by as much as three notches over his own 'approximate' six feet. Yet her attraction went much deeper than a mere clawing at his carnal senses. Humour constantly simmered in Martha's blue-green eyes, her face radiated so much health that make-up was a non-essential, and her complete zaniness was marked by the pointless black plastic hairband that permanently adorned her frenzy of short blonde hair. From the very first day she had started working in the coffee shop, Jamie had considered her his ultimate woman. The only slight problem was that, during their many brief encounters, he had found out she had six years on him and had been in a steady relationship for three of them. But inaccessibility only made the crush grow deeper.

The coffee shop was enjoying good custom that afternoon, but with the hometime rush yet to start, there was no queue at the counter. Martha caught his entry and immediately turned to one of her colleagues, slumping her shoulders and raising a long-suffering eyebrow. Jamie saw her every move, but undeterred by her lack of amorous reciprocation, he approached her with a broad grin.

'Hi, there, Martha.'

When she turned at his greeting, Martha gave him only the briefest of smiles. 'Well, James, what is it you're wanting this afternoon?'

'Black coffee to go, please.'

Martha turned to the espresso machine, and unclipping one of the coffee strainers, she banged it forcefully on the waste tray to rid it of the old coffee granules. 'So what's been going on today? Still home alone, are you?'

'Nup, not any more. I've managed to get two of the bedrooms rented out.'

Martha glanced over her shoulder and shot Jamie a more meaningful smile that succeeded in floating butterflies around his stomach. 'That'll please the bank manager then.'

'Too right.' He dug in the pocket of his trousers for some change. 'And what about you? Busy as ever?'

Martha placed the styrofoam cup on the counter and pushed on a lid. 'Working at full throttle,' she said, holding out her hand for the money. 'We didn't close up until midnight last night.'

Jamie handed her the exact change. 'No more cameras going missing then,' he said with a laugh.

Martha narrowed her eyes at him as she rang up the amount. 'That's a very bad joke.' She shut the drawer of the till with force. 'It's not good for business, having people come in here and nicking things.'

'No, I reckon not.' He picked up the cup from the counter. 'Well, I'd better head back in case one of my punters arrives. I'll see you later.'

'Nothing in life could be more certain,' Martha replied quietly through clenched teeth as she turned to serve another customer.

Seeing the taxi pull away from outside his flat, Jamie ran the last thirty yards along London Street and spun around the railings that led up to his front steps. An elderly man, smartly dressed in a tweed jacket and cavalry-twill trousers, was standing at the entrance door with a large suitcase by his side, pressing one of the bells on the brass-panelled intercom.

'Are you Mr Hartson?' Jamie asked.

The man turned with a start and appraised the young man standing in front of him in the calf-length shorts, white baggy T-shirt and flip-flop sandals. 'Yes?'

'Hi, I'm Jamie Stratton. Sorry I wasn't here. I was getting myself a cup of coffee.'

'No need to apologise,' Leonard Hartson replied with a shake of his head. 'I have only just this moment arrived.'

Jamie pulled a bunch of keys from the pocket of his shorts and unlocked the door. Holding it open with a foot, he reached out his un-coffee-ed hand and grabbed the handle of the man's suitcase.

'Oh, I can manage that,' Leonard said, making a move to take the suitcase from Jamie's grasp.

'It's no bother,' Jamie replied. 'I'm used to carrying heavy loads up these stairs. The flat's on the third floor, so I'm afraid you've got a bit of a climb.'

Leonard laughed. 'In that case, I am sincerely grateful that I have a fit young landlord.'

By the time the man had made the stairs, Jamie had opened the shutters on the large windows and given the bedroom a quick visual appraisal, letting out a loud expletive when he saw the well-breasted front cover of a copy of *GQ* peeping out from under the valance of one of the beds. Picking it up, he rolled it up into a tight scroll in his hand and went out into the hall just as Leonard Hartson entered the flat, puffing with the effort.

'Oh, my word, that is some climb,' Leonard said, resting his hand on the sideboard.

'Yeah, sorry about that. Better to take it in stages.' Jamie held out a hand to guide Leonard towards the bedroom. 'You're in here, Mr Hartson. It's on the quiet side of the building, so you won't hear the traffic. The bathroom is on the left just outside your bedroom door, which I hope you don't mind sharing with me. The kitchen is down the hall on the right, and there's a large sitting room at the other end with satellite television which you're welcome to use whenever you like.' He looked around the room, wondering if there was anything he had missed. 'Does this seem all right for you?'

Leonard nodded his approval. 'Perfect.' He glanced a smile at Jamie. 'Almost as well appointed as my room at the Sheraton

Grand.' He walked across to the window and looked out on to the small gardens that were enclosed by the surrounding buildings. 'Very pleasant indeed.' He turned back. 'And what about cost?'

'Well, erm . . .' Jamie had given this some thought. The agency was to be charging £40 per room per night, minus their commission, from the start of the festival, but he had to try to make up some of the shortfall. 'How about fifty pounds per night?'

Leonard nodded. 'Would you consider sixty pounds a night and allow me use of your telephone? Only for calls within the United Kingdom, of course.'

Jamie raised his eyebrows thoughtfully. 'Yeah, sounds good to me. We have a deal.'

'Good.'

Jamie leaned his back against the wall and folded his arms across his chest. 'So, are you going to be here for the whole of the festival?'

'Yes, I am.'

'To see the events?'

'No. I'm going to be working.'

Jamie furrowed his brow, wondering what type of work an elderly man, obviously well past retirement age, would be undertaking at the festival. 'And what is it you do?'

'I'm a lighting cameraman.'

'Is that right?' Jamie replied, suitably impressed. 'What a fascinating job. What type of films do you make?'

'Well, I've worked on every kind of film in my time, but right now, I'm up here to do a documentary.'

'So you've done features as well?'

'I have, yes.'

'Would I know any of them?'

'Not unless you're a fan of very old movies.' Leonard chortled. 'The last feature I worked on was made long before you were born.'

'In that case, I'll bet my father would know it. He's a complete movie buff.'

Leonard nodded slowly. 'Is that so? I wouldn't suppose your father has any contacts up here in the film industry?'

Jamie laughed. 'No way! Dad's a farmer. Why do you ask?'

'Because I'm looking for someone to assist me, and I'm not really very sure where to begin.' He scratched a finger down the side of his lined face. 'I don't suppose you know of anyone who might be looking for a job for the next three weeks? Experience isn't really very necessary. I just need someone who has a bit of muscle and a bit of common sense about them.'

Jamie shrugged his shoulders. 'I'm afraid not. All my university friends have either headed off to jobs or they're on summer vacation. I'll have a think about it, though.'

'That would be most kind,' Leonard replied.

Jamie pushed himself away from the wall when he heard the front-door buzzer sounding in the hall. He excused himself from Leonard and walked quickly along the hall and picked up the receiver.

'Hullo?'

'Is that . . . Jamie Stratton?'

Jamie winced at the distorted voice that rang in his ear, the woman obviously having her mouth pressed hard against the speaker of the entry phone.

'Yes.'

'This is Rene Brownlow. I'm standing outside your front door.'

'Right. When you hear the buzzer going, push the front door open. I'm on the third floor.'

'What? I can't get this wretched suitcase one inch further. My arms have stretched that much in length, ye'd think my dad was an ape!'

Jamie chuckled. 'All right, hang on there. I'll be down in a sec.'

He jammed the doormat in against the door to stop it from shutting and headed down the stairs at his customary speed. He opened the front entrance door and a woman with short straight hair, her small but ample frame swathed in a loose-folded coat that appeared to have been manufactured from a couple of multi-coloured rag rugs, jumped back with surprise.

'My, that was quick! You must 'ave wings on your feet!'

'I'm used to taking those stairs at speed,' Jamie said, picking up her suitcase. 'By the way, I read your review this morning. Pretty good.'

Rene stared open-mouthed at the ease with which he had lifted her enormous Samsonite burden. 'Ah, well, nice of you to say so,' she replied distantly.

Jamie cocked his ear, catching the sound of a telephone ringing up the stairwell. 'Dammit, that's my phone. I'd better see if I can get it, so just make your own way up.' He turned and began taking the stairs two at a time, as if he were carrying nothing heavier than a paper bag.

Rene remained on the front steps for a moment, watching the point where he had disappeared. 'That lad must be superhuman,' she said, shaking her head in disbelief before starting her ascent to the flat at a much more sedate pace.

Dropping the suitcase with a thump on the flagstone floor at the door, Jamie crossed the hall and made a dive for the telephone. 'Hullo?'

'Good afternoon, Jamie. It's Gavin Mackintosh here.'

Jamie caught his breath before replying. 'Hi, Gavin. Sorry about the delay. I was down at the bottom of the stairs when you rang.'

'Is my timing a bit inconvenient?'

'No, not at all.'

'Good. I was just ringing to see if you managed to find any tenants for the festival.'

'Well, funny you should say that,' Jamie replied, glancing around to see that Mr Hartson's bedroom door was closed and Rene Brownlow was yet to make it to the top of the stairs. 'Two have just arrived today.'

'Oh, excellent. So does that mean you'll be all right for your mortgage payments?'

'Yeah, I've worked out I should be OK until the end of September.'

'I take it, then, your tenants will be there for the whole of the festival.'

'Probably not both of them. One is doing a show on the Fringe, so she could well leave before the final week. The other guy's a cameraman who's making some sort of documentary at the festival, so I reckon he'll be around for the duration. Talking of which, Gavin, you don't have any contacts in the film industry up here, do you?'

'No, I'm afraid that's away out of my network, Jamie. Why do you ask?'

'Well, this cameraman is an old boy and he's in need of an assistant, so he asked me if I knew anyone up here. I think he's a bit desperate because he said he'd be happy to take someone with no experience.'

'Nothing springs to mind, Jamie, but I'll certainly keep my thinking cap on.'

'That'd be great. Cheers, Gavin.' Jamie waved a greeting to Rene as she entered the flat and sat down with a flump on her suitcase. 'By the way, did Dad get hold of you?'

'No. What would that have been about?'

'A possible game of golf at Muirfield tomorrow evening, I think.'

'Ah, in that case, I'll have to tell him I won't be able to make it. Jenny and I are going to a concert to hear Angélique Pascal play.'

'She's the French violinist, isn't she?'

'Exactly.'

'Yeah, there was a photograph of her on the front page of the newspaper this morning, arriving at Edinburgh Airport. She's pretty fit-looking.'

Gavin laughed. 'You're not wrong there. I had the pleasure of being in her company at a reception yesterday evening and she is an extremely captivating young lady.'

'Sounds as if you're a bit hooked there, Gavin. Maybe you should consider ditching Jenny tomorrow evening and going it alone.'

'Ah, Jamie, I think maybe this would be an apt time to finish this call before you come up with any other suggestions, and

I'm tempted to charge you for my time. We'll keep in touch, though.'

'Right you are. Thanks, Gavin.'

Jamie put down the receiver and turned to his new tenant, who still sat on the suitcase catching her breath. 'Sorry about that.'

Rene held up a hand. 'Not at all. I'm not used to all this exercise. Living in Edinburgh is like being at a bloody 'ealth farm.' She got slowly to her feet. 'I tell you, I'm going to be returning to 'Artlepool a mere shadow of my former self.'

Jamie smiled at her as he picked up the suitcase. 'Come on, I'll show to your room and you can recover in a bit more comfort.'

Twenty-One

The police panda car was sitting at traffic lights in Stockbridge when the report of suspicious behaviour came through on the radio from the control room. Being only four streets away from where the supposed incident was taking place, WPC Heather Lennox took the call while her male colleague switched on the blue light, gave a short wail on the siren and swerved out of the queue, swinging the car left across the red light.

As they approached the street, the driver killed the blue light and drove slowly around the corner, hoping for an element of surprise in their arrival. He flicked the headlights on to full beam, illuminating the two youths who turned with expressions of panic on their faces, immediately stepping away from the car into which they were only a moment away from gaining entry. As the panda car accelerated towards them, the two boys took to their heels like a couple of frightened gazelles, and as the car drew level with them their desperation pushed them to perform a near impossible feat, scrambling up and over a seven-foot wall before disappearing from sight.

The driver unclipped his seat belt and threw open the car door, making ready to give chase, but was stopped by WPC Lennox.

'Dinnae bother, Jim. We'll never catch 'em.' She turned around in her seat and stared out of the back window. 'Did ye see onything a bit odd back there when we turned intae the street?'

The policeman shrugged.

'I'm sure there was some'dy standing in that end doorway watching everything that was going on wi' something like a pair of binoculars.' She swung round and unslotted the radio handset. 'Come on, I think it's worth checking it. Better get the car turned so we don't have to reverse out o' here.'

The police driver spun the steering wheel back and forth until he had managed to turn in the tight space between the rows of parked cars. He drove to the end of the street and stopped at the junction with the road.

'Which way?' he asked.

WPC Lennox craned forward in her seat and glanced up and down the street. She could make out a number of pedestrians walking beneath the orange glow of the street lights, mostly in couples. There seemed to be only one person walking alone.

'That could be him up there on the left. Wait for a couple of cars to come and slot in between them, then just drive past at normal speed so I can tak' a look at him.'

Sixty yards away, Thomas Keene junior was still chuckling to himself. It had been the third time he had videoed those two boys from his housing estate attempting to nick a car, but that one really had to take the Oscar. He had had the zoom set right in to record every detail of the theft and consequently had seen the expressions of horror on the boys' faces when they turned to look up the street. Sensing then that something was going on out of frame, T.K. had zoomed out, catching the police car approaching, and he had kept the camera switched on until the two lads had disappeared from sight over the wall. He could not have captured the scene better, so well in fact that he could not resist the temptation of reviewing the whole hilarious scene right then and there. Opening up the viewfinder, he rewound the tape and pressed 'playback', studying the screen as he walked, oblivious to the cars that passed him on the street.

'Well, speak o' the devil,' WPC Lennox breathed quietly, as the car passed the slow-moving figure on the pavement.

'D'ye know him?' her colleague asked.

'That, Jim, is one Thomas Keene junior, a young man from Pilton Mains who has mair stolen cars to his name than the Queen of England has jewels.'

'Ye'd think he'd notice us, then. What was he doing?'

'I don't know. He was holding something in his hand, but I couldn't work out what it was.' She gestured with her hand. 'Turn into the street on the left here and we'll just wait to ask the lad a few questions, shall we?'

T.K. was so distracted by his latest masterpiece that he missed the step down on to the street at the end of the pavement and landed awkwardly on his foot. Wincing with pain, he closed the viewfinder on the camera and bent down to rub at his throbbing ankle. It was at that point he became aware of the two shadows that darkened the area around him.

'Evening, Keene,' the policewoman said in an airy manner. 'Remember me, dae ye?'

Thomas slowly lifted his head and saw the two uniforms standing above him. Shit, he thought to himself, the bloody polis. His first fleeting thought was that at least he was innocent of all crime, but then his eyes glanced down at the stolen video camera that lay by his right foot. Hell, he couldn't get caught with it. He'd stayed out of trouble for so long, he wasn't going to get pulled in for something as petty as that.

'Could you stand up so that we can ask you a few questions, Keene?' the policewoman asked, taking a step towards him.

'Ma ankle's sare.'

'Just get to yer feet, sonny,' the policeman said sternly, backing up his colleague's request.

T.K. put his hand on the camera and manoeuvred his feet into a position that was as near as possible to that of a hundred-metre sprinter about to push off from his blocks. The policeman sensed the lad's intentions and reached down to grab his shoulder, but his hand closed on thin air. Thomas Keene junior had taken off like a scalded cat.

'Bring the car. I'll get him,' the policeman called out to his colleague as he ran off in pursuit of T.K. After fifty metres he wondered if he hadn't been a bit premature in the surety of his statement because the gap between him and the wee bastard was increasing with every second.

T.K. glanced quickly behind him. He was certainly putting welcome distance between himself and his pursuer, but the policeman was still in full view, which meant T.K. wasn't yet in a position to jettison the camera unseen. He had to get out of sight.

T.K.'s knowledge of every short cut to the north side of the New Town was infinite, and so he knew from the moment he turned into the small mews street that he had made a fundamentally suicidal mistake. The cobbled lane, which was lined with small, pleasantly symmetrical stone houses with brightly painted garage doors, came to an abrupt end at an eighteen-foot-high wall that was topped, for some ridiculous reason, with a spiral of razor wire. Left with no other alternative, T.K. kept running until he came to the wall. He turned, at bay against it, thankful that the street was only lit at its entrance. He looked frantically around. To one side were a couple of potted bay trees at either side of the front door of the last house. No time to start digging, he thought to himself. On the other side was a cluster of pristine rubber dustbins tucked away into the corner of the wall where the house owners would deem them least unsightly. He dragged one of them out, pulled off the top and pushed the camera down deep amongst the plastic bags. Then a spur-of-the-moment decision made him retrieve it. Losing the stolen apparatus was unfortunately a necessity, but he was damned if he was going to lose his precious videotape. He ejected the cassette and once more rammed the camera back into its hiding place, and then, squatting down behind the dustbin, he slid the cassette down the side of his battered trainer shoe. He leaned back against the wall, drew up his knees and took in a deep, calming lungful of air. It was all he had time for. He watched the beam from the powerful torch light up the profile of the dustbin, hitting him full in the face ten seconds later. He held up a hand to protect his eyes, hearing the policeman's rasping breath.

'All right, lad, are ye going to come quiet now or am ah going tae have tae use a bit o' persuasion?'

Gavin Mackintosh rose to his feet along with the rest of the audience in the Usher Hall to give tumultuous applause to the performance of Mozart's Violin Concerto No. 3 in G Major. With outstretched hand, the conductor directed the acclaim toward the young soloist, then swivelled on his plinth and gave her a short Germanic bow. Angélique Pascal, dressed in a black strapless cocktail dress that hugged her small but curvaceous figure, reciprocated by blowing him a kiss before continuing on in similar style to the packed auditorium encircling the stage.

Gavin continued to clap until his was the last to echo feebly around the vast domed concert hall, his eyes fixed on the departing orchestra. Jenny, his wife, already with her coat on and her handbag shouldered, touched his arm to draw his attention to those others in their row who were waiting to get past him. Gavin held a hand up in apology, slipped the evening's programme into the inside pocket of his jacket and followed his wife up the steep staircase to the exit.

Outside, a cool wind blew up Lothian Road, swerving with force around the curved walls of the Usher Hall. Fastening the centre button of his suit jacket, Gavin took hold of Jenny's arm and manoeuvred a path for them through the crowds, at the same time taking his mobile phone from his breast pocket and switching it back to 'general' ring. It was as well he had remembered to turn it on to 'silent' before the concert because he had felt it reverberate against his chest halfway through and it had taken a steely glare and a brisk shake of the head from his wife to curtail his immediate reaction to answer it. Pressing the play-back number, he listened to the message as he walked.

'Damnation,' he muttered, slipping the mobile back into his pocket and guiding Jenny over to the side of the pavement.

'Don't say you have a call-out,' she said in a voice which expressed both disappointment and long-sufferance.

'I'm afraid so. One of John Anderson's Legal Aid cases. The lad's been taken into Gayfield Square Police Station.' He held up a hand to hail one of the few taxis on Lothian Road with their 'For Hire' lights still on. 'It shouldn't be too complicated, but I'll have to stop in at the office to see if I can unearth some files on the boy. You take this taxi home and I'll be back as soon as I can.' As the black cab pulled up alongside them, Gavin opened the door and gave his wife a kiss on the cheek. 'At least this year we managed to *get* to see the concert.'

Jenny smiled knowingly at him. 'Just as well, too. I think you might have been in a bit of a grump if you'd missed out on both Madamoiselle Pascal's musical *and* physical attributes this evening.'

Gavin laughed. 'My dear, it is nothing more than a boyish infatuation.' He closed the door, and with a quick wave of farewell as the taxi pulled away from the pavement, he headed off down towards Princes Street, glancing behind him from time to time in the hope of spying another vacant taxi.

Thomas Keene junior sat slumped on the hard wooden chair in the windowless interview room, chewing hard on a fingernail that was already bitten down to the quick. God, how he hated the stink of these places. They were always the same, the sour aroma of disinfectant doing little to cover the ingrown stench of fear. It always made his stomach knot up in agitation, and this time his unease was exacerbated by the fact that he was beginning to break out in a cold and clammy sweat, being a good hour overdue with the methadone.

He glanced at the pair of battered trainers that sat incriminatingly on the table. 'Ah, fa *fuck's* sake!' he yelled out, thumping his elbows on the desk and slapping repeatedly at his face. Why in the name of hell had he kept the tape? He should have known they would give him a thorough search. Now, if he ever got out this bloody mess, his life wouldn't be worth shit. There was enough evidence on that tape to put at least nine lads in front of the juvenile court, and it wouldn't take long before everyone on the Pilton Mains estate knew exactly who was responsible for supplying the evidence. He leaned back in the chair, clasping his hands behind his head. He'd asked to see his solicitor the moment that damned policewoman had held up the video cassette between finger and thumb, eyeing it as if she was bloody Sherlock Holmes. 'What do we have here, then, Keene?' she had asked. 'A miniature timing device that'll blow yer hand aff in twa seconds,' he had wanted to answer, but then felt it wouldn't have helped his case any. Where the hell had that damned Mr Anderson got to? The polis must have put the call through a good hour and a half ago.

The door of the interview room opened and WPC Lennox entered, barely able to cover the smirk on her face. 'Your solicitor is here, Keene.'

A large man in a dark-blue pinstriped suit walked in and thumped a buff-coloured file down on the table. T.K. stared at him in alarm.

'Where's Mr Anderson?' he asked, a note of panic in his voice.

'On holiday, I'm afraid, Thomas. I'm Mr Mackintosh. You're going to have to make do with me.'

T.K. let out a groan of hopelessness on hearing the gruff tones of his new solicitor. This is it, he thought. There's no way ye're goin' tae escape dae'n time now.

Gavin turned to the policewoman. 'Constable Lennox, would you be good enough to allow me two minutes with my client?'

The policewoman flicked her head uncertainly. 'We should really just get on wi' it, Mr Mackintosh, but I'll give ye a couple of minutes, as long as ye don't hold back on anything during the interview.'

Gavin nodded. 'You have my assurance.'

As the door closed, Gavin pulled out one of the chairs opposite T.K. and sat down. He took a pair of half-moon reading glasses from his pocket, put them on, and then, flicking the bands off the file, he spent a moment in silence scanning through the reports on the first few pages. Pushing the file to one side, he leaned forward on the desk and eyed the young man over his spectacles. 'Well, it doesn't look too good, does it, Thomas?'

'Ah didnae dae onything,' T.K. mumbled disgruntedly.

Gavin found it difficult to suppress a laugh. 'I wouldn't know about that. On that videotape, you seem to have supplied the police with enough evidence to cut car crime in Edinburgh by half overnight.'

'Ah, *shite*,' T.K. spat out, throwing back his head and closing his eyes tightly.

'What happened to the camera, Thomas?' Gavin asked.

'Ah dropped it in the chase.'

'You didn't dump it, did you?'

'How should I? It wis mine.'

'Why did you take the tape out then?'

T.K. managed to pause only fractionally before replying. ''Cos I'd just loaded it wi' a new one.'

'You know Constable Lennox's colleague went back to look for the camera. There was no trace of it.'

'Some thievin' gypsy must hae picked it up then. That cost us a packet, that did.'

'What model was it, Thomas?'

'A JVC digi'al compact.'

Gavin nodded. He had a half inkling to believe the boy. His experience was that those who stole cameras usually had no idea or interest in what model or make it was, only in what money they could raise from its sale.

'You seem to be bit uncomfortable, Thomas. Are you back on the hard stuff?'

'No, I'm clean. I'm just sweatin' 'cos ah'm due ma "script".'

'Could you tell me why you've been filming people stealing cars?'

T.K. eyed the solicitor distrustfully before shrugging a silent reply.

'It would help your cause if you gave me some sort of answer, Thomas. How did you know who was going off to steal cars?'

T.K. sighed and stared up at the bare fluorescent ceiling light. 'They meet uvvy night on the estate. They talk aboot how they nick the different cars, some o' them learn themselves, others learn fi' the boys they meet in detention centres in other cities. That's how it works.'

'It's like a club, then?'

'Aye, s'pose.'

'And you were in this club, then?'

'No!' T.K. replied with vehemence. 'If ye want proof o' that, tak' a look at the film. I never went near 'em.'

'Are you running some kind of racket, Thomas?'

'Whit?'

Gavin leaned over and leafed through the pages in the file. 'Car theft does seem to be your speciality—'

'It wis,' T.K. cut in.

'Well, your knowledge of how it's done is probably infinitely greater than the lads you've been filming, and even I know that anti-theft devices on modern cars are making it more and more difficult to break into them, so I'm wondering to myself if you're not running some kind of elaborate training scheme.'

T.K. scoffed out a laugh. 'Ye're talking crap, mister. Ah dinnae wanna steal cars onymair, d'ya unnerstand that, ah wanna film stuff. Whit else is there tae shoot when ye live in a shitehole like Pilton Mains?'

Gavin studied the gaunt, loose-lipped face of the young man. 'Is that the truth, Thomas?'

'Aye, it is,' T.K. replied quietly, avoiding eye contact with the solicitor as if embarassed by what Gavin had just drawn out of him. 'Ah'm tryin' ti go straight, eh, but the breaks dinnae come easy.'

170

Gavin nodded and reached over and drew the buff file towards him. He closed it, replaced the rubber bands with a twang and got to his feet.

'Where you aff tae?' T.K. asked, sitting bolt upright in the chair, a sudden look of desperation in his eyes.

'I think it's time we started the interview, don't you, Thomas?'

T.K. held his arms across his chest to stop the shakes that were developing due to his condition and to the thought of what was going to happen to him. 'Honest, Mr Mackintosh, I didnae dae onything. Ye've gotti believe me.'

Gavin winked. 'Just stay cool, Thomas, and answer the questions. I'm on your side, lad.'

Fifteen minutes past the hour of midnight, Gavin walked out of the police station into the cool night air and stood on the pavement listening to the breeze rustling the leaves on the trees that stood in the grassed centre of Gayfield Square. A moment later, he heard the door of the police station open and he sensed someone come to stand beside him. He turned to see T.K. stick his hands into the pockets of his baggy threadbare jeans and pull in a long breath of relief.

'Cheers fae that, Mr Mackintosh,' he said, nodding appreciatively. 'I'm no' sure what ye said in there aifter the interview, but . . . cheers onyway.'

'I did stick my neck on the block for you in there, Thomas, and judging from your notes, Mr Anderson has done likewise in the past. However, I was willing to take the risk because I think you probably are making an effort to keep out of trouble. Just don't disappoint me, Thomas.'

T.K. shook his head and glanced up and down the street. He knew he wasn't out of the shit yet. He now had to go back to Pilton Mains, and God only knew what kind of reception would be waiting for him there. No doubt the police would have been knocking on doors already, which meant it would be highly unlikely he'd get by the evening without getting knifed or having a broken bottle slice open some part of his body.

He turned to Gavin and shot him a sad smile. 'Mr Mackintosh, I dinnae like tae ask ye, but is there any chance you could gie's some cash tae get hame? Ah'm skint.'

Gavin sucked on his teeth. 'Where'd you keep your methadone, Thomas?'

T.K. frowned quizzically at the solicitor's unrelated question. 'In ma bedroom in the flat. How?'

'Well,' said Gavin with a slow, pensive nod. 'I'm going to suggest we take a taxi back to my house, pick up my car and you can then show me where you live. Once I've fetched the methadone from your bedroom, I'm going to bring you back uptown and take you to a hostel for the night. It's no five-star hotel, I'm afraid, but I reckon it'll be a whole lot safer than you returning to Pilton Mains right now.'

'Ye're no' kiddin me,' T.K. mumbled disconsolately.

Gavin flicked a forefinger at the boy, gesturing for T.K. to walk with him up the road towards Leith Walk. 'I don't do this for all my clients, you know, T.K., but in your case, I do happen to have an ulterior motive.' He fixed the lad with a stern glare. 'I have a real aversion to being called out to police stations at a time when I should be in my bed, and if I can do anything to avoid it, I will. So tomorrow morning, I shall come and pick you up at the hostel at nine-thirty sharp. Is that clear?'

T.K. nodded dolefully.

'Because then I'm going to try out an idea of mine which, if it comes to a favourable conclusion, might hopefully result in my never having to encounter you in a police station ever again.'

Twenty-Two

Albert Dessuin arrived just over three quarters of an hour late for the post-concert reception in the Sheraton Grand. His mobile had rung almost the moment he had walked out of the Usher Hall and he had sought out the quietest corner of Festival Square so that he could placate his mother as she reeled off her trials and tribulations for that particular day. He had listened and reasoned and accepted responsibility for gross negligence, and when eventually he had exhausted every form of appeasement, he had abruptly ended the call with a stab of his finger and made to hurl the mobile phone as far across the square as he could. Now, as he entered the function suite, he could sense the black cloud of frustration and irritation that resulted from such a call descend upon him.

He swept a glass of champagne from the waitress's tray at the entrance door, downed it in one gulp and took another before skirting the outside of the room, hoping to locate Angélique Pascal and spirit her away before being engaged in conversation. He did not get far. A small grey-haired lady with a friendly smile approached him almost immediately and began to twitter away to him in bad French about the various concerts she and her husband had attended so far during the festival. Smiling disinterestedly at the woman, Dessuin looked up over the top of her head and scanned the assembled crowd, eventually fixing his eyes on the cluster of men who gathered around the unused bar in the corner of the room. In the midst of them, Angélique and another girl sat up on the high counter, chatting and laughing, and Dessuin immediately recognised the girl as being Tess Goodwin, the marketing assistant from the International office with whom Angélique had struck up a friendship at the welcoming reception two nights before. He watched as Angélique turned to Tess and, with cupped hand, whispered something in her ear. The girl reacted by staring at the young violinist with a wide-eyed, open-mouthed look of sheer disbelief, before both dissolved into fits of laughter. The men dutifully followed suit, even though they could have had no idea as to what had been said.

Albert left the woman still talking, hearing her conversation trail off to a stunned silence as he moved into a position where he could see the two girls more clearly, noticing immediately that the short length of their skirts and the high angle at which they were sitting no doubt afforded a greater attraction to the men than anything that was being said. Taking another glass of champagne from the tray of a hovering waitress, Albert started to walk across the room towards the group, but was waylaid by a hand on his arm, and he was introduced to the main sponsor of that evening's concert, a small man with an almost tangible air of self-importance, dressed in a perfectly cut dinner jacket with a deep-red Thai silk waistcoat. He had at his side a woman with long straight blonde hair and an over-tanned face, who not only had to be twenty years his junior, but also towered over him by at least four inches. Albert smiled and pretended to listen to what was being said, but his eyes kept glancing across the room to Angélique, his mind boiling over with anger and jealousy.

Ever since the concert in Munich two weeks ago, he had begun to notice unwelcome changes in the way Angélique was behaving towards him, and he had come to realise that she was no longer the pliable little working-class girl from Clermont Ferrand who, from the moment she had appeared at the Conservatoire, had held hard to his coat-tails in everything that she did. This new, grown-up Angélique Pascal was beginning to show too much independence and self-reliance, often questioning his judgement on a matter or taking little heed of the advice he gave her concerning her playing style. What's more, she had begun to display an obvious aversion to those congratulatory embraces that had been commonplace between them since he had first started to teach her. And that was something he could not allow to continue. She had, after all, become his property, he had invested his life in her, and eventually he wished to possess every part of her, even though sixteen years separated them in age, because he knew it was the one way he could truly prove to his mother that he was of some worth and importance in the world, and not just an impotent lackey as she had so often described him. And how that would succeed in rankling her! It was therefore imperative to his own interests, and to his financial survival, that he should continue to keep Angélique reined in, under his control.

Nodding his appreciation to the sponsor and his wife, Albert took his leave of them and turned to watch Angélique at the very moment she placed her hand on the shoulder of one of the men, drew him towards her and kissed him on his forehead. She then threw back her head with a laugh and pushed him away, waving her hands as if dismissing him from her presence. This action did nothing to help Albert's already darkened mood. It was indicative of yet another unwelcome change in the character of Angélique Pascal as she demonstrated awareness of what both her status and her sexuality could do for her. She was learning the arts of flirtation and manipulation, qualities that were no different from the cunning deception employed by the whores in the Quartier Latin to attract their clientele each night. And if that was the way in which she wished to behave, then it was obvious to Albert that now was the time to forgo his kind, fatherly influence and educate her in ways other than simply playing the violin.

Wiping beads of perspiration from his forehead, Albert made his way purposefully towards the group.

'Albert?'

He turned to the person who greeted him with forceful words of dismissal ready to bubble like a hot geyser from his lips, only to gulp them back when he found a smiling Sir Alasdair Dreyfuss standing beside him.

'I'm sorry, I've been rather negligent of you this evening,' the director said, putting a hand on his arm. 'I'm afraid Signor Montarino seems to be under the impression this whole party is for his own considerable self alone and he has rather commandeered my attention up until this point.'

Albert took in a deep breath and smiled at the director. 'Please do not worry. I have also been engaged in numerous conversations.'

'And most of them would have been about the concert tonight, I am sure.' Alasdair Dreyfuss glanced in the direction of Angélique. 'Quite startling. She seems to be becoming more accomplished every time I hear her play. You really are to be congratulated, Albert.'

'Thank you,' Albert replied distractedly as he too turned to stare at his protégée.

Alasdair eyed Angélique Pascal's manager concernedly. 'Are you all right, Albert? You're looking a bit pale.'

Albert shook his head. 'No, it is only a bit of a headache, but I was thinking I might slip away to lie down in my room for a while.'

'Well, I'd be grateful if you might just spare me a moment before you go,' the director said, taking his arm and guiding him away from the young violinist's admiring group. 'I want to have a quick word with you about the late concerts Angélique will be performing. Let's head over to the recess by the window so we won't be disturbed.'

And as Sir Alasdair led him across the room, Albert heard Angélique's laughter sound out once more and he turned with paranoid fury burning in his eyes as the distance grew between them.

As Tess stood by the door of the function room, thanking the departing guests for their attendance, she heard her mobile phone ringing in her handbag. She left Sarah Atkinson to carry on the duty and walked down the carpeted steps and into the centre of the nearly deserted room, scrabbling in her bag for the phone. She glanced at the screen, took in a long steadying breath and pressed the 'receive' button.

'What are you doing?' she whispered angrily, cupping a hand around the mobile and casting a furtive glance over to where Alasdair Dreyfuss stood chatting to a group of late departers. 'I said I'd be the one to make contact.'

'I know,' Peter Hansen replied, 'but I wanted to let you know I've booked a table for a week today in La Hirondelle at eight-thirty. I thought that as it used to be our favourite restaurant, it would be a good place to renew our friendship.'

'It's not going to happen, Peter. The only reason I agreed to have dinner with you is because I love my husband and I love my job and I am certainly not going to lose either because of you. Is that understood?'

'Come on, Tess, there's no reason to be like that. Let's just take one step at a time. I have made it my plan not to leave Edinburgh without mending all our differences.' Tess heard one of his slow, seductive laughs, the very thing she had been idiotic enough to find so attractive at the outset of their relationship. 'And I thought maybe you might wear that blue dress I bought for you? You always looked very beautiful in it.'

'What? You think I'd keep that?' Tess laughed derisively. 'I chucked that ages ago.'

There was a brief silence. 'OK, no matter, then,' he said, the tone of disappointment in his voice satisfying Tess. 'I am sure you will look wonderful in whatever you wear.'

'I have to go, Peter. Our guests are leaving.'

'All right. A week today, then, eight-thirty at La Hirondelle. I shall be there waiting.'

Tess did not bother to say any word of farewell. She ended the call and slipped the phone into her handbag, and then, taking a moment to compose herself, she fixed a smile on her face and returned to stand next to Sarah Atkinson.

Twenty-Three

Still dressed in the black cocktail dress she had worn for the concert, Angélique Pascal lay huddled on the bed in her hotel bedroom, staring at the distorted image of her violin case on the cream Regency-style chair that sat against the wall. The side of her face felt wet and sticky, due to the tears of frustration and fatigue that had been shed on her pillow, but she had neither the energy nor the inclination to make any move.

She had never before had such a row with Albert Dessuin. She had played her heart out at that evening's concert, and had consequently felt unusually buoyant in spirit during the reception afterwards, dissipating the smog of exhaustion that had enveloped her over the past month. But it had only lasted until the moment she had returned, or had *been* returned, to her hotel bedroom by Albert, who had caused an embarrassing scene at the crowded reception by extricating her from the room like a naughty schoolchild who was being marched off to see the headmaster. All she had said was she wanted to go out that night for a couple of drinks with Tess and her husband, and that was when Dessuin had lost his temper. In the privacy of her room, he had set about berating her for the sloppiness of her performance and the way she had acted both on stage in the concert hall and at the reception. And then, displaying an almost disturbing irrationality, he had literally *ordered* her to start practising part of the Szymanowski Violin Concerto, a piece not scheduled to be performed until the concert in Singapore in ten days' time. It was at that point she had retaliated. She did not lose her temper, she did not scream, she just told him in a quiet, controlled voice that she'd had enough. When Edinburgh was finished, she wanted to take a complete break.

'What do you mean by that?' Dessuin had blurted out, his eyes narrowed in anger.

'Albert, you must understand that I cannot go on like this, playing night after night. It is becoming too . . . automatic, impersonal, for me, and it affects the way I feel about the music. You are probably right to criticise me, although tonight I made a great effort to play well, but it does not make me happy, Albert, to have to *make* that effort and not have it come naturally to me. I need a rest. I want time to go back to Paris to see some of my friends, and also to return to Clermont Ferrand to stay with Madame Lafitte. I know that she would help me get my perspective back and help me regain my enthusiasm for music.'

'*Pah*, that ancient old crow could give you *nothing* now.'

'Albert, you have no right to call Madame Lafitte such—'

'*Tais-toi et écoutes-moi.* You will not go back to Paris, nor to Clermont Ferrand. You will continue to play until I tell you to stop. It is as simple as that.'

'But there is absolutely no way—'

'Exactly, there is no way you can back out of your obligations at this stage. Can you not imagine what the press would say about you? It would spell the end of your playing career.'

'Could we not just say that I am sick?'

'But you are not sick, are you? And I am not going to be party to such subterfuge. No, the tour continues, and let that put an end to all this *merde*. Now, once you have changed out of that dress, which I have to tell you makes you look like a tart, please get on with your practising.'

Angélique let out a short, quiet laugh and shook her head slowly. 'Oh, Albert, sometimes you are so like your mother.'

'How *dare* you say such a thing!' Dessuin screamed at her, raising his hand as if to strike her backhanded across the face. Falling back on to the bed to avoid the blow, Angélique crawled away from him, pushing herself against the headboard, and stared at him with horrified astonishment. He dropped the threatening hand to his side, turned on his heel and stormed out of the room, slamming shut the door that connected their bedrooms. And then, in the ensuing silence, Angélique had keeled over on the bed, exhausted and frightened.

Sitting up, she glanced across at the radio alarm clock on her bedside table. It was a quarter past midnight. Two hours had passed since Dessuin had left the room. She shuffled her bottom over to the edge of the bed and pushed herself to her feet. Intending to have a shower, she slipped out of her dress as she walked across to the bathroom, her nakedness spared only by a black lace thong.

She turned with a start at the sound of the connecting door being thrown open, and her immediate reaction was to cover her breasts with her hands and push her legs together in an attempt to hide what the thong did little to cover.

'Albert, what the *hell* are you doing?' she said to Dessuin, who stood framed in the doorway, one hand against the doorpost to steady himself. In the other, he clutched a bottle of J&B whisky by the neck. 'I am naked, so please get out of here *now*.'

Dessuin gave a short, scornful laugh. 'Oh, look at you, Miss

Modesty,' he said in a slow, slurring voice, 'trying to cover yourself up as if you have something to hide from me.'

Angélique turned to get into the bathroom, but drunk as he was, Dessuin still made it across the room, blocking her path before she was able to seek refuge. She backed away into the centre of the room, shaking with uncertainty and fear.

'Come on, Angélique,' he laughed derisively. 'Why bother acting so cold with me? You would have no doubt loved to have given one of those young men who clustered around you tonight the chance to see you as I am now seeing you.'

Angélique squatted down on her haunches, cupping her hands to her face and covering her breasts as best she could with her elbows. 'Albert,' she sobbed quietly, 'please leave me alone.'

'Leave you alone?' he whined. 'Why should I leave you alone?' He came and leaned over her, and she could smell the alcohol surrounding him like a poisonous cloud. 'I *own* you – and so you will never get rid of me.'

Angélique took her hands from her face and stared up at him, her eyes now afire with disillusionment and hatred. 'My God, you are a screwed-up *bastard*, Albert Dessuin. I am beginning to realise it now. You are nothing more than a worthless, drunken *cochon*!'

The force of the blow was so great that it knocked Angélique on to her side and rolled her across the floor. She lay with her head spinning, trying to orientate herself, trying to work out how she could avoid the next blow. She began to pull herself into a fetal position to protect herself when he grabbed her by the arm and yanked her to her feet. Angélique let out a cry of pain as he dug his fingernails into her arm, dragging her across to the desk so that he could rid himself of the bottle of whisky. Then, with both hands free, he picked her bodily off the ground and threw her spreadeagled on to the bed.

'Right, Mademoiselle Pascal, world-famous musician, if you choose to call me that name, I will show you exactly what a *cochon* excels at!'

He clumsily unbuttoned his trousers and pushed them to the

floor, but as he pulled his legs up to step out of them, the cuffs caught on his shoes, and in his inebriated state he lost his balance and fell heavily to the ground. Angélique, seeing her moment to escape, jumped off the bed and grabbed her dress from the floor. As she ran towards the door, a hand grasped at her ankle and she fell forward on to the desk, splaying out her hands for support and knocking over the whisky bottle in the process. It toppled from the desk and hit heavily against a metal wastepaper basket, shattering its neck and spraying whisky liberally over the wall and on to the carpet. Putting his near-spent energy into one final heave, Dessuin brought Angélique crashing to the ground, but even in his drunken stupor, the ensuing scream cut through to his inner senses and he immediately released his grip on her ankle.

Dessuin crawled over to the wall and leaned his back against it, and with lolling head fixed his drunken gaze on Angélique. All thoughts of protecting her modesty now long gone, Angélique sat on the floor with her legs apart, staring at her hand and at the blood that flowed down her arm from the wound.

'Oh, *mon Dieu*, what have you done? What have you *done*?' she cried out, her desolate sobs shaking every part of her body. 'You have just ruined my *life*!'

'Oh, Angélique,' Dessuin said, his voice slurring heavier than before. 'I'm so sorry, *ma chérie,* I did not mean . . .' He tried to make a move towards her, but the violent struggle and the amount of alcohol that was now coursing through his body took its toll and he toppled over unconscious.

Never taking her eyes off her hand, Angélique got slowly to her feet and stepped over Dessuin's prostrate form. She went into the bathroom and turned on the cold tap, wincing with pain as she held her palm upturned under the gushing stream. She held her hand up to the light to see if there was any glass still embedded in the wound. The gash was long and deep but, as far as she could tell, it was clean. Taking a white hand towel from the rack, she bound it tightly around her hand and then, for the first time, viewed her shivering, naked form in the large

181

mirror above the sink. Oh, Angélique, what has just happened in there? Everything has changed, everything has gone in the past few minutes. What are you to do now? You cannot stay here, not with this man who has betrayed your trust and put an end to your wonderful dream. But maybe you provoked it. Maybe everyone would believe it was your fault. He would certainly do everything to manipulate the story for it to appear so.

You have no alternative but to leave now, leave everything behind you. But where do you go? Where do you seek refuge when you are completely alone, knowing nobody in a vast foreign city?

She peered round the door of the bathroom and looked down at Dessuin. He lay gently snoring with his mouth open, his glasses pressed awkwardly into the side of his face. She noticed two small patches of blood on the carpet beside the desk and decided there and then to cover her tracks, removing as much evidence as she could of the struggle.

Moving guardedly around Dessuin's prostrate form, Angélique wiped away the blood from the carpet and soaked up the whisky with the help of half a roll of lavatory paper before flushing it away. She then took the whisky bottle and its broken neck through to Dessuin's bedroom and put it in his wastepaper basket. Returning to her room, she picked up her dress from the floor and stepped into it. Taking a linen jacket from the wardrobe, she pulled it awkwardly around her shoulders and kicked her feet into a pair of flats. She glanced over at the small card that lay next to the telephone on the bedside table, and then walked across the room and picked up the receiver. She started to dial the number on the card, but then halted and put down the receiver. It was impossible for her to call Tess. She was too involved, and if she were to see her in this state, then questions would be asked and the story would be on the front pages of every international newspaper within days. And that was something Angélique knew she could never allow to happen.

She moved over to the door, and then turned to take one last fleeting look at those things that were now useless to her – Albert Dessuin, her former tutor and manager, and the black violin case that sat on the cream Regency-style chair against the wall.

For a moment, Angélique eyed the room key that lay on the desk, but then decided she would not take it. She would never have any need to return here again. She closed the door behind her and hurried along the corridor. She pressed the button for the lift, and as she waited for it to make its journey from the ground floor, her face crumpled and tears streamed unguarded down her cheeks, in the full realisation of all that she was leaving behind and the terrifying uncertainty of what she would face in her future and much-changed life.

Twenty-Four

During the three hectic weeks of the Edinburgh Festival, the city itself rarely succumbs to rest. At every hour of the day and night, each street corner, each darkened lane on both sides of the bridges becomes a venue for some aspiring musician, actor, comedian or entertainer, attracting an ever-shifting audience from the vast crowds that throng the streets and creating an inescapable cacophony of sound that drowns out even the constant drone of traffic. In the small hours of the morning, an ambling pedestrian on Princes Street, which would be as crowded as on the last Saturday before Christmas, might find himself first striding out in proud military style to the stirring skirl of the bagpipes before gliding rhythmically past a string quartet playing a Strauss waltz; and then staggering away in laughter from the comedian whose act had been conducted from the confines of a council wheelie bin. He might then be reduced to tears of compassion by a couple of teenage actors, using a long fold-away table as their only prop, performing the death scene from *Romeo and*

Juliet with as much passion and fervour as one might ever witness in the velveted splendour of the Old Vic.

And intensifying this atmosphere of revelry and bonhomie are the blazing lights that shine out from every misty-windowed restaurant, crammed public house, queued-up café and buzzing street stall, each staying open until the hour when city licensing laws stipulate their closure or when the last of their customers see fit to adjourn to their smart hotels and homely boarding houses, sparse lodgings and shared bedrooms.

It was against such a backdrop that Jamie Stratton, having spent the whole evening reviewing a plethora of Fringe shows at the Pleasance, made his way back to the London Street flat. A distant bell rang out two o'clock as the sound of the never-ending street theatre faded away behind him. As he walked briskly down Broughton Street, he heard the frenetic finale of an Irish jig band floating out through the open doors of his local pub, and his initial thought was to cross the road to squeeze in one final pint before closing time. But then he noticed that the lights of The Grainstore coffee shop were still ablaze farther down the road, and knowing that Martha usually closed up at midnight at the latest, his curiosity as to why it should still be open dispelled the need for another drink.

The coffee shop appeared to be completely deserted, with all the chairs upturned on the tables and the floor swept and mopped. And there was no sign of Martha. Suspicion gripped at his stomach as he slowly pushed down on the door handle. It was locked. He retreated back on to the pavement, his mind racing. What if that junkie who stole the camera had returned? Maybe he had waited until Martha was alone and then come in and robbed the place and left her tied up at the back of the shop. Maybe Martha was in real need of his help.

He approached the door once more and beat his fist on the wooden frame. 'Martha, are you in there?' he yelled. 'Martha? Can you hear me? Are you all right?'

He pressed his face to the glass, squinting through The Grainstore logo, and then, with relief, he caught sight of Martha, looking up over the counter from her seated position behind it. Getting to her feet, she placed a thick dog-eared paperback on top of the microwave oven behind her, and then, with a disconsolate frown on her face, came round the counter and approached the door. She unlocked it and opened it only a fraction.

'What do you want, Jamie?'

'God, you had me worried. I thought something had happened to you.'

'Why?'

'Because you're usually closed up by now and I saw all the lights on, and I thought, well . . .'

'You thought what?'

'That you'd been robbed or something.'

Martha laughed mockingly. 'Ah, and I suppose you were going to do your 'Sir Galahad' bit and rescue me.'

'Well, no, but I was just . . .' He scratched self-consciously at the back of his head. 'Why *are* you open so late, then?'

Taking a quick glance behind her, Martha opened the door and came out on to the doorstep. 'Listen, Jamie,' she said in a quiet voice. 'Do you really want to be a help to me?'

Jamie shrugged. 'Yeah, sure. What d'you want?'

Martha jabbed a thumb over her shoulder. 'There's a girl in there who won't leave. I can't get rid of her. Every time I think she's about to finish up, she orders another cup of coffee. And I'm knackered and I want to go home and get to bed.'

Jamie peered through the window of the coffee shop. 'I can't see her.'

'Of course you can't. She's sitting at the table behind the drinks cabinet.'

'Oh, right. Well, why don't you just tell her to leave?'

Martha raised her eyebrows. 'Because I think she's French, or something foreign anyway, and I don't know what to say to her.'

'So you want me to tell her to leave – in French.'

'Da-ra!' Martha sang out, flicking open her hands, as if Jamie had just answered the million-dollar question correctly.

Jamie bit at a fingernail as he tried to recall some suitable

185

phrases from his sparse GSCE French vocabulary. 'Well, I suppose I could give it a go.'

'You do that,' Martha said, jumping off the doorstep and walking round behind her saviour. She put two hands on his back and pushed him forcefully into the coffee shop. 'I'll go to the loo and get my things while you get rid of her.'

As he approached the counter, Jamie saw for the first time the dark-haired girl who sat at a table in the far corner behind the drinks refrigerator. She seemed oblivious to his arrival, staring out of the window into the darkened alleyway that ran alongside the coffee shop and slowly spinning her empty coffee cup around in its saucer.

Jamie walked across to the girl's table and leaned his hands on the back of the chair opposite her. '*Excusez-moi, mademoiselle? Êtes-vous française?*'

From the moment she turned to face him, Jamie knew there was something very wrong. Her eyes were swimming with tears, and the only colour in her pallid features came from an ugly bruise that spread purple across her right cheekbone. She sat awkwardly, hunched forward, keeping one hand hidden in the folds of something bulky inside her linen jacket.

'*Tout est bien, n'est-ce pas?*' Jamie asked.

'*Oui,*' the girl replied unconvincingly.

There was something strangely familiar about her, but he could not work out what it was, his thought process being taken up with trying to recall a few more relevant French words. '*L'heure est très tarde, mademoiselle, et mon amie veut fermer le café.*'

The girl nodded slowly, smiling apologetically at him. 'Yes, of course. I am sorry to have stayed so long.' Her grasp of English far outmatched Jamie's stuttering attempt at her own native tongue. 'I will leave immediately.'

'Ah, I'm sorry, I didn't realise you spoke English. I'm sure Martha would have talked to you if she'd known.'

'Please don't worry,' the girl said, dismissing his remark with a light wave of her exposed hand. 'Anyway, I was very distracted myself.' As she pushed herself to her feet, Jamie noticed her screwing up her eyes, as if she had just suffered a sharp stab of pain. 'Maybe you would be kind enough to give me some advice before I leave?'

'Of course.'

'Would you know if there is a hotel close to here where I might get a room?'

Jamie began to explain that there was little chance of her finding anywhere to stay, never mentioning the fact that he himself had a spare room in his flat, because, as he spoke, he studied the girl's face, digging deep into his memory, trying to think where he had seen her before. And then suddenly, out of nowhere, the image on the front page of the newspaper came to him and he clicked his fingers in recognition.

'For heaven's sakes,' he exclaimed. 'You're Angélique Pascal, aren't you?'

Jamie witnessed the girl's eyes widen in alarm the instant the question had been asked. She lowered her head as if to avoid further recognition and walked past him towards the door. 'I must leave now, but thank you for your kindness.'

'Hang on a minute,' Jamie said with such force that the young violinist froze in her tracks. He moved quickly to put himself between her and the door. 'Listen, it may be none of my business, but why are you looking for a hotel? You, of all people, must have somewhere to stay tonight. You're one of the star attractions at the festival this year, so you have to be booked into one of the big hotels.' Jamie paused, giving her time to answer, but she continued to stare down at the floor. He took a step towards her, dipping his head to try to see her face. 'Something's happened, hasn't it? What's gone wrong?'

Angélique Pascal took a step to the side to make for the door. 'I must . . .'

Jamie moved to block her path once more. 'I think you're in quite a bit of pain, aren't you? What have you done to your hand?'

The violinist shot a frightened look of entrapment at the young man who stood in her way, and then renewed tears welled in her eyes. 'I have cut it,' she sobbed. 'Very badly, I think.'

Jamie put an arm on her shoulder. 'Come on, you're not in any fit state to leave. Let's go and sit down again.' He guided her back to the table, and once she had resumed her seat, he pulled round a chair and sat down next to her. 'Right,' he said, with hand outstretched, 'let me have a look at it.'

Angélique undid her jacket and slowly pulled out her hand wrapped in the bloodstained towel.

At that point, the door of the restroom banged shut and Jamie turned to see Martha staring at him transfixed, her handbag held limply at her side. 'What are you doing?' she mouthed at him. 'Get rid of her.'

'Martha, just come here for a sec.'

Rolling her eyes heavenward, Martha walked quickly over to the table, desperate to get the coffee shop closed up as fast as possible, and then she saw the girl's bandaged hand. 'Oh, for God's sake,' she murmured, immediately turning away from the bloody sight.

'Right,' Jamie said gently to the violinist, 'just lean your elbow on the table. I'm going to remove the towel really slowly, OK?' He carefully unwrapped the towel and handed it to Martha, who took it as if she were handling a garment newly stripped from a leper. Jamie narrowed his eyes at her and shook his head, and Martha reciprocated with a mouthed expletive.

As Jamie slowly unclenched Angélique's hand with his fingers, blood immediately dripped from the wound on to the table, and the young violinist cried out in pain. 'Martha, get me some paper towels to wipe this up and also something really clean to cover it with.'

Sighing impatiently, Martha dropped her handbag on the ground and clumped off behind the counter. Meanwhile, Jamie studied the uneven gash that ran across the violinist's now-swollen palm. 'Ow, that looks quite deep. How on earth did you do it?'

'I fell over on to broken glass,' Angélique answered in a faltering voice.

'Where? On the street?'

'No, in my hotel bedroom . . .' Her voice trailed off almost to silence as she cast a worried glance between Jamie and Martha, who had returned to the table with a large kitchen roll and two clean white tea towels.

Jamie bit at his lip as he studied the violinist's face. 'Well, let's just take one thing at a time. First, we need to get this cleaned up and then stitched. You'll probably need a tetanus jab as well.'

'I'm sure it does not need all that,' Angélique said quickly, trying to draw her hand away from Jamie.

'Oh, yes, it does,' Jamie said, exerting enough pressure on her hand to stop her. 'I've seen hundreds of wounds like this, and they all needed stitches.'

'Are you a doctor?' Angélique snuffled.

Jamie let out a short laugh. 'No, I'm a rugby player.' He pointed a finger at the wound on her hand. 'There are cuts like this in every game.'

As Jamie began to rebind the wound with one of Martha's tea towels, Angélique studied the face of the well-built young man who was being so kind, noticing now the small scars of battle that were quite familiar to her. 'My brothers used to play rugby as well, for a club in Clermont Ferrand, but they are now both too old.'

'Jamie played rugby for Scotland, didn't you, Jamie?' Martha stated knowledgeably from a distance, 'or that's what I was led to believe.'

Jamie looked quizzically at Martha, never having realised before the acerbity in her tone. 'Only for the under-twenty-one team.'

'*C'est vrai?*' Angélique asked, obviously impressed. 'You are quite famous then?'

Jamie laughed. 'Not nearly as famous as you.' He rose to his feet. 'Right, Martha, we'd better get Angélique to A and E at the Royal Infirmary, and—'

'What do you mean, "we"?' Martha cut in.

Jamie turned fully in his chair, his back to Angélique. 'You've got a car, Martha, and I don't.'

'Listen,' Martha said in a whisper, 'I've got to get this place opened up at half past eight tomorrow morning. Can't you take a taxi?'

'For God's sakes, just do us a favour and drop us off,' Jamie hissed at her. 'We'll get a taxi back once the girl's been treated.'

Martha stood looking at Jamie, taken aback by the vehemence of his reply. 'All right, then. You don't have to get on your high horse. You'll have to give me time to get her table cleared and the till locked up.'

Jamie gave her a short, sharp nod. 'OK, then.'

As he watched Martha sweep away the coffee cup from in front of Angélique, Jamie felt saddened by the shattered illusion he had of Martha, thinking that the next time he set foot in The Grainstore, it would be for coffee and nothing else.

'Listen, Angélique, I'm trying to work things out in my head. Who else knows you've cut your hand?'

Angélique shook her head. 'Nobody.'

'Right,' Jamie said, rubbing hard at his forehead with his fingers, 'this is how I see it. I know for a fact you were playing in a concert in the Usher Hall this evening, and I'm pretty sure you've got another one tomorrow. Trouble is I think it's quite obvious to both of us you won't be able to play with your hand in that condition.' He paused, catching the look of unease in the violinist's expression. 'So, I suppose we should tell someone you're going to be out of action.' Angélique dipped her head once more at the suggestion. 'What about that man who was in the photograph with you?' Jamie continued. 'Is he your manager or something? Do you think we should let him know?'

'No! Don't do that!' Angélique cried out, jerking up her head to glare at him with fear burning in her eyes.

Jamie held up his hands to calm her. 'All right, all right, we won't do that.' He let out a long sigh and shook his head. 'Angélique, I haven't got a bloody clue what's gone on this evening, but if you're trying to hide away from someone or something, the press will get wind of it the moment you don't turn up for your next concert, and I'm afraid they'll come looking for you. There's a spare bedroom in my flat which you're more

190

than welcome to have for a night or two, but I can't hide you there for ever unless I know who or what I'm hiding you from.' He leaned forward on the table when Angélique Pascal made no reaction to his reasoning. 'So, what do you want me to do?'

The violinist did not answer for a moment or two, but sat staring at her bandaged hand. 'Listen, maybe,' she said eventually, looking up at him, 'for an hour or so?'

Jamie nodded. 'OK, I'd be happy to.' He glanced round as Martha came out from behind the counter and scooped up her bag. 'Let's leave it for now,' he said quietly, giving Martha a nod.

She walked over to the entrance door and pulled it open. 'Come on then,' she said resignedly. 'Let's get you to the hospital.'

Twenty-Five

Cathy Dent and Phil Kenyon were deep in conversation when they walked into the office of the Exploding Sky Company just as the clock that hung amongst the framed photographs on the far wall clicked on to nine o'clock. Both stopped talking when they realised that Roger was already there, sitting with his feet up on the desk, a mug of coffee in hand, and staring out of the rain-lashed window at the dark Cotswold landscape.

Taking it that the boss was in one of his morning moods, Phil pulled a long face at Cathy before walking over to Roger and giving him a hearty slap on the shoulder. 'How're things this morning, mate?' he asked jovially. 'Raring to go, are we?' He dumped the files he had been carrying on to the desk and then went through to the small kitchen that led off the room to make some coffee for himself and Cathy.

Cathy pulled out the chair next to Roger and sat, pushing the button on her computer to boot it up. She looked across at her husband, who was yet to acknowledge her entry. 'You all right, love?' she asked with a hint of concern.

He turned to her and smiled. 'Yeah, I'm fine.'

'I didn't hear you get up this morning.'

'I know that. I've been here since six o'clock.'

'What have you been doing?'

'Nothing much. Just thinking.'

'About what?'

Roger shrugged his shoulders. 'This and that.'

Phil came through from the kitchen carrying the two mugs of coffee. Handing one to Cathy, he pulled across a wheeled secretary's chair from the other desk and then reached across in front of Roger for the schedule diary before sitting down. He placed his mug on the edge of the desk and opened the diary at the paper clip, moving it across to mark the page for the seventeenth of August. 'Right, so it looks like we're getting gear ready for Edinburgh today.'

Sliding his feet off the desk, Roger leaned forward and put his own mug on the desk. 'We're doing a bit more than that, Phil.'

Phil frowned questioningly at Cathy, but she answered only with a shake of her head. 'And what's that supposed to mean?'

Roger picked up the pile of papers in front of him, evened them up with a hard tap on the desk and handed them to his colleague without looking at him. 'Tell me what you think of that.'

Phil glanced through them quickly. 'This is the firing plan for Edinburgh.'

Roger nodded.

'You've changed it.'

'Yeah, I have.'

'But you've gone and added stuff.'

'I know.'

Phil went back to the beginning of the firing plan and silently studied Roger's alterations in detail. When he eventually turned over the final page, he blew out a long breath of frustration. 'Mate, this is going to screw up all the timings.'

'No, it's not. All the new firings will be simultaneous with those already programmed.'

Phil tossed the papers on to the desk. 'But we're completely full up on the slave units, Rog. There's no room for this lot.'

'I'm going to increase the number of slaves from thirty-seven to forty. That should do it.'

'And complicate the whole thing to hell as well. Jeez, mate, this isn't going to be easy to set up.'

'I know. That's why I'm rescheduling our departure from here for the twenty-sixth of August. That'll give us a day extra.'

Phil flipped through the pages of the diary. 'That's only in nine days' time!'

'Yes, so we've got a bit of work to do, haven't we?'

'And how! What about the crew? Are they going to be able to make it?'

'Not sure yet. Cathy can send round an e-mail to tell them about the change in plan. If not, then we'll just start rigging without them.'

Cathy had sat silently watching her husband during the inter-change between the two men. Getting up from her chair, she went to stand behind her husband, encircling his neck with her arms and giving him a kiss on top of his thinning pate. 'Is this what I think it is?' she asked.

'Yeah, love, this is it.'

Phil let out a short laugh and shook his head. 'OK, you two, what's cooking? I'm obviously being kept in the dark about something.'

Roger held hard to his wife's hands as he looked across at his colleague. 'My swansong, old friend. I've decided Edinburgh's going to be my last show.'

Phil stared at his boss, open-mouthed. 'You're joking, Rog.' He paused. 'Aren't you?'

'No, I'm not.' Roger unwrapped his wife's hands from around his neck and rose stiffly to his feet. 'I've been doing this for twenty-five years now and I'm just . . . dog-tired of it all. This is a young man's game, Phil. This constant shifting around the country, the intensity of the workload, it's all getting too much for me. I just feel the time's right to move on. I want to take it easy, spend some quality time with Cathy, and maybe do something completely different.'

'Like what?'

Roger chuckled as he stuck his hands deep into the pockets of his chinos. 'I've always fancied the idea of breeding pigs.'

Phil threw back his head in laughter. 'Mate, you cannot be serious! What the hell do you know about breeding pigs?'

'About as much as I did about putting on a firework display when I first started out.'

'He's actually very knowledgeable,' Cathy interjected. 'He's been reading up on it for the past year.'

Phil shook his head in disbelief. 'God, is that how long you've been planning all this?'

'Maybe a bit longer,' Roger replied. 'It was one of the reasons I bought this place out here in the country. The thirty acres that were included in the sale are all I'm going to need.'

Phil sucked on his teeth. 'My word, Rog, you don't half take the wind out of a bloke's sails.' Discarding the diary on to the desk, he pushed himself to his feet and scratched at the back of his head. 'So, that's it, then. The end of the Exploding Sky Company.'

'Doesn't have to be,' Roger replied, picking up a lengthy typewritten document from the desk and handing it to the tough little Australian.

'What's this?'

'A partnership agreement.'

'Saying what?' Phil asked, glancing at the front page.

'That I keep a vested interest in the Exploding Sky Company, but hand over forty-nine per cent of the company to my new partner. The business is doing well, so there's no reason why he shouldn't be able to pay for his shareholding over a ten-year period on a no-interest loan basis.'

Phil's eyes never left the page. 'My name's on this.'

'Of course it is,' Roger replied with a laugh. 'I wouldn't take anyone else on as a partner. You, Cathy and I have built up the Exploding Sky Company together, Phil, and if you're not going to take it on, then I'd rather close the whole damned shooting match.' He shrugged. 'But it'd be a pity, especially seeing we're at the top of our profession.'

Phil stood for a moment in silence, biting on his bottom lip as he ran briefly through the pages of the agreement. 'It's a bit of a no-win situation for you and Cathy, ain't it?'

'Not at all. We have a company that keeps going and we retain a controlling shareholding. We don't lose out at all.' He eyed his colleague. 'So what d'you think?'

Phil shrugged his shoulders. 'What d'ya think I think! I'll go for it, mate, without a whimper of doubt.'

Roger put out his hand and the Australian grabbed it and shook it forcefully.

'Only thing is,' Roger said, holding up a finger, 'part of the payment is this.' He pointed at the new firing plan for Edinburgh. 'I want to put together a display that's going to break new ground, one that's just going to knock 'em all dead, and I want you to make it work.'

Phil laughed. 'You wanna go out with a bang, mate.'

Roger slid an arm around Cathy's shoulders. 'Quite literally, old friend, quite literally.'

Twenty-Six

While Gavin Mackintosh retrieved a parking ticket from the machine on the corner of the street, Thomas Keene junior stood next to the solicitor's Volvo, tentatively surveying his surroundings, wondering if there might be some ominous reason behind Mr Mackintosh's choosing to park his car in the exact location where, just over two weeks ago, T.K. had bid a hasty retreat with the stolen video camera. There seemed no interest in his presence there – cars passed noisily along London Street's wide cobbled thoroughfare, and a few pedestrians strode unconcernedly to and fro on the pavements – but to T.K.'s distrustful eye, it was the normality of it all that posed the greatest threat.

Sticking the ticket on to the windscreen of the car, Gavin shut the door and glanced across at T.K., witnessing the obvious unease in the boy's manner, but taking it solely as an attack of nerves at the thought of the imminent meeting. Gavin walked over to him and gave him a light, reassuring slap on the back. 'Come on, then. Let's go meet the man.'

They crossed the street and climbed the three wide stone steps that led up to one of the many entrance doors in the row of smooth-stoned, tall-windowed Georgian buildings. Running his finger down the list of names on the polished brass panel, Gavin pressed one of the buttons and stood back, whistling gently to himself.

'This is the residence of Mr James Stratton,' a woman's voice crackled from the speaker, affecting a smart upper-class accent quite unconvincingly. 'How can I be of assistance?'

Gavin chuckled to himself and pressed the button. 'Is Jamie there, please?'

'I 'aven't seen him this morning,' the voice replied, now in a strong Yorkshire accent. ''E's probably still in his bed.'

'I see. Well, my name is Gavin Mackintosh and I'm Jamie's solicitor, and I do need to see him quite urgently, so I would be most grateful if you could let me in.'

'OK then, hang on a mo'.' There followed an amplified crash and a distant expletive at the other end of the line, and after a few seconds the voice said, 'Oops, sorry 'bout that. I dropped the receiver.' A long pause then ensued. 'I don't suppose you 'ave the faintest idea 'ow this wretched thing is supposed to work?'

'I think there's a button on top of the phone you have to press.'

Immediately there was a long buzzing sound and Gavin pushed open the heavy entrance door. With T.K. following at his heels, he made his way up the three flights of well-worn stone stairs to Jamie's flat, where a small plump woman with short streaked hair was waiting to greet them at the door.

'Good morning,' Gavin said, holding out a hand to the woman. 'You must be one of Jamie's new tenants. I'm Gavin Mackintosh.'

'Rene Brownlow,' the woman replied, taking his hand and giving it one strong brief shake. 'Pleased to meet ye.'

Gavin revealed his young companion, who was lurking behind him. 'And this young man is Thomas Keene junior.'

Rene nodded a short, querying greeting at the boy before stepping back into the flat. 'Well, you'd better both come in, then.' She shut the door with a bang when Gavin and T.K. had entered. 'As I said on that phone thing, I 'aven't seen Jamie this morning. D'you want me to knock on his bedroom door?'

'Not necessarily straightaway,' Gavin replied, tilting his head thoughtfully. 'You wouldn't happen to know Jamie's other tenant, would you?'

Rene shook her head. 'No, not really. We've passed once or twice in the corridor, but we haven't got as far as a formal introduction yet.'

Gavin sucked on his teeth. 'Well, not to worry. Would you have any idea if he's here or not?'

'Aye, I know that for a fact.' She pointed to a door at the end of the corridor. 'I saw 'im go into the sitting room about ten minutes ago.'

'Right,' Gavin replied with a slow nod as he eyed the door, 'but you can't help me with his name?'

'I'm afraid I 'aven't a clue.' There followed a brief moment before enlightenment shone on Rene's face. ''Ang on a mo' though. I'm pretty sure Jamie's written it down on the wall chart in the kitchen.' She walked past them into the first room on the left. 'Aye, 'ere it is,' her muffled voice called out from behind the door, 'Leonard 'Artson.' She reappeared back in the hall seconds later. 'Did ye get that? Leonard 'Artson's 'is name.'

Gavin smiled broadly at her. 'Thank you.' He pointed at the sitting-room door. 'What I'm going to do then is just pop in there to see Mr Hartson with Thomas, and hopefully by the time we finish, Jamie might have surfaced from his bedroom.'

Rene shrugged. 'Fine by me. Do you want a cup of coffee or summat to take in with ye? I've just put the kettle on.'

Gavin shook his head. 'That's very kind, but I think we'll give

197

it a miss. Thomas and I have something pretty important we need to discuss with Mr Hartson.'

Rene stood and watched as Jamie's solicitor, shadowed by the strange young man, walked down the hall and knocked on the door of the sitting room. When it was answered, he pushed it open and peered around the side. 'Mr Hartson?' she heard him ask, 'I hope I'm not disturbing you. Might I come in for a moment?'

Half an hour later, seated at the kitchen table, Rene looked up from the aged copy of *Hello!* she had been leafing through to see Jamie enter the room dressed in nothing but a bath towel tucked in around his waist. Seemingly oblivious to Rene's presence, he made his way over to the sideboard as if working on automatic pilot and switched on the kettle. Rene smiled as she cradled her cup of tea in her hands. 'Ye shouldn't go walking round the place like that, Jamie, when ye've got impressionable ladies as your 'ouse guests.'

Turning with a start, Jamie folded his arms across his chest as if attempting to cover his semi-nakedness and peered at Rene through bleary eyes. 'Yeah, sorry about that. I had a bit of a late night. I'm not really with it yet.'

'Out on the booze, were ye?'

'I wish,' he replied, turning to take a mug from the cupboard above the sink. He spooned in a large heap of instant coffee and filled it to the brim with boiling water, and then, walking across to the table, he pulled out a chair and sat down with a sigh of exhaustion, as if the very action had drained the last remaining cell of energy from his being. 'I had to take someone to the hospital.'

Rene looked concerned. 'Nothing too serious, I 'ope.'

'Not really. Three stitches in a cut hand.' Jamie replied, leaning forward on the table and rubbing at the gritty tiredness in his eyes. 'But that turned out to be only half the story.'

'Tell me about it.'

Jamie smiled at her. 'Well, I would, but . . . it's all a bit secretive, really.'

Rene nodded understandingly. 'OK, but let me know if there's anything I can do to 'elp.'

'Yeah, I will. Thanks.' He glanced at his watch and pushed himself up from the table. 'Listen, I've just got to make a phone call.'

At that point, a door slamming shut at the far end of the corridor jogged Rene's memory. 'Damn, I almost forgot to tell ye. Yer solicitor called in about 'alf an 'our ago, along with some dozy-looking young lad. They're in the sitting room right now with that gentleman who's staying 'ere.'

Jamie frowned quizzically at Rene. 'Gavin Mackintosh?'

'Aye, that's yer man.'

'He's here in the flat?'

'That's right,' a voice said from behind him, and Jamie turned to see the solicitor's portly frame standing in the kitchen doorway.

Jamie gave his head a quick disbelieving shake. 'How weird is that? I was just about to call you. What on *earth* are you doing here?'

'Just a bit of worthwhile networking. I've managed to find someone to give your Mr Hartson a hand.'

'What?' Jamie asked, still baffled by Gavin's presence in the flat. 'Who?'

Gavin came into the kitchen and flumped himself down on the sagging sofa that was pushed hard against the wall next to the fridge. 'A young man called Thomas Keene. I doubt you'd know him, Jamie.' He let out a short laugh. 'Not quite in the university scene, this one.'

'And what did Mr Hartson think?'

'He reckons Thomas will suit his needs extremely well, and all I can say is I hope to hell he's right.' Gavin crossed his legs and stretched his hands along the back of the sofa. 'Mind you, I was pretty amazed just how well the lad managed the interview. I doubt he's ever undergone one like that before in his life.'

'So what's he been doing up until now?'

Gavin wagged a finger at Jamie. 'Ah, that's between myself,

Thomas and Mr Hartson for the time being. Let's just say we're in a probationary period.'

Rene laughed. 'I think I understand where ye're coming from. I've known a lot of lads like that in my time.' She got up from her chair. ''Ow's about I make ye a nice cup of tea or coffee now then, Mr Mackintosh?'

'I think a black coffee would go down a treat, Rene. Thank you.' Gavin turned to Jamie. 'So what were you going to call me about?'

Jamie scratched a hand at the back of his neck and glanced furtively in Rene's direction. 'Well, it's a bit . . . delicate.'

'Don't worry,' Rene said, having caught the look, 'I can take a hint. I'll make myself scarce.' She made up the mug of coffee and handed it to Gavin. 'I've got to come up with some more funnies for my show tonight, any road.'

Jamie leaned his bottom against the work surface and folded his arms. 'Yeah, how's it all going? Did the newspaper review help?'

'A bit. I'm playing to about half capacity now, but it's still a struggle.' She smiled at the two men. 'But that's my problem, in't it? I'll let you get on with yer own.'

As she closed the door behind her, Gavin looked questioningly at his young client. 'What problem are we about to discuss now, Jamie?'

Walking back to the table, Jamie pulled out a chair, spun it around to face Gavin and sat down. 'Well,' he started, and then, with a brief shake of his head, he leaned forward on his knees. 'Gavin, you are *not* going to believe who I've got sleeping in the free bedroom.'

'Tell me.'

'Are you ready for this?'

'I'm all ears, Jamie,' Gavin replied, taking a sip from his coffee cup.

'Angélique Pascal.'

Gavin almost choked on his coffee. He hurriedly set his mug down and took a handkerchief from his jacket pocket.

'I think you're having your leg pulled, lad,' Gavin laughed, wiping his mouth.

'It's no joke, Gavin.'

Gavin stared at Jamie open-mouthed. 'Are you really being *serious*, Jamie?'

'Yeah, course I am.'

'In that case . . .' Gavin shook his head, momentarily lost for words, '. . . what in the name of goodness is she doing here?' He cast a calculating eye over Jamie's state of undress. 'You haven't, erm, become . . . involved with—'

'No, of course not,' Jamie remonstrated. 'It's nothing like that. I met her in a café last night, and me and this other girl ended up taking her to hospital, and then afterwards . . .'

'You had to take her to *hospital*? Why?'

'She'd cut her hand quite badly.'

'Her hand?' Gavin's eyes suddenly clouded over with consummate concern and he shook his head slowly. 'Oh, no, Jamie, she can't have cut her hand. Not *her* hand.'

Jamie bit at his bottom lip. 'Yeah, I know what you mean. That's why *she* was so terrified to go to the hospital. She really thought she was going to be told she'd never be able to play the violin again. However, as it turned out, it wasn't nearly as bad as it looked. The doctor said no tendons had been touched and that the swelling in her fingers would soon go, so I reckon she won't be out of action for too long . . . probably won't do anything else at the festival this year, though.'

'*You* reckon, Jamie? I'd be more interested in hearing the doctor's considered opinion.'

Jamie paused for a moment, caught in the solicitor's steely glare. 'Actually, Gavin, we never mentioned to the doctor that Angélique was a violinist. In fact, I did something that's probably against the law. I gave her a false name when we registered her at the hospital.'

'You did *what*?'

'Listen, she insisted on it. I couldn't go against that. She said she didn't want anyone to know who she was, because she was frightened the press would find out about her injury, and . . . she didn't want her whereabouts to be known either.'

Gavin tried to unscramble the baffling rationale behind the violinist's presence in the flat.

'Jamie . . . Jamie,' he stuttered, holding up his hands as if trying to steady his thought process. 'I'm completely in the dark as to what is going on, so could you please just start at the beginning and tell me everything that happened last night?'

'OK, but it could take some time. I was up until five o'clock this morning listening to the whole saga.'

Gavin nodded. 'Right,' he said, pushing himself up from the sofa. 'I think I'd better cancel all my appointments for this morning.' He thumped at the pockets of his suit jacket. 'Hell, I must have left my mobile in the car. Can I use your telephone?'

Jamie pointed at the door. 'It's out there on the sideboard.'

When Gavin had left the kitchen, Jamie got up and went to make himself his customary second black coffee of the morning. As he poured water into the mug, he heard a single knock on the door and turned to see Leonard Hartson standing outside in the hall with a tall, straggly-haired youth peering over his shoulder.

'I thought I'd let you know I have found myself an assistant,' Leonard said, 'due to the kind endeavours of your solicitor. I just wanted to thank you for putting the word around so promptly.'

'Glad it all worked out, Mr Hartson,' Jamie replied, carrying his coffee over to the door and leaning a shoulder on the doorpost. 'Hope all goes well for you. Are you going to start filming today?'

'No, not yet. My immediate plan is to give young Thomas here a crash course on all the equipment.' The cameraman turned and smiled up at the youth. 'It'll be a steep learning curve, but I am counting on my new assistant to be a very fast learner.'

Jamie gave Thomas a friendly smile which went unreciprocated. Studying the gormless expression on the assistant's face, it struck him that Thomas looked anything *but* a fast learner. 'Well, best of luck then, to you both.'

As he watched the two move off towards the front door, Jamie was taken by the almost comical incongruity of this new partnership, the tall lanky figure of the new assistant, with his threadbare hooded sweatshirt and baggy jeans worn at half mast, towering menacingly over the diminutive but dapperly dressed figure of the elderly cameraman. And then, for the second time in so many hours, Jamie found himself searching his mind for some glimmer of identification, knowing that there was something vaguely familiar about the boy – especially, for some reason, from the back view.

'Right,' said Gavin Mackintosh, taking a diary and pen from his inside pocket as he pushed purposefully past Jamie into the kitchen. 'The rest of the morning is yours, Jamie my lad, so shut the door behind you and let's be having the whole story.'

An hour later Jamie welcomed the chance to rest his voice as Gavin, with brow furrowed, sat in silence leafing through the copious notes he had written in the back of his diary.

'And that's about it, is it?' the solicitor asked eventually, glaring seriously at Jamie over his spectacles. 'She told you nothing else?'

'Well, it's not word for word, but near enough.'

When Gavin once more resumed the examination of his notes, Jamie began drumming his fingers on the table. 'So what do you think we should do?' he prompted quietly, eager to know what was going through the solicitor's mind.

Lobbing the diary on to the table, Gavin took off his spectacles and twirled them back and forth in his fingers as he stared thoughtfully out of the window. 'A very good question, Jamie. A very good question.' He let out a long sigh. 'I don't think anything can be done until I've spoken with Angélique myself and ascertained exactly what course of action she wants to take.'

Jamie pushed himself to his feet. 'I'll go and wake her then.'

'That would be the best idea,' Gavin replied, 'and if you wouldn't mind, I think I should speak to her myself. There could be some quite complicated legal procedures involved in this whole affair, and consequently it should remain as confidential as possible.'

'OK,' Jamie replied, quite content in letting Gavin take on responsibility for Angélique. 'Do you want me to do anything?'

'Not immediately, but I'd suggest you head off and get yourself showered and dressed, because I could well be in need of your assistance after I've spoken to her.'

Five minutes later, Jamie ushered Angélique into the kitchen. Her eyes were drowsy and the oversized dressing gown she was wearing trailed behind her across the flagstoned floor like the train of a wedding dress.

'She's a bit out of it, I'm afraid,' Jamie said. 'The doctor gave her some pretty strong painkillers last night.'

As Jamie settled her on a chair, Gavin smiled kindly at the violinist to put her at her ease, but his eyes were registering deep anger at the sight of the purply-black bruise that spread down one side of her face and the white elastic bandage that was bound around the palm of her left hand. He waited for Jamie to leave the kitchen before he sat down opposite her.

'Angélique, I don't know if you remember me, but my name is Gavin Mackintosh. We met the other night at the reception at the Sheraton Grand.'

'*Bien sûr*,' she replied woozily. 'You are the lawman.'

'That's absolutely right.'

Angélique's attention drifted to her unfamiliar surroundings and she gazed foggily around the kitchen before fixing Gavin with a look of bewilderment. 'What are *you* doing here? You do not live in this place as well, do you?'

Gavin laughed. 'No, I don't.'

The drowsiness faded instantly from the violinist's face and she glared at him, wide-eyed with panic. 'Then who told you I was here?' she exclaimed, pushing herself clumsily to her feet. 'How did you find out?'

'It's all right, Angélique,' Gavin said in a slow, calming voice, holding up his hands to steady her anxiety. 'You are perfectly safe. Nobody knows you are here, except Jamie and myself.'

Gavin fixed himself with his most reassuring smile as she studied his face to try to detect any sign of deception, and then, very slowly, she sat back down on her chair.

'Let me explain,' Gavin said, leaning forward on the table and interlocking his fingers. 'It just happens by chance that I am Jamie's solicitor. I have been a friend of his father for many years, and consequently have always handled the family's legal affairs. Now Jamie, quite rightly, was going to call me to ask advice about your . . . predicament, but it just happened that I had to pay him a visit this morning for a completely different reason.'

The violinist took in a faltering breath. 'So now Jamie has told you the whole story,' she said quietly.

'Yes, he has.'

'He is a very kind person.'

Gavin nodded. 'You were extremely lucky to bump into him last night.'

'I know that,' Angélique breathed out almost indiscernibly. 'I had been to so many places before, but they were all filled with a lot of people and a lot of noise, and I just wanted to be alone. I saw the café was empty when I passed by, so I went in. I did not realise it was about to close. Martha was very kind also, because she kept it open for me and she drove us to the hospital.'

'But Martha wasn't present when you told your story to Jamie?'

'No, she had gone home, but when she dropped us off at the hospital, Jamie made her promise not to say a word about me to anyone. He was quite . . . *brusque* with her. I do not think he likes her very much.'

At that moment, Gavin had no interest in Jamie's likes and dislikes. His greatest concern was for this vulnerable young girl whose world, in the past twelve hours, had been turned upside down and whose trust in her manager, tutor and companion had been decimated. He let out a long, disheartened sigh. 'Angélique, I am so sorry this has happened to you.'

Angélique averted her eyes from the solicitor and began fiddling with the cord of the dressing gown.

'How does your hand feel today?'

She shrugged her shoulders. 'It is quite sore.'

'I'm sure it is.' Gavin stroked a finger thoughtfully across his mouth. 'Angélique, I know this is a difficult question to put to you, but I'm afraid that it has to be asked. What action do you wish to take against your manager, Mr Dessuin?'

She jerked her head up and looked at him questioningly. 'What do you mean?'

'Well, I know that he has been your tutor and manager for many years, but in my opinion I think his immediate actions would suggest that he could well pose a real threat to you in the future, and accordingly my advice would be that we seek a restraining order against him as soon as possible.'

'How would you do that?'

'You and I would have to go to the court here in Edinburgh to ask for what is called an interim interdict.'

'I would then be in the newspapers?'

'It's not usual for the press to be at the initial hearing, but of course I can't guarantee that, especially when the case involves someone who is as much in the public eye as yourself.'

'Then I cannot let it happen.'

Leaning back in his chair, Gavin folded his arms and puffed out his cheeks. 'Can I ask you why not, Angélique? My real concern is that he might well try to repeat his actions of last night.'

Angélique shook her head. 'You do not understand Albert Dessuin. He is very . . . how would you say . . . complex?'

'I'm sure he must be, judging from what he's done to you.'

'No, what I am meaning is that *I* understand him very well, even though he probably would never believe it. If something bad was to be written about him in the newspapers, I know he would do something very stupid.'

'In what way?'

Angélique paused momentarily. 'He would probably try to harm himself.'

'You mean he would attempt suicide?'

Angélique shrugged. 'It is very possible. It is in the family, after all, because I found out that his own father had killed himself. And, besides that, there are so many *irrationalités* in Albert's head. I know, because I have been subjected to every one of them during the years we have been together. So, even though he treated me so badly last night, I cannot do anything to hurt him. It would always then be my fault.'

Gavin scratched frustratedly at his forehead. 'But you must understand I cannot allow you to leave Edinburgh with him. It would then be *my* fault if something were to happen to *you*.'

The violinist shook her head. 'I will not be leaving Edinburgh with Albert. It is all finished between us. I decided that even before I left my hotel bedroom.'

'And what will you do? Tour the world by yourself?'

Angélique appeared uncertain. 'I suppose I will have to find another manager.'

'But what about Dessuin, Angélique? You are a famous person. It wouldn't be difficult for him to find out where you are at any time of the day or night. You said yourself he is a complex person, and your leaving him could well spark off considerable paranoia in his mind – and if that were to be the case, you would never be safe from him.'

Angélique looked up at the solicitor with sad eyes. 'I know this, but I can never be the reason for him doing harm to himself.'

Gavin leaned back heavily in the chair and folded his arms. 'So, what *are* we to do then?' he murmured. 'What *are* we to do?'

'I do not know,' Angélique mumbled in reply.

Gavin got up from the table and began to pace the floor. 'OK, I shall reluctantly leave that issue aside for now. What we have to do, as a matter of urgency, is somehow break the news that you won't be playing tonight, nor probably for the rest of the festival. Because of the present circumstances with Dessuin, we must do it in such a way that nobody need know what really happened, and we certainly should not reveal your whereabouts.' He waved his hands as he thought. 'We could just say you've cut your hand in an unfortunate accident and you've had to return home to France to recover.' He pondered this for a moment. 'Actually, that's not such a bad idea. It might even act as a red herring for Dessuin.'

'A herring? What is that?'

'A false trail. It'll certainly get him away from the hotel and, at best, out of the country. You do have your passport with you, don't you?'

'Yes, it is in my handbag.'

'Good. That means he could quite easily take the bait. The only problem is your clothes. Jamie said you left everything in the hotel bedroom.'

'And my violin as well.'

'And the key to your room?'

'I left it there too,' Angélique replied sheepishly.

Gavin shook his head. 'Not to worry. We'll just have to find a way of getting everything out of your room while Dessuin is not about.' He blew out an anxious breath. 'My word, the plot thickens by the minute, doesn't it?' he murmured.

'Gavin, will I really be returning to France?'

'Well, it's entirely up to you, Angélique, but I would suggest it would be better if, for now, you just stayed here in Edinburgh and kept a very low profile. It'll give you time to recover, and at the same time it'll give *me* the chance to monitor Dessuin while you're still under my watchful eye.'

'But where would I stay?'

'No better place than where you are right now. I don't think it would be very wise for you to come to my house under the present circumstances. I'm quite seriously bending the rules of my profession with all this subterfuge, so it's better if I'm seen to be taking more of an impartial stance. Anyway, nobody else is using that bedroom you slept in last night, and I know for a fact Jamie's going to be around until the end of

September. I don't think you'd find anyone better to look after you.'

'But he might not want me to stay. I could make his life quite difficult with so much secrecy.'

Gavin smiled at her. 'I'll have a word with him. I'm sure he'd be more than delighted.'

'I could pay him, of course.'

Gavin clicked the fingers of both hands simultaneously. 'Jumping Jupiter, there's a problem.' He sat back down on the chair, clenching his fists together on the table. 'Angélique, does Dessuin handle your finances?'

The violinist shook her head. 'No, everything is managed by the lawyers of Madame Lafitte in Clermont Ferrand. They give me an allowance each month and pay Albert his salary.'

Gavin puffed out a breath of relief. 'Well, that's one thing less to worry about, but we'll have to notify them in due course.' He pushed himself to his feet once more. 'So what about this story we've concocted for the press? Would you agree to it?'

'Yes, I think it would be a good idea.'

'Right,' Gavin said, walking over to the window and gazing down at the bustling activity in London Street. 'So, all that remains for me to do is to find a journalist with a bit of integrity.' He gave a short, cynical laugh. 'Now, that is a tall order.'

Angélique sat in silence for a moment, her brow creased in thought. 'I know of a man, a journalist, here in Edinburgh. He has been trying to interview me for many years, but Albert would not allow it. Maybe we could ask for his help?'

'Do you know his name?'

The violinist stared up at the ceiling. '*Qu'est-que c'est? Qu'est-que c'est?* He met us at the airport.' She held up her hand as a name flashed into her mind. 'Will, I think is his surname. No, Wills. He is called Harry Wills. He seems to be a nice man, although I know that he does not care much for Albert.'

Gavin nodded. 'Good, sounds like the perfect contact.' He bent over the table and wrote down the journalist's name in his diary. 'I don't know him personally, but I've read his articles in the *Sunday Times*. I'll see if I can arrange a meeting with him straightaway, because it's imperative that we get this story into the *Evening News* tonight. I'm also going to ask Mr Wills to liaise with the International office as well. They'll need to be told as soon as possible so that they can arrange for another soloist for the concert tonight.'

A sudden pinpoint of clarity shone in Angélique's eyes. 'Of course, he must speak with Tess Goodwin. Do you remember her?'

Gavin stared bemusedly at her for a moment. 'No, should I?'

'She was the person I was speaking to at the reception when you came to talk to me.'

Gavin nodded. 'Ah, yes.'

'She works at the International office and she has become a friend of mine. I was going to call her on the telephone last night, but I was frightened the true story would then be put in the newspapers.'

Gavin wrote down the second name in his diary. 'Yes, I think you were probably wise not to call her. We won't involve Tess right now.' He slipped both the diary and the pen into the inside pocket of his jacket. 'The only other person I am going to tell about this incident is my doctor, who is a good and trusted friend of mine. I'll get him to come round to see you and he'll be able to keep an eye on that very special hand of yours.' He smiled at the young violinist. 'Now, I want you to take yourself back to bed and rest well, and don't worry about a thing. We have it all under control now. If you want to contact me at any time, just speak to Jamie. In the meantime, I'll make sure he looks after you.'

As he turned to leave, Angélique got up from her chair and moved across the room towards him, putting a hand on his arm. 'Gavin?'

'Yes?'

'I was very lucky to meet you at the reception the other night. Thank you for being such a kind friend.'

Gavin grinned broadly at her. 'My dear,' he said, 'the circumstances are not what I would wish for, but it is indeed a pleasure to be of some assistance to you.'

Twenty-Seven

Albert Dessuin sat slumped forward on the chair in his bedroom, his throbbing head cradled in shaking hands, trying desperately to trawl through his befuddled thoughts for some recollection of what had taken place the previous night. Coming round from his alcoholic stupor, he had found himself on the floor of Angélique's bedroom, but his memory of the events that had led him to being there had been completely wiped out. Evidence only showed that Angélique's bed linen was rumpled, but not slept in, and the bottle of whisky he must have consumed was in two pieces in the wastepaper basket in his own room.

He tried to convince himself that nothing untoward had happened. He always drank in private – he had never allowed Angélique to see him in an inebriated state – so maybe he had come into her room last night just to check on her, and found she wasn't there. But if that was the case, where was she now? No, it was more likely he had only been lying there for an hour or two and that Angélique had risen early from her bed and had left the room before he had come in. But then that didn't add up either. She had not slept in her bed – unless she had made it up herself. And why would she do that in a hotel?

He got to his feet and moved slowly across the room to the bathroom, clutching his arms around his shivering body. A cold shower was what he needed. It always helped to clear his head.

At the top of Lawnmarket in the Old Town, on the fourth floor of the Hub, Tess Goodwin sat at her desk in the International Festival office, listening, open-mouthed with disbelief, to the gravelly male voice at the other end of the telephone line. When she ended the call, neither a word of thanks nor salutation passed her lips. She was too shocked to speak.

Getting to her feet, she moved around the desk and hurried over to the door that led into Sir Alasdair Dreyfuss's office. His meeting with Sarah Atkinson and the morose director of the Estonian National Symphony Orchestra was scheduled to run for another half-hour, but this was something that definitely could not wait. She gave one cursory knock on the door and walked in without waiting for a reply.

Both Alasdair Dreyfuss and Sarah Atkinson looked up at her immediately, enquiry and annoyance in their eyes, while the Estonian turned his corpulent figure around in the armchair with a flatulent squeak of leather.

'I think you might have your time wrong, Tess,' Alasdair Dreyfuss said pointedly, pushing back the cuff of his shirt and consulting his wristwatch. 'I said we wouldn't be free until midday.'

'I'm sorry to interrupt, Alasdair, but something extremely important has come up, and I wonder if I might just have a couple of minutes with you and Sarah.'

'Can't it wait, Tess?' Sarah asked tersely, but she was stopped from enquiring further by a hand on her arm from the director, who could tell from the troubled expression on his marketing assistant's face that something was seriously amiss.

'Valdek, would you please excuse us for two minutes,' he said, getting to his feet. 'I do apologise for this.'

The man in the leather armchair gave his consent with a flick of his pawlike hand, and both Alasdair Dreyfuss and Sarah Atkinson followed Tess out of the room and into the open-plan office.

'Now, what's wrong, Tess?' the director asked, as he closed the door behind him.

'I've just had a journalist on the phone who says that Angélique Pascal had an accident last night. She's cut her hand pretty badly and she's heading back to France.'

'What?' her two superiors exclaimed in unison.

'He said the story's going to be on the front page of the *Evening News* tonight, and that he was only telephoning the International office to give us warning so we could find another soloist to take over from Angélique Pascal at tonight's concert and rearrange our programme for the rest of the festival.'

'Is this genuine information, Tess?' Sarah Atkinson asked. 'Who was the journalist?'

'He didn't give his name, and I'm afraid I didn't recognise his voice.' Tess shook her head. 'I can't believe this has happened. I spent the whole evening at the reception with her last night. She was going to come out afterwards with Allan and me, but then her manager spirited her away.'

'Maybe it's some kind of hoax, then,' Sarah Atkinson said, glancing between Tess and the director.

Alasdair Dreyfuss stood staring intently at Tess, lost in thought as he chewed on the nail of a forefinger. 'We've got to take it as being true,' he said eventually. He turned to his marketing director. 'Sarah, you head back to my office and give my humblest apologies to our Estonian friend and finish off the meeting with him, and once you've done that, get hold of Julia Parfitt and put her on standby for tonight's performance.'

'What are you going to do, Alasdair?' Sarah Atkinson asked.

'First off, I'm calling the *Evening News* to see if they're genuinely going to run with this story, and if so, then I want to get hold of Albert Dessuin and ask him what the hell is going on and why he hasn't let me know about this sooner.' He took off his spectacles and rubbed a hand across his face. 'Dammit, I thought everything was going too smoothly.'

Albert Dessuin stood in the middle of the hotel dining room and scanned the few tables that were still occupied for break-fast. Apprehension gripped at his stomach when he realised Angélique was not there, and he hurried out of the room and down the stairs to the reception area. There was a queue of people shuffling their suitcases forward as they waited to check out, but he bypassed them and went straight up to the desk.

'Excuse me,' he said ungraciously to the young female receptionist who was trying unsuccessfully to swipe a credit card.

'I'm sorry, sir,' she replied with a smile, 'but there is a queue. I'm afraid you'll have to wait your turn.'

'I have not time to wait. You must tell me, have you seen Angélique Pascal this morning?'

The girl looked questioningly at him. 'Do you mean the violinist, sir?'

'Of course I mean the violinist. There is no one else of that name staying here, is there?'

Dessuin's tone made the receptionist's face colour. 'I'm sorry, sir, I've only just come on duty, and I certainly haven't seen her this morning.'

Dessuin snorted angrily. 'Well, then, who *was* on duty? I need to speak to them immediately.'

'I'll see if I can find out, sir.' She smiled apologetically at the couple with whom she was dealing and walked off to the door at the side of the desk. Before entering the room, she turned back to Dessuin. 'Can I ask who you are, sir?'

'I'm her manager, Albert Dessuin. Now go and find out if anyone knows where she is. This could be a very serious matter, you know.'

'Excuse me, Mr Dessuin,' a voice said from the far end of the reception desk.

Albert turned to the other receptionist, who stood with her hand cupped over the mouthpiece of a telephone. The expectant guests in the queue were now regarding him with increasing impatience.

'Yes?'

'There's a telephone call for you.'

'*Enfin!*' Dessuin exclaimed, striding along the desk and causing the man at the front of the queue to take a hurried step back to avoid being forcibly thrust out of the way. 'Thank you,' he said to the receptionist, jerking the receiver from her hand, and meeting her surprised look with the thinnest crease of a courteous smile. He turned his back on his hostile audience. 'Angélique, where the hell are you?' he hissed into the receiver.

'Oh, so *you* obviously don't know what's happened, then, do you?' a man's voice replied.

'Who is this?' Dessuin demanded.

'It's Alasdair Dreyfuss, Albert.'

For a moment Dessuin stood speechless, his eyes screwed up tight with embarassment. 'Ah, Alasdair – I apologise,' he stuttered out eventually. 'I have had rather a bad morning. I did not mean to be so abrupt with you.'

'What on earth is going on, Albert?'

'I'm sorry?'

He heard the director let out a sigh of impatience. 'Albert, I have just been on the telephone to the *Evening News* and they are about to run a front-page piece about Angélique Pascal.'

'No – no, that could not be right.'

'It's very right, I'm afraid, Albert. Seemingly Angélique had an accident last night. She cut her hand quite badly and is flying back to Paris as we speak, which of course means she'll be unable to fulfil her commitments here at the festival. How on earth did you not know about all this, Albert . . . Albert? . . . are you still there?'

The words of the director of the International Festival were enough to start clearing the fog of alcoholic amnesia from Dessuin's brain. He saw Angélique's naked form flash into his mind, the raised hand coming down with force on the side of her face. He slowly clenched and unclenched his fist, noticing a tightness in the skin on the back of his fingers which he had not noticed before. 'Oh, no,' he murmured, dropping the receiver limply to his side. 'Oh, no, what have I done?'

'Albert, for God's sake, are you still there?' Alasdair Dreyfuss's distant voice asked again.

Dessuin slowly brought the receiver back to his ear. 'Yes,' he replied weakly.

'This has put me in an extremely difficult position, you know,

Albert. It's one thing rearranging the late concerts for next week, but trying to find another soloist at the eleventh hour for the concert tonight . . . well, it really would have helped if you—'

As if in a trance, Dessuin reached across the desk and dropped the receiver back onto its cradle. He turned and walked across the reception area to one of the chairs that were grouped around a low glass-topped coffee table and sat down. Covering his face with his hands, he began to piece together all the missing scenes of what had taken place the previous night, and then tears of remorse and shame began to flow. 'Oh, Angélique,' he sobbed quietly to himself, 'I did not mean to hurt you. I never wished to hurt you. Please do not tell anyone I have done this terrible thing. *Please* do not tell.'

He felt a hand press lightly on his shoulder. 'Are you all right, sir?' a female voice asked.

Dessuin uncovered his face and looked up at the young receptionist who had left to find out about Angélique's whereabouts. 'I am fine, thank you,' he replied in a quavering voice.

'I'm afraid I can't get hold of any of the receptionists who were on duty last night.'

Dessuin shook his head. 'It does not matter now.' He reached for the girl's hand and held it tight. 'Would you do something else for me, please?'

'Of course, sir,' the girl replied in an uncertain voice as she eyed her clamped hand.

'Angélique cannot leave without me. I need to find her.'

'I know, sir,' she replied quietly. 'We're doing everything possible.'

'No, what I mean is, can you please find out for me what flights leave from Edinburgh to Paris today?'

There was relief in the girl's smile on seeing her chance to get away from the strange Frenchman. 'Yes, sir. I'll get on to the Internet straightaway.'

'Thank you very much,' Dessuin said, releasing her hand. 'I will go to my room now.' Pushing himself to his feet, he made his way across to the stairs and began to climb them, moving like an old man, every tread an effort as he dragged himself up on the broad wooden banister rail. Halfway up, his mobile rang and he eagerly glanced at the screen, hoping that it would be Angélique.

It was not. He continued to climb the stairs, allowing the mobile to ring in his hand, not answering until he reached the next floor. He pressed the 'receive' button as he walked along the thick-carpeted corridor towards the lift. 'Bonjour, Maman. Ça va?'

The other four people in the lift would hardly have known he was engaged in a telephone call had it not been for the fact that he had his mobile held to his ear. He never spoke, but listened with an empty, forlorn expression on his face. When the lift eventually stopped at his floor, he walked out and waited for the doors to close.

'Listen to me, you spoiled old woman. When will you ever consider how I am feeling? You never do. Never, never!'

He punched the button to end the call and dropped the mobile into his pocket, and as he walked along the corridor to his room he felt the weight of hopelessness and despair bear down upon him, realising that he had now succeeded in alienating himself from the only two people who played any part in his sad, pathetic life. Just as his father had done.

Twenty-Eight

In the middle of the vast empty warehouse deep in the docklands of Leith, Thomas Keene junior sat uneasily on the silver camera box, a look of painful concentration on his face as he felt around in the black changing bag on his lap, attempting to load the dummy roll of film into the camera magazine for about the twentieth time in the past hour. He glanced at the wristwatch Leonard Hartson had left hanging on a light stand for him to time his progress, but it only served to remind him that it was nearly three o'clock in the afternoon and his stomach was aching with hunger.

He shut his eyes trying to envisage what his fingers were doing inside the bag as he threaded the film through the slot into the pick-up chamber of the magazine and doubled over the end so that it sat tight in the spool before clicking the spring catch closed. When he thought all was in place, he pulled his arms free from the constraints of the elasticated armsholes, just as the fire door at the far side of the warehouse opened and banged shut again, stretching a momentary beam of bright sunlight out across the floor. Pulling back the Velcro flap on the changing bag, T.K. watched Leonard Hartson pick his way over the electric cables, ducking to avoid the lights that they had already set up earlier that day.

'There you are,' the cameraman said, handing T.K. a brown paper bag and a can of Sprite. 'Two ham-and-cheese rolls.' He sat down opposite T.K. on a long lighting box. 'How did you get on this time?'

'I think ah've go' it,' T.K. replied, putting the black bag to one side and making to flick back the ring pull on the can.

'Don't do that yet,' Leonard said sharply.

T.K. glared at Leonard. 'How no?'

The cameraman pointed a meaningful finger at his assistant. 'Another golden rule, Thomas. Never handle food or drink while you're loading a film magazine. If one single foreign body gets into that changing bag, it could gum up the whole roll of film.'

'Ah've finished loadin' onyways.'

'No, you haven't. What did I tell you? Magazine out of the bag, check it's secure, tape it up and write on it the stock number and film roll. That's the order of things.'

T.K. let out a disgruntled sigh and, with great deliberation, put down his can and picked up the black bag.

'I'm sorry, Thomas,' Leonard chuckled. 'I told you it was going to be a steep learning curve.' He leaned across and gave the boy a solid pat on his knee. 'But don't worry, you're doing well.

You've had more thrown at you in one day than many assistants would have to learn in about a month.'

T.K. undid the zip on the changing bag and pulled out the magazine. As he placed it on his knee, the cover on the load reel fell off in his hand. 'Aw, *shite!*' He glanced apprehensively at Leonard. 'Ah mean, sorry.'

Leonard raised an admonishing eyebrow. 'Don't worry. It's only an end-roll, but remember, you must check the cover plate is fitted securely into its grooves before you lock it. If you'd just loaded that magazine with an unexposed roll, we would've had to throw it away.'

'Ah'm no' goin' tae get a-haud o' this,' T.K. murmured solemnly.

Leonard studied the boy's face for a moment, trying to judge the meaning of T.K.'s last sentence by the expression on his face. Eventually, he just shook his head. 'Thomas, if our partnership is to work successfully over the next couple of weeks, I think it's going to be of paramount importance that we understand what we're saying to each other. Now, please believe me, I'm not saying anything derogatory about the Scottish accent and it is probably my fault entirely that I have never taken the time to study the colloquial intricacies . . .' He stopped mid-sentence when he saw a broad grin stretch across T.K.'s face. 'What's the smile for?'

'Are ye saying that ye cannot understand what I am sayin'?' T.K. asked, mouthing out the words in laborious fashion.

Leonard nodded. 'That, I'm afraid, is exactly what I'm saying.'

'That's good, 'cos I wis goin' tae say the same thing tae you.'

They eyed each other for a moment before both burst out laughing, rocking back on their makeshift seats.

'Well,' Leonard said eventually, taking a handkerchief from the breast pocket of his jacket and wiping a trickling tear from his cheek. 'I think we might have just had a breakthrough there, Thomas.'

Still smiling, T.K. carefully pulled the film out of the maga-zine and placed everything back in the changing bag. 'You can call me T.K.,' he mumbled as he refastened the zip and pressed down the Velcro flap.

'What was that?' Leonard asked.

'T.K.' His cheeks flushed with embarrassment as he once more pushed his hands through the elasticated armholes. 'All my friends call me tha'.'

In that instant, Leonard realised there had been more than just a breakthrough in their language barrier. 'In that case, I would be delighted to call you T.K.'

'Ah think ah've got the hang o' this now.'

'All right,' Leonard said, reaching out to take his wristwatch from the light stand. 'I'll time you.'

Just under two minutes later, T.K. pulled his hands free of the changing bag, opened it up and held the loaded film magazine out to Leonard. First checking that the covers were secure, the cameraman then opened up both sides to make certain the threading of the film was correct.

'Perfect. Couldn't have done better myself,' he said, handing the magazine back to T.K. 'After you've had your lunch, you can have a go at loading the real McCoy.'

Whilst Thomas Keene junior had happily found gainful employment that day, the case was not the same for Rene Brownlow's husband, Gary, in Hartlepool. Having dropped Robbie and Karen off at their school in the morning, he had taken a bus downtown and spent the best part of the day sitting in the Employment Exchange staring vacantly at the plethora of posters that told of the consequences of being caught 'working on the fly' while drawing unemployment benefits. Then, when his long-awaited interview eventually did take place, he had to leave halfway through to get back to the school to pick up the kids again. His parents were busy that afternoon, his father at his mate's allotment, his mother doing the weekly shop at Morrison's, so he had no alternative other than to head back into town with the kids in tow.

When he entered Andersons Westbourne Social Club, his

immediate impression was that the spacious lounge bar was completely deserted. There was nobody up at the bar and the two women who stood behind it were idly chatting away before both turned at the sound of the swing doors banging shut. It was only when he heard the clink of dominoes from the table near the stage at the far end of the room that he surmised that some, if not all, of Rene's 'Fringe committee', were there.

He walked over to the bar and shot a wink at the elder of the two women. 'Hi, Mags. I 'ope ye don't mind me bringing the kids in. I just wanted to see Terry Crosland for a moment.'

'Aye, they'll be fine,' Mags replied. 'Mr Prendergast is away for the day, so ye've got nowt to worry about.' She glanced over Gary's shoulder and her glossy lipsticked mouth stretched into a broad grin. 'Was it just Terry ye wanted to see, or the whole bang shooting match?'

Gary turned round to find that the five domino players had left their table and had come to gather around him, their faces alight with enquiry.

''Ave ye 'eard 'ow Rene's doing?' Stan Morris, the self-appointed chairman of the committee, asked.

'All right,' Gary replied noncommittally, catching Terry's eye and greeting him with a brief nod.

' 'As she been on telly yet?' Skittle asked, squinting up at Gary through his bottle glasses.

'No, not yet.'

'Give 'er a chance!' Stan Morris said, glaring at Skittle. 'It takes time to build up fame.' He pushed his hands into the pockets of his tweed jacket. 'Now, I remember the time I appeared on the television—'

He was interrupted by sombre Derek Marsham's disparaging laugh. 'We all know about that one, don't we? All ye did was walk back and forth behind the reporter when 'e was doing that bit on the marina, just so ye could get yer ugly mug broadcast.'

Stan Morris's face puffed with indignation. 'I'll 'ave ye know that I was asked to be—'

'All right, let's give it a rest, lads,' Terry Crosland cut in, pushing past Stan and leaving him to swallow his explanation. He gave young Robbie's hair a firm ruffle. 'Ye're wanting a word with me, mate,' he said to Rene's husband.

'Aye, if ye can spare a couple of minutes.' Gary replied, glancing briefly at the other members of the committee, who pressed claustrophobically around them.

Terry turned to his fellow domino players and waved his raised hands towards their table, as if guiding back a reversing car. 'Go on, lads, just get on with the game. I'll be over once I'm through talking with Gary.'

'But what if it concerns Rene?' Stan blustered out. 'I am the chairman—'

'I know y'are, Stan,' Terry interjected in a quiet, diplomatic tone, 'and if any part of our discussion might have some relevance to those business matters over which you 'ave jurisdiction, then of course I will inform you of them accordingly.'

'Right,' Stan said, shrugging up his tweedy shoulders importantly. 'That's fair enough. Come on, lads, let's return to the table and allow Terry time to converse with Gary.'

'Sorry about that,' Terry said to Gary once he had seen the four members of the committee settle themselves back at the table. 'Stan likes to do things by the book.'

'Might be better if someone 'it 'im over the 'ead with one.'

Terry laughed. 'Aye, ye might be right.' He leaned an elbow on the bar. 'Fancy a pint or summat?'

'Just a Coke would do me, thanks.'

'And what about you lot?' Terry asked, looking down at Gary's children. 'Shall we make it four rounds of Coca-Cola?'

Robbie and Karen nodded in agreement to the idea.

Terry turned to the bar girl. 'Mags, make it four glasses of Coca-Cola and give the kids a set of those darts ye keep behind the bar. They can knock 'ell out of the dartboard for a moment while Gary and I have a chat.'

The two men carried their glasses over to the table in the furthest corner from where the game of dominoes had resumed and sat down.

'So, 'ow 'ave things been with you?' Terry asked. 'Any luck yet on the job front?'

Gary shook his head. 'Not yet.' He lit up a cigarette and then looked around the interior of Andy's, as if embarrassed to make eye contact with Terry. 'Listen, mate, I never said owt to you that day we put Rene on the train, but the first thing I want to do is to apologise for being bloody rude that time ye came round to see 'er. I 'ad no right.'

Terry waved his hand dismissively. 'No need to do that, lad. As I said then, I understand your situation.'

'Aye, maybe, but ye shouldn't 'ave been the one to cop the flak for my frustration.'

'Enough said,' replied Terry, taking a drink from his glass. 'So 'ave you 'eard from 'er?'

'Aye, I 'ave.'

''Ow's she getting on?'

'Not too good, I don't think.'

'Oh?' Terry leaned forward on the table, a look of concern on his thin face. 'What's gone wrong?'

'It's just not working for her. I spoke to 'er two nights ago and she said she's not getting the punters coming to 'er show and she's dead worried she's going to end up 'aving to foot the bill at the end of the run.'

'She don't 'ave to worry about that!' Terry exclaimed. 'That's all taken care of!'

'Aye, well, that's just one of 'er problems. She's living in some bloody awful out-of-the-way place and she 'as to be out of the 'ouse for most of the day.'

'Can't she find some place else to stay?'

'She was going to 'ead off this morning to see if she could find out about that, but I tell you, Terry, it took all me limited powers of persuasion to stop 'er from packing 'er bags and coming 'ome.'

'Oh, bloody 'ell,' Terry murmured, running a hand lightly over his Teddy-boy quiff. 'That doesn't sound too good, does it?'

'Not really.'

'Mind you, there's another week and an 'alf to go. If she can stick it out, things could change.'

Gary shrugged. 'Aye, they could, but it's my way of thinking what she could do with is a bit of encouragement from the 'ome crowd.'

'What are ye saying?'

'Well, it's the last thing I can afford to do, but I'm going to take the kids up to Edinburgh at the weekend to go see Rene's show. Give 'er a bit of moral support, sort of thing.' He stubbed out his cigarette in the ashtray. 'I was wondering if ye might like to come with us.'

Terry repeatedly sucked on his teeth as he contemplated Gary's suggestion. 'Mate, I don't think there's any way I can make it this weekend. I've got that much work on. I don't suppose you could leave it until the following one?'

Gary's laugh had a cynical edge to it. 'There's nowt pressing in my life right now, Terry. I could make it any weekend. The only thing about that is we'd be only there for Rene's last show, but I don't suppose it would matter too much.'

'You could all travel back to 'Artlepool together then.'

'Aye, that's true.' He pulled another cigarette from the packet and lit it. 'OK, let's make it next weekend.'

Terry flicked his head towards the group of domino players at the far end of the room. 'What about that lot? I don't think I'd make myself that popular if I 'eld back on telling them our plans.'

Gary took a long drag on his cigarette. 'Tell 'em then. I don't mind if they all come. They deserve it, really, 'aving raised all that money for Rene. Anyway, it'll help swell 'er audience, even if it is only for the last night.' He drained his glass of Coca-Cola and got to his feet. 'Well, I'd better take the kids back to do their 'omework.'

''Ow're you planning on getting up to Edinburgh?' Terry asked.

'I 'adn't really thought. Probably by train, though I sure as 'ell can't afford it.'

'In that case, I suppose we could take me van. Strictly illegal, but I'm quite 'appy to risk it.'

'D'ye reckon it would make it?'

Terry laughed. 'Aye, I reckon. I'll do a bit of tinkering with the engine beforehand and get a new exhaust stuck on. It's long overdue.'

'We'll be needing to fix somewhere to stay as well, won't we?'

'That's true,' Terry replied, rubbing thoughtfully at his chin. 'I'll 'ave a word with Stan Morris. 'E's always going on about 'is great contacts, so let's see what 'e can come up with.'

Gary nodded and stuck out a hand to Terry. 'I appreciate yer 'elp, mate.'

Terry stood up and shook it. 'Don't think anything of it.' He looked over to the far table where the four other members of the committee were now staring at them expectantly. 'Well, I'd better get over there and give me report.' He shot a wink at Gary. 'I doubt there's going to be much dominoes played for the rest of the afternoon.'

Twenty-Nine

In the space of one day, the world had suddenly become a brighter place for Thomas Keene junior. That evening, having first accompanied Leonard Hartson back to his lodgings in a taxi, he now made his way across town to the hostel, walking with a purposeful spring in his step and his shoulders held high, a young man displaying an element of pride in himself.

And he had every reason to feel that way. Not only had he now found himself a job, he had also received considerable praise from his new boss in the way he had picked up so much technical information during the course of the day. 'I called it a steep learning curve,' the old cameraman had said to him in the taxi, 'but, so far, you seem to have diminished it to nothing more than a gentle incline.'

As he walked, T.K. went over in his head all the skills that he had learned that day. The loading of the magazine and how to slot it on to the back of the camera, the threading of the film in the camera gate, leaving the correct-sized loop above and below, the raising and lowering of the tripod legs and the levelling of the 'head', and the assembly of the lights on their stands. When he turned into the street where the hostel was situated, he was so preoccupied with his thoughts that he never clocked on to the two boys who were leaning against the railings on the opposite side of the street. As soon as they saw him, they began to make their move. They crossed over to meet him at a diagonal, keeping their faces turned away to avoid recognition.

T.K. only became aware of their presence behind him when he had begun to climb the stone steps leading up to the door of the hostel. He felt a hand grabbing his arm, another on his shoulder and he was spun round and slammed against the railings with such force that he let out a scream of pain as the ironwork jarred against his spine. One of the boys took hold of the neck of his sweatshirt and twisted it in his hand, and T.K. found himself choking for breath as it tightened like a noose.

'Whit the fuck hae *you* been dain', ye bloody toe rag?' the boy said, his face contorted with hatred.

'Jeez, Lenny, let go,' T.K. gasped out in a high-pitched voice, his face beginning to turn puce. 'Ah cannae breathe.'

'Tha's the whole idea, ye wee bastard. Ma younger brither wis takin' aff by the polis this mornin', and guess wha the cause o' that wis?'

''Onest, Lenny, it wisnae—'

The other boy stepped forward and backhanded T.K. hard across the cheek. 'Dinnae ye try tae fuckin' well deny it, mon. A'body kens it wis you. The word's a-roond the estate, a' aboot you takin' videos o' the lads nickin' the cars.'

T.K.'s eyes filled with tears of terror and his legs gave way underneath him. He began to slide slowly down the railings to the ground. 'It wis a mistake, Rab. Ye gotta believe me.'

Lenny eased off the pressure on T.K.'s neck. He didn't want

him to black out just yet. 'An fuckin' mistake!' He let go T.K.'s sweatshirt and aimed a violent kick at his side. T.K. let out another cry of agony.

A man dressed in a dark suit and carrying a leather briefcase slowed down as he passed by, a look of concern on his face. Rab turned and flicked a thumb at him. 'Git on yer way, mister. This is private business.' The man shot a glance at T.K., then back at his shaven-headed assailants. The sight of the ragged tattoo on the neck of the youth who glared at him quickly dissipated any thought of further intervention on his part and the man continued on his way up the street with quickened step.

Lenny squatted down on his haunches, his face only a few inches away from T.K.'s. 'So ye thocht ye could hide awa' frae us, did ye? Jist yer luck, then, that auld Peesy McGill from ma block decided tae get guttered last night and ended up in yer fuckin' dosshoose. It wis him wha' saw ye and him wha' telt me.' He gave T.K. a knowing wink. 'As Rab said, Thomas Keene, the word's oot. A'body's efter ye. Ye're bloody done fer, pal.'

The door of the hostel was suddenly flung open and a huge man appeared on the doorstep. He was wearing a vast pair of jogging pants and a dirty white T-shirt that strained hard to cover his enormous belly, yet the size of his arms seemed to be in complete proportion with the rest of his body. 'Whit the hell's goin' on here?'

'It's naine of yer business, fatty,' Rab said, pointing a hostile finger at the man.

The man stepped down from the threshold and seized the lapel of Rab's denim jacket with one hand, lifting him almost clear of the ground. 'A'thing that happens on these steps is ma business, ye wee tosser,' he said through clenched teeth, glancing momentarily at T.K.'s sprawled form on the step, 'especially if it's tae dae wi' wan of ma lads.' He jerked the youth closer to him. 'And whit's mair, ah dinnae like bein' called "fatty", so if ah wis you, ah'd git the hell oot o' here afore I call the polis, is that understood?'

He let go his grip on the lad, giving him a violent push that made him stumble down the steps. Lenny stood up and backed away to join his colleague on the pavement. He balled his fist and flicked out a thumb, affecting the action of a switchblade. 'Ye'll be gettin' it comin' tae ye, Thomas Keene. You canna hide awa' fae us.' He cleared his throat noisily and then spat at T.K. with such force that the gob passed more than a foot above the head of its intended target.

'Get awa' wi' ye!' the caretaker yelled out with an angry wave of his hand. He stood watching after the two boys as they ambled off down the street, every so often casting a glance behind them, and then, letting out a long sigh, he looked down at T.K., who lay on the steps rubbing at his aching ribs. 'Ye dinnae half pick yer friends, dae ye, lad,' he said with a shake of the head. Leaning over with effort, he put a hand under T.K.'s armpit and pulled him to his feet. 'Ye'd better get yersel' inside and ah'll hae a look-see whit damage they've done tae ye.'

'Ah'm fine,' T.K. replied dolefully. He took in a long deep lungful of air. 'Ah'll jist stay here fer a minnit and catch ma breath.'

The caretaker gave a brief nod of his head. 'A'right. Come in when ye're ready,' he said as he turned and walked back into the house.

T.K. waited until the man's huge frame had disappeared from sight, and then, casting a quick glance up the street to make sure the two boys had gone, he descended the steps and headed away in the opposite direction, clutching a hand to his side.

Even though T.K. was only one amongst the thousands of people who crammed the centre of Edinburgh that night, he kept walking until well after midnight, never being too sure that somewhere, a hundred yards back on the crowded pavements, the two boys weren't following him. Eventually, he took the risk of ducking down a dimly lit alleyway off the bustle and noise of Rose Street, where he squatted uncomfortably behind a large industrial refuse bin for a good half an hour, waiting to see if his fears were to be justified. There did come a moment when he was set ready to make a dash for freedom, hearing two male voices talk quietly to each other only twenty feet away from him, but then he heard a splattering noise on the cobbles and realised that it was just a couple of revellers finding an unseen corner to relieve themselves. After they had gone, he left it for five minutes before quitting his hiding place. Rubbing at his aching legs, he began to make his way back along the narrow street, walking unexpectedly into the warming blast of air coming from a heating duct set into the side of one of the buildings that fronted on to Princes Street. He stood in its comforting folds for a moment, feeling its warmth penetrate his chilled body and relieve the aching in his side, and his eyelids began to give way to fatigue. He realised then that he would be unlikely to find a more comfortable place to pass the night than right there on that spot. Returning to the refuse bin, he pulled out a couple of cardboard packing cases and carried them back to a recessed doorway where he could still feel the warmth from the duct. Laying one on the ground, he pulled up the hood of his sweat-shirt and drew the strings tight around his face. He sat down on his hard, unforgiving bed, propped his back against the wall and covered himself with the other piece of cardboard, punching it with the side of his hand to mould it around his legs and body. He then leaned his head back and, with a deep sigh of despair, focused on the clear, cool starlit sky. Please, he thought to himself, if there's onybody up there, please gi' us a break. Dinnae let it end like this . . . please.

His head lolled heavily to one side and he fell into a deep, near-comatose sleep, blanking from his mind all the frustration and anger he felt at the innumerable injustices the world had heaped upon him.

Thirty

Albert Dessuin stood in the queue at the British Airways desk at Edinburgh Airport, his face lowered as he looked over the top of his dark glasses to see if there was any sign of movement up ahead. Gone was the bravado and impatience he had displayed the previous morning when he had pushed his way to the front of the queue at the hotel. Now, he was prepared to stand and wait, not wishing to draw attention to himself.

Since being informed of Angélique's injury and her unscheduled return to France, Albert had hidden himself away in his bedroom in the Sheraton Grand, not daring to leave, even though the receptionist had given him details of at least three direct flights that would have taken him to Paris that day. He had sat in the armchair staring trance-like out of the window, not wishing to watch the television in case it featured some damning news item about himself and not even glancing toward the small refrigerated minibar that was built into the corner of the wardrobe. When he had eventually left the room early that morning to check out, he had even averted his eyes from the complimentary newspaper lying on the ground outside his door. He just couldn't bring himself to learn whether Angélique had spoken to anyone about what had happened two nights before.

As the queue inched forward, he bent over and pushed the two suitcases along the ground, making sure the violin case remained hidden between them. He could hardly bear to look at it. It was only when he had returned to Angélique's bedroom in the hotel after speaking with Alasdair Dreyfuss the previous day that he had realised how serious a situation had arisen. Under those appalling circumstances of the preceding night, he could well understand why she had run off without taking any of her clothes, but to abandon her most treasured possession, the violin, was beyond comprehension. Oh, Angélique, he thought to himself, I cannot believe I allowed myself to do such a thing to you. Please let me find you so that I can try to make amends.

He did not mean to look round. It was just that he was so filled with guilt and self-loathing at that particular moment that even looking at the violin case brought the now clear memory of what had happened on that fateful night back to mind. He found himself staring directly at a man dressed in jeans and a multi-pouched body warmer, a large camera slung around his neck, who leaned against a pillar in the centre of the departure lounge, idly scanning the long queues that formed at the various check-in desks. The man glanced briefly in his direction, looked away, and then did a double take. He pushed himself away from the pillar and made his way quickly over to Albert.

'It is Mr Dessuin, isn't it?' the man asked, adjusting the dials on his camera and taking the cap off the lens.

Albert did not reply, pretending that the photographer had mistaken him for someone else. The camera flashed and Albert reacted instinctively, holding up his hand to shield his face. It was all the verification the photographer needed.

'Mr Dessuin, why are you travelling alone?' the man asked. 'Where is Angélique Pascal?'

The other people who stood in line at the British Airways desk had now begun to take interest in what was going on, turning to look at the tall man wearing the sunglasses and the belted mackintosh with the collar turned up, to whom the questions were being directed. Leaving his bags on the floor, Albert walked quickly away from the queue, and then turned to confront the photographer, who had followed, hot on his heels.

'I have no comment to make about anything,' Albert hissed at the man. 'I'm sure your newspapers have said it all.'

'It's all a bit airy-fairy, though, Mr Dessuin. All that's been reported is that Angélique Pascal had an accident and was returning to France.'

Dessuin bit at the side of his mouth as he contemplated what the photographer was telling him. Maybe Angélique had not disclosed the true facts after all. If so, for what reason? Maybe, despite all he had done, she was still displaying a sense of loyalty, protecting his reputation. If that was the case, there was hope of reconciliation after all. He decided to go along with that assumption, making a mental effort not to display the sense of elation he was feeling to the photographer. 'And that is all that happened. Mademoiselle Pascal has returned to Paris, and I am about to catch a plane to join her, so if you will now please excuse me . . .'

The photographer put a hand on his arm as Albert prepared to return to his place in the queue. 'That's all very well, but I can tell you Angélique Pascal has definitely not returned to Paris.'

Albert stared at the man. 'What do you mean?'

'Mr Dessuin, over the past twenty-four hours my colleague and I have been doing shifts here at the airport waiting to get a photograph of her, and there hasn't been one person who even vaguely resembles her booking in for a flight to Paris, or anywhere in France for that matter.'

Albert shook his head. 'You are mistaken.'

'No, I'm not. I've even had an acquaintance of mine check the passenger lists. Angélique Pascal has not left from this airport.'

Albert looked around at the queue. Those who were behind him were now moving forward, skirting around his luggage on the floor. 'She has obviously then been directed to a flight from another airport.'

The photographer let out a short, disbelieving laugh. 'Mr Dessuin, this is big news, you know. The festival's top performer has an accident preventing her from fulfilling her engagements, and heads off home to Paris. The word's got round to every freelance news photographer in Scotland. We've had all major airports and train stations covered for the past day, and there's not been even a glimpse of her. Now, having seen you here by yourself, it just confirms to me my own journalistic instinct on the matter.'

'Which is?'

'That Angélique Pascal is still in Edinburgh. The whole story about her returning to France is a sham, for some reason or other. Have you any idea why that might be, Mr Dessuin?'

Albert stood looking at the man, speechless, working through the logic of his reasoning. If the photographer was indeed correct, then where was Angélique? She knew no one in Edinburgh except those she had met at the receptions, and certainly Alasdair Dreyfuss was under the impression that she had returned to France. Of course, there was that girl, Tess Goodwin. Angélique seemed to have become friends with her, but how was he to find out? It could be that Angélique had confided in the girl, in which case he didn't want to question her, otherwise she might declare to the press the true events of that night.

He realised now, though, that he had to remain in Edinburgh to find Angélique, but first he had to think of a way of throwing this photographer off the scent. He could not allow press speculation to continue on her whereabouts. If she was still in Edinburgh, he needed the time and space to find her.

Albert smiled at the man and shook his head. 'The story is not a sham. I know that for certain.'

'How, may I ask?' the photographer asked, his eyebrows arched in uncertainty.

'Because I planned for Mademoiselle Pascal to leave before me, and I spoke with both her *and* my mother on the telephone last night. They are together in my house in Paris.' He cocked his head at the man. 'So, it would seem you have not been so efficient after all. Mademoiselle Pascal must have eluded you.' He gave a short bow of his head. 'So if you will now excuse me, I should like to continue with my plans to return to Paris and allow you to get on with some more lucrative work than standing around this airport all day.'

He left the man and walked back to the queue. Those who had been standing behind him had now shuffled forward past his luggage, but he was not concerned. It gave him time to see if the photographer had fallen for his ruse. He watched him out of the corner of his eye, studying his body language as he talked on his mobile phone. When the man had finished, he never turned to look in Albert's direction, but walked quickly over to the revolving doors and left the terminal.

Letting out a sigh of relief, Albert flicked back the cuff of his shirt and glanced at his watch. He would give the photographer five minutes' grace, and then he himself would take a taxi back to the city.

Thirty-One

In the London Street flat, Jamie Stratton sat cross-legged on a large threadbare Turkish carpet that covered only a fraction of the floor space of the cavernous sitting room, scratching perplexedly at his thick mop of blond hair as he stared at the backgammon board on the low cluttered coffee table.

'You've done it again, haven't you,' he said, eyeing his opponent with suspicion. 'You can't tell *me* you haven't played this game before.'

Leaning her elbows on the table, Angélique cupped her face in her hands and grinned at him. 'Not very often.'

'Hah! I knew it!' Jamie exclaimed, pointing an accusing finger at her. 'You're nothing more than a damned hustler.'

Angélique laughed. 'Of course,' she said, getting to her feet and immediately flopping back into the drape-covered sofa. 'There is no other way to be in life.'

Jamie pushed himself away from the table and leaned his back against an armchair. 'OK, so you'd better tell me about your other hidden talents, just so as I don't get duped again,' he said, smiling at her.

Angélique pulled the large towelling dressing gown tight around her neck and tucked up her feet on the sofa. 'Well, I could tell you all the names of the French rugby fullbacks all the way back to Serge Blanco.'

'You're joking.'

'I am not. My brothers thought it was a very necessary thing for their little sister to know. Shall I tell you the names?'

'No, spare the details, I'll believe you,' Jamie laughed, holding up his hands as if to defend himself from what was to come.

Angélique challenged his cowardly rebuff by wrinkling her

nose disdainfully at him. 'You are just frightened that I might know more about rugby than you.'

'Probably,' he replied, watching her closely as she ruffled her short dark hair, still wet from the shower, with the fingers of her unbandaged hand. It was funny, he thought to himself, how he had always been magnetically drawn to tall, shapely blonde girls with sparkling blue eyes in the past. Martha in the coffee shop was certainly a case in point. But now, having spent two days in the isolated company of Angélique Pascal, he realised that this preference had been narrowing the field quite unnecessarily. He studied the brown eyes that mischievously stared back at him, the downy softness of the sallow-skinned cheeks that were creased with humour, and the small dark-lipped mouth that challenged him with its smile. Everything about her – her diminutive size, her boyish figure – was a complete antithesis to those qualities that had fulfilled his youthful fantasies, but now he was beginning to see this young French violinist as one of the most mysteriously attractive and outrageously captivating members of the opposite sex he had ever clapped eyes on.

'Anything else?' he asked.

Angélique rocked her head from side to side in consideration. 'I suppose I am quite good at playing the violin as well.'

Jamie smiled. 'Maybe you should take it up professionally then.'

'I suppose it's a consideration,' she replied quietly, the smile on her face fading away and Jamie realised immediately his joke had been crass and badly timed, a stark reminder of her present situation.

'Sorry, that was a stupid thing to say.'

Angélique shook her head. 'No, I understand you did not mean it that way. I can only imagine everything would be much worse if I hadn't met you and Gavin.'

'Yeah, well,' Jamie replied, dismissing the remark with a wave of his hand, although his true feeling was that their meeting was one of the more fortuitous things that had happened to him. 'So, how's the hand feeling today?'

Angélique flexed the fingers of her bandaged hand. 'It seems to be better. I do not have so much pain now.'

'In that case, I've got something for you,' he said, clambering to his feet. He walked over to the fireplace and began tipping out the contents of each of the chipped china bowls that lined the dark polished granite mantelpiece. 'Where the hell is it? I know it's in one of these.' He eventually found what he was looking for in the last bowl. 'Here you are.' He turned and lobbed something small and black to Angélique. She caught it by instinct and then turned the object around in her fingers, studying it with a baffled expression on her face.

'I think this is a ball for playing squash,' she said.

'Yeah, it is.'

Angélique laughed. 'So, are you now challenging me to a game of catch or something?'

'No, but it's not such a bad idea. I might have a slight advantage over you with two good hands.' He pushed the backgammon board to one side and sat down on the table in front of Angélique. He took the ball from her hand and began squeezing it repeatedly in his fist. 'Last year, this enormous rugby prop forward from one of the Borders teams decided it would be fun to grind his studs into my hand during a game. By the time I'd been helped off the field of play, my fingers had lost all feeling and had swollen to the size of sausages. I used this squash ball to get them working again, and I was back on the rugby pitch within two weeks.' He put the ball back in her bandaged hand and gently folded her fingers over it. 'How does that feel?'

Angélique's mouth screwed to one side, as if she was trying hard to suppress a laugh. 'Very nice. Quite sensual, actually.'

Jamie smiled at her in surprise. 'Just keep squeezing it. You'll find it does help.' He got to his feet and pushed his hands into the back pockets of his jeans. 'Listen, I've got to get on with writing some of these reviews. I'm a day behind and I have a deadline for this afternoon, so I hope you don't mind if I leave you to fend for yourself for an hour or two.'

Angélique swung her legs off the sofa. 'Jamie, have you heard yet from Gavin?' she asked concernedly.

'No, I haven't.'

'So we don't know what Albert is doing.'

'I'm afraid not.'

Angélique nodded. 'It's just that I would really like to have my violin. I have never been parted from it for so long, and I feel . . . lost without it.'

Jamie scratched thoughtfully at his head. 'I don't think we should do anything until Gavin gets in touch, but tell you what; if I don't hear from him by midday, I'll give him a call.' He walked over to the door and opened it. 'In the meantime,' he said, turning back to her, '*work the ball!*'

An hour later the telephone began to ring shrilly in the hall, making Jamie type faster than his fingers would allow as he tried to commit to his computer's memory what he knew was the perfect description of the Fringe comedy show before it faded from his mind. He swore under his breath when he looked up and saw nothing but a plethora of misspelled words on the screen. Pushing himself out of the chair with a frustrated yell, he ran through to the hall and made a dive for the telephone.

'Hullo?'

'Jamie, it's Gavin here. How's everything today?'

'Oh, good enough,' Jamie replied absently, picking up a biro to scribble down the sentence on the back of an unopened envelope. When the biro refused to write, he threw it with force against the wall. '*Bugger!*'

'Obviously not a good time,' Gavin laughed.

'Sorry, I was just trying to write something down before I forgot it.'

'Do you want me to call back?'

'No, don't worry. I'll probably remember it.'

'How's Angélique this morning?'

'Doing OK.'

'And the hand?'

'On the mend, I reckon. She's not in so much pain now.'

'A good sign, then. Listen, Jamie, I think our little plan about getting her luggage back from the hotel might have backfired.'

'In what way?'

'Dessuin didn't leave the Sheraton Grand yesterday, so that's why I never called you about collecting Angélique's belongings. Now it would appear that he's gone and checked out of the hotel at about eight o'clock this morning and taken a taxi to the airport. I can only deduce from that that he's following her back to Paris.'

'He hasn't taken Angélique's stuff with him, has he?'

'That I can't tell you. My source of information couldn't confirm it one way or the other, but I'm afraid it's highly likely.'

'So, what happens now? Angélique was just saying she was desperate to get her violin back.'

'Well, let's not write off everything at this point in time. Dessuin will have been pretty distracted before leaving, so there's the slimmest chance he might have left something behind. I would suggest you just go round to the Sheraton Grand and see what's what.'

'OK, but what do I do if he *has* taken everything?'

Jamie heard Gavin sigh resignedly at the other end of the line. 'Then we'll just have to consider what our next step is going to be, but let's just rule out one thing at a time, shall we?'

'All right. I'll call you when I get back.'

'You do that. Thanks, Jamie.'

Jamie replaced the receiver and turned to go back to his bedroom but stopped when he saw Angélique leaning against the door of the sitting room, silently watching him.

'How long have you been standing there?' he asked.

'Long enough,' she replied.

Jamie nodded. 'Right, well, you probably gathered I'm going to try to pick up your things this morning.'

'If they are still there.'

'Yeah, that's right,' he replied, moving off towards his bedroom door. 'I'll go as soon as I've finished off writing that review.'

'Jamie?'

She had not moved away from the door, but was following him with her dark-brown eyes.

'What?'

'Do you want me to leave?' she asked quietly.

'No. Why do you ask?'

'Because I am causing you a lot of problems. It would be easier for you if I was not here.'

Jamie shrugged. 'Yeah, that's true.' He grinned at her. 'But life would be a helluva lot more boring.'

'Do you mean that?'

'Course I do. Anyway, you can't go.'

'I know that Gavin says I should not—'

'It's got nothing to do with Gavin. You're not leaving here until I've beaten you at backgammon.'

The haunting shadow of worry evaporated from Angélique's face as she contemplated this challenge, eventually answering it with a shrug of her shoulders. 'I cannot be here for ever, you know.'

Jamie narrowed his eyes and jabbed a finger in her direction. 'Tonight, Mademoiselle Pascal, you are history.'

'Ça m'étonnerait!' Angélique exclaimed, pulling back her arm and throwing something at him with force. Jamie ducked to one side as the squash ball thudded against the wall behind him. She rushed forward and bent down to retrieve it, and as she straightened up she stood on her toes and planted a kiss on his cheek. 'You were supposed to catch it,' she said, her face so close to his that Jamie felt her breath brush past his ear. He had time to see one small, squint-toothed imperfection in her teasing smile before she turned and walked assuredly back towards the sitting room. 'That, I'm afraid, is another game I have won.'

Leonard Hartson adjusted the knob on the back of the 1K Redhead to balance the contrast of light hitting the chalk-white face of one of the Japanese dancers and the reflective gold thread that was intricately woven through the silk of her deep-red kimono. He walked forward to the dancer and scanned her with his light meter before returning to the row of canvas chairs T.K. had set up beside the camera, two of which were occupied by the dance company director, Mr Kayamoto, and Claire, his young interpreter.

'Right,' Leonard said, slipping the light meter into the pocket of his jacket. 'I think we're about ready to shoot.' He smiled reassuringly at Kayamoto as Claire translated his words. 'And I would suggest that after we've finished this particular scene, the company breaks for lunch. That'll give me time to reset the lights for some close-ups.' He glanced towards the unlit area of the warehouse behind the camera. 'Right, T.K., if you could start the music and then mark the scene.' He stepped up on to the camera box he had positioned behind the tripod legs to give him extra height, set the aperture on the lens, checked his focus through the eyepiece and waited for the music to start. Nothing happened. He turned and looked across to where the darkened shape of his assistant leaned forward in front of the rack of amplifying equipment. 'T.K., when you're ready.'

Again, nothing happened. Leonard heard a scrape of chairs as both the director and his interpreter turned to see why the music hadn't started. He stepped stiffly off the camera box and walked away from the dazzling pool of light. In the few seconds that it took him to reach his assistant, Leonard's eyes became accustomed to the obscurity of the warehouse and he could tell immediately that T.K. had not heard a word he had said. He placed a hand on the shoulder of the boy's slumped form and gave it a gentle shake. 'Are you all right, lad?'

T.K. jumped to his feet too quickly, lost his balance and fell hard against one of the large loudspeakers. It toppled over with a low resonant thump.

'Sorry about tha',' T.K. said, heaving up the speaker and gingerly returning it to its position. He dipped his head, not wishing to make eye contact with the old cameraman. 'Sorry, Leonard. Ah think ah drapped aff.'

Leonard stared hard at the boy. Because T.K. had not turned

up that morning until well after the dance company had arrived, Leonard had decided to hold back from saying anything to him about his general state of appearance and his sloppy, wordless demeanour during the morning's shoot, but he certainly would have to address it during the lunch break. T.K. was wearing the same clothes he had worn the day before, his hair was greasy and dishevelled, and his whole being emanated a sour smell of body odour and unkemptness.

'Yes, well,' Leonard said curtly, 'if you're ready now, maybe you would be good enough to turn on the music and then come and mark the scene.'

It took three takes before Leonard managed to put the shot in the can. He noticed that one of the dancers had looked straight at the camera during the first, a jerky camera pan put pay to the second, but the third worked beautifully. Having congratulated the director and the company on a good morning's work, accompanied by many a reciprocated bow, he watched as the little ensemble in their bright, out-of-place clothes filed through the fire door at the side of the warehouse and closed it behind them.

'Shall ah turn the lights aff?' T.K. asked, his voice tentative as it echoed around the vast empty space.

Leonard took off his spectacles and let them drop to his chest on the neck cord. He rubbed a hand at his eyes, unaccustomed as they were now to working under the glare of the lights, and then pressed it to the slight pain he felt at the left side of his ribcage. Maybe it had been a foolhardy idea of his to take on the making of the film in this way. Of course, both he and Gracie knew he had to take this one-off, God-given opportunity to show the world that Leonard Hartson, the once famous director of photography, had not lost his touch. But maybe it was all happening twenty years too late, and trying to do it now was really biting off more than he could chew. If he had a full working crew as was originally planned, things would be different, but to have only this young lad who knew little about what he was doing and who could hardly keep his eyes open

241

was going to test both his patience and his fading stamina to the full.

He turned and made his way back to the studio floor. 'What was that, T.K.?'

'Ah didna know if ye wanted me tae turn aff the lights.'

Leonard let out a despondent sigh. 'Yes, you can do that.' He walked over to the camera and unlocked the tripod legs, allowing them to sink down, and spun the lens round to face him.

T.K. switched off the last light and came to stand beside him. 'If ye're goin' tae check the gate, ah've already dunnit,' he said quietly. 'It's clean.'

Leonard smiled at the young lad. He was trying his best. 'Well done. I had forgotten to do it.'

T.K. hunched his shoulders and stuck his hands deep into the pockets of his sagging jeans. 'Ah'm sorry ah dozed aff, Leonard. Ah'll no dae it again.'

Leonard shook his head. 'Listen, I do understand you're being thrown in at the deep end here, but before we go any further, there are a few things we've got to get straight.'

'It wis jist that . . .'

'I know,' Leonard said, holding up his hand to curtail T.K.'s further excuses. 'Just hear me out, if you would. When one is making a film, T.K., it is extremely important that you are seen to be totally professional in everything you do, because that is what impresses the client. Now, this not only makes itself apparent in the way you work around the set, but also in the way you present yourself. I know you'll probably think my dress sense is a bit old-fashioned, and I wouldn't dream of asking you to wear a jacket and tie like myself, but tomorrow I want you not only to turn up for work on time, but also having smartened up your appearance quite considerably.' Leonard paused, seeing the lad dip his head in embarrassment at the reprimand. 'Now, I don't want you to get disheartened. You had one slip-up today – that was all. Other than that, I thought you worked pretty well.' He put a hand on the boy's shoulder. 'Appearances are crucial, T.K., so when you finish up this afternoon, I want you to go home,

242

get yourself cleaned up, look out some clean clothes and then have an early night. Is that understood?'

The young man nodded dolefully in reply.

'Right, enough said,' Leonard said, turning to check the footage left in the film magazine. 'Let's get ourselves set up for the next scene. I want to do some close-ups on the faces, so if you could move the camera forward to the edge of the dance area . . .'

'Leonard?'

Leonard turned back to the boy. 'Yes?'

T.K. stood with his head still lowered. 'Ah don' like tae ask ye this, because ah know ah havna earned it yet, but could ye lend us some money so as ah can turn up fer work tomorrow?'

Leonard looked questioningly at him. 'Would this be for a bus fare, T.K.?'

T.K. shook his head. 'So's ah can get ma claithes washed.'

'Do you not have a washing machine at home?'

'Aye, it's just that . . .' T.K. scratched the back of his greasy head. 'Ah'm no' livin' at haim at the minnit.'

'Oh, right, I understand. And there's no washing machine in the place you're staying now, is that it?'

T.K. moved over to the camera, swung it round and locked off the tripod head. 'Ah'm no' stayin' onyplace,' he said quietly. He picked up the apparatus and began pushing the tripod spider towards the dance area with his foot.

'T.K., would you just leave the camera for a moment?'

The boy settled the tripod back into the grooves on the spider and turned slowly to face the cameraman.

'What do you mean, you're not staying anyplace? Where did you spend last night?'

T.K. shrugged his shoulders and began pushing one of the snaking electrical cables into a loop with the toe of one of his dirty white trainers.

'Where did you spend last night?'

'Jist aff Rose Street,' he mumbled.

'What do you mean, just off Rose Street?'

'Doon the back o' Marks and Spencer's. There's a hot-air duct comin' oot the back o' the building, so it's good an' warm, but people kept walking past so ah didna get much sleep.'

Leonard let out a long sigh, understanding now exactly what the boy was saying to him. 'You're sleeping rough, aren't you, lad?'

T.K. nodded.

'How long have you been doing this?'

'Jist the once. Mr Mackintosh had paid fer me to stay in a hostel fer a week, just so's I could get started wi' you.' He paused, his head lowered as he scratched at his downy stubble. 'But ah didna want tae go back there.'

Leonard sat down heavily on one of the lighting boxes. 'And why would that be?'

''Cos there's folk wha are efter me. They know ah wis staying there.'

'And what's the reason for these "folk" being after you?'

'Jist because.'

Leonard nodded, realising the boy did not wish to elaborate on the circumstances. 'So, in a nutshell, you have nowhere to stay and you have no clothes other than those you're standing up in, is that right?'

'Aye, ah suppose,' T.K. muttered.

Leonard leaned forward on his knees and covered his face with his hands. 'Oh dear, oh dear, oh dear,' he stated rhythmically. This was certainly the last thing he needed. The making of this film was going to take up enough of his time and energy without having the additional hassle of sorting out both the accommodation and security problems of this young waif-and-stray. He felt the lid of the lighting box sink slightly as T.K. came to sit beside him.

'Ah'm sorry, Leonard. I wis hopin' you widna find oot.'

The old cameraman reached across and patted the boy's knee. 'That's all right. I'm glad I did sooner rather than later.'

'Ah could always sleep here, if ye'd allow me tae. Naebody wid find me here, and ah could look efter a' the equipment.'

'No, that would not work. You'd be no better off.' He looked across at his assistant, studying the sad, hopeless expression on his face. 'T.K., do you really want to work with me?'

The boy jerked round his head, a look of alarm on his face. 'Aye, ah do, Leonard. Ah promise ah won't be late again, and ah'll get masel' sorted oot, honest ah will.'

'I can't have you sleeping rough.'

'Ah willna dae it,' he replied, his voice rising in agitation at the thought of losing his one big chance.

'No, what I mean is that I can't *allow* you to sleep rough. If you work for me, then you are part of my crew, and it is my responsibility to find you lodgings.' Leonard rubbed his wrinkled hands on the knees of his cavalry-twill trousers. 'Trouble is I can't really afford to pay for your accommodation, and what's more, I doubt I'd find anywhere for you stay right now . . .' He paused a moment before murmuring, '. . . which leaves only one option.' T.K. got to his feet and took a couple of paces towards the lighting stage. He stood with his back to Leonard, his shoulders slumped dejectedly and his hands thrust into the pockets of his jeans.

'Ye're goin' tae say ah canna work fer ye, aren't ye?' he sniffed.

'No, I am not. I'm certainly not going to find anyone else to assist me at such short notice, and anyway, I offered you a job and I'll stick by that, so you have no worries on that account.'

T.K. turned to the cameraman. 'So, whit did ye mean aboot the wan option?'

Leonard clambered wearily to his feet. 'Well, it's certainly not the most ideal arrangement and I'll have to clear it with my landlord, but there are two beds in my room, and—'

'Whit are ye sayin'? That ah can come and stay wi' you?' T.K. stared at Leonard, wondering if he had misunderstood what the old cameraman was saying, but desperate to grab at any opportunity.

'I don't think there's much alternative, is there?'

T.K. eagerly approached Leonard, realising now all was not lost. 'If ah did that, I widna be a nuisance tae ye, ah promise, and ah dinna snore or a'thing, and onyways, it's a good idea 'cos we can talk aboot whit we're goin' tae dae the next day, so ah can get ready fer it in ma heid . . .'

Leonard smiled and held up a hand to halt T.K.'s exuberant outburst. 'All right, let's take one thing at a time, lad. After we've finished shooting this afternoon, I would suggest we go uptown and get you kitted out with a few things, including a pair of jeans with a decent belt. I don't want you to continue exposing half your backside to our assembled company every time you bend down to unplug a light.'

As if trying to make amends already, T.K. pulled up his own drooping trousers and ran a hand around the waistband to tuck in his grimy T-shirt. They immediately slipped to their original position when he launched himself at the cameraman and grabbed hold of his hand. The shake it received was so enthusiastic that Leonard had grave worries a serious shoulder dislocation was imminent. 'Cheers, Leonard. I willna let ye doon, ah promise.'

The result of T.K.'s energetic arm action was to immerse Leonard in a suffocating waft of body odour. He pulled his hand free from the boy's grip and took a few paces back to escape the unsavoury cloud. 'And the first thing you do when we get back to the flat is have a long hot shower, is that under-stood?'

T.K. grinned broadly at him. 'Aye, ah will.' He turned and hefted the tripod and camera up on to his shoulder and kicked the spider across the floor. 'Tell us how far ye want this in now.'

Shrugging on a corduroy bomber jacket, Jamie descended the stairs of the flat and flung open the front door. Without lessening his speed, he ran out on to the broad stone steps, managing to swerve in time to avoid a thumping collision with the small solid figure that swung around with alarm at his sudden appearance, crumpling an open street map of Edinburgh against her ample chest.

'Is there ever a time when ye slow up?' Rene Brownlow asked

as Jamie's momentum took him clear off the three remaining steps to the pavement.

'Yeah, waking up in the mornings is a pretty slow affair, as you've witnessed,' Jamie laughed.

Rene pulled a long face and glanced about her. 'More's a pity there's no one about to 'ear you say that,' she said, stretching out the map in front of her with a flick of her wrists.

'Where are you off to?'

'I thought I'd try to find a quicker route uptown than the one I've been taking the last couple of days.'

'Come with me, if you like. I'm heading up there now.'

'At what speed?' Rene asked, folding up the map and slipping it into her large shoulder bag.

'I'll let you set the pace,' Jamie replied with a smile.

'That'll do me,' Rene said, descending the steps and pushing her hands into the pockets of her rag-rug coat. They headed off side by side along the street. 'So, did ye manage to get it all sorted out with your nice lawyer chap yesterday?'

'We're getting there.'

'Don't think I'm prying, like, but has it got something to do with that nice French violinist who's staying in yer flat?'

Jamie's step faltered as he fixed her with an open-mouthed look of amazement. 'How come you know about *her*?'

'Well, ye could 'ardly stave off our eventual meeting, Jamie. Yer flat is large, but it's not exactly Buckingham Palace.' She shifted her bag up on to her shoulder. 'Any road, to answer yer question, we bumped into each other this morning on the way to the bathroom.'

'What did she say?'

'Well, I can't remember her exact words, but it was something like "Please, you must use ze basroom first."'

Jamie was too eager to hear what had passed between them to react to her light-hearted quip. 'And that was it?'

'No. I asked what she'd done to 'er 'and and she told me she'd cut it on glass and 'ow sad she was because she wasn't going to be able to play the violin for a bit.' Rene slowed her pace as they

247

started up the incline of Dublin Street. 'And then when I got back to my bedroom I was leafing through some of the festival brochures and suddenly there she was, staring out of the pages at me. Angélique Pascal, world-famous violinist. I tell ye, ye could 'ave knocked me down with a feather. It's not every day ye get to talk with someone like that, let alone share a bathroom!'

Jamie kept walking without passing comment. It had never occurred to him that Angélique might talk to one of his tenants. He had only foreseen problems coming from without the sanctuary of the flat. Not that it was the fault of either Angélique or Rene. They were just making normal conversation with each other, and like as not, Rene would still have found the photograph of Angélique in the brochure. But it did add up to a huge complication. If Rene was to keep her ears and eyes open, she was bound to find out sooner or later that Angélique's presence in Edinburgh was contrary to everyone else's belief. She seemed to be a decent, down-to-earth sort of person. Maybe his best option was just to confide in her.

'Oh, thanks for that,' Rene gasped, taking Jamie's reason for stopping at the corner of Heriot Row as a chance for her to catch her breath.

'Listen, Rene, if I tell you something about Angélique, will you honestly swear to me you won't mention it to anyone else, most of all the press?'

'My, this all smacks of intrigue, don't it?'

'Do you promise?'

'Jamie, I don't 'ave an 'otline to *News at Ten,* you know, and I don't reckon the press will be queuing up to ask Rene Brownlow, small-time comedienne from 'Artlepool, for her weighty views on world affairs.'

'If they discover you're living in the same flat as Angélique Pascal, they'll find what you have to say pretty important, I can tell you.'

Rene nodded. 'Right,' she said, realising now that her young landlord was seriously concerned about something to do with the violinist's welfare. 'In that case, of course I promise. Ye've been me bloody saviour up here in Edinburgh, Jamie Stratton. The last thing I'd want to do is get ye into trouble.'

So, as they continued on their way up to the lights on Queen Street, Jamie told Rene about his chance meeting with Angélique in the coffee shop. By the time they turned into George Street and he had told her of the assault the violinist had suffered at the hands of her manager, Rene was so captivated by the story she forgot all about her lack of fitness and made sure she kept pace with Jamie, even breaking into an awkward trot at times to avoid missing one word of what he was telling her. When the one-o'clock gun thundered out from the battlements of Edinburgh Castle and the pigeons, sitting high on the flat stone ballustrades of the buildings, rose momentarily in panic, Rene listened on, seemingly immune to the sudden, ear-pounding disturbance. They stepped off the pavement in unison to avoid the disorderly but boisterously good-natured queues that meandered along the street, readying themselves with plastic beer glasses in hand to squeeze into unlikely basement venues for the early afternoon Fringe performances. And then, on reaching Charlotte Square, where crowds mingled on the grass outside the white marquees of the Book Festival, dappled with shadow under their sun-glistened umbrella of trees, Rene let out a loud expletive describing her thoughts on Albert Dessuin and stepped out into the street without looking. Had it not been for Jamie's restraining arm, she no doubt would have ended her days beneath the wheels of one of the vehicles in the ever-constant stream of traffic, with the vulgar word frozen on her lips.

'So, this is where they were staying, is it?' Rene wheezed when they eventually came to a halt, looking across Festival Square at the glass-fronted rectangle of the Sheraton Grand.

'Yeah, it is,' Jamie replied distractedly as he cast an eye around the packed area.

'Do ye think 'e's still somewhere abouts?'

'No, I'm pretty sure he's headed back to Paris.'

'So what're ye going to do?'

Jamie exhaled a deep breath. 'Just go in, I suppose.'

'D'ye want me to come in with ye?'

'No, don't worry. You should go off and do what you've got to do.'

'Oh, I've got nowt pressing. Anyway, ye've got me 'ooked now, lad. I want to 'ang around and see the outcome.'

Jamie smiled at Rene, secretly pleased she was there with him as an accomplice, her quirky banter calming the nervousness he felt at carrying out the task in hand. 'All right. Maybe you could stay here then, just in case I am followed out of the hotel.'

'D'ye think that's likely?'

'Anything's possible.'

Rene shot him a wink. 'OK, then, consider it done. I'll 'ave a seat over there at the café and keep me eyes peeled.'

As Jamie hurried across to the steps and entered through the swing doors of the hotel, Rene walked across to the café, put her bag on an empty table and flumped down into one of the metal chairs facing the hotel entrance so that she had an unhindered view of all that was going on in Festival Square. She was taking this whole 'private eye' business pretty seriously.

And had she not been so attentive while waiting for her cup of cappuccino to arrive, she would never have noticed the woman with the wild mass of red hair and the huge pink scarf wrapped around her neck get up from the table beside her, nor the brown leather purse that lay dropped beneath her chair.

'Excuse me!' Rene called out, pushing herself to her feet. She leaned over awkwardly and picked up the purse. The woman had not heard her, continuing on in the same direction as Jamie had taken five minutes before. Rene bustled off across the square after her. 'Excuse me!' she called out again, this time much louder.

The woman turned and looked back at her, a querying frown on her freckled, moon-shaped face.

'Ye dropped yer purse,' Rene said as she approached her. 'It was under yer seat.'

The woman's mouth dropped open in horror. 'Oh my God!' she said, taking the purse from Rene's outstretched hand. 'I can't believe I'd do that. My whole life's in this purse. How can I ever thank ye?'

Rene smiled at her. The woman spoke with an accent not dissimilar to her own, and although Rene could tell she didn't hail from Yorkshire or County Durham, just the very tone of her voice was like a homecoming, a comfort to hear.

'Think nowt of it,' Rene replied with a shrug of her shoulders. 'Lucky I saw it.'

'Well, let me at least buy you a coffee.' The woman flicked a thumb behind her towards the Sheraton Grand. 'I'm going into that 'otel there.'

Rene shook her head. 'Thanks, but ah can't. Ah'm waiting for someone. Any road, ah've just ordered a cappuccino back there at the café.'

'Right, well, in that case, what can ah say other than thanks.'

Rene stuck her hands deep into the pockets of her huge coat. 'It was a pleasure.'

A quizzical frown came over the woman's face once more. ''Ave we met before?'

'Ah don't think so.'

'It's just that you look quite familiar.'

'Maybe you've seen my double in *Vogue* or summat like that.' The woman laughed. 'Aye, maybe that's it.'

'Ah'm always being mistaken.'

'Ah'm sure y'are.'

Rene turned to see the waiter put her cup of cappuccino on the table. He lit the patio warmer that stood next to it, and then glanced around for his customer. She caught his eye and raised a hand. 'Ah'd better get back, then,' she said, pointing a finger.

'Aye, ye'd better. And thanks again for the purse. That was a real lifesaver.'

Giving her a brief wave of farewell, Rene turned and walked back to her table.

She was savouring every sip of her frothy cappuccino, floating with an overabundance of flaked chocolate, when she saw Jamie appear back through the swing doors of the hotel and cast a searching look around the square. When he caught sight of Rene, he beckoned for her to come quickly. She stood up, her eyes darting back and forth between him and the inviting cup of coffee. 'Oh, damnation!' she said under her breath, rummaging in her handbag for her purse. She showered some coins on to the table, slung her handbag on to her shoulder and hurried over to the steps.

'What's up?' she asked.

'Bloody Dessuin's standing in the queue right now at the reception. He was meant to have gone back to Paris.'

''Ow d'ye know it's 'im?'

'Because I've seen his picture in a newspaper. Anyway, he's also got her blue suitcase and the violin with him.'

'But I thought yer lawyer had said he'd booked out.'

'I know. That's what's puzzling me. He must have come back, which means . . .'

Rene saw the gaunt look of realisation on Jamie's face. 'Means what?'

'Somehow he's worked out Angélique is still here in Edinburgh.'

Rene blew out a long breath. 'Aye, that *would* seem the logical answer. So what should we do?'

'Only one thing for it. I've got to get her suitcase and violin now. There's never going to be another opportunity.'

'But 'ow?'

'I'm not sure yet,' Jamie replied, turning back towards the swing doors. 'Come on, you'd better come with me. If the worse comes to the worst, you'll have to set up some kind of diversion.'

Rene pushed through the swing doors in pursuit of Jamie and scurried along the carpeted corridor to catch up with him. ''Ow do I do that?'

'I have no idea,' Jamie said as he descended the wide black-banistered staircase leading down to the reception area. 'Hopefully it won't be necessary, but you'll just have to use your imagination, if need be.'

'We're not going to break the law, are we?'

But Rene got no answer to her question. She stood transfixed on the final landing of the stairs, watching Jamie as he made his way over to the reception where a tall thin man with a belted mackintosh was in heated debate with the young receptionist, his hands gesticulating in annoyance as he tried to put his point across to her.

Rene slowly descended the remaining few steps in a knee-knocking trance of panic, her eyes never leaving Jamie as he nonchalantly reached down to pick up the blue suitcase and the violin that stood in the row of luggage behind the man. This is not going to work, she thought to herself.

'Oh, I've suddenly come over all faint,' she said shrilly to no one in particular, theatrically grabbing hold of the large square banister knob and weaving her body in a circular motion, not unlike a spinning top that was coming to the end of its centrifugal momentum. The true fact was that the tension of the whole situation was making her feel particularly light-headed, which helped to reassure her of the realistic nature of her performance. Unfortunately, though, she delivered her line with such clarity and volume that she not only attracted the attention of all those who were present in the hotel lobby but also the very person whom Jamie was so far doing a very good job of evading. There was a brief moment when he glanced over to her with an agonised look on his face before he made a fast and furtive dart for the back entrance of the hotel, clutching Angélique's suitcase and violin. Through her oscillating vision, Rene watched as the Frenchman's unsympathetic glare turned from her, the lady in distress, to Jamie, the boy in quick retreat, his expression changing in an instant from annoyance to open-mouthed horror.

'Hey, you, come back with those!' he yelled out at the top of his voice as he took off after Jamie, who had by this time disappeared out into the street. Rene glanced down at the floor, measuring her distance, and with a final, desperate prayer that the Sheraton Grand had not scrimped on its furnishing budget and that the carpet was indeed a plush, top-of-the-range

Axminster with a deep spongy underlay, she fell poleaxed to the ground, on the very spot where Dessuin was about to plant his neat black, highly polished shoe. Like a racehorse that had an obstacle the size of a Grand National fence suddenly dropped in front of it, Dessuin could do nothing to avoid the prostrate form. His foot caught the side of Rene's body with such force she momentarily opened her eyes wide, muffling a cry of pain, as Dessuin's charcoal-worsted legs flew over her in a horizontal arc. As she heard the thump of his body coming to rest next to hers, she hurriedly closed her eyes and feigned serene unconsciousness, hoping that her face was giving off the colour of insipid magnolia rather than the much more likely raging red of a well-stoked brazier. She sensed people gathering around her, some giving helpful commands like 'Stand back and give her air,' and then, rather alarmingly, hands started to undo the top buttons of her shirt. If ye go to the next one down, she thought to herself, I'm going to slap yer bloody 'and away, regardless. And then she heard a female voice, further away from those surrounding her, say something that certainly had the effect of draining any excess colour from her face.

'I'll call the police immediately, sir.'

'No, don't do that,' came the immediate reply. 'I do not want to involve the police.'

'But, sir, you've just had some luggage stole—'

'I said I do not want you to call the police.' Rene heard Dessuin let out a short unconvincing laugh. 'It is all a bit of a misunderstanding. I know who has taken the cases. I will get them back from him.'

There was a pause, during which someone raised Rene's head off the floor and slipped a soft cushion underneath it.

'Well, if you're sure, sir.'

'Quite sure. I will deal with it all once I am in my room.' Rene heard the man's soft tread skirt round the foot of her supine body. 'Does anyone know who this woman might be?' he asked.

Oh, no, Rene thought to herself, this is it. I've been found out. This must 'ave been 'ow it felt for a member of the Resistance to be picked up by the Gestapo. I wonder 'ow I'll 'old up under interrogation. Oh, please, God, all I ask is that I can get to go to the loo first.

'Aye, she's a friend of mine,' a female voice replied, very close to Rene's head. 'We were about to have tea together when she said she was feeling faint and headed off to the ladies' toilet.'

There was a pause before the Frenchman's voice replied, 'Very well,' and then Rene heard him walk away. She flickered one eye, trying desperately to see who it was that had come to her rescue. Through the diffusion of her eyelid, she could make out the wild tangle of curly red hair and the huge pink scarf.

'That's about five minutes now,' the woman's voice whispered to her. 'I reckon that's sufficient time to be in your so-called faint. Just flutter your eyelids a bit like you're seducing Brad Pitt and then let out a bit of a moan.'

Rene smiled, her eyes still tightly shut. 'I'm 'oping those were your 'ands that were getting dangerously close to my cleavage.'

'No such luck, pet. That was Brad Pitt.'

Rene fought hard to suppress a giggle, but it spluttered out nevertheless.

'I said moan, you daft cow, not laugh!'

Rene did as was requested, and with a dazzling flicker of eyelids looked up into the round freckled face of the woman whose purse she had returned. There was such an expression of hilarity in her greeny-grey eyes that Rene had a strong urge to burst out laughing there and then. Not that it would probably have mattered. She realised the woman was now the only person who was paying any attention to her.

'Ye're Lancashire, aren't ye?' Rene said, seeing no reason now to speak in hushed tones. 'I've just worked it out.'

'Aye, and you're Yorkshire . . . or were at one time.' The woman wrinkled up her squat little nose. 'I remembered where I recognised you from. Ye're Rene Brownlow, aren't ye? I've seen yer show.'

Rene raised her eyebrows in astonishment. 'Well, fancy that. Fame at last.'

'You should write that fainting bit into your repertoire,' the woman said, giving Rene's arm a light shove with her hand. 'It was one of the funniest things I've seen in years.'

'I thought it was quite convincing,' Rene replied, feigning pique.

'Well, if you're ever thinking about getting a bit part in *ER,* you'd have to improve on that performance.'

Rene grinned at the woman. 'Thanks for stepping in just then. I thought my cover was blown.'

The woman shrugged. 'One good turn deserves another. Anyway, us comediennes had better stick together, isn't that right?'

'Oh my word, is that what ye do too?'

'Aye, every day, every night.' The woman stuck out her hand. 'Matti Fullbright.'

Rene took the hand and shook it. ''Ullo, Matti Fullbright. Listen, while ye've got an 'old of me 'and, d'ye think you could 'eave me back up on to me pins?'

'Aye, sure, but you'd better make it look as if you're still a bit unsteady, just for authenticity's sake, OK?'

Rene accomplished the upward movement and held hard to Matti's hand as she weaved her body round once more.

'Right, you can stop that now,' Matti said, glancing around her. 'No one's taking a blind bit of notice. Listen, how d'ye fancy a nice cup of tea?'

Rene flicked her head to the side. 'I'd really like that, lass, but I think I'd better get back to me flat. I've got to make sure of a few things.'

'Like if your young friend made it back there with the suit-case and violin?'

Rene smiled. 'My, what intuition you 'ave, Matti Fullbright.'

'Can I ask what the hell all that was about?'

Rene bent down and picked up her handbag. 'I can't tell you right now, but believe me, we were both doing someone a good turn.'

'Aye, I'm sure you were,' Matti replied. 'I didn't like the look of that man from the moment he came into the hotel. He gave me the once-over as he walked past, and from the expression on his face ye'd think he'd just stepped in a bloody great dog's mess. Took every ounce of my female gentility not to give him the finger.' She took hold of Rene's arm. 'Come on, let's get out of here. We'll go out the front, so it don't look as if we're following in the path of the suitcase snatcher.' As they began to climb the stairs, Matti stopped and turned round. 'Who'd give a damn anyway?' she said, surveying the people who criss-crossed the reception area. She shook her crazy mop of red hair. 'Typical, in't it? Ten minutes ago you were the centre of attention, and now not one person's paying you the blindest bit of notice.'

Rene shrugged. 'That's an entertainer's life for you.'

They turned and made their way up the staircase, both unaware that the person with the dark-rimmed spectacles and the belted mackintosh, who had been sitting out of sight on the other side of the staircase, had paid a great deal of notice to everything that had passed between them during the previous five minutes.

Halfway across Festival Square, Rene stopped and looked back at the imposing frontage of the hotel. 'So what were *you* doing in that place? A bit posh for the likes of us, in't it?'

'I had a meeting with my agent.'

Rene looked suitably impressed. 'Really? My word, you must be at the top of the game.'

Matti stuck her hand into her blue canvas tote bag, pulled out a leaflet and handed it to Rene. 'Come and see the show sometime. I'll make sure it's a freebie, all right?'

Rene glanced at the leaflet. ''Eaven's sakes, you're on at the Smirnoff Underbelly!' she said in astonishment. 'That's one of the top venues, in't it?'

Matti shrugged her shoulders. 'Well, I've been lucky. I was there last year and they asked me to come back.'

'You must be damned good, then.'

Matti reached out and squeezed Rene's arm. 'Come and see for yourself.'

'I will,' she replied, pushing the leaflet into her handbag, 'and thanks again, lass, for yer help back there.'

'And likewise, thanks for my purse. See you around, I hope.'

And as Matti Fullbright strode off across the square, Rene let out a long, satisfied breath as she watched her go, realising that her lonely existence in Edinburgh had taken a change for the better over the past hour or two. Jamie had *needed* her confidentiality and help that morning, and she liked nothing better than to feel *needed,* to take over, step into the fray, just like when that singer never turned up at Andersons Westbourne Social Club and she took to the stage for the first time. And then in meeting Matti Fullbright, with her peculiar zany looks and wild sense of humour, Rene realised that, for the first time ever, she had come across a person who was *just like her.*

She smiled to herself as she saw Matti disappear out of sight. 'Aye, see you around,' she murmured.

Thirty-Two

Albert Dessuin flicked back the net curtain of his newly designated bedroom, situated now on the fourth floor of the hotel but still with the same wide panoramic view over Festival Square. Even through the diffusion of the curtain, it had been easy enough to single out the bumbling little figure with the loose-fitting multicoloured coat that threaded its way through the crowds and then turned down Lothian Road towards Princes Street. Letting go of the curtain, he took off his mackintosh and threw it on to a chair. He was not unduly worried by the way things had turned out. In fact, they could not have turned out much better.

This was contrary to the blisteringly angry mood he had been in when he had arrived back at the hotel an hour earlier. Whilst returning from the airport in the taxi, he had had time to mull over all the facts leading up to Angélique's disappearance, and it had slowly begun to dawn on him that, from the start, she had been playing him along in a cruel and calculated game of deception, making him feel wretched and guilty for something that had never been his fault in the first place. She had orchestrated the whole affair, displaying her naked body in front of him like that, knowing that he had already admonished her for her sluttish behaviour. His reaction of fury was totally natural, one that came from a deep sense of protection for his protégée, but she had twisted his motives, using them as the very reason for which to walk away from him, from everything that he, Albert Dessuin, had bestowed upon her. And this story about her having cut her hand and returning to France was just another way in which she was trying to manipulate him, to put him off the scent and literally to blackmail him into keeping away from her by not disclosing the full story, which they both knew to be nothing more than a harmless row between them. Well, she had made a grave mistake. She certainly would not get rid of him that easily.

There was no chance of him ever being able to recognise the young man who took the suitcase and the violin, save for the fact that he had blond hair and was stockily built. He was undoubt-edly one of those who had clustered around Angélique with their tongues hanging out at the post-concert reception, their eyes fixed on the glories that lay beneath her short dress as she sat on the bar, shamelessly crossing and uncrossing her legs. But then his instincts had been right about that red-haired girl. He had seen her the moment he had walked into the reception area on his return from the airport. She had been sitting on one of the sofas lining the walls of the hotel lobby, talking across a low coffee table to a dark-haired woman dressed in a sombre pencil-skirted suit worn over a cream cashmere polo-neck sweater. Beauty and the Beast, he had thought to himself. He did not like red-haired girls. He had always thought them the unattrac-tive product of recessive genes, and this one in particular had not one redeeming feature to speak of, with her wide-set eyes, her moon face and a nose which made her look as if she had walked at speed into a plate-glass window. And her dress sense had been almost offensive to the eye. Why would anyone choose to wear a pink scarf with hair that colour?

He knew she had never before laid eyes on the fat little woman who had foiled his pursuit of the young man. That's why he had decided to hang around, out of sight but within earshot, after the mêlée had died down. He hadn't been able to decipher everything they had said to each other in their brogueish accents, but he had understood enough and had heard every derogatory word she had had to say about him.

He walked over to the bed and picked up the thick copy of the Fringe show guide that he'd found on the display stand next to the reception desk. He opened it up at the index and ran a manicured fingernail down the first column, and then the second. He found what he was looking for halfway down. He memorised the venue reference number and leafed through the guide until he came to the correct page. 'Hilarious Comedienne from Hartlepool' was the strapline above the photograph of the woman whose face he had first seen as she lay flat out on the carpeted floor of the hotel lobby. *Mon Dieu,* she must be bad, he thought to himself, if she can come up with no better advertisement for her act than that!

Creasing the guide open at the page, he spun it on to the desk and walked over to the minibar and took out a miniature of Scotch and a bottle of mineral water. It was really too early to start drinking, but what the hell! His plans had changed now. There was no reason for him to go off immediately in search of Angélique Pascal. He would take his time, let the heat die down. After all, the show was on every night in the Corinthian Bar.

Pouring himself a drink, he let out a short quiet laugh and raised his glass. 'Here's to you, Rene Brownlow. I'm sure in time you will prove very useful to me.'

Thirty-Three

Desperate to get away from the vicinity of the hotel as quickly as possible, Jamie had bundled himself and Angélique's luggage into a passing taxi and slumped down into the seat beneath the level of the rear window, expecting to hear at any moment the ominous sound of a police siren threading its way through the traffic towards them. He was actually quite amazed he had got this far. Because of Rene's extraordinary outburst in the hotel, he knew that Dessuin had caught sight of him before he had even left the place. Under normal circumstances, he was sure he could have outpaced the man quite easily, but burdened with the suitcase and violin, he thought he would have had the Frenchman breathing down his neck before he'd even reached the street. Maybe Rene had managed to set up some kind of diversion, but he couldn't imagine how. There had only been a moment for her to react.

By the time the taxi dropped him outside his flat, Jamie was beginning to have serious concerns about the comedienne's welfare, realising now that it had been both unwise and unfair to have involved her to such an extent. It would have been pretty obvious to anyone with half a brain in the hotel foyer that her coming over all faint at the very moment when he was making a run for it with the suitcases was more than coincidental, and he was convinced she would now be closeted in some back office at the hotel being interviewed not only by the police, but by a very interested Albert Dessuin as well. And if that was the case, then not only would she be forced to identify Jamie as the 'mastermind' behind the bag snatch, but also Angélique's where-abouts as well.

Having paid off the taxi, he let himself in through the entrance door and ran up the stairs, his heart in his mouth as he tried to work out his next move. Maybe he should ring Gavin straight-away and tell him what had happened. At least then, if the police did come to arrest him, Gavin would have had time to prepare some sort of defence for him and get him out on bail. He wasn't too sure what police procedure would be. Or maybe he should hang fire for twenty minutes or so, just in case Rene came back by herself.

He entered the flat and hurried over to the telephone. He

couldn't risk waiting for Rene. He picked up the receiver and began to dial the number of Gavin's law firm, but just before he hit the fourth digit he stopped, his finger poised in mid-air, and stood listening to the low reverberation of voices coming from the sitting room. He slowly replaced the receiver as he heard Angélique speaking a long, drawn-out sentence before it was answered by the lower and much more resonant tones of a male voice. Jamie exhaled with relief, realising it could only be his solicitor, and he walked quickly along the hall passage to the door of the sitting room and threw it open.

'Gavin, thank goodness you're—'

Angélique and a heavily built middle-aged man in a gabardine raincoat were sitting on one of the sofas, their mouths frozen in mid-conversation as both looked round in surprise at his sudden entry, the man's ballpoint pen still hovering above a spiral notepad.

'What's going on?' Jamie demanded, his eyes ablaze with both concern and distrust for the man. 'Who are you?'

Angélique quickly uncurled her feet from underneath her and stood up. 'It's all right, Jamie. This is Harry Wills. He is a journalist who is an acquaintance of mine. It was he—'

Jamie shook his head, never taking his eyes off the man. 'I told you not to let anyone into the flat. What the hell's the point of me trying to hide you away if you allow any Tom, Dick or Harry into the place?'

He knew as soon as he had said it, it was the wrong metaphor to use. Angélique frowned at him and unwittingly capitalised on it. 'Who is Tom and Dick?'

'This is not a joke, Angélique.'

Harry Wills flipped over his notebook and stood up. 'I'm sorry, this is my fault. You're absolutely right. I should never have come round without giving you both some warning.'

'How did you find out she was here, anyway?' Jamie asked abruptly.

'If you will just listen to me for a moment, Jamie, I shall tell you,' Angélique said, her voice rising in frustration at his hostile attitude. 'It was Harry who wrote the story about me having cut my hand and leaving the country. I suggested his name to Gavin, and they both met to work out what should be written in the newspapers. Harry knows what has happened, Jamie. He is helping us, along with Gavin.'

The explanation did little to lighten the thunderous expression on Jamie's face as he glanced from one to the other. 'Well, that's just great. Maybe it would have been an idea to let *me* know about all this as well.'

Angélique bit at her bottom lip in an effort to stop smiling at his moody reaction. She walked over to him and gave the sleeve of his corduroy jacket a tug. 'I am very sorry. It was very bad of me not to tell you, and I promise I will not overlook such a thing again.'

'I'm being quite serious, actually,' Jamie mumbled.

Angélique pulled a long face, stood to attention and gave him a brisk salute. 'I quite agree, and I am now taking it very seriously, don't you think?'

Jamie smiled reluctantly. 'Oh, get lost,' he said, waving a hand in the general direction of the hall. 'Your suitcase and violin are out there.'

'*Oh, ce n'est pas vrai!*' Angélique exclaimed. She jumped forward and gave him a quick peck on the cheek before rushing out into the hall.

Jamie turned to the journalist when she had left the room. 'Sorry about the misunderstanding.'

Harry Wills waved his notebook dismissively. 'No bother. Anyway, you were quite right to question my presence here. You're obviously doing a good job of looking after her.'

Jamie shrugged off the compliment. 'Were you doing an interview?' he asked, nodding towards the notebook.

'Not about immediate events, I can assure you, and anyway, nothing will get printed until this whole situation has rectified itself.'

'Well, we've a long way to go before that happens,' Jamie murmured ruefully.

'What makes you say that?'

Jamie pushed his hands into the pockets of his jacket and took a backward step to glance along the hall, just in time to see Angélique beam him a broad smile as she disappeared into her bedroom with the suitcase and violin. He closed the door of the sitting room with a shove of his foot and turned to the journalist. 'Listen, Dessuin's figured out that the story about Angélique returning to France is untrue. He knows she's still in Edinburgh, and by now he could very well know she's here in this flat.'

Harry Wills's expression showed immediate concern. 'Why do you think that?'

'Because I've just seen him booking himself back into the Sheraton Grand. What's more, he saw me, or at least the back of me, when I took Angélique's cases.'

'You took the cases from in front of his eyes?' the journalist asked incredulously.

'No, they were actually sitting behind him. I reckon I would have got away with it, only . . . well, let's just say he turned round at the wrong time.'

'But he didn't follow you?'

'No, for definite.'

'Then what gives you reason to believe he might find his way round here?'

Jamie told him briefly of Rene's involvement in the suitcase snatch and his uncertainty as to what had happened to her. When he had finished, Harry Wills stood in silence, slapping his notebook rhythmically against the side of his raincoat.

'Well,' he said eventually, 'this poses a bit of a problem for us all, doesn't it?'

Jamie felt almost angry at this ridiculous understatement of facts. 'Of course it poses a problem – especially for me! I could well get arrested for what I've just done.'

Harry waved a hand at him. 'I don't think you need worry about anything like that happening. If the worst comes to the worst, then we'll tell the true story. Remember the only reason we're in this situation is because Angélique wanted to protect

Dessuin's name. My instinct tells me the man will do his utmost to avoid involving the police, just for that very reason.'

Jamie stood for a moment considering the journalist's logic before breathing out a sigh of relief. 'Yeah, that would make sense, wouldn't it?' He clicked his fingers as a thought came into his head. 'But wait, we're forgetting about Rene. If Dessuin knows she was helping me, then he'll surely find out from her where I'm living, or even if he *doesn't* question her, he could still just follow her around here.'

'Would there be any reason for Dessuin to think she *might* have been helping you?'

Jamie blew out a derisive laugh. 'God, yes! She would have been as well having a notice hanging round her neck saying, "*Hey, look at me! I am the thief's number-one accomplice*"!'

While Harry looked thoughtful over this new predicament, Jamie heard Angélique in her bedroom play a cautious scale on her violin. Although the notes were clear and resonant, the speed at which she played them seemed falteringly pedestrian. Nevertheless, Jamie knew it was a major achievement and a boost to the violinist's shattered confidence, and if he hadn't been so concerned with the seriousness of the situation, he might well have felt like letting out a whoop of triumph there and then.

'Is there anyplace you and Angélique could lie low for a couple of days?' the journalist asked.

'Here in Edinburgh, d'you mean?'

'No, preferably away from the city.'

Jamie looked dubious. 'I'm not sure. I'm meant to be writing Fringe reviews, but I suppose I could get out of that. What about my tenants, though?'

'Hopefully, it would only be for a few days. I'm sure they could fend for themselves during that time.' He paused, seeing Jamie still vacillate over making a decision. 'I'd strongly recommend the idea.'

Jamie shrugged his shoulders. 'In that case, I suppose we could go to my parents' place in East Lothian.'

'That will be good,' Harry said, nodding his approval of the idea, 'and then while you're away, I'll stick myself outside your flat and keep an eye out for Dessuin turning up here.'

'Really? Would you mind doing that?'

Harry laughed. 'I was an investigative journalist for a good number of years, Jamie, so I'm quite used to spending many a lonely hour sitting in my car outside people's houses.'

Jamie stared at the man for a moment. 'Can I ask you a question?'

'Shoot,' Harry replied.

'Why are you willing to give us so much help? Surely, with the festival on, you've got a hundred better things to be doing with your time?'

Harry sat his sizeable bottom down on the arm of a sofa. 'Quite simply because I have absolutely no time for Albert Dessuin. He happens to be one of the most discourteous human beings I've ever had the displeasure of meeting.'

'You *know* him?'

'Let's just say there have been numerous occasions over the past few years when I've been party to the more unpleasant side of his nature. Ever since Angélique Pascal left the Conservatoire in Paris, I have been trying my damnedest to get a personal interview with her and Dessuin has always been there to thwart my attempts.' He clicked the top on his ballpoint pen. 'Does that answer your question?'

'Yes, I suppose it does,' Jamie replied with a smile.

'OK, so what I suggest is that if there's been neither sight nor sound of the man over the next few days, then I'll give the all-clear for you both to return to the flat. Do you have a number I could contact you on?'

Jamie reeled off the number of his mobile and the journalist wrote it down before slipping his pad into his coat pocket and getting to his feet. 'Right, you and Angélique should get yourselves ready to go as soon as possible.'

'Which brings us to another problem,' Jamie said tentatively. 'I don't have wheels.'

Harry pushed back the folds of his raincoat and delved into

a trouser pocket. 'In that case,' he said, taking out his own mobile phone, 'I think it's time we involved Gavin Mackintosh.'

The sound of the front door slamming shut had both men looking questioningly at each other. Jamie walked over to the sitting-room door, opened it a fraction and squinted down the hall. 'Oh, hell! It could be too late!' he exclaimed quietly, glancing round at Harry. 'It's Rene.' He opened the door fully to see the comedienne stagger exhaustedly along the passage towards him.

'Glad to see ye made it back,' she said, taking off her coat as she walked past him into the sitting room and dumping it, along with her handbag, on to a chair. She gave a quick nod of greeting to Harry Wills before flopping herself down on to a sofa and kicking off her shoes. 'I am absolutely dead beat,' she puffed out, awkwardly pulling a stockinged foot up across her knee and giving it a rub. 'That's far too much excitement for one day.' She glanced up at Jamie and Harry, who had now come to stand side by side in front of the fireplace, observing her closely, trying to work out from her demeanour whether they had an imminent problem to face. 'So, aren't you going to introduce me to yer friend, Jamie?'

'Oh, yeah, sorry; this is Harry Wills.'

'Nice to meet ye, 'Arry,' Rene said, holding out the hand with which she had been rubbing at her foot. She then thought better of it and just waved it at him. 'Let's just forgo that formality.'

'Rene, what happened?' Jamie asked, eager to ply her for information. 'Why didn't Dessuin come after me?'

'Because I set up a diversion, just like ye asked me.'

'How?'

'I pretended to faint right in 'is path.'

Jamie pulled his hands across his head in desperation. 'Oh, God. What did he do?'

'He gave me a kick in the ribs, and then flew through the air and fell with a thump to the floor.'

'OK, but what happened then? Were the police called? Were you questioned at all?'

Rene closed her eyes tight as if in deep concentration. 'I think the answer to that is, nothing, no, no,' she replied before resuming her foot massage. 'It was all a bit odd, really. I was lying on the floor with me eyes closed, pretending to be out for the count, when some girl – I think it was probably the receptionist – asked if she should call the police, and the Frenchman went all sort of panicky and said he didn't want them involved. He said he knew who ye were and 'e'd sort it all out later.'

Jamie frowned apprehensively at the journalist, who answered it immediately with a dismissive shake of his head.

'That's exactly what I thought he'd do,' Harry said, 'and he was just bluffing when he said he knew you, so don't worry about it.'

Jamie turned his attention back to Rene. 'But he must have known you were helping me. Weren't you asked any questions at all?'

'No. Mind you, I've little doubt I would 'ave been, if it 'adn't been for this girl coming to my rescue.'

'How?' both Jamie and Harry asked in unison.

'Well, when I was still flat out on the floor, the Frenchman asked, in a sort of general way, whether anybody knew me, and this girl said she did and that I was a friend of 'ers, and we were going to have a cup of tea together when I'd come over all faint.'

'And Dessuin believed her?' Harry asked.

'I'm certain of it. 'E just stormed away after that, probably went straight up to 'is room.'

Harry and Jamie glanced at each other, relief written on their faces.

'So, there's absolutely no chance Dessuin could have followed you back here?' Jamie asked.

'Why would 'e want to do that? The girl made it pretty clear I was just an innocent bystander. Anyway, I had to stop off in a pub on the way back to go to the loo, and when I came out I certainly didn't see anyone lurking about.' She let go of her foot and stood up. 'Now, unless you've got some more furtive action planned, I think I might just get back to my normal pace of life.'

Jamie approached the comedienne and planted a kiss on her

268

hot round cheek. 'Thanks, Rene, for being a real star. I could have ended up in deep shit if it hadn't been for you.'

Rene smiled at him. 'Glad to be of assistance,' she said, moving off towards the door. 'Just don't expect me to do it every day, right? Otherwise I'll 'ave to be charging ye the full union rates for a thief's assistant.'

When she had left the room, Jamie turned round to the journalist. 'Looks like we're in the clear, then,' he remarked hopefully.

'We might be,' Harry replied with a reserved flick of the head.

'You don't think so?'

'Let's just say Dessuin is no fool. He's now back in Edinburgh on a mission, and as yet he has no leads. He doesn't want to involve the police and he certainly won't want to involve the International office, so I reckon he'll be looking to grasp on to any small oddity or coincidence. Maybe Rene and her friend did manage to convince everyone in the hotel with their act, but it just could be that Dessuin saw it all as being a bit suspect.'

'So what are you saying? That he could be standing outside the flat right now?'

'No, I'm pretty sure Rene was right in saying she wasn't followed here. However, we don't want to give Dessuin any opportunity to be doing clever things behind our backs, so I think we should still continue with the plan for you and Angélique to leave Edinburgh. If he doesn't show up here over the next two days, I reckon then, and only then, we can probably say we're in the clear.' He thumbed a couple of buttons on his mobile phone. 'OK, so let's see now if we can't get hold of Gavin Mackintosh.'

Thirty-Four

Leonard Hartson had a smile on his face as he climbed the steps to the entrance of the London Street flat. It had been there ever since T.K. had appeared out of the small barber's shop next to The Jeans Warehouse on Princes Street, where, on his own insistence, he had had his greasy mane reduced to a very presentable and very clean fuzz of hair. It had had the immediate effect of not only transforming his features, but some of his more unsavoury characteristics as well as if, in its cutting, T.K. had rid his body of some virulent, energy-sapping, brain-numbing amoeba. His vacant eyes now looked alert, his pallid cheeks flushed with colour (although Leonard knew that that was initially due to T.K.'s embarrassment at his new look), and there was even a determined rigidity to his loose-lipped mouth. But the most extraordinary by-product of the barber's clippers had been to unlock the floodgates on a verbosity Leonard would never before have thought to exist in the lad's slow-witted head.

With the shopping bags bearing his new purchases gathered round his feet in the taxi, T.K. had questioned Leonard incessantly on all aspects of film-making, hardly waiting for a reply before he was on to the next query. Even now, while Leonard extracted the keys of the door from his jacket pocket, T.K. stood beside him eager to find out how long it had taken Leonard to be considered proficient enough to operate a camera. While the cameraman paused in his action of putting the key in the lock, casting his mind back over countless years in an attempt to come up with an accurate answer, the entrance door flew open and his young landlord appeared, shouldering a rucksack. His presence had the immediate effect of cutting off T.K.'s verbal assault, which Leonard greeted with a clandestine sigh of relief, likening it to that first brief moment of silence after a plug has been pulled on a blaring radio.

'I'm glad I've caught you, Mr Hartson,' Jamie said, as he came down on to the steps, his eyes momentarily glancing with astonishment at T.K.'s incongruous new hairstyle. 'I have to head off for a couple of days, so just use the flat as your own. I've left my mobile number on the hall table if you need to contact me for any reason.'

Leonard was about to speak when Gavin Mackintosh, the solicitor who had introduced him to T.K., appeared at the entrance door carrying a canvas zip-up overnight bag and a violin case. 'Ah, Mr Hartson, I do hope everything's going well for you both,' he said, before catching sight of T.K. and almost doing a double take. 'My word, Thomas! You've changed into a dapper-looking fellow. Well done, you!' He gave T.K. a pat on the arm before hurrying off down the steps. He was closely followed by a young girl who had appeared through the door wearing a short jacket with the collar turned up and a large pair of sunglasses that obscured her features. Gavin opened the back passenger door of a Volvo estate car and waited for the girl to get in before walking around to the back to put her luggage in the boot.

While this furtive operation was in progress, Leonard noticed Jamie casting searching glances up and down the street. 'Right,' he said, making a move to join them once the man was seated behind the driving wheel. 'I'll see you when I get back.'

'Could I just have a moment of your time?' Leonard asked quickly, realising there seemed to be a degree of urgency in their departure.

Jamie paused on the bottom step. 'Sure,' he replied, turning.

'I had hoped to get the chance to explain this in more detail, but I do see you're pressed for time, so I'll be as brief as possible. It's just that T.K. here has unfortunately found himself to be temporarily without lodgings, and I wondered, therefore, if you might have any objections to him making use of the other bed in my room.'

Jamie bit on his bottom lip to stop himself from laughing at such an absurd idea. He immediately had this mental vision of them both tucked up in the two beds gazing into the darkness whilst they indulged themselves in a bit of Deep Meaningful Conversation.

'Yeah, that's fine by me.'

'Of course, it goes without saying that I shall pay a bit more for the rent of the room.'

'Oh, don't bother about that,' Jamie replied, dismissing the suggestion with a shake of his head.

'No, I insist. What would you say to eighty pounds per night for the both of us?'

'Seventy-five,' Jamie said in reply as he made his way to the pavement and opened the front passenger door of the Volvo. He dumped his rucksack into the footwell and glanced back at the two roommates. 'That's my final offer.'

Leonard smiled at him. 'That's very kind. Thank you.'

'Ring me if you have any problems,' Jamie called out as he got into the car, which began to move out into the street before he had even time to shut the door.

Leonard turned and raised an eyebrow at his crop-haired assistant. 'Well, looks like we're in business then.'

While T.K. went off to have his much needed shower, Leonard made use of the telephone in the hall to speak with Nick Springer in London, telling him of the progress he had made during the initial day's shooting and giving him the name of the courier service that would be delivering the exposed film stock to his office the following morning. Although Nick sounded pleased to hear from him, Leonard could sense from the producer's lack of reciprocative chat that he had caught him at a busy time, so he kept the call short. He then rang Grace and gave her a more in-depth account of what had passed that day, including news of the unavoidable, but somewhat irregular, sleeping arrangement he now had with his young assistant, T.K. He did not, however, mention to his wife the facts that led to this happening, knowing that it would only perturb her to hear he had taken a young vagrant off the streets, simply giving the reason that T.K. lived too far away for him to travel to work every day. Neither did he mention to her the doubts he had harboured earlier in the day about taking on both such a physical and financial burden at his advanced stage in life, and he certainly was not going to tell her about the pain that had begun to nag intermittently at the left side of his chest. Nevertheless, as if by telepathy, while he now pressed a hand to the troublesome area, Grace told him that he was not to overdo it and asked him if he was remembering to take his pills. 'Of course I am, my dear,' he replied. 'Don't worry about me, I'm quite capable of looking after myself.'

When he replaced the receiver after the call, Leonard turned to find a young man standing in front of him whom he hardly recognised. His own expression must have been enough to convey this because T.K.'s face immediately broke into a broad grin.

'What d'ya think, then?' he said, his arms outstretched as he gave himself the once-over.

Leonard nodded approvingly as he appraised the new-look T.K., with his clean white T-shirt, stiff new Levi's tightened at the waist by a wide belt with a Harley Davidson buckle, and the virginal-white pair of Adidas trainers. Slung over his shoulder, a finger through its hanging loop, was the new Timberland jacket at which T.K. had gawped longingly in the shop while Leonard was paying the bill for two identical pairs of jeans, six white T-shirts, a four-pack of boxer shorts and a six-pack of white socks, one cotton sweatshirt, one belt, and a pair of Adidas trainers. 'And I think we'd better take that jacket as well,' Leonard had said quietly to the shop assistant.

'Well?' T.K. asked again.

'I think you look very . . . clean.'

'Is that a'?' T.K. exclaimed.

Leonard laughed. 'No, I really am very impressed, T.K.'

T.K. smirked bashfully. 'Cheers, Leonard.'

'And I think it's only right that we should celebrate your new and much improved appearance by searching out a suitable eating establishment that can provide us with some well-earned sustenance.'

'Eh?' T.K. remarked, reverting too easily to his imbecilic look, his mouth curled up at one side.

'How would a very large beef steak and a glass of beer suit you?'

'Oh, aye, tha' sounds great,' T.K. replied enthusiastically, his face brightening with comprehension. He swung the new jacket off his shoulder and shrugged it on.

A door opening at the far end of the hall made them both turn, and their fellow tenant appeared, her attention caught up with trying to find something in her large handbag. Rene looked up and saw them.

'My word!' she said, her eyes fixed on T.K. as she came along the passage. 'What 'appened to you? Did ye fall in front of a street cleaner or summat?'

Leonard held out a hand as she approached them. 'We've met in passing, but not yet introduced ourselves. My name's Leonard Hartson.'

Rene shook his hand. 'Nice to meet you, Leonard. Rene Brownlow.'

'Are you just on your way out?'

'Aye, I am.'

'In that case, you wouldn't care to join us for something to eat? T.K. and I were just going out to celebrate a very successful day's work.'

Rene sucked her teeth disappointedly. 'Oh, what a grand thought, but I can't, luv. I've got to do a show in 'alf an 'our. Maybe another time.'

Leonard opened the front door and stood aside to allow her to leave the flat first. 'Well, consider it a firm invitation then.'

'I'll tell you what, though,' Rene said as she walked past him. 'Seeing as Jamie's gone and left the lot of us 'ome alone, what about me cooking us all a meal tomorrow night? Wouldn't be until after me show, but if about nine o'clock would suit?'

Leonard glanced at T.K., who answered with a shrug of non-commitment. 'Well, I think that would suit us both very well,' Leonard replied with a nod. 'We shall look forward to it.'

'Right,' the comedienne said as she began to descend the stairs. 'In that case, see you tomorrow night at La Maison de Rene.'

Thirty-Five

During the journey out to East Lothian, what little conversation there was in the car was between the two men in the front, although Jamie would occasionally glance round and ask Angélique if she was all right, sensing she might be feeling somewhat excluded from proceedings. She was not, however, in a great mind to talk. At first, when the car was travelling slowly through the sprawling, colourless suburbs of Edinburgh, her mood had been rock-bottom, the road seemingly taking her further and further away from her previous life, and there was a moment when she wanted to end all this craziness and tell Gavin to turn the car around and take her back to the Sheraton Grand, regardless of the consequences. But then, as the fast dual carriageway left behind the city, her spirits improved as the endless rows of houses and industrial estates gave way to open countryside, and it dawned on her that this was almost the first time since leaving the Conservatoire she had not been viewing a country from thirty-three thousand feet up in the air. Her troubled thoughts and heart-aching doubts subsided as she looked out of the window, shielding her eyes against the glare of the early evening sun that shone gold on the ripe rolling wheat fields and glinted off the bulky bodies of the combine harvesters that cut their laser-straight paths through the crops. And when the car turned off at Haddington and breasted the hill above the village of East Linton, Angélique could not help but let out a quiet breath of wonderment as she looked out across the wide panoramic view of the rugged Lammermuir Hills shouldering in the velvet-green coastline as it bent its way southward, leaving nothing but the endless expanse of the North Sea before it.

Gavin swung the car to the right, curtailing Angélique's enjoyment of the vista, and took a narrow high-banked road that wound its way up towards the hills. They drove through a small village boasting both a pub and a post office but hardly of a size to merit the thirty-mile-an-hour speed limit, and then turned left down a smooth dirt-track road with overgrown verges, past a number of long, low livestock sheds with slatted sides and tidy concrete aprons. A hundred metres on, they entered through a stone-pillared gateway leading on to a gravelled drive bordered by well-tended lawns that were shadowed long by the sprawling limbs of two ancient cypress trees. For a moment they hid from sight the tall white house with steep slated roof and craw-stepped gable ends that stood proudly defensive of a broad circular sweep.

As Gavin brought the Volvo to a scrunching halt in front of the house, a couple of black-and-white sheepdogs appeared from nowhere, made a beeline for the car and started biting ineffectually at the front tyres with bared snarling teeth. Jamie immediately opened the door and gave them a yell as he got out, but it did little to stop their attempted mauling of the car. It was only when a voice like thunder rang out around the grounds, so loud it echoed off the side of the house, that the dogs ceased their endeavours and slunk off to lie side by side on the lawn, their eyes fixed on the quad bike that came at a breakneck speed up the drive. Angélique got out and stood gazing at her new surroundings as the bike swung round at the back of the Volvo, spurting up gravel that landed dangerously short of the car's gleaming paintwork.

'Hey, quit that, Stratton!' Gavin shouted angrily as he jumped out and stomped round the back of the car to inspect it. 'If there's so much of a scratch, I'll have you foot the bill for a complete respray.'

Angélique smiled at the grinning man who sat astride the mud-spattered quad. He was dressed in a heavy cotton lumberjack shirt and waterproof trousers pulled over wellington boots, a battered baseball cap jammed back to front on his head. He put a dirt-ingrained hand up to his ear and delicately dislodged an earphone. The thumping beat that emanated from it was so loud that Angélique could hear it quite clearly from where she was standing. 'I'm sorry,' the man said, looking at Gavin with a bemused expression on his tanned weather-beaten face. 'I didn't quite catch that. Did you say anything of interest just then, Mackintosh?'

'God, he's such a lad,' Angélique heard Jamie mutter as he came to stand beside her. He raised a long-suffering eyebrow at her. 'Come on, I'll introduce you to my father.'

They walked over to where the two men were already engaged in a friendly but sparring banter.

'Dad, this is Angélique Pascal.'

The man swung a leg over the handlebars of the bike. 'Good to meet you, Angélique,' he said, taking her by surprise by flipping off his cap and landing a bristly kiss on both her cheeks. 'I understand you're a bit of a violinist.'

'A bit of a violinist!' Gavin exclaimed. 'God, you really are an uneducated heathen, Stratton.'

'Not at all,' Rory laughed, encircling his son's shoulders with a pair of wiry arms and giving him a welcoming hug. 'Just because our tastes in music differ somewhat.' Moving over to the car he opened up the boot, and took out Angélique's bag and her violin case. 'Come on, then,' he said, heading off towards the house, 'I reckon it must be time for a drink.'

'Count me out, Rory,' Gavin said, closing the boot. 'I have to be getting back to Edinburgh.'

Jamie's father turned, a disappointed frown on his face. 'Not even a quick one?'

'Can't do, I'm afraid. I have a mountain of work to get through in the office before I call it a day.'

'Oh, how deadly boring of you.'

Gavin smiled at his old school friend. 'Maybe another time, but give my love to Prue and tell her I'm sorry to have missed her. I'll call you about golf, as well.' He waved to Angélique as she followed Rory towards the house before turning back to Jamie. 'How have you left things with Harry Wills?'

277

'He's going to call me in a couple of days' time if all's well.'

'And you can make your own way back?'

Jamie nodded. 'I'm sure I can persuade Dad to give us a lift.'

'Right, well, give me a call if you need anything.'

'Will do, and cheers, Gavin, for bringing us out here.'

'My pleasure,' the solicitor said as he got into the car. 'Let's hope this whole business has resolved itself by the time you get back.'

'Yeah, let's hope,' Jamie replied, giving him a wave of farewell as he turned towards the house.

The large, ornately furnished sitting room was warmed by the dusty rays of the setting sun streaming in through the three west-facing windows. When Jamie entered he found his father standing in jeans and stockinged feet in front of the unlit fire, a large glass of whisky in his hand.

'Where's Angélique?' Jamie asked.

'Your mother's showing her to her bedroom.' Rory took a healthy swallow of whisky and cocked his head to the side. 'Nice-looking girl, that.'

'Yes, she is,' Jamie replied indifferently, walking over to the drinks table and removing the ring pull from a can of beer.

'*Very* nice-looking, in fact,' Rory continued, a smile on his face as he eyed his son.

Jamie shook his head. 'Leave it out, Dad.'

Rory laughed. 'Just a bit of a leg-pull.' He sat down heavily in one of the pale-blue loose-covered armchairs. 'Oh, by the way, I bumped into Gordon McLaren in Dunbar today and told him you were coming out for a couple of days. He said there's a pre-season warm-up game tomorrow evening at the club if you wanted to play.'

Jamie shrugged. 'I suppose I could. I'm not that fit, though.'

'Do you some good, then, wouldn't it? Give him a call, anyway, and in the meantime you can start your fitness training early tomorrow morning by going up on to the hill and looking round the sheep for me. I've got some lambs going through the ring at Kelso, so I won't be able to do it.'

'Thanks for that, Dad,' Jamie replied morosely.

'Well, seeing you're home, you may as well do some work! Anyway, it's not that much of a slog. You'll be able to get the quad as far as the gate above the high burn and then walk from there. You should take Angélique with you, as well. I'm sure she'd appreciate a taste of the Scottish wilderness.'

The door of the sitting room opened and Angélique entered with a small blonde woman dressed in a long denim skirt and white cotton shirt. Her face lit up when she saw Jamie and she came over to him, her arms outstretched. 'Darling, how are you?' she said, giving him a kiss on either cheek that left traces of her pale-pink lipstick.

'I'm good, Mum,' Jamie replied with a smile, 'except Dad's giving me grief as usual.'

Jamie's mother looked over at her husband, her expression turning to one of horror. 'Rory!' She hurried over to where he was sitting and delivered a resounding thwack to one of his knees. 'I'll give *you* grief, you dreadful man. Get out of that chair!' Rory leaped to his feet as if suddenly finding himself sitting on hot coals, and Jamie's mother dusted off the vacated seat with her hand. 'How many times do I have to tell you *not* to sit on these new loose covers in your filthy jeans?'

Rory twisted himself round to inspect his backside. 'They are *not* filthy. They were clean on this morning. Anyway, I've been wearing overtrousers all day.'

'That's as may be,' Jamie's mother said, puffing up the flattened cushions, 'but you still stink like an old tup.'

Rory pulled a schoolboy face at Angélique that made her smile unwittingly. 'I hope you've been treated a bit better by my wife.'

'Prue could not have been kinder to me,' Angélique replied.

'Just you wait. After two days in this house you'll be bossed around like the rest of us.'

'Oh, you do talk such rubbish!' Prue scoffed, taking hold of his arm. 'Come on, you old moaner. You can give me a hand to get supper ready.'

'See what I mean,' Rory said over his shoulder as his wife led him to the door. 'Boss, boss, boss.'

'They are very lovely people, your parents,' Angélique said to Jamie when they were alone in the room.

'Yeah, they're good. I wonder sometimes how she puts up with him, though. He's incorrigible.'

'They are very happy, I think. A good mixture.'

'Probably. Talking of mixtures, what can I get you to drink?'

'Just a Coke, if you have one.'

While Jamie searched the drinks tray, Angélique walked around the room, running her fingers lightly over the furniture. 'I love your house, Jamie. It is filled with so many old things.'

Jamie clinked ice into a tall glass and poured in the contents of the can. 'Well, everything's been here for quite a long time. I think about four or five generations of Strattons have lived with this furniture.'

'It reminds me very much of Madame Lafitte's house in Clermont Ferrand.'

'Who's she?'

Angélique traced a finger around the central diamond-shaped pane of glass in a tall veneered display cabinet. 'She is the lady who started me playing the violin. She is very old now, but she is the kindest, most wonderful person I know.' She turned and smiled at Jamie. 'You would like her very much.'

'Is she a relation of yours?' Jamie asked, handing her the glass of Coke.

'No, but I suppose she is as close to me as any of my family. It was Madame Lafitte who paid for me to go to the Conservatoire in Paris.'

'Really? A bit of a fairy godmother, then. How did you come to meet her?'

Angélique walked over to the sofa and sat down. 'My mother worked for her in the house.'

'What did she do, your mother?'

'She was Madame Lafitte's cleaner.'

Jamie was so taken aback by this revelation, he could not help but stare aghast at Angélique. 'Oh, I see.'

Angélique smiled at him. 'Your look is very disapproving,

Jamie. Is it because you now learn I am from a very humble background?'

Jamie shook his head. 'Don't be silly. Of course not. Anyway, look at you now, a world-famous concert violinist. That's an incredible achievement for someone . . .'

'Whose mother was a cleaner?' Angélique suggested, a teasing glint in her eyes.

'That was *not* what I was going to say,' Jamie replied, raising his eyebrows. 'Tell me more about Madame Lafitte. Have you seen her recently?'

The light expression on Angélique's face seemed to change immediately to one of deep sadness. 'No, I have not. My schedule has never allowed me the time. She suffered a stroke just before I finished at the Conservatoire and she is now confined to a wheelchair in her house. It is my greatest regret that she has never been able to come to one of my concerts.'

'Are you still in touch with her?'

'Oh, yes, every week I either write to her or speak with her on the telephone. She talks very slowly because of the stroke, but her brain is as sharp as ever, even though she is in her ninetieth year.'

'She sounds a pretty remarkable person.'

Angélique smiled at Jamie. 'That is exactly what she is, and that is why I long to see her again.' She paused, rubbing a finger against the strapping on her hand. 'It was one of the reasons why Albert Dessuin got so angry on that night.'

Jamie nodded understandingly. 'You wanted to go back to France to see her.'

'I did not think it was so much to ask.' She lowered her face to hide the tear that ran down her cheek. 'I just have this very bad feeling that I will not be seeing her again.'

Jamie walked over and sat down on the low kilim-covered stool in front of her. 'Hey, don't think that,' he said, giving her knee a couple of gentle but reassuring thumps with his fist. 'Of course you'll see her again. Sounds to me as if she's strong as an ox.'

Looking up at him, Angélique wiped her cheek with the cuff

281

of her shirt and forced a smile on to her face. 'Why is it, Jamie, that you always manage to say the things I most want to hear?'

'Well, maybe because . . .' His forehead creased in thought. '. . . no, sorry, I've no idea.'

Angélique snuffled out a laugh. 'I think it is because inside that tough exterior of a rugby player you are covering up the heart of a *romantique*.'

'Oh yeah?' Jamie said with a quizzically distasteful look. 'That sounds just like me.'

'Hah, you are not prepared to admit it, are you? I think you are very fortunate to have such a perfect balance in you. For me, playing a violin is not just a physical process. I cannot rely on my hands alone. I must use every bit of my soul to understand the emotions that a composer has written into a piece, and sometimes I must make my violin take me to a . . . a different level of maturity and understanding to achieve the balance between the emotional and the physical. And when I do achieve it, it is the most beautiful feeling. It is like . . . how do you say it? . . . an "out-of-body" experience?'

Jamie scratched at the back of his head. 'Yeah, I can understand that, but I don't think you can compare it with playing rugby. If I walked out on to a pitch and was confronted by fifteen socking great lads who knew I had "the heart of a romantic", I'd be subjected to an "out-of-body" experience within the first five minutes of the game!'

Angélique shook her head. 'Now I am beginning to see a great similarity between you and your father. You are as incorrigible as he.'

'Maybe,' Jamie laughed. 'By the way, talking about your violin, I heard you playing it this morning.' He pointed to her strapped hand. 'How's it getting on?'

'It is feeling much better. Look' – she leaned back on the sofa and delved into the pocket of her jeans – 'I still have the squash ball.' She began squeezing it in her hand. 'I used it all the way out here in the car.'

'That's good, but you should be trying to increase the pressure a bit more.' He wrapped his hand around hers and gently closed his fist until he could feel the ball flatten against the palm of her hand. 'Is that OK?'

'I don't feel any pain,' Angélique replied.

He opened up her hand and inspected each of her fingers. 'Bruising's almost gone and so has the swelling.' He scowled seriously at her. 'It is my considered opinion, mademoiselle, that you will very shortly be resuming your career as a concert violinist.'

Angélique grinned at him. 'It would never have been possible, *monsieur*, without your wonderfully inventive cure. How can I ever repay you?'

'Don't worry, I shall be sending you an enormous bill which should keep me in squash balls for forty years.'

'In that case, I had better start to play my violin as soon as possible.'

Their faces had been edging closer together during this interchange, so when the door of the sitting room burst open they sprang apart and began to act with unnatural nonchalance.

'Oh, sorry,' Jamie's father said, glancing from one to the other. 'Hope I wasn't interrupting anything important.'

'No,' Jamie replied, leaning back on his hands on the stool, and fixing his father with a challenging stare, daring him to say anything about what he had just witnessed. Rory answered the look with an understanding raising of his eyebrows, a thinly disguised smirk and an almost imperceptible wink at his son.

'Well, in that case,' he said with a brief, subservient bow of his head, 'if you would care to follow me, I shall show you to the kitchen where your evening meal awaits you.'

Thirty-Six

T.K. lay in bed with a contented grin on his face, staring up at the fixed shaft of orange light that shone through the gap in the curtains and cast its funnelled shape on to the bedroom ceiling.

All was quiet except for Leonard's fast, shallow breathing in the bed next to his. He could not believe a room could be so quiet. Back in Pilton Mains, there was always constant movement and the banging of doors outside in the stark, echoing corridor, or raised voices coming through the paper-thin wall that divided his room from the next apartment, or the whine of a police car somewhere on the estate. He moved his feet back and forth over the smooth, clean undersheet, feeling the weighty warmth of the duvet moulding itself around his body. He slowly pressed three fingers, one after the other, into the soft, springy mattress, counting out under his breath as he went. Three days. What was that in hours? He imagined the multiplication sum in his head. Three times four is twelve, carry one; three times two is six, plus one is seven. Seventy-two hours. In seventy-two hours, everything in his life had changed. Out of nowhere, out of a hopeless situation when all that faced him was a lengthy spell in the slammer, he had, by some extraordinary turn of fate, got the break he so longed for. And here he was now, not huddled beneath a torn cardboard packing case at the back of a city centre department store, but experiencing, in this warm, quiet room, a level of comfort he had never before dreamed could have existed. And across from him was the decent old bloke who had given him that break, who treated him . . . like he was worth something.

'Leonard, are ye awake?' he whispered.

He heard the cameraman catch his breath before letting out a long, sleepy groan. 'Did you say something, T.K.?'

'Aye, ah asked if ye wis awake.'

Leonard turned laboriously over in his bed. 'Well, I am now. What is it?'

'I wis just thinkin' aboot whit we did today.'

'Yes?'

'Will we get the chance tae see the stuff we shot?'

'Not until it's finished. Once it's gone through the film laboratory, it'll go straight to the cutting room in London.'

'That's the master copy and the black-and-white cutting copy, is it no'?'

'Good for you,' Leonard said sleepily. 'You were obviously listening.'

T.K. grinned smugly to himself and linked his hands behind his head on the pillow. 'Dae ye no' get worried that nothing's goin' tae come out on the film? I mean, it's no' like video, is it, when ye can see whit ye've shot the moment ye've dunnit.'

'No matter how long one is in the business, T.K., one constantly worries. Sleeping is enough of a problem without . . .'

T.K. listened for Leonard to finish the sentence. 'Without what?'

Leonard let out a long breath. 'Never mind.'

T.K. looked over at the darkened shape of the old cameraman. 'Leonard?'

'Yes, T.K.,' Leonard replied with drowsy impatience.

'Are ye all right?'

'Sorry?'

'It's just that ah saw ye kept hauding on to yer side a' day. Have ye got a pain there or somethin'?'

'Just old age, T.K. Just old age.'

'Aye, but ye're fit, Leonard, aren't ye? Ye're as fit as onyone wha's twenty years younger than ye. Ye're fitter than ma dad and he's only fifty-twa, but that's no' surprisin' 'cos he does bugger all except sit in his chair watching TV and he gets through aboot fifty fags a day.'

'Good night, T.K.'

T.K. stretched out his legs and once more smiled contentedly to himself. 'Good night, Leonard. See you in the morning.'

Leonard flickered his eyes open and glanced at the luminous hands of his alarm clock. 'I do believe, young man, that we've just had that pleasure.'

Thirty-Seven

The quad bike ascended the hill at speed, kicking up loose stones as it went and brushing before it the tall fescue grass that grew in the centre of the deep-rutted track. Unused to rising from her bed at such an early hour, Angélique stifled a yawn as she sat astride the small pillion seat behind Jamie, her arms tightly encircling his waist. The sun ribbed the high-clouded sky in pinky red, promising warmth for the day, but as it had yet to appear above the top of the hill, she shielded her face from the freshening wind by pressing her cheek against Jamie's back. The high-revving engine of the quad cut out any possibility of conversation, but Angélique was happy to watch the view down onto the low ground unfold before her and feel the comforting warmth of Jamie's body radiate into hers through his sleeveless fleece body warmer.

They came out into the sun at the head of a long deep gully that frothed with clear fast water tumbling down the hillside. Jamie left the track and drove alongside a wire fence that followed the contours of the top of the hill, dipping and rising until it fell away from sight over the horizon. When they came to a wide metal gate swung between new pine strainer posts, Jamie turned the quad to face out over the view and cut the engine. In the resultant silence Angélique could hear the sound of sheep bleating beyond the fence and the throaty cackle of a pheasant somewhere down in the bracken that lined the bottom of the gully.

'What d'you think of that?' Jamie said, sweeping his gaze around the view.

Keeping her arms around his waist, Angélique rested her chin against his shoulder. She took in a deep inhalation of air, the sweet smell of the damp vegetation on the moor mingling with the faint aroma of shaving cream on the side of Jamie's face. Without moving, she focused her eyes on the mass of blond hair, pushed back behind his ear and curling down to his shirt collar, and she wanted, there and then, to reach up and push it to one side so that she could press her mouth against his warm downy neck. 'That is one of the most beautiful sights I have ever seen,' she replied eventually to his question, without averting her gaze.

'That's the North Berwick Law over there,' Jamie said, pointing to a conical-shaped rock that jutted up along the coastline.

'What would that be?'

Jamie looked over his shoulder and smiled at her. 'Do you really want to know?'

'Of course.'

'OK, it's a carboniferous volcanic plug, composed of phonolytic trachyte and formed over three hundred and thirty-five million years ago.'

'How very fascinating.'

Jamie laughed. 'Not at all. It's about the only thing I remember from my geography lessons at school. Local interest and all that.'

'There are some extinct volcanoes where I come from, too. Les Monts Dôme, les Monts Dores, and les Monts de Cantal.'

Jamie shot a quizzical frown at her. 'Where on earth are they?'

'In the Massif Central. Your geography is obviously not so good if you did not know Clermont Ferrand lies in the heart of one of the most beautiful mountain ranges in Europe.'

'Right,' Jamie said with a nod. 'In that case, the good old North Berwick Law is a just a bit of a bump to you.'

'But it is a very nice bump, as far as bumps go.'

'Well, thank you for saying so. And I guess this view will be pretty unspectacular to you as well.'

'I think it is . . . different.'

Jamie sighed. 'I'm beginning to wonder why the hell I bothered bringing you up here in the first place.'

Angélique laughed and tightened her grip around his stomach. 'I would not have missed it for all the world.'

Jamie gave her hands a light slap. 'Come on, let's go check these sheep out.' Swinging a leg over the handlebars, he took a beaten-up duffle bag from the wooden box strapped to the front pannier rack on the quad.

'What do you have in that?' Angélique asked as she clambered off the bike.

'Well, besides the usual veterinary stuff, there's a Thermos flask filled to the brim with undrinkable coffee and a couple of tepid bacon rolls.'

'Ah, breakfast on the moor. That is a wonderful idea.'

'Actually, it was the old man's. I think he's taken a bit of a shine to you ever since he found out it was you who was playing the violin on the one classical CD that he owns.'

'He is then surely a man of impeccable taste,' Angélique remarked airily.

'On that account, I think you should leave off judgement until you've tried his coffee,' Jamie replied doubtfully.

Three quarters of an hour later they sat in the warmth of the morning sun with their backs against a large smooth-sided boulder, looking out over a small loch that was surrounded by grazing sheep and on to which wild duck noisily landed and took off as frequently as planes at Heathrow Airport. Pouring out two cups of coffee from the Thermos, Jamie handed one to Angélique and waited for her to take her first mouthful.

'What's your verdict, then?'

'It's' – she swilled the liquid round in her mouth and then licked her lips – 'quite disgusting, actually.'

'There you are, I told you it would be,' he laughed, taking the bacon rolls from their foil wrappers and passing one over to her. 'Not really Parisian café quality, is it?'

Angélique smiled at him. 'No, it is not,' she answered quietly.

Jamie took a bite of his roll. 'You miss Paris, don't you?'

'Yes, I do. I miss it very much.'

'Will you head back there after all this is over?'

She took a small piece from the side of her roll and began rolling it between her thumb and forefinger. 'I don't think so. I have commitments to fulfil.'

'Where?'

'All over the world.'

'D'you reckon you'll be able to do them by yourself?'

Angélique sighed. 'For now, I don't think I have any other choice.'

'What about getting a new manager?'

She threw away the rolled ball of dough and turned her head away from him. 'I actually don't know how to start to find one . . . one that I will be able to trust.'

'Yeah, under the circumstances I can understand that,' Jamie said, taking a mouthful of coffee. 'Dessuin's really succeeded in messing up your life, hasn't he?'

Angélique turned and looked at him with glistening eyes. 'I have been with Albert Dessuin since I was thirteen years old. I suppose I revered him for all that time. It is very difficult when someone like that shatters all your illusions.'

Jamie could only nod his head in reply. He knew he didn't have the experience or understanding of life to come out with anything that wasn't going to sound crass or light-hearted, but he did wish he could have the pleasure of meeting Dessuin alone down some secluded alleyway one dark night.

He felt a hand settle on his knee. 'And what about you, Jamie?' Angélique asked, a brave smile on her face. 'Are you going to stay in Edinburgh?'

'No, I'm heading down to London in September to start a job.'

'That will be good fun for you. I would very much like to live in London.' She paused, toying once more with her now-cold bacon roll. 'Maybe we could meet up if I have a concert there?'

'Of course. I'd like that.'

'I would too.' She threw away what was left in her cup and handed him the bacon roll. 'You have this. I'm not very hungry.' She lay down, resting her head on his lap and tucking herself up into a ball. 'I hope you don't mind.'

'What? Eating your fingered bacon roll?'

She hit him playfully on the leg. 'You know what I mean.'

A flight of ducks whistled over their heads and Jamie munched on the roll as he watched them coast down on to the loch, breaking the dark water in parallel wakes.

'You know, last night was the best fun I have had for a very long time,' Angélique said. 'Being with you and your parents, I sensed what it would be like to be part of a close and contented family, and I have not experienced that very much. When I was a little girl in Clermont Ferrand, there was always something wrong in my house. Either my father was in a very bad mood because he had drunk too much, or he and my brothers were arguing over some industrial problem at the factory; and then, of course, my mother was *always* complaining about how she did not have enough money to feed everyone. So that's why last night shall become a very special memory for me.' She paused before letting out a long, sad sigh. '*En fait*, I really don't want it to end.'

Jamie looked down at the side of her face, seeing one curved eyelash flick open and shut and her short dark hair lying wind-blown against her cheek. 'What don't you want to end?' he asked, putting the last of the roll into his mouth.

She turned her body and looked up at him. 'Any of it. Being up here alone with you. Being so far away from all the travel-ling from one country to another.' She smiled wistfully at him. 'When one does not know any other way of life, it is easy to accept. But now, with all this happening, I don't know if I will ever be able to return to the normal things again. I feel . . . very lost, Jamie.'

Jamie took hold of her bandaged hand and rubbed a finger against the strapping. 'Listen, you'll do OK,' he said, smiling down at her. 'You've got a lot of healing to do, not just this hand here but . . . well, in yourself as well. When all that's happened, you'll be crying out to get yourself back in there and you'll find your-self playing your violin better than ever before.'

'Why would you think that?'

'Because you'll be a free spirit, because your life will no longer be ruled by that creep Dessuin, and I know you have the courage and the talent to go it alone.'

Pulling her hand free from Jamie's grip, Angélique reached up and pressed a finger to his chin. 'There goes that heart of yours saying all the right things again.' She pushed herself upright and shuffled her bottom over so that she sat between his legs. Leaning back against his chest, she pulled his arms around her. 'I think that I will have to tell all your rugby-playing friends about it this afternoon.'

Jamie pushed his fingers deep into her side, making her let out a short scream and squirm her body to the side. 'If you do that, it'll be the end of our friendship.'

'I don't think so,' Angélique said, rubbing her hand against the soft blond hairs on his muscled arm as she looked out across the sunlit moor.

'For Chrissakes, lads, what the hell are you doing?' the coach of the Dunbar First XV yelled as he stood at half-time in the middle of the crouched semicircle of sweating bodies, everyone of them heaving with effort. 'This lot's a division below us and you're letting them walk all over you!' He slapped a hand frustratedly against his forehead and let out a long breath to steady his anger. 'Right, Billy,' he said, addressing a giant of a man whose muddy face was covered with congealed blood from a gash above his left eye. 'Their game plan seems to be based on kicking for touch, so I want you to contest every line-out. Get up in the air, spoil their tactics. If you have to, use an arm to keep the other jumper down, but keep it subtle, like. I don't want you sin-binned.' He pointed at a player who leaned forward, his hands on his knees, revealing a neck that was as thick as a bullock's. 'Callum, you're letting that tight-head prop control the scrum. You've got to get on top of him, otherwise there's no way we can get good ball to the three-quarters, is that clear?' The player raised his shaved head and nodded. 'And you, Jamie,' the coach continued, staring fixedly at his stand-off half, who was tipping the contents of a water bottle down his throat, 'I know you're used to playing in dizzier ranks than this motley crew, but their backs are lying flat, so I want you to break the gainline by running every ball, is that understood?' Jamie nodded, wiping a dirt-streaked arm across his mouth. 'Right, just go out there, you lot, and start working as a team. I want this deficit turned round in the first fifteen minutes of the second half, otherwise you won't have a hope in hell against the team next week.'

As the coach stomped off the field, the semicircle broke up and the players dejectedly sloped off to their positions to wait the few minutes until the referee restarted the game.

'There's someone over there trying to attract your attention, Jamie,' the inside centre said as he stretched a leg up behind him to keep his muscles from seizing up.

Jamie turned and looked over to the touchline where Angélique was waving at him. He lifted a hand to acknowledge her, but it only made her beckon more frantically.

'You'd better go,' the inside centre said with a teasing smile. 'I don't think she can wait until after the game.'

Jamie raised a finger at him as he ran over to the touchline. 'Yeah? What is it?' he asked Angélique.

'You are playing very well,' she said, a broad grin on her face.

Jamie pulled a hand across his head and rubbed at the back of his neck. 'We're losing, Angélique.'

'I know, but *you* are playing very well.' She gazed over to where the opposing team were thumping one another on the back in congratulations of a job well done so far. 'How fast is your left wing?' she asked.

Jamie turned and looked across at the player on the far side of the pitch. 'Andy? He's fast. Beats me by about two seconds over a hundred metres.' He turned back to her. 'Why do you ask?'

'Their three-quarter line is lying very flat.'

Jamie eyed her with amusement. 'That's what the coach has just said.'

'Well, I was just thinking that if Michalak was playing in your position and he had a very fast player like Dominici on his left wing and he saw a gap behind the three-quarter line of the opposition, he would put the ball there for Dominici to chase.'

Jamie smiled at her. 'You do know about this game, don't you?'

'I have told you that before.'

'Well, I'm afraid your idea doesn't match our coach's. He wants us to run every ball.'

Angélique shrugged. 'In that case, you will lose the match.'

Jamie crossed his arms. 'I'm glad you're so confident. Anything else you want to say?'

'No, but if you do not try it, I shall embarrass you,' she said with a wicked smile.

Jamie pulled his mouth guard from the pocket of his shorts. 'Just watch your step, Mademoiselle Pascal,' he said before placing it in his mouth and running back to his position just as the referee readied himself to blow his whistle to start the second half.

Five minutes later, after Jamie had started a number of abortive three-quarter-line movements, a scrum was called right in front of Angélique. She found herself standing next to the coach, who had been patrolling the touchline yelling out ineffectual orders at his players.

'Go on, lads, you've got one against the head! Hold it there now, hold it there.'

Angélique glanced over to the opposition's three-quarters and saw that their fullback had joined in the line as it edged forward to cover their opposing backs. 'Try it now, Jamie,' she yelled out at the top of her voice.

As the scrum half waited for the ball to be released from between the number 8's feet, the coach turned to Angélique, a querying look on his face. 'Try what, love?'

The scrum half picked up the ball from the base of the scrum and spun it at speed out to Jamie.

'Now move it down the line!' the coach yelled. 'Oh, no! What the effing hell are you doing?' He clapped both hands to his head as he watched Jamie kick a lobbing cross-field ball over the heads of the gawping opposition. The coach spun round and buried his face in his hands, not wishing to see the outcome of such an insane tactic.

Jamie's left wing was indeed a flyer. Timing his run to perfection, he scooped up the awkward-bouncing ball in one hand and tucked it under his arm, swerving his heels to avoid the last desperate attempt at a tap tackle by his opposing wing. Once he realised he had a clear path to the try line, he changed his running angle towards the centre of the posts and touched the ball down unchallenged between them. The cheers that erupted from the small crowd of home spectators made the coach turn slowly to watch what was going on.

Angélique jumped up and down, clapping her hands. 'It worked perfectly!' she said excitedly to him.

The coach stared at her open-mouthed for a moment before turning with a shake of his head and walking off in subdued silence down the touchline.

At the end of the game Jamie ran across the pitch to Angélique, pulling a sweatshirt over his head. 'Well, that was quite a turn-around, wasn't it?' he laughed. 'I owe you one. That tactic of yours really screwed them.'

'I told you it would work,' Angélique replied smugly. She took hold of the neck of his sweatshirt and pulled his head down towards her and gave him a kiss on the cheek. 'You played well. In fact, it is a pity you were not born a Frenchman.'

'That'd be no use. I have a phobia about snails,' Jamie said, giving her a wink before he turned and looked over to where his team was standing, watching them both. 'The lads want to have a drink with you in the clubhouse.'

Angélique shook her head. 'No, you go by yourself. I will wait for you in the car.'

'Come on, why not?'

'Because I do not know them . . . and they might know me.'

Jamie took hold of her arm and gave it a squeeze. 'Listen, *I* know them all and I can guarantee there's not one of them who would say a thing. Anyway, the person they're more concerned with meeting is the great rugby tactician who's just won them the game, not a world-famous violinist.'

Angélique looked over towards Jamie's teammates. 'Are you sure it's all right?'

'Yeah, of course it is. You're more likely to be offered a contract to sign rather than be asked for your autograph.'

'All right, then,' she replied and began to walk beside Jamie across the pitch. 'I hope you all take a shower first, though. I don't want to be drinking with a lot of sweaty men.'

Jamie laughed. 'Well, better get used to it, then,' he said, putting a filthy rugby-sleeved arm around her shoulders and pulling her tight in against him.

Thirty-Eight

Albert Dessuin threw a pound coin into the cardboard box of the young juggler who shared his stance in the doorway of Marks & Spencer on Princes Street, and without acknowledging the boy's gratitude he turned and looked into the brightly lit store, wondering if he shouldn't go in to try to find the woman. He had every reason to do so, because the place was packed with shoppers and there was a good possibility she could slip out of a back entrance, but nevertheless he decided to wait. It had been four days since he had first encountered her sprawled on the floor of the reception area in the Sheraton Grand, and so far that evening, he had done a good enough job of keeping himself out of sight, even in that dank little cellar where he had suffered a gruelling hour listening to her appallingly incomprehensible show. Because of that alone, he wasn't going to risk ruining his chances at this stage.

He moved away from the doorway, pulling up the collar of his mackintosh and thrusting his hands into the pockets. The wind was getting up and there was rain in the air. He looked up towards the castle where the vast bank of spotlights, lighting the Esplanade for the evening performance of the Military Tattoo, spilled upwards on to the dark threatening clouds rolling in from the west of the city. The audience would be getting wet tonight, he thought to himself. Later on, the streets leading down from the castle would be thronged with people wearing the free refuse-sack rainwear the organisers handed out, looking like an army of pink-shrouded ghouls sent forth from the ancient ramparts to ransack the town. He could not understand why they never went better prepared for an open-air show in the first place.

He saw her coming out of the store and standing in the doorway, her arms weighed down by two bulging plastic bags. It was the coat he recognised, that extraordinary multicoloured dog rug of a creation, a fitting garment, he thought, for someone as unattractive as she. He quickly turned towards the castle once more, watching her out of the side of his eye. She looked one way and then the other, maybe judging her moment when to step out into the crowded street or perhaps vacillating as to which way she should go. She moved off away from him, west-bound on Princes Street, lumbering along with her shoulders hunched and her coat-tail trailing along the grubby pavement.

It was easier than he could ever have imagined. She gave no indication that she might have suspected she was being followed, no furtive backward glance, no quick escaping dash into a darkened side street. It was child's play. As she laboured her way up the gentle slope of Hanover Street he decided to make it more interesting for himself and hurried his pace so that he was no more than twenty feet behind her, close enough to hear her gasping breath, stopping when she stopped and starting again when she continued her plodding ascent. He laughed quietly as he closed the gap further. It would be fun to go up and touch her on the shoulder, just to see her reaction when she turned round.

And then, as she reached the junction with George Street, the handle on one of her overloaded shopping bags gave way and the contents fell with a clatter on to the pavement. He stood frozen as he watched a tin can roll down the street towards him and veer off into the gutter, and then she turned to face him, bending down to retrieve her goods. At this point, he quickly moved over to the side of the pavement and pretended to study the window display of a fast-print photographic shop.

'Oh, bugger, bugger, bugger!' said Rene as she watched the tin of oxtail soup roll off down the road and disappear over the edge of the pavement. 'That's all I need.' She put the shopping bags on the ground and bent down to try to fashion a makeshift loop out of the broken handle. 'I hope this bloody well holds,' she mumbled irately to herself as she picked up the dirt-spattered packets and returned them to the bag. She straightened up, gingerly testing the strength of the new handle. 'Right, should get me 'ome. Now where on earth did that oxtail soup get to?'

She had taken no more than two steps down the street when her attention was suddenly caught by the figure of a man, not more than twenty feet away from her, studying intently the display in the window of a small photographic shop. It was the coat she recognised, a Maigret-style mackintosh with a double fold across the shoulders and a belt that was done up so tight that it puckered the material around his waist. And then she saw the high cockscomb of hair and knew instantly who it was.

'Oh, bloody 'ell!' she murmured to herself, and without even bothering to attempt to retrieve the lost can of soup, she took off across the street, dodging the traffic, and with her head bowed low as if trying to evade sniper fire, she scurried away along George Street as fast as her tired legs would carry her.

Albert Dessuin looked down at the bottom left-hand corner of the shop window as a way of being able to snatch a glance up the street, and then spun round fully when he realised the woman had gone. After a quick appraisal of Hanover Street, he ran up to the junction with George Street, and in his haste collided with a jovial group of beer-carrying young men.

'Oh-oh, watch it, mate!' one of them exclaimed as he steadied his plastic pint mug at arm's length. 'That's expensive stuff, you know.'

'I am sorry,' Albert replied curtly, holding up his hands in apology. He waited until the group had moved off before continuing his search for the woman. The full length of the street, however, was heaving with jostling pedestrians competing for space on pavements narrowed by queues awaiting entry into show venues. There was no sign of her. Albert smiled to himself. Maybe she had seen him, maybe not, but it did not matter. There was always another night, and he had the time to wait.

Rene peered tentatively round the side of the shop doorway and looked along the length of George Street. A momentary gap opened up in the mass of people and she caught sight of the mack-intoshed figure of the Frenchman standing at the junction, leaning his head one way and then the other as he searched the street.

'Oh, 'eck, it is me 'e's after,' Rene murmured to herself as she hurried off down the street once more, weaving her way in and out of the crowds to keep herself hidden. 'You've got to get yourself off the street, lass.'

She passed by a long queue formed outside a wide glass-doored entrance. She veered off towards the brightly lit haven only to feel a hand grasp at her shoulder.

'Hang on, love, you need a pass or a ticket to get in here.'

Rene looked up into the faces of two black-shirted, shaven-haired bouncers, both wearing earpieces with curly leads that disappeared down their collars.

'What kind of pass do I need?' Rene asked in desperation. She transferred her shopping bags to one hand and delved into the folds of her coat, pulling out the Fringe pass she had suspended around her neck. 'Is this any use?'

'That's all we need,' one of the bouncers said, pushing open the door for her. 'You'll find the bar at the end of the hall.'

Rene didn't quite know how the man knew she was gagging for a stiff drink but she wasn't going to hang around to question him. She bustled her way across the pillared, stone-floored hall and entered the double doors at the far end.

The bar was crammed with people, every inch of seating space taken up – on sofas, chairs, even on the tables. She pushed her way towards the bar and set her shopping bags down on the floor, blowing out a long breath of nervous exhaustion.

'Rene!'

Her immediate reaction on hearing the voice was to make ready to get down on all fours and crawl round the side of the bar to hide, but then it dawned on her that the caller's tone was distinctly female. She stood up on the footrest and scanned the room, seeing no one that she knew, and she was just coming to the conclusion there must have been someone else called Rene in the place when she spotted the bobbing mass of red hair threading its way towards her. A few seconds later, Matti Fullbright appeared at her side, a broad grin on her large freckled face.

'Hi, there, girl. How're you doing?'

'Matti Fullbright, am I pleased to see you!' Rene exclaimed, rolling her eyes in relief.

'You look all in. Let me get you a drink.'

'Aye, I'm needing one bad, luv,' Rene said, leaning heavy-elbowed on the bar. 'Bacardi and Coke would go down a treat.'

With a click of her fingers, Matti attracted the attention of the barman and ordered up two drinks. 'So what's been going on?'

'Ye won't believe who I've just seen out there in the street.'

'Not the bloody Frenchman!'

'Aye, right first time. The bloody Frenchman.'

'What was he doing?'

'I don't know, but I think 'e might 'ave been following me.'

The barman put the two drinks down on the bar and Matti handed Rene her Bacardi and Coke.

'I doubt there's any way he could have been doing that. It's just a coincidence, that's all.'

'Some bloody coincidence!' Rene exclaimed, taking a hefty slug from her glass. 'Edinburgh's a damned big place to go bumping into someone like that.'

'It happens all the time during the festival. I'm forever meeting people I know on the street.'

'Oh, well, I suppose ye could be right,' Rene said with a flick of her head. 'After all, 'ere's you and me meeting up again. That's pretty extraordinary, in't it?'

Matti screwed up the side of her mouth as she scrutinised the naivety of Rene's remark. 'That's not so out of ordinary, you know.'

'What d'ye mean?'

'Haven't you been here before?'

Rene gazed around the bar. 'No, never. Why should I?'

'Because this is the Assembly Rooms. All the Fringe acts congregate here at the end of the day.'

'Really? D'you mean all these people . . . ?'

'Yeah, they're either Fringe performers or guests.'

Rene shook her head in disbelief. 'Would you credit that? I'd no idea this place existed.'

'In that case, you didn't read all that bumf you were given.'

'Obviously not.'

Matti laughed. 'So, how did the act go this evening?'

'Same as ever. Three foreigners who couldn't understand one word I was saying and a drunk who slept all the way through.'

Matti sucked her teeth despondently. 'I know what you mean. It's not been a brilliant time for me, neither. I think I might have overstayed my welcome here.'

'Ye're not being serious, are ye?'

'Too right I am. I reckon I'll have to do a major overhaul of my act quite soon, but I'm not sure how.'

Rene's face broke into a smile. 'Maybe you should try doing it in the nude.'

Matti almost choked on her mouthful of gin and tonic. 'For God's sake, I'm trying to woo my audience, Rene, not have them run screaming for the exits!'

The laughter that ensued between the two women was so loud it made those that stood around them stop mid-conversation and turn to stare. Matti blew out a deep breath to control herself. 'Oh, my word, it does you good, don't it?'

'Tell that to the audience,' Rene replied with a giggle.

'Aye, maybe we should.' Matti took a drink from her glass and then turned to Rene, her eyes narrowed in thought. 'Listen, what're you doing tomorrow afternoon?'

Rene shrugged. 'Nowt at all.'

'Right, d'ye know the Royal Scottish Academy on Princes Street?'

'No, but I s'pose I could find it.'

'Good. Meet me there at, say, one-thirty.'

'Why?'

'I want you to come to see my new show.'

'What? Ye've worked something out already?'

'I think I might have just done that very thing, Rene, my girl,' Matti replied, swallowing the last of her drink and slamming her glass down on the bar. 'Come on, let's set up another round.'

Rene shook her head. 'I can't, thanks, lass,' she said, bending down to pick up her shopping bags. 'I've got be off. I've sort of taken on the evening cooking duties for these two lads in the flat.'

'Right,' Matti said disappointedly. 'Oh, well, I'll just have to drink alone.'

'Sorry.'

Matti shot her a conciliatory smile. 'See you tomorrow, then, and watch out for skulking Frenchmen.'

Rene raised her eyebrows. 'Oh 'eck, I'd almost forgotten about 'im.'

'Oh, don't let him get your knickers in a twist. If he's still around, I suggest you just run straight up to him and throw your arms around his neck and give him an enormous tongue sandwich. That should make him hightail it back to his lair in the Sheraton-bloody-Grand!'

'Right, that's it,' Rene said, her mouth drooping in disgust. 'I'm leaving before you make me physically sick.'

Thirty-Nine

Why this evening of all evenings, Tess Goodwin thought to herself as she leaned over in her seat to get an unrestricted view through the windscreen of the bus, hoping to see what had caused it to remain stationary for the past ten minutes. There was no traffic coming down Hanover Street, so she knew there had to be some sort of blockage up ahead. She glanced at her wristwatch. It was half past seven. She was going to be so late and the last thing she wanted to do was to arrive at the restaurant in a flustered state. Tonight she had to be in the mood to play it ultra-cool, bordering on iceberg-cold.

Getting to her feet, she slung the strap of her laptop case on to her shoulder and walked down the aisle to stand by the driver. 'Are we going to be moving soon?' she asked, peering up the street.

'Nae idea,' the driver replied, masticating heavily on a piece of gum. 'Looks like an accident. Ah've just seen a police car head down past the roundabout on George Street.' He turned to her. 'How far are ye goin'?'

'Dundas Street.'

'D'yae want tae walk then? Ye'd be better tae.'

'Yes, I think you're right.'

The doors opened with a swish and Tess jumped down on to the pavement and began half walking, half running up the incline.

This had to be the most imperfect climax for what had already proved to be a gruelling week. The dinner date with Peter Hansen had been permanently at the forefront of her mind. She was distracted at work, forgetting to attend at least three meetings and to organise press calls that would normally have been second nature to her, and then, because Peter had gone against his word and had kept calling her constantly, she had become near paranoid about her mobile phone ringing. She considered turning it off altogether, only she knew it was her constant lifeline during the festival.

But the worst had always been when her day's work was over and she had gone home to Allan. She tried to act as naturally as she could with him, but everything that she said or did seemed so false, so deceiving, that eventually she resolved to plead utter exhaustion and keep all conversation between them to a minimum, hoping that he would not question the sudden change in her mood and character. So every night she would lie beside him in bed, her eyes fixed on the television but taking nothing in, while he would give up on his nightly attempts to make love to her and fall asleep, resigned to his sudden celibacy, with his head leaning heavily against her shoulder. She dreaded the coming of the day when she would have to meet Peter Hansen at the restaurant, yet she also longed for it so that she could put an end to this appalling charade and get her life with Allan back to normal.

Just before arriving at the flat, she took her mobile from her bag, thumbed the keys and put it to her ear. Her call was answered immediately. 'Yes, it's Tess,' she said in a voice that was distinctly cryogenic. 'I'm going to be late . . . I don't know, maybe half an hour, depends on the traffic . . . can't do that, I'm on my way home now. I want to have a shower first . . . no, Peter, you read nothing into that. You really could not be more wrong.'

Angrily, she put the mobile back into her handbag as she shouldered open the entrance door. She ascended the stairs quickly, praying she still had time to get changed and away from the place before Allan came back from the office. Tonight, she thought to herself, when this whole thing is over and done with, I'll make it up to him.

Her heart sank as soon as she walked into the flat, dropping her case on the chair in the hall. She could hear the blare of the television coming from the bedroom. She took off her coat as she walked along the passage and entered the room. Allan was lying propped up on the bed drinking a mug of tea, still in his suit trousers but with stockinged feet and his tie loosened. An open newspaper lay beside him. His eyes momentarily left the television screen and she saw immediately the deep sadness in his eyes.

'Allan?' she asked quietly, feeling her heart give a jolt of apprehension. 'What's happened?'

He smiled at her. 'Nothing.' He zapped the television with the remote. 'Just been watching the end of some stupid romantic film. Got to me a bit.' He dropped the remote on the bed beside him. 'I came home early 'cos I thought we could go out to dinner.'

Tess bit at her bottom lip. 'I can't, Allan. I've got to attend another reception tonight. I've just come home to change.' Feeling her face colour, she turned away from him and walked back over to the door. 'I'm just going to have a quick shower.'

She returned five minutes later wrapped in a towel, her skin tingling from the scalding she had given herself in the hope it would purge away her guilt. Allan was still sitting on the bed, still looking at her. She smiled at him as she walked over to the open wardrobe and took out a dark-red silk cocktail dress on a hanger.

'We need to talk,' Allan said.

Tess glanced round at him. 'What about?'

Allan shrugged. 'Anything you want. We haven't communicated for about a week, or maybe you haven't noticed.'

Tess placed the dress on a chair and walked across to the bed and sat down next to him. 'I know and I'm sorry. It's just—'

'Work,' Allan interjected morosely.

She put a hand on his arm. 'After tonight, things will be different, Allan, I promise. We could go out for dinner tomorrow night?'

Allan shrugged and picked up the newspaper. 'Have you any idea what happened to Angélique Pascal?' he asked, the change of subject seeming to Tess a ruse to avoid giving her an answer, yet she was glad of it. She shot a glance at the radio alarm on the bedside table. It was almost eight o'clock. Peter Hansen would no doubt be sitting in the bar at the restaurant waiting for her.

'No,' she said, getting to her feet and walking over to a chest of drawers and taking out a pair of pants and a bra, 'other than she's returned to France.'

Allan let out a hollow laugh. 'You're really a strange one, Tess. A week ago you were beside yourself with worry about her, and now you're acting as if you couldn't give a damn.'

Dropping the towel to the ground, Tess slipped on her pants

and her bra, and then stood for a moment staring at her reflection in the mirror that sat on top of the chest. He was right, of course. She hadn't given Angélique another thought ever since she'd left. She was too preoccupied with her own damned problems. 'I *am* concerned about her,' she said, picking up the dress from the chair and slipping it off the hanger. 'It's just that—'

'*How* concerned are you?' he cut in.

'What do you mean?'

'Well, it's been over a week since she left Edinburgh,' Allan replied, giving the newspaper a thump with the back of his hand, 'and we've heard nothing more about her. Wouldn't *you* think, as someone who deals with the press all the time, that a story about a world-class violinist who has had to cancel a whole load of concerts because she'd cut her hand badly would be pretty big news? I mean, there's been no follow-up story, no progress report, not even a photograph. Don't you think that's a bit weird?'

Tess rubbed her fingers against her brow. Again, he was absolutely right. Even though she'd had her nose buried in the newspapers for the past week looking out for reviews and articles on artistes, it had never occurred to her there had never been a mention of Angélique.

'Maybe she's asked for some privacy during her convalescence,' she offered hopefully. 'She is quite a private person, after all.'

'Come on, you know as well as I do the paparazzi don't give a damn about the privacy of *any* celebrity. It's all just money to them. And don't you think it's quite odd she hasn't been in touch with you? You became pretty chummy with her and she did have your mobile number.' He closed the newspaper, spun it on to the floor and then folded his arms. 'I think you should try to find out more about her, because to tell you the truth, *I'm* concerned even if no one else appears to be.'

Tess gazed at him for a moment. 'You're right. She should have been in touch.'

'I know.'

She glanced once more at the time on the radio alarm. This was an issue she was not going to be able to avoid. Peter Hansen was just going to have to wait for a bit longer. Pulling on her dress, she walked over to the door and left the room. She returned a few moments later with her mobile phone and address book. She sat down on the bed next to Allan, turned quickly through the pages and then began dialling a number.

'Who are you calling?' Allan asked.

'A reporter called Harry Wills,' Tess replied, putting the phone to her ear. 'I tell you, this is really breaking a cardinal rule. I never ask information from the press.'

Allan swung his legs over the side of the bed and got to his feet. 'D'you want a cup of tea?'

'Hullo, is that Harry Wills?' Tess asked, shaking her head at Allan's offer.

Five minutes later, Allan returned to the bedroom, a brimming mug of tea in his hand, to find Tess staring thoughtfully out of the window, her mobile held limply in her hand. 'How did you get on?' he asked, putting the mug down on the bedside table.

'He's coming round here now.'

'Why? What did he say?'

'Well, to begin with, he seemed quite adamant that Angélique had gone back to Paris, but then when I told him she was a good friend of mine and that I couldn't understand why I hadn't heard from her, his whole attitude changed.'

'In what way?'

'He just started asking me a whole load of questions about how I'd met her and when was the last time I'd seen her, and then when I told him I worked in the International office, he just immediately said he thought it would be best if he came round to see me.' She laid the mobile and the address book down on the bedside table. 'Funny thing is, I think I now recognise his voice. I'm pretty sure it was him who called the International office to break the news about Angélique's accident.'

'Sounds as if I was right, then,' Allan said, sitting down on the edge of the bed and rubbing his face with his hands. 'My word, there seems to be a hell of a lot of cloak-and-dagger stuff going on at the festival this year.'

He said the remark in such a strained voice that Tess shot him a worried glance out of the corner of her eye. She decided silence to be the only fitting reply.

Forty minutes later, Tess closed the door of the flat behind Harry Wills and walked back along the corridor and into the bedroom. Allan was pulling on his suit jacket, studying the piece of paper the reporter had ripped out of his notebook.

'Where are you going?' she asked.

'Out to East Lothian. Someone's got to go see Angélique.'

Tess bit at her lip. This was decision time, but already, in her heart, she knew where she had to go. 'I'm coming too.'

'Don't bother,' he said, studying her face intently. 'You'd better go to your reception.'

She glanced at her wristwatch. A quarter to nine. It was all too late now anyway. She didn't know what Peter Hansen's next step would be, but she was prepared to face the consequences. She picked up her handbag from the chest of drawers. 'No, I want to come.' She walked towards the door. 'I'll just make a quick phone call to Sarah Atkinson to say I won't make the reception.'

It was not a good time to be attempting to cross over to the other side of Edinburgh. The streets were clogged both with traffic and with pedestrians, and for the greater part of the journey through the city Allan drove in silence, only breaking it to mutter some oath under his breath as the traffic lights incessantly changed to red as he approached them. Tess didn't care. Her mind was completely set on the confrontation that was now inevitable between herself and Sir Alasdair Dreyfuss. She kept imagining the scene of her being called to his office, trying to work out what she would say when he questioned her about her affair with his friend, Peter Hansen, knowing that whatever she said in reply would make little difference. Her future as an employee of the International Festival would be considered untenable.

When she had spoken to Peter Hansen on the telephone before leaving the flat, he had been surprisingly understanding of her reasons for not being able to turn up at the restaurant. 'How disappointing,' he had said. 'In that case, we should make it another night.' And she had replied, 'Maybe.' Now she thought to herself how much easier, how much more self-preserving it would have been to have answered, 'Yes, of course we can,' but then she glanced across at Allan, shaking his head in frustration as he edged the car forward another few feet, and she knew she had made the right decision not to continue with this stupid, foolish, damaging game any longer. Her job was expendable, but not her husband. This was the man she loved, and this was the man she did not want to lose.

She didn't want to think about it any longer. She switched her mind to Angélique and wondered if she should ring her at the house in East Lothian to warn her they were on their way out to see her. She took her mobile from her handbag and picked up the slip of paper next to the gear stick on which Harry Wills had written the address and the mobile number of Angélique's friend, Jamie Stratton. She read his name again, trying to work out why it seemed so familiar, and then her mind registered on the meeting she had had in the Hub café with the elderly cameraman who had been desperate to find somewhere to stay in the city. Distractedly she put her mobile and the piece of paper back beside the gear stick and leaned her head against the window, thinking to herself how extraordinary it was that she'd already spoken to this man.

The next thing she knew she was jolting herself awake, blinking her eyes to accustom them to the glare of the oncoming headlights. The car was now travelling at speed along a dual carriageway. To her left she could see the illuminated block of the power station at Tranent. She reached across and squeezed Allan's hand. 'Sorry about that. I dropped off.'

'You must be exhausted,' he said.

'I am quite.'

'Too many late nights, burning the candle at both ends.'

Tess frowned. There was almost a frenetic edge to his voice. 'Not really.'

'Are you sleeping with him again then?'

Tess felt her face go on fire. 'What?'

'Peter bloody Hansen. You just can't stop yourself, can you?'

Tess swallowed hard. 'I don't know—'

'Of course you know what I'm bloody talking about. I saw him this evening. He was round at our flat knocking on the door when I got back from work. He recognised me and scuttled off like the rat that he is.'

Tess shook her head. 'Allan, I—'

'Don't even start to tell me you didn't know he was here. Who was it you called just before you left the flat? Sure as hell wasn't Sarah Atkinson, was it?' He picked up her mobile phone from beside the gear stick and punched at the buttons. 'Look,' he said, holding the screen inches from her face. 'Lo and behold, if that isn't the name of Peter Hansen. Now, are you going to tell me that's just coincidence?'

Tess closed her eyes tight. 'Stop the car.'

'Why? Do you want to get out here and walk all the way back to his loving arms? Is that what the hell you want?'

'Please, just stop the car.'

Allan swerved into a lay-by at speed and slammed his foot on the brake and turned off the engine. The silence was absolute. Tess heard him let out a deep, quivering groan and turned to see him slump forward on the steering wheel, his head in his hands.

'I really didn't know he was going to turn up, Allan. He just did and the arrogant bastard expected everything to be exactly as it was before.'

Allan raised his head and looked at her.

'And was it?'

'No, of course it wasn't. Why would it ever be? I'm married to you now. I don't want anyone else in the my life, least of all him.'

'But you were going to go out with him tonight, weren't you?'

Tess paused, realising at that moment how badly she had handled this whole situation. She should never have kept it from him. 'Yes, I was. I was going to have dinner with him.'

'Jesus!' Allan muttered angrily, thumping his hand against the steering wheel.

'Let me finish – please! I agreed to have dinner with him only because he, in so many words, threatened to tell Alasdair Dreyfuss about our' – the word momentarily stuck in Tess's throat – 'relationship. I didn't want to lose my job and I certainly didn't want to lose you. I was going to have dinner with him and, I really mean this, Allan, that was going to be the end of it. I hate the man and I hate myself for getting involved with him in the first place, because I nearly lost you as a result. I decided not to tell you about him being here, because . . . well, I thought I could handle it myself.'

'Why? Did it never occur to you that this all involves me as well? If you screw up your life, you screw up mine as well.'

Tess looked down into her lap, feeling tears of stupidity and hopelessness begin to well up in her eyes. 'I know, and I'm really sorry. I should have told you.' She opened the glove box in front of her and took out a box of tissues. She pulled out a wodge and wiped her eyes. 'I have hated this week more than any in my whole life. I've felt I've been betraying you every moment of it, and to do that to someone you really love is just the most painful thing to bear.'

There was a long silence before Allan broke it. 'I don't know what to say, Tess. Maybe it's slipped your mind, but after we'd sorted everything out last year, I thought we'd made an agreement we would never hold back secrets from each other. Hell, that was the fundamental reason we got married! And now you've just blown the whole thing out the window, as if all those endless talks we had on trust and reconciliation were just trite and totally expendable. And yes, that's exactly how you always end up making *me* feel – totally and utterly expendable.'

Tess reached across and laid a hand on his arm. 'Please, you must never, ever think that. I know I've made a hash of things but you have to remember that nothing happened, Allan, and nothing similar will ever happen again in the future, because you are the only person I want in my life.'

With a shake of his head, Allan turned the key in the ignition, pumping his foot on the accelerator and making the engine roar angrily to life. 'We'd better go find Angélique.'

'Can't we call a truce first?' Tess asked quietly

Allan considered her question for a moment before turning to her. 'OK, but for your friend's sake only, because, Tess, you think back on what you've just said about nothing similar happening again. You used almost exactly the same words last year.'

'I know what is going to occur next,' Angélique said as she and Jamie lay on the sofa in the sitting room, the only source of the light coming from the television.

'OK, go on then, let's hear it.'

'The man with the beard who was on the bus with her has followed her home and has got into the house.'

'How?'

'I don't know. Through an open window, maybe?'

'Wrong.'

Angélique lifted her head from his chest and turned to look at him. 'Why do you think that?'

'Could be intuition.' He smiled at her. 'Or could be because I've seen the film before.'

'Oh, you are such a cheat!' she exclaimed, reaching for a

cushion. The imminent blow never struck its target, as her arm stopped mid-arc when the door of the drawing room opened and the lights were turned on. Both she and Jamie turned to see Rory Stratton standing there in his dressing gown.

'Hi, Dad,' Jamie said. 'I thought you'd turned in.'

'Yes, well, I was on my way upstairs when I heard a car arriving. You've got visitors.'

The news brought them both immediately to their feet. Jamie stared in bewilderment at the young couple that entered the room, having never set eyes on either of them before. Both were dressed as if they had been to a party, the man in a suit, the girl in a dark-red cocktail dress with her face made up. Jamie spun round when he heard Angélique let out a gasp of astonishment.

'Tess!'

She ran across the room and flung her arms around the girl's neck.

'Hullo, Angélique, how are you?' the girl said, giving her a kiss on both cheeks. 'We've only just found out what happened to you. We came straight out to see you.'

Angélique pushed herself away. 'I cannot believe this. How did you know I was here?'

'Yeah, good question,' Jamie said, still looking suspiciously at the couple.

'Well then, find out over a drink, Jamie,' his father retorted, still standing by the door as he shot a steely glare of disapproval at his son's lack of welcome. 'I'm off to my bed, so I'll bid everyone good night.' He was about to leave the room when he glanced back at Jamie. 'If you want to talk into the small hours, Allan and Tess can stay the night if they want. The double bed's usually made up in the top spare room.'

Jamie nodded. 'Thanks.'

As Rory shut the door behind him, the two girls walked across to the sofa and sat down, already engrossed in a deep private conversation. Still nonplussed as to what was going on, Jamie forced a smile on his face as he approached the man, his hand outstretched. 'Hi, we haven't met. Jamie Stratton.'

The man shook his hand. 'Allan Goodwin.' He pointed over to the girl sitting next to Angélique. 'That's Tess – my wife.'

'Right . . . so, what can I get you to drink?'

'A beer would do me fine.'

'And for Tess?'

Allan shrugged. 'Just something soft. She's driving home.'

'Where exactly *is* home?' Jamie asked as he walked over to the drinks tray, not yet willing to extend his father's offer of a bed until he had found out more about the couple.

'Edinburgh,' Allan replied, following him across the room. 'In fact, Tess says she knows you.'

'Really?' Jamie shot a quizzical glance at the girl seated next to Angélique. 'I can't say that I ever remember—'

'She spoke to you on the telephone.'

'Concerning what?'

'Renting a room to a Mr Hartson? She said he was a cameraman.'

Jamie stared hard at the man. 'I seem to remember that call came from the International Festival office.'

'It would have done. Tess works there.'

'Oh, I see,' Jamie replied, glancing apprehensively at the girl. 'But it couldn't have been Mr Hartson who told you we were here. He had no idea where we were going.'

'No, that information came from a reporter called Harry Wills.'

'*Harry Wills?*' Jamie exclaimed incredulously, just stopping short of overflowing a glass of Coke over the floor. 'Excuse me for asking this, but why did he think it necessary to tell her?'

'Because Tess hadn't heard one word from Angélique since she left for France. She called Harry because she knew he'd had contact with Angélique in the past.'

'And Harry . . . told you everything?'

'Yes, he thought it would be safe enough now. He said he'd stopped his vigil outside your flat about three night ago.'

'Yes, I know that, but I didn't expect him to start telling people we were here.'

'Don't worry, neither Tess nor I will be breathing one word on her whereabouts to anyone.' Allan studied the look of distrust on Jamie's face as the young man carried the glass of Coke across the room and handed it to Tess. 'I think, quite honestly,' Allan continued quietly when Jamie had returned to pour him his beer, 'that, until this whole situation with Angélique is well and truly over, the more allies you two have in your camp, the better. Tess has become a good friend of Angélique, and she would never do anything to jeopardise either her safety or her privacy.'

Jamie handed Allan his beer, and then looked over to where Angélique and Tess were chatting, seemingly oblivious to his and Allan's presence in the room. He gave a shrug. 'I had no idea Angélique knew anyone else in Edinburgh. I wonder why she's never mentioned Tess to me before.'

Allan shot a withering look at Tess and shook his head. 'I'm afraid that's the female mind for you,' he said, raising his glass of beer in salute. 'They have a bloody awful habit of keeping secrets from us men.'

Even though Jamie had no way of knowing the poignancy of Allan's remark, it was sufficiently male-bonding to break the unease Jamie had felt since the young couple's unexpected arrival at the house. He too raised his glass to the man. 'Listen, sorry about being a bit . . . well, unfriendly towards you. I was completely thrown into this whole game and I suppose it's just made me quite . . . protective towards her.'

'Yes, I can see that,' Allan replied, glancing briefly at Angélique before turning back to Jamie with a grin on his face, 'and I think I can probably understand the reasons why.'

Jamie felt his face colour instinctively at Allan's quip. 'So, how about it?' he asked, deciding to change tack to avoid further discussion on the subject. 'Do you want to stay the night? As my father said, the bed's made up.'

'That's very kind, but we wouldn't want to impose ourselves on you.'

314

'No imposition at all,' Jamie replied, looking over at the two girls on the sofa. 'I doubt we're going to stop those two talking for a while.'

'Looks that way, doesn't it?'

'So you'll stay?'

Allan shrugged his shoulders. 'All right, why not?'

'Good,' Jamie replied, walking over to the drinks tray. 'In that case, we have no excuse now not to hit the hard stuff.'

Forty

'Hang on, lass, stop kicking around,' Rory Stratton muttered, squeezing his legs tighter around the body of the upended ewe to stop her from trying to make a break for freedom. He heaved her round in the pen so that he could cast light on the infected foot from the reddened glow of the early morning sun. 'Right, let's see if we can't get you back into shape.' He took a penknife from the back pocket of his jeans and began paring away the side of the hoof, wrinkling his nose at the foul smell of the foot rot. 'My word, that's not a good one, is it? I should have spotted you before.'

He turned round to pick up the aerosol can of antibiotic from the ground and started when he saw the figure standing behind him. Holding hard to the ewe's feet, he stood upright, stretching out his aching back and looked across at the young man whom he had welcomed to the house the previous evening.

'You're up bright and early,' Rory said, giving the aerosol a shake as he appraised the man's attire. 'Not the ideal clothes to wear for a visit to a sheep pen.'

Allan glanced down at his dark-blue suit and the expensive black loafers, already spattered with mud, and then smiled at the man. 'Yeah, you're right, but I just felt like getting out of the house and having a walk.' He leaned on the wooden railing,

315

clasping his hands together. 'Do you always talk to them like that?'

Rory laughed. 'A bit mad, eh?' He bent down and gave the ewe's foot a spray. 'My wife sometimes accuses me of speaking more to my sheep than I do to her. She calls them the other women in my life.'

Allan pushed his hands into the pockets of his trousers. 'At least your wife only has to compete with a load of woolly animals,' he said, turning round to look back at the house.

Rory glanced briefly at the young man, detecting an obvious tone of melancholy in his voice. He eased the ewe forward on to her front feet and let her go and watched as she ran to the far side of the pen, turning to eye him distrustfully. He walked over to the railing and put the aerosol can in the bag that hung on one of the strainer posts. 'That sounds as if you've experienced a similar problem.'

Allan let out a long sigh. 'Sort of.'

Rory took a towelling rag from the pocket of his padded waistcoat and wiped his hands. 'Have you been married long?'

Allan turned and stared questioningly at him. 'Why do you ask?'

Rory leaned an elbow on the railing. 'Well, it's probably none of my business, but I just saw that shiny new ring on your finger and wondered why someone would prefer trudging around a muddy farmyard at this time in the morning, rather than be tucked up in bed with a beautiful young wife.'

Allan bit at the corner of his bottom lip as he studied the weather-beaten face of the farmer, wondering whether he should rise to this line of questioning. 'Sometimes things just don't appear how they seem, if you get my meaning.'

Rory laughed. 'I know exactly what you mean! I'm afraid, my friend, that's just one of the anomalies of marriage. You'd think after twenty-seven years of being wedded to my wife, there'd be an almost Zen-like plane of understanding between us and we'd go out of our way to avoid the pitfalls which we know put us at loggerheads – but no, we both still get attracted to them like moths to a light bulb. What you've got to consider, though, is how boring it all would be without those little annoyances and niggling differences.' He flashed a wicked smile at the young man before pushing himself away from the railing and walking across the pen to release the ewe into the adjacent paddock. 'I think it's much more healthy to have a bit of fire in a marriage rather than let it smoulder aimlessly along. That can lead to problems.'

'And what about trust?' Allan asked.

'That's fundamental to any relationship.'

'So there should be no secrets, nothing hidden?'

'That depends on their context, whether they're being deployed for deception or protection. One represents total breakdown in communication, the other pure love.' Rory took the bag from the strainer post, slung it over his shoulder and climbed over the railings. He smiled at the young man. 'Look, don't think marriage is always going to be a bed of roses, but it's infinitely better than sitting on a dung heap by yourself for the rest of your life.'

Allan smiled at the farmer. 'That's a good quote. I might use it sometime.'

'Well, remember where you heard it first. It's a Stratton original.' He nodded his head in the direction of the house. 'I think you might have company.'

Allan turned to see Tess coming towards them, her arms crossed as she walked along the road from the house. He glanced back at Rory. 'We'll be heading back to Edinburgh quite soon, so if we don't see you, many thanks for letting us stay the night, and, erm . . . for the advice as well.'

'My pleasure,' Rory said, shooting him a wink. 'Have a good journey back.' He made his way across the concrete apron to the lambing shed and hung up the bag on a nail inside the door, and then walked over to the grain store to turn on the drying plant for the day. Ten minutes later he was back in the lambing shed, climbing astride the quad bike. He fired up the engine and drove it outside. A hundred yards away, he spotted the young couple still standing in the middle of the road talking with each other, and then he witnessed the man putting his arms around his wife's waist, drawing her into him and kissing her long on the mouth. Rory grinned with satisfaction at the sight, gave a brief self-congratulatory nod of his head and then set off at speed up the dirt-track road towards the hill, trailed closely by his two fleet-footed sheepdogs.

Forty-One

Sir Alasdair Dreyfuss placed the cup of coffee on his desk and sat down, leaning forward on his elbows and rubbing at the fatigue that was smarting in his eyes. For the past ten days, the earliest he had been to his bed was two o'clock in the morning, and it was really beginning to tell on him. He pulled forward his diary and glanced through the appointments he had listed for the day. The telephone began to ring and he muttered angrily under his breath, wondering why, at nine-fifteen in the morning, it had yet to be switched off night service.

'Oh, where the hell is everyone?' he exclaimed, grabbing the receiver on its sixth ring. 'Hullo, International Festival.'

'Alasdair?' a woman's voice asked.

'Yes,' the director answered, a quizzical frown on his face. 'Who is this?'

'It's Birgitte Hansen.'

'Birgitte!' Alasdair exclaimed, leaning back in his chair, relaxing immediately in the knowledge it was to be a social call. 'What a lovely surprise. How are you?'

'I am good.'

'And the family?'

'All busy doing different things. Kirsten is working close to us here in a restaurant in Charlottenlund, making some money before she goes back to university, and Henning starts his new school next week, so there is a lot to do, as you can imagine. I don't seem to have stopped all summer, so I am very much looking forward to our holiday with you and Paula and the kids in Lillehammer next April.'

Alasdair laughed. 'That goes for me too. We're bang in the middle of the festival here and it's chaos in the office. So, tell me, how's Peter getting on?'

His question was met with a long silence, and for a moment, he thought the line had gone dead. 'I'm sorry,' Birgitte said eventually. 'What did you say?'

'I wondered how Peter was?'

'But you should know how Peter is. He is with you in Edinburgh, is he not?'

Alasdair sat forward in his chair. 'Peter? I don't think so, Birgitte.'

'Of course he is. He is directing some plays for you.' Alasdair began to note a rising level of desperation in her voice. 'I am sending him something in the post today as a surprise, but I do not know the address of his hotel and I don't want to contact him on his mobile phone, so I wondered if you might be able to tell me.'

Alasdair rubbed at his brow. 'Birgitte, I'm sorry, but if he's here in Edinburgh, I'm afraid it's for a different reason other than the festival, because I haven't seen him and he certainly isn't directing anything for me.'

He heard her mutter something forcefully in Danish, and deciphered the word God as part of the phrase.

'Birgitte, are you all right?' he asked concernedly.

There was a long sigh. 'Yes, I'm all right,' she replied in a resigned, almost sad voice. 'Tell me, Alasdair, do you know of a girl called Tess?'

'Well, I suppose you'll be referring to Tess Goodwin. She works in the office here.'

'Ah, she still works there, does she? I found out she was quite a friend of Peter's.'

'I suppose she was. She looked after him a couple of years ago, when he first came here to direct.'

'And she did a very good job of that, not just for one year, but for two.'

Alasdair frowned. 'I'm not sure quite what you mean by that, Birgitte.'

He heard her letting out a deep breath. 'Peter had an affair with this girl. It went on for the two years he was in Edinburgh and I found out about it just before the end of the festival last year.'

Alasdair stared with shock at the door of his office. 'Are you sure about all this?'

'Of course I am. I heard it from Peter himself. He is like a little boy, Alasdair, he cannot keep secrets. He has to tell me everything to . . . what is that word? . . . to . . . to exonerate himself.'

Alasdair ran a hand across his head. 'Birgitte, I had no idea. I'm so sorry.'

'Oh, it is not new. It has happened before. He goes off to work abroad and I never know what he is going to tell me when he gets home.'

'Why on earth do you stand for it?'

'Because of Kirsten and Henning and because – this may sound stupid to you – but because he is so honest about his indiscretions.' She sighed again. 'However, it looks like his affair with this Tess has continued, so maybe this time I have to make a decision.'

'Birgitte, to be quite honest, I really don't think you're right on this one. Tess got married earlier this year and I know she's head over heels in love with her husband. I can't see her jeopardising that relationship.'

'Do you know how long she went out with her husband before they got married?'

'Yes, quite some time. I think about three—' Alasdair stopped abruptly when he realised what he was saying. He pressed a hand to his forehead and closed his eyes. 'Oh, Birgitte, I really don't know what to say.'

'It's all right. It is my problem, not anybody else's. I shall speak with him and find out the truth.' She laughed quietly. 'He will no doubt tell me. Goodbye, Alasdair.'

He returned the farewell and thumped the receiver back on its cradle, and then sat drumming his fingers slowly on the desk, lost in his thoughts. The telephone began to ring again, this time it was an internal extension that flashed. He answered it.

'Hullo?'

'Good morning, Alasdair.' It was Sarah Atkinson. 'I've got Peter Hansen holding for you on line one. Do you want to speak to him?'

'Well, speak of the devil. Yes, I most certainly do. Sarah, is Tess coming in this morning?'

'She's just arrived. She had phoned in to say she was going to be a bit late.'

'Would you send her into my office as soon as I've finished with this call?'

'Will do.'

As soon as she had hung up, Alasdair heard the smooth voice of Peter Hansen greeting him with his usual self-confident charm.

'Peter,' Alasdair cut in vehemently, 'I've just spoken to Birgitte, and if I were you, you stupid bastard, I'd zip up your trousers and get back to her as fast as you bloody well can.'

He slammed down the receiver and jumped to his feet, and thrusting his hands into his trouser pockets, he turned and looked out of the window, trying to steady his anger and gather his thoughts before Tess came in. He had no more than a moment because there was an immediate knock on the door.

'Come in!'

He turned as Tess walked in and he could tell from the apprehensive expression on her face that Sarah had obviously warned her some kind of confrontation was imminent.

'Take a seat, Tess,' he said, gesturing towards the wooden armchair at the other side of the desk. He watched as she sat down, nervously smoothing her skirt over her knees. 'Are you all right?'

'Yes, fine. I just had a few glasses of wine over the top last night, but,' – she blew out a long breath – 'I'm ready now for what the world has to throw at me.'

'Right.' He cleared his throat. 'Tess, there's no real easy way to ask this question, but did you . . . or maybe I should say, have you been having an affair with the creative director Peter Hansen?'

She nodded slowly. 'You've obviously spoken to him.'

'Very briefly, but as it happens, it was his wife who's just broken the news to me.'

Tess closed her eyes tight and lowered her head. 'I had no idea she knew.'

'So it's been going on for three years.'

She jolted up her head. 'No, it all finished last year. I had no idea he was going to turn up again. He rang you out of the blue, don't you remember, about a week and a half ago, and you put him through to me?'

'He was here in Edinburgh at that time?'

'Yes, and he quite literally forced me into meeting with him.'

'How did he do that?'

'By implying that he would tell you about our affair if I first didn't see him, and then later, go out for dinner with him.'

Alasdair pressed a finger to his brow. 'For heaven's sakes, that's as good as blackmail.'

'I know,' Tess replied quietly.

'But, Tess, you didn't, er, succumb to him this time?'

Despite the seriousness of her predicament, Tess could not help but smile at his formality. 'No, of course I didn't. I'm married now, Alasdair, I'm extremely happy and I certainly wouldn't put all that at risk for a man like Peter Hansen.'

The director nodded. 'I'm glad.'

'I agreed to have dinner with him last night, but that's all. I've no doubt he viewed it as the necessary stepping stone in order to rekindle the affair, but it was going to be my opportunity to tell him to get the hell out of my life.'

'And did you say that to him?'

'No. For one reason or another, I didn't turn up.'

Alasdair nodded slowly, beginning to piece together Peter Hansen's resultant actions in his mind. 'So that's obviously why he called me this morning. To let the cat out of the bag.'

'I'm sure of it.' Tess leaned forward, resting a hand on the desk. 'I don't even know how to start apologising to you, Alasdair. I know he's a great friend of yours and I can't imagine what his wife is thinking right now . . .'

'Well, she's thinking it was all still going on.'

'I promise you, that's not true. It all ended pretty acrimoniously last year, but nevertheless, I do still feel so guilty for allowing it all to happen and letting you down so badly.'

Alasdair gave a dismissive wave of his hand. 'Tess, you've no reason to feel that way. *I'm* the one that's guilty.'

She stared at him, perplexed. 'I'm sorry?'

'I didn't admit knowledge of it to his wife, but I've known for years that Peter is a philanderer. He's had girls in every country he's worked in. I should *never* have put you in charge of him for that first year. I realise now it was as good as sending a lamb to slaughter. So, you see, it's me that owes *you* the apology.'

Tess remained silent for a moment. She could never imagine he would have reacted in such a way. 'Thank you,' she said quietly. 'I can't tell you how good that makes me feel.'

Alasdair smiled at her. 'And how bloody awful it makes me feel.'

Tess sat back in the chair and rubbed nervously at the palm of her hand. 'And . . . what about my job? Do you want me to continue?'

The director stared incredulously at her. 'Of course I do. Did you think you were in danger of losing it?'

'To be quite honest, yes.'

He shook his head slowly. 'How dreadful – not, I may add, because you thought you'd lose your job, but I realise now how little you understand my ways.' He stopped prowling around behind the desk and sat down, linking his hands in front of him. 'You have become a very important part of the team here, Tess.

323

I would go so far as to say you're invaluable, and I think, quite honestly, you could not have handled this appalling situation with Peter Hansen any better.'

'Yes, I could.'

'Why do you say that?'

She paused for a moment. 'I told Allan last year about the affair and that was the main reason we spurred on the marriage, but I never told him about Peter Hansen returning again and he found out.'

'Oh, my word, no,' Alasdair replied quietly. 'Has it caused great difficulties?'

'There was a moment when I thought I'd blown it completely, but we eventually managed to reason it out. If there's any upside to this whole stupid situation, it has to be that it's made me appreciate even more what a special person Allan is and just how much I love him.'

'Well, what a lucky girl you are to have hooked him.'

Tess grinned. 'Yes, I know.'

Alasdair shook his head. 'Well, I can only reiterate how sorry I am that this all took place, Tess, and if you feel you can, I really hope we might be able to treat this whole episode as water under the bridge.'

'I'd be happy to.'

'And if Mr Hansen ever so much as utters one word to you again, will you let me know?'

'Without a moment's hesitation.'

'Good.' The director thumped a hand down on his diary and smiled at her. 'In that case, maybe the time has come for us both to get on with some work.'

Forty-Two

Following hard on the heels of Matti Fullbright, Rene entered the Smirnoff Underbelly at the top door beneath a narrow tubular archway from which a sign of an upside-down cow with gravity-defying teats was suspended, and descended the stone steps into a claustrophobically small, but brightly painted reception area.

'Is this it?' Rene asked as she looked around, wondering why so much hype surrounded this Hobbit-sized venue.

'Just you wait,' Matti replied, beckoning her on. 'Don't make a judgement until you've seen the whole place.'

She led the way down a circular stone staircase, hardly wide enough for two undernourished people to pass without contact, each step worn into a curve by centuries of use. Spotlights played on the thick dark walls, plastered from top to bottom with posters advertising the acts that were being staged. At the bottom of the flight it opened out into a small but crowded space, off which led two doors hung with signs reading 'Quiet, please. Show in progress,' each attended by a girl wearing a red T-shirt emblazoned with the inverted-cow logo.

'Come on, keep up,' Matti said as she led on down another identical flight of stairs.

'I don't know if I'm enjoying this very much,' Rene said, putting her hands against the cold dank walls to steady her descent. 'It's like we're going into the bowels of the earth.'

'Aye, it does feel a bit like that,' Matti replied as she momentarily disappeared from sight.

'What is this place?'

'Old bank vaults,' Matti's disembodied voice echoed up the stairwell. 'They're supposed to be haunted.'

'Oh, bloody 'ell,' Rene mumbled, hurrying her step to catch up with her tour guide.

They continued to descend more winding stairs, each one ending on a floor packed with show-goers, standing outside venues or crammed into bars with low-vaulted ceilings that rang with laughter and conversation.

'How big is this place?' Rene asked as she squeezed past a portly American woman who had picked an inopportune place to stop and study her programme.

'Ten venues, three bars and a nightclub,' Matti replied. 'I think they continuously stage about one hundred and thirty shows a day.'

They eventually ran out of staircases, coming out into a large bar that was again filled to bursting point.

'This is the famous Beer Belly,' Matti said as she pushed her way through to the blue-fronted bar. 'I'll get us some drinks up and meet you outside in the yard.' She pointed a finger towards an entrance at the far end of the room.

Rene threaded her way through the crowd and walked out the lower entrance door into a narrow cobbled alleyway, its fifty-metre length strung with a dazzle of lighted bulbs. Small open-doored rooms and arched alcoves lined the street, each set up as a temporary coffee stall or fast-food kitchen, their wares being consumed at wooden tables that sat against the walls of the ancient stone buildings. Rene stopped in front of a huge board that showed the full programme of events, smiling at the clever puns that gave names to each of the venues – Belly Button, Belly Dancer, Delhi Belly. She scanned the list of acts, eventually finding Matti's name under a column headed Belly Laugh.

'Here y'are,' Matti said as she arrived beside Rene and handed her an enormous glass brimming with spitting bubbles.

'What is it?' Rene asked, holding it away from her and studying its swirling contents.

'A very large Bacardi and Coke.'

''Eavens, lass, I'm not used to drinking in the middle of the day.'

'You're going to need it,' she said, grabbing Rene by the arm. 'Come on, I'm running late.'

The musty-smelling changing room was as small and sparsely furnished as a nun's cell, yet it was a hundred times more salubrious than the conditions Rene had to endure at the Corinthian Bar. 'Take off your coat and sling it on a chair,' Matti said as she hurried to get herself ready, 'and then go out on stage and have a squint through the curtains. I need to know if there's anyone out there.'

Shrugging off her coat, Rene walked out of the room, around the side wing and out on to the stage. She tiptoed over to the curtain and pulled it aside a fraction, catching her breath when she saw that the auditorium was jam-packed. She dropped the curtain and scuttled back to the changing room.

'It doesn't look as if there's a spare seat in the place!' she said to Matti, who was leaning over in front of the mirror on the makeshift dressing table, trying to fix a red rose in her hair with a kirby grip.

'Fantastic!' she exclaimed, picking up the plastic bag she had brought with her. 'Just what I wanted.' She extracted a white rose and another kirby grip from the bag and handed it to Rene. 'Stick that in your hair, girl.'

'What for?'

'Don't ask, just do it.'

Moving over to the mirror, Rene arranged the rose above her right ear and secured it with the grip. She stood back, swinging from side to side as she admired herself. 'Look at that – a touch of Carmen, don't ye think?'

'You look perfect,' Matti said, pulling Rene by the arm out towards the stage as the announcer began his rambling introduction.

'I'd better go try find a seat out there,' Rene said, trying to wrest her arm free from Matti's grip.

'Leave it to the last minute, would you? I'm feeling dead nervous about my act today.'

'. . . so, ladies and gentlemen,' the announcer's voice crescendoed through the sound system, 'will you please welcome that red-haired lady from Lancashire, MATTI-I-I-I FULLBRIGHT!'

As the curtains drew back and the audience burst out into applause and loud whistles, Rene tried once more to free herself from Matti's vicelike hand.

'I'd better get off now,' she said.

Matti turned round to face her, a broad grin on her freckly face. 'Too late. We're on.'

She gave Rene an almighty heave that nearly took her off

her feet. The next thing she knew she was standing in the middle of the stage in front of the largest audience she had faced since being in Edinburgh.

'Good evening, everybody, good evening!' Matti yelled out, waving her hands in the air in acknowledgement of the thundering applause. 'OK, calm down, calm down.'

She turned to Rene and eyed her in a strangely hostile way as the noise abated. 'I decided tonight to bring along a friend with me. Well, not really a friend, actually. How could she be?' She nodded knowingly. 'She's from Yorkshire.' She turned and walked towards Rene, giving her a wink as she approached. 'Ladies and gentlemen,' she said, putting her arm around Rene's shoulders, 'this is Rene Brownlow, one of the funniest women I know, but unfortunately' – she reached down and patted Rene's stomach – 'coming from Hartlepool, she's too fond of her fish suppers.'

As the audience burst out laughing, Rene looked up at Matti, aghast that she could have said such a thing, but then her fellow comedienne smiled and leaned over and whispered in her ear, 'Come on, defend your rose.'

And then Rene understood. The red rose of Lancashire, the white rose of Yorkshire. Matti was setting up a double act. No rehearsals, no scripts. She wanted a duel of head-to-head ad-libbing, one bouncing off the other. The audience was suddenly deathly silent, waiting for the riposte, waiting for the next scheduled line to be spoken. But there was none. She slowly unwound Matti's arm from around her shoulders and stood her distance from her, appraising her from head to foot. 'You're a fine one to talk, ye red-'aired tramp. Bad breeding, that's what it is' – she held out her hands to the audience – 'but what can ye expect, coming from Lancashire.' And with that, the partisan spirit of the audience was unleashed with whoops of support and cries of umbrage.

It was the perfect ice-breaker, but neither Matti nor Rene could keep up the animosity during the performance. There was too strong a rapport between them, too much good humour, and they settled into an off-the-cuff routine that had both the audience and themselves in fits of laughter. They kept it going without one faltering moment for a full hour, and at the end of the show the audience would not allow them to leave the stage, clapping and banging their feet for a full ten minutes before the curtain finally fell on the two bowing performers.

'Read that!' Matti exclaimed, striding across the bar in the Assembly Rooms and throwing a copy of the *Evening News* at Rene.

'What is it?' she asked, leaning forward on the sofa and putting her drink down on the table.

'I'm not telling you,' Matti said, her face aflame with excitement. 'Just read it and see.'

Rene watched Matti move off with a spring in her step towards the bar before spreading the folded paper on her knee. She scanned the newsprint, trying to find what she was meant to be looking for, and then her own name bounced out at her. She moved quickly to the start of the small review article, entitled 'War of the Roses'.

This had to be written today, it read. *It couldn't wait. At two o'clock this afternoon, the Belly Laugh venue truly lived up to its name when two comediennes took to the stage for a raucous side-splitting, hour-long ad-lib session.*

Wacky-haired Lancastrian Matti Fullbrook, a favourite with audiences at the Underbelly for the past three years, teamed up with feisty little Yorkshire lass Rene Brownlow (currently appearing at the Corinthian Bar in West Richmond Street) to produce one of the most pulsating double acts seen so far on the Fringe this year. And rumour has it that it's not going to be a one-off either, so go beg, steal or kill your best friend for a ticket. It's just a pity they hadn't pooled their considerable talents before now, because there's no doubt they would have been up there with the front-runners contesting the Perrier Comedy Award for this year.

'Did you find it?' Matti asked, placing two wineglasses on the table in front of Rene before applying all her strength to prising the cork out of a bottle of Cava.

Rene could not reply. She read through the article again, taking in every word, every accolade, every nuance of what the reviewer was implying.

'What have we done?' she asked eventually, her eyes registering total incomprehension.

'We've cracked it, Rene, that's what we've done.'

'But what's all this about the show continuing? We never said that.'

Matti grinned as she overflowed the glasses with frothing liquid. 'I did.'

Rene dropped the newspaper on the sofa and stared at Matti in disbelief. 'Why?'

'Why not? We're electric, Rene. We've taken the punters by storm. I've never had a reaction to any of my shows like that. Have you?'

Rene looked at Matti open-mouthed. 'Are ye saying that . . . we should team up, like?'

'Of course I am! We've got it made, girl!' The grin slid from her face, taking Rene's blank expression as one of rejection to the idea. 'What's the matter? Don't you want to?'

Rene slowly shook her head. 'Matti, ye're successful. Ye've been working the Fringe for years. For God's sakes, ye've even got an agent! It's a really wonderful thought, lass, but ye don't want to be saddled with me.'

'What d'you mean, saddled with you? Rene, it's vice versa! I told you I had to change my act. I need you. Obviously though, the question is do you need me?'

'But . . . what about my own show in the Corinthian? What do I do about that?'

330

'Ditch it! You said yourself you weren't getting the punters in. If we team up, we'll go fifty-fifty on everything. That'll cover all your costs and more, I know it will.'

Rene bit hard at her bottom lip to stop herself from bursting into tears. It didn't work. She got up from the sofa, walked around the table and put her arms around Matti's neck. 'Thanks, lass, thanks so much.'

Matti chuckled. 'Do I take that as a yes, then?' she asked, pushing Rene away from her.

Rene snuffled out a laugh. 'Aye, why not? Let's go for it.'

'Oh, that is great, girl!' Matti said, punching her fists in the air. 'You and I are just going to take this whole damned world apart!' She picked up the two glasses from the table and handed one to Rene. 'Here's to us, my love, here's to the War of the bloody Roses!'

Forty-Three

On the Thursday, two days before the last acts of the Festival Fringe were to be staged and nine days before the final curtain was brought down on the International Festival, four white trucks, each emblazoned with the Exploding Sky Company logo, drove slowly across the castle esplanade through a chevron of tourists. They lined up, one behind the other, waiting while the first truck was guided through the low tunnel leading into the inner sanctum of Edinburgh Castle, its roof having barely six inches clearance at either side of the ancient stone archway. Once it was parked in the inner courtyard, drawn up in front of the portcullis gate, Roger Dent jumped down from the cab and stretched his arms above his head, ridding himself of the stiffness in his body after the ten-hour drive. He walked over to the battlements and looked out across the all-too-familiar view of the New Town while the other trucks came through the tunnel and drew in close to his own. As the drivers disembarked, Roger pushed himself up on to the wall and sat watching as they made their way over to him.

Every one of his crew had at least two years' experience of doing this particular job with him, each choosing to spend his two-week summer holiday helping him to put the show together. They were really a crazy bunch of misfits – Dave Panton, a weapons expert for the Ministry of Defence; Graham Slattery, a computer programmer with IBM; and Annie Beardsley, an air traffic controller at Gatwick Airport – but they seemed to gel as a team with both humour and ease, their work of setting up the display a far cry from the stress and worries of their everyday employment.

And it was just as well he had an experienced team with him this year. The programme he and Phil Kenyon had eventually devised for the climax of the Edinburgh Festival was to be the most complex and work-intensive display his company had ever dared to stage, the intricately timed detonation of over five tonnes of fireworks in thirty minutes. It was to be his swansong, his final flourish, but yet, even now, the thought of the logistics involved was enough to make his stomach knot tight in trepidation.

'Right, before we adjourn to the pub,' Roger began, a remark that received an immediate cry of approval from his attentive audience, 'I'm afraid there's a good bit of work to be done. We'll start by unloading all the workshop equipment and get it set up under the stairs in the master gunner's office. There's no need to change a plan that works, so lay it out exactly as we've done in previous years – all electrical gear at the far end of the store, radios near the sockets for recharging, and the firing plan and safety regs on the wall above the table. If we get all that done this afternoon, we'll start loading the small-calibre shells first thing tomorrow morning.' He pushed himself off the wall. 'OK, make a move.'

As the crew headed back to their respective vans, Phil Kenyon appeared from a small doorway at one end of the narrow terrace and made his way across to Roger.

'All looks good,' the stocky little Australian remarked, handing Roger a clipboard with pad attached. 'No new safety measures, so we can just go ahead as planned.'

'When are the riggers due to arrive?'

'First thing Saturday morning. I reckon the briefing will take most of the day, so we won't start getting the multicore cabling laid out until Sunday morning.'

'And when are you due to meet up with the score reader?'

Phil shot him a wink. 'The beautiful Helen, d'ya mean?'

Roger narrowed his eyes at his colleague. 'Just watch it, Phil, don't cause a fallout, this of all years.'

'No worries, mate, I'll keep it under wraps. She's coming across from Glasgow tomorrow afternoon, so we'll make a start then on the timing plan.'

'It could take quite a while. A lot of those new cues will be completely alien to her.'

'We'll make it, as long as we don't have too many unscheduled interruptions.'

As Phil said this, a young woman dressed in a dark business suit came through the castle tunnel and strutted meaningfully towards them, a gash of a smile on her lipsticked mouth.

'Oh-oh, I spoke too soon,' Phil said, turning his back on the woman. 'You deal with her and I'll go help the others.'

As Phil headed off to the vans, Roger crossed his arms and leaned back against the wall, watching as Pauline McCann, the PR coordinator for the Scottish Bank, the main sponsor of the Fireworks Display, approached him. 'Hi there, Pauline, how're things with you?' He gave her a welcoming peck on the cheek.

'Working away, Roger,' the woman replied jovially. 'No rest for the wicked, and all that.'

'I'm surprised to see you. I thought you were planning on leaving the SB to set up your own agency.'

'You're right, it was a thought,' she said, digging a hand into her large shoulder bag and extracting a Moleskin notebook, 'but then the company made me an offer I couldn't refuse.'

She undid the elastic band on her book. 'Right, let's get down to business. First off, I have a few messages for you. Jeff Banyon wants to meet with you at the Scottish Chamber Orchestra office tomorrow evening, so he asked if you give him a call. And Sir Raymond Garston, the conductor, will be here on Tuesday morning and would like to meet up around lunchtime at the Balmoral Hotel.' She turned a page. 'Now, the International office has scheduled the press call this year for Monday morning at ten o'clock. I know this is a bit earlier than usual, but the weather forecast for Tuesday and Wednesday is a bit iffy, so I thought it would be a safer bet for the photo opportunity. Does that sound all right for you?'

Roger shrugged. 'As long as you keep it as brief as possible.'

Pauline smiled at him. 'I'll do my best.' She closed the note-book and put it back in her bag. 'Now, I'll need to send out a blanket e-mail to all the papers, so is there anything you can tell me about what you've got planned for this year?'

Roger let out a quiet laugh. 'It's going to be the largest and the most complicated display I've ever staged.'

'Really? That's quite a statement.'

'I'm throwing every bit of caution to the wind this year.'

'Any reason for that?'

Roger nodded slowly. 'It's to be my last show.'

'*What?*' Pauline exclaimed, her eyes wide in disbelief. 'But you can't . . . you've been doing it for . . .'

'This is the twenty-third year,' Roger offered.

'So . . . does this mean it's the last year the Exploding Sky Company will be doing the Fireworks Display?'

'I hope not. Phil Kenyon is taking on the business, so I suppose it'll be up to him and the Scottish Bank as the sponsors. In fact, you'd be doing me a favour in letting them know before the story hits the press.'

'You don't mind me using it as a hook, then?'

'Not at all. You can entitle it "Going out with a bang!"'

Pauline laughed. 'That's not such a bad idea, actually.

Maybe you should think about starting a second career as a journalist.'

Roger rubbed a hand against his beard. 'Listen, by the time this show is over, I reckon the only establishment that will invite me into its folds is a secure lunatic asylum.' And he turned with a wave and headed off towards the vans to help the crew, eager to finish off the day's work as quickly as possible so he could get to the pub for the first of many pints of beer that evening.

About the same time as the clientele of the Queen's Head in Grassmarket was swelled by the ranks of the Exploding Sky Company, a mud-spattered, long-wheel-based Land Rover was pulling up outside the flat in London Street. Killing the engine, Rory Stratton clambered out and walked around to open up the back door. Jamie was already waiting there on the pavement with Angélique, ready to pull out the luggage.

'Thanks for the lift, Dad,' Jamie said, hoisting the straps of the two bags on to his shoulder and taking the violin case in his hand. 'Do you want to come up for a drink?'

Rory shook his head. 'No, I'll head home. I half promised your mother to take her out for a meal in the village pub this evening.'

'You should do that. It'll give her a break. I don't think she realised she was going to have to put up with us for a whole week.'

Rory put a hand on his son's shoulder. 'It was a great time. We both loved it.' He walked over to Angélique and gave her a kiss on either cheek. 'And what a bonus meeting you, my beautiful French girl. See and keep in touch with Jamie's old fogies now, won't you?'

'Of course I will,' Angélique replied, reaching up and putting her arms around Rory's neck and giving him a long hug. 'Thank you so much for having me to stay, Rory. It has been the most wonderful time.' She pushed herself away from him. 'I will send you some more CDs that I think you will like. Maybe you can play them along with the Rolling Stones?'

Rory smiled. 'I'll make a point of it.' He turned back to Jamie. 'I hope you don't have any more problems with . . . you know who,' he said quietly.

'I doubt it very much. Harry Wills was outside the flat for three days. Never saw a thing.'

'Good.' Rory put his arms around his son's shoulders and gave him a squeeze. 'Look after yourself, boy, and keep in touch.'

'Will do, Dad, and thanks again for everything.'

They waited on the doorstep until the Land Rover had pulled away from the kerb before Jamie put the key in the door and they both entered into the building.

No more than twenty seconds after the door had closed behind them, a dishevelled figure hurried across the street and up the steps and pressed his hands against the door, as if willing it to open. Albert Dessuin turned away, his fingers splayed against his throbbing head, and slowly slid his back down the door to sit on the cold stone step, feeling the damp seep through the fabric of his raincoat. He cared little for that, or for the general grubbiness of his appearance, because now, at last, he had found Angélique Pascal.

Five days had passed since he had followed the fat little comedienne back to this address. It had been luck that he had made the decision to wait for her in the bar at the Corinthian, rather than in the theatre, because for some reason she had not performed that night, only turning up long enough to have a word with the blonde girl at the box office before she had left again. Five days. How his whole life had changed in that time. At first, he thought the refusal of his credit card at the restaurant in Randolph Place had been a mistake, a mere fault of the electronic banking system, but then when he had tried it in four different automatic machines without success, he knew something was definitely amiss. Returning to his hotel, he had phoned his bank in Paris and was informed that his monthly cheque had not been paid in and would he therefore write a letter immediately, authorising them to transfer money from his deposit account to cover the weekly standing order made to his mother's account. Because of the embarrassment and inconvenience this had caused him, anger blinded any consideration of the outcome of the next telephone call and he had instantly rung the lawyers of Madame Lafitte in Clermont Ferrand, demanding to know why his salary had not been paid. Even before he had finished haranguing the female receptionist he was transferred to a Monsieur Chambert, who introduced himself in a quiet but frosty voice as the recently appointed secretary of the trust set up by Madame Lafitte for Angélique Pascal. Albert could do nothing but listen in mute horror as the man recounted to him in a controlled, precise manner every detail of what took place between himself and Angélique on the night of the sixteenth of August in the Sheraton Grand, and, as a result of which, it was considered by the trustees that he, Albert Dessuin, was an entirely unsuitable chaperone for Angélique Pascal and that his contract of employment was to be terminated with immediate effect and that no consideration should be given to financial compensation. At that point, Albert Dessuin could hear the change in the lawyer's voice as he spat out his closing line with such vehemence and hostility that Albert was left shaking as the receiver buzzed in his ear. 'And if you ever chance to go near Mademoiselle Pascal again, I will make sure every police force in the world has knowledge of what you have done and I can guarantee there will be no safe haven for you. Goodbye, Dessuin.'

He had booked himself out of the hotel immediately after the telephone call, realising that he could no longer continue to afford to stay there and wanting desperately to distance himself from the place. Monsieur Chambert had confirmed to him for the first time that Angélique had been divulging the true facts of what had happened that night, and consequently others would no doubt know about it here in Edinburgh. From that moment on he could sense a thousand pairs of judging eyes upon him, watching his every move with distrust and loathing.

He had eventually ended up staying in a grubby, stale-aired room above a pub in Tollcross. It was being used as a storeroom, but the barman, who had taken pity on the drunk foreigner who sat alone with his suitcase in the corner of the bar, had cleared out the boxes and the empty beer crates and had then gone back to his own flat, returning with blankets and sheets to put on the metal-framed bed with the sagging mattress. There were no washing facilities on the upper floor, so Albert had to make use of the rank-smelling gents' lavatory downstairs, only being able to do that during the time when the pub alarm was switched off. Consequently, he had spent many a lonely hour in those sordid surroundings, his self-esteem shattered and his mind becoming increasingly embroiled with hatred and revenge, having too much time to think about the hopelessness of his situation and about those whom he knew to be responsible for it all happening.

He put a hand into the folds of his mackintosh and pulled out a half bottle of whisky from the inside pocket. He held it up in front of him, studying the inch of amber liquid still remaining in the bottle. This now was his only true solace, a mind-numbing refuge from all his crazy, distorted thoughts. Unscrewing the cap, he tilted it to his mouth and drained the bottle in two gulps. He placed it on the step beside him, carefully resting the cap upside down on the top, a small token of order in his disordered world. He got to his feet and steadied himself on the cast-iron handrail as he descended the steps. After five days, the waiting was over. He had found Angélique Pascal. A few more hours, even a few more days would make no difference. Eventually he would be able to confront her and ask her why, after all those years he had sacrificed for her, she had chosen to ruin him completely.

The delicious aroma of roast chicken was floating around the hallway when Jamie and Angélique entered the flat. Dumping the bags on the ground, Jamie followed the herb-laden smell to its source, pushing open the door of the kitchen. Rene Brownlow, Leonard Hartson and his young assistant, T.K., were seated at the table, all in the throes of eating, a glass of red wine in front of each. The conversation halted when he and Angélique walked in, and his three tenants turned to look their way.

'Well, if it's not our absentee landlord,' Rene said with a smile.

'Yeah, sorry about that,' Jamie replied, scratching embarrassedly at his head. 'We sort of stayed a bit longer than was expected.' He eyed the plates piled with food on the table. 'You seemed to have been coping all right, though.'

'Aye, well, someone had to play mother for these poor starving lads.' She laid down her knife and fork and pushed herself to her feet. ''Ow about some for yourselves?'

Jamie held up a hand. 'No, don't worry. I can make something up for Angélique and myself.'

'Don't be stupid. There's masses left over.' Grabbing a cloth from the sideboard, Rene opened the door of the oven and took out an enormous roast chicken, one side of it still untouched. 'Come on, join the party.'

'Are you sure?' Jamie asked.

'Of course you must,' Leonard Hartson cut in, getting to his feet and pulling an unoccupied chair away from the table. 'Move yourself round the table, T.K., and allow the young lady a bit of space beside you.'

'Hullo, we have not met,' Angélique said, reaching across the table to shake hands with the two men, young and old. 'My name is Angélique Pascal.'

'Ah, my word, what a pleasure!' Leonard said, bowing his head as he took her hand. 'I have long been an admirer of your wonderful playing.' He introduced both himself and T.K. to Angélique.

Rene placed two steaming plates brimming with chicken, vegetables and potatoes on the table. 'Right, grab yourselves a knife and fork and get stuck in.' She took two wineglasses from the cupboard above the worktop and put them next to the plates.

'And I'm sure Leonard wouldn't mind if you had some of 'is wine.'

'I'm afraid it's only a very humble Bordeaux,' Leonard said, smiling apologetically at Angélique as he leaned across to pour her a glass. 'I'm sure you will notice that as soon as you try it.'

Sitting down next to T.K., Angélique took a sip from her glass. 'It is delicious. You are obviously quite knowledgeable about wines, Leonard.'

'Leonard knows a lot aboot everythin', don't ye, Leonard?' T.K. stated with pride.

Leonard laughed. 'Flattery will get you everywhere, T.K.'

As Jamie took his seat, he looked across the table at the cameraman. Although he appeared to be in good spirits, the old man seemed to have aged visibly since Jamie had last seen him. His eyes were twinkling with enthusiasm, but they were set deep into a face that was lined with either worry or pain, its colour drained to an unhealthy chalky-white.

'So, how's it going with the filming?' Jamie asked.

'We're doing reasonably well,' Leonard replied. 'A little bit behind in our schedule, but hopefully we'll be able to complete everything in the next nine days.'

'The stuff we've shot so far s'been great, isn't that right, Leonard?' T.K. said, looking eagerly at the cameraman.

'I think it would be safer to say that the reports from London have been quite encouraging.' He shot a clandestine wink at Jamie. 'My assistant is not only an invaluable asset to me whilst shooting, but also a constant boost to my morale.'

Jamie swallowed a mouthful of food. 'Well, I'm glad all's been going so well while we've been away.'

'Aye, an' for Rene, too,' T.K. said.

Jamie turned to the comedienne. 'Really?'

'Go on, Rene, tell 'em whit's happened tae you's,' T.K. prompted.

Rene's face flushed to a colour similar to that of the wine she was drinking. 'I've . . . erm . . . started a new show.'

'What?' Jamie asked perplexedly. 'Where?'

'In the Underbelly.'

Jamie stared at her. 'You're kidding!'

'What is an Underbelly?' Angélique asked.

'Only probably the best Fringe venue in the whole of Edinburgh.' He turned his attention back to Rene. 'How did you manage that?'

'I teamed up with another girl who was doing a show there. We're now on as a double act.'

'Who is she?'

'A lass from Lancashire, Matti Fullbright.'

Jamie's jaw dropped. 'Matti Fullbright! Rene, she's fantastic! I reviewed her show last year when she was short-listed for the Perrier Comedy Award.'

It was Rene's turn to gawp. 'Ye're kidding me! She never told me that!'

'Well, all I can say is that you've got yourself teamed up with one of the funniest women I've ever seen. Is this to be a permanent partnership?'

Rene shrugged. 'I reckon it could be. We've been playing to packed audiences every day. They've even shifted our act on to twice daily.'

'How did they organise that?'

'They found someone who was quite 'appy to move to my old venue at the Corinthian.'

Jamie nodded slowly. 'You've got it made, Rene. That's great news. What do the folks back home in Hartlepool think about it all?'

Rene grimaced. 'I 'aven't actually told them.'

'Why not?'

'Because there's a lot to discuss before I make a decision one way or t'other,' she replied, and not wanting to enlarge on the problems her new partnership would doubtlessly cause in her already troubled domestic life, she left it with a smile and turned to Angélique. 'So, 'ow's your 'and getting on, luv?'

Angélique held up her injured hand, showing no sign of a strapping, only a small pink scar across the palm. 'It is back to normal, I think.'

'Oh, that looks brilliant,' Rene said, taking the violinist's hand in hers and scrutinising the healed wound. 'You'll be back to playing the violin in the blink of an eye.'

'She already is,' Jamie said. 'In fact, Angélique reckons she's ready to play in public again, so we're just hoping the International office can arrange for her to do one of the late concerts next week, just before the close of the festival.'

'Oh, I'm glad to 'ear that, lass,' Rene said, giving Angélique's hand a pat. 'Ye're doing exactly the right thing, jumping back on that 'orse straight after ye've fallen off it.'

Jamie thumped his hands down on the table. 'Right, I think all occupants of number seven London Street have got quite a bit to celebrate, so how's about we adjourn to the local pub and have a drink?'

There was no voiced approval to the idea but all jumped to their feet and started to clear away the plates. All, that is, except Leonard. 'If you don't mind,' he said quietly, 'I think I might just give it a miss on this occasion.'

T.K. clattered the plate he was carrying down on the sideboard and stared at the elderly cameraman. 'Whit's up, Leonard?' he asked concernedly.

Leonard held up a hand. 'Nothing at all, T.K. I'm just a little tired. Nothing a good night's rest won't cure.'

Jamie glanced worriedly at Rene. 'We don't need to go out.'

'Of course you must!' Leonard replied heatedly as he got slowly to his feet. 'I'm perfectly capable of looking after myself.'

'Ah'll gie ye a hand tae the bedroom,' T.K. said, putting a supporting hand under Leonard's elbow.

'Really, T.K., there's no need.'

'Aye, there is,' T.K. replied resolutely. 'Ye're goin tae yer bed.'

Leonard smiled at the rest of the party. 'Quite an assistant, is he not?'

'Do you think he's all right?' Jamie asked, pulling on his jacket as he came down the steps to join Rene and Angélique on the pavement.

'I'm not that sure,' Rene replied as they began walking up London Street side by side. 'To be quite 'onest, I think 'e's bitten off more than 'e can chew. 'E told me this is the first film job 'e's done for about twenty years.'

'Never!' Jamie exclaimed.

'Aye, and what's more, 'e was meant to have a whole load of people 'elping 'im, and now it's just 'im and the young lad.'

'Maybe we should ask that nice doctor who treated my hand to come round to see him,' Angélique suggested.

'Good idea,' Jamie replied. 'We'll see how the old boy's getting on in the morning and make a decision then.' They turned the corner and began walking up Broughton Street. 'Come on, let's take a short cut,' he said, turning down a narrow cobbled street lit only by a few dim lamps fixed high on the dark walls of the surrounding buildings. It was deserted save for a large ginger cat that jumped clear of an open dustbin and disappeared down some steps as they passed.

'Ooh, I'm glad I'm in the presence of a tough young man,' Rene said, wrapping her coat around her. 'I wouldn't fancy walking down 'ere by myself.'

'Do you think T.K. will know where we are?' Angélique asked.

'I don't know if he'll come, but anyway I told him the name of the pub before we left. He should find it.' There was the sound of footsteps running quickly up the street behind them. Jamie turned. 'Speak of the dev—'

The force of the blow to his shoulder was so great that it made him spin round through three hundred and sixty degrees. He put out his hands to try to grab hold of something that would keep him on his feet, but he knew immediately it was a lost cause. The side of his head hit hard against the cold stone of the building and his knees gave way, his eyes swimming in and out of focus as he slowly sank down the wall to the ground. Clutching his head in his hands, he heard Angélique scream and Rene shout, their voices sounding to him as if both were standing in an echo chamber. The words 'Let go of 'er!' resonated through his brain, followed by a hollow slap like a fish being thrown down on to a wooden chopping board. A heavy weight fell across his legs and through blurred vision he saw Rene lying in front of him, whimpering and clutching at the side of her face. 'Albert, stop this! Please, stop this!' he heard Angélique cry out.

The name rammed into Jamie's brain, causing an adrenalin rush that cleared his head and brought feeling back to his legs. Pulling himself free of Rene's weight, he levered his body up the wall and staggered towards Dessuin, who had Angélique gripped firmly by the wrists. He was yelling at her in French, his eyes demonic with hatred and rage. It was only then Jamie realised that, in all the physical encounters he had experienced on the rugby pitch, he had never been rendered quite so hopelessly weak. Dessuin turned to see him approach and let go of Angélique.

'You filthy bastard!' he spat out, as he came towards Jamie. 'You think you can turn her against me?' He grabbed hold of Jamie's hair with force and yanked his head down, at the same time bringing his knee up into the pit of Jamie's stomach. Jamie keeled over, fighting for breath, but still Dessuin was not finished with him. He pulled his head up by the hair and slammed Jamie against the building, clutching him by the lapel of his jacket. Jamie saw the fist being drawn back and knew now that he was without the energy either to duck or to parry the blow. His only act of resilience was to keep his eyes open while the finishing blow was administered.

But it never came. He suddenly saw Dessuin spin round in front of him and the Frenchman's head rock backwards. He turned slowly back to face Jamie, clutching at his nose as blood spurted out between his fingers, and Jamie watched as he sank down to his knees on the cobbled street. Gulping in air, Jamie now focused on the figure that stood before him.

'Jeez,' T.K. groaned as he rubbed hard at his forehead. 'Ah never got the hang o' the head butt.'

Jamie shook his head. 'You did bloody well, mate. I owe you

one.' He looked past T.K. to see Angélique enveloped in the bearlike folds of Harry Wills's arms. 'God, the cavalry arrived in the nick of time, didn't it?'

Jamie stumbled round Dessuin's hunched form and squatted down beside the little comedienne's supine body. 'Rene,' he said gently, taking hold of her hand, 'are you all right?'

Rene opened one eye. 'Aye, I'm fine. I just decided to play dead until that bloody French madman had gone.'

Jamie smiled at her. 'Well, you're safe enough now,' he said, pulling her to her feet and giving her a hug. 'Sorry about that. I wasn't much good.'

Rene glanced down at Dessuin with a sneer of disgust. 'You didn't get much of a chance, lad.' She leaned over Dessuin's hunched form. 'The little sewer rat played dirty, didn't ye?'

Jamie felt an arm slip around his waist and he turned to find Angélique looking up at him, her face puffy and stained with tears. 'Are you badly hurt?' she sobbed.

'No, I'm fine. Just aching a bit,' he replied, putting an arm around her shoulders and giving her a squeeze. 'Don't worry. It's all over and done with now.'

'I'm sorry about all this, Jamie,' Harry Wills said, coming to stand beside Dessuin and looking down at him with pure dislike. 'I never saw sight nor sound of him while I was outside your flat. I really had no idea he knew where you lived.'

Jamie shook his head. 'No matter. Where did you spring from, anyway?'

'I dropped in at the flat just after you'd left to go to the pub. I was coming round with T.K. to join you for a drink.'

'Just as well,' Jamie replied, clutching a hand to his aching stomach. He nodded towards Dessuin. 'So what are we going to do with him?'

Harry Wills bent down and heaved Dessuin to his feet. He put a hand into his pocket and pulled out his mobile phone. 'I think this game we've been playing has run its course. It's time to call in the police.'

As he began punching in a number, Angélique glanced at

Albert. He still clutched at his nose, covering his face with his hands, but she saw new tears well up in his eyes.

'Please wait, Harry. Don't do it just yet.' Walking over to Dessuin, she reached up and took a hand away from his face and held it in hers. 'Albert, you must understand it's all over. Please, will you go home now? I promise you not one other person will ever know about what happened between us. You are such a talented man and you must use that talent to help others as you have helped me. And Albert, you must find someone else to look after your mother because she will continue to make your life a misery and you do not deserve that. So, please, Albert, go back to Paris and find yourself some happiness there.'

Dessuin lowered his face and his body suddenly heaved with sobs. 'I'm so sorry, Angélique,' he cried. 'I'm so sorry.'

Putting a hand on either side of his face, Angélique lifted it up and planted a gentle kiss on his cheek. 'Will you go?'

Dessuin bit hard at his bottom lip to control himself. 'I would do anything for you.'

'I know you would.' She pressed his face between her hands. 'You are not a bad man, Albert. You must take courage and start on a new life without me.'

Harry Wills slipped the mobile back into his pocket. 'I'll take him back.'

'What d'you mean?' Jamie asked. 'To Paris?'

Harry nodded. 'I feel responsible for tonight, so it's the least I can do. Anyway, I'm not quite so forgiving as Angélique, and I'll not rest easy until I've seen this chap out of the country. I'll have him stay with me tonight so as I can keep an eye on him and then we'll get the first flight out tomorrow.' He gripped Dessuin firmly by the arm. 'Come on, let's make a move.'

'Harry?'

The reporter turned round to Jamie. 'Yes?'

'Could you give me a call tomorrow before you leave? There's something I want to discuss with you.'

346

Harry nodded. 'Sure.' He shot them a smile. 'I'd get to bed, you lot. I think you've all had enough excitement for one night.'

Having watched Harry guide Albert Dessuin down the street and round the corner, Jamie leaned over, resting his hands on his knees, and took in a couple of deep breaths. 'Angélique, would you head back to the flat with Rene?'

'Why? What are you going to do?' she asked.

'Just recover for a moment. T.K. and I will be along soon.'

Angélique took the comedienne by the arm and they walked off slowly down the street.

'Hell, I didn't want to let on,' he said to T.K. once they were out of earshot, 'but that bloody man's really managed to hurt me.'

'D'ye need a hand?' T.K. asked.

'No, just give me a minute.' He looked up at T.K. 'Can I ask you something?'

'Whit?'

'Have we met before . . . I mean, before you came round to the flat with Gavin Mackintosh?'

T.K. grinned at him. 'Aye, we coulda done.'

'Where?'

'I think it wis you I bumped intae roond the corner there. Ye were carrying somethin' in yer hand and ye drapped it.'

Jamie nodded slowly as the mental picture of the paint cans rolling off the side of the pavement came to mind. 'Of course. That was it. You went haring up London Street.'

T.K. laughed. 'Aye, I thocht someone wis efter me.'

Jamie scrutinised him. 'It wouldn't have had anything to do with a stolen video camera from the coffee shop, would it?'

T.K. scratched at the back of his head. 'Aye, well, sort of.'

Jamie had a sudden fit of coughing and he gripped the side of his ribcage in agony.

'Whit's the matter?' T.K. asked. 'Are ye all right?'

Jamie lifted his head. 'Yeah, don't worry. I'm just laughing and it bloody hurts.'

'Whit's so funny?'

'Nothing, really,' he said, pushing himself upright and giving T.K. a thump on the shoulder, 'only that both you and I have damned good reasons not to set foot inside that coffee shop ever again.' He began to walk slowly down the street. 'I could kill for a pint of beer. What about you?'

T.K. smiled to himself and then hurried to catch up with Jamie. 'Aye, why not?'

Jamie felt the relieving effects of the two power-plus painkillers, swallowed with the aid of a large malt whisky, drift over his body like healing hands as he lay in the darkness of his room. He was only a moment away from deep, restful unconsciousness when it happened, so he could not tell whether it was an incipient dream of unrequited desire rather than sublime reality. It started with a beam of light falling across his face for a brief second before darkness enveloped him once more. A sliver of cold air hit him as the duvet was lifted away and he felt the mattress sink to the pressure of another person and the form of a female body melt its contours into the arch of his back. He lay there without moving, sensing every part of her on him, the push of her breasts and the squeeze of her stomach against his spine. He smiled to himself in total contentment and then turned to face the truth.

'Hi,' Angélique whispered.

'Hi,' he replied, leaning up on an elbow and reaching out a hand to the silk-soft skin of her face.

'Did you know it was me?'

Jamie grinned into the darkness. 'Well, as much as I like her, I was hoping it wasn't Rene.'

Angélique muffled a laugh into the duvet. 'How is your head feeling?'

'Throbbing.'

'And your body?'

'Aching.'

'Shall I make you feel better?'

'How do you plan to do that?'

He sensed Angélique raise her head from the pillow and then felt the pressure of her lips against his mouth. 'I don't think you really need to ask,' she breathed out.

Forty-Four

Gavin Mackintosh sat in the Hub café toying with his empty coffee cup as he watched the group of Japanese tourists at the next table sifting through the pile of festival leaflets they had laid out before them and discussing with incomprehensible excitement their viewing plan for the day.

'Gavin?'

He turned to find the young woman whom he had first seen talking with Angélique at the welcoming reception at the Sheraton Grand. He stood and offered a hand. 'Tess, how good to meet you at last.' He pulled out a chair for her at the table and sat down next to her. 'I just felt I should come to see you in person to say how grateful I am for all your help during the past week. The confidence and support you have shown towards Angélique has been invaluable to us all.' Gavin stopped talking when a waiter came and hovered beside him. 'What can I get you?'

'A cappuccino, please.'

Gavin ordered two cappuccinos and then leaned forward on the table. 'No doubt you've been in touch with Angélique?'

Tess nodded. 'I had a long chat with her this morning. It seems all your fears over Dessuin were well justified.'

'They were, and I think we were very lucky it didn't all turn out a great deal worse than it actually did.'

'How's Jamie? I hear Dessuin gave him quite a beating.'

Gavin smiled at her. 'He's a tough lad. He'll make a speedy recovery.'

'And Angélique?'

'Despite what happened, she seems a very different person this morning. I think a whole weight has lifted off her shoulders with the departure of Dessuin.'

Tess raised her eyebrows. 'I can well believe that, and I—' She stopped when the waiter approached their table and placed the two cups of cappuccino in front of them. She waited for him to leave before continuing. 'I'm just so glad it's all over for her.'

Gavin took a sip from his cup. 'She's ready to play again, you know.'

'Yes, she told me. I'm going to see Alasdair Dreyfuss this afternoon and break the news to him. It's going to be tricky to arrange it all, but there's no doubt he's going to be over the moon.'

'What will you say to him?'

'Just that Angélique's hand has healed much faster than was expected, and she's decided to return here from France so that she can at least fulfil a small part of her commitment.'

Gavin nodded. 'Yes, I think you're right to keep it quite simple.'

Tess blew out a breath. 'I have to. One way and another, I've been keeping too many secrets back from Alasdair this year. Anyway, once we've rescheduled one of the concerts, I'll get Sarah Atkinson, my boss, to arrange rehearsals for her. And then we can publicise it.'

Gavin drained his cup of coffee. 'I'm sure it will be a sell-out within hours of you doing that.' He glanced at his watch. 'Now, I really must fly,' he said, pushing back his chair and getting to his feet. 'I have a meeting in fifteen minutes.' He took out a five-pound note from his wallet and placed it on the table. 'It's been good meeting you properly, Tess.'

They stood and shook hands. 'And you too, Gavin. I know how much you've done for Angélique.'

'For me, it's been nothing but a pleasure.' He held on to her hand, laying his other one across it. 'Actually, Tess, there is one other thing. Would you be able to reserve two tickets for me for this concert before the word gets out?'

Tess laughed. 'Consider it done,' she said, 'and seeing you've paid for the coffee, I think we can put them on the house.'

Forty-Five

Jamie and T.K. stood up from the kitchen table as the tweed-suited doctor walked into the room, unhooking his stethoscope from around his neck and slipping it into the leather case he was carrying.

'How is he?' Jamie asked.

The doctor gazed seriously at them both over the top of his spectacles. 'Rest, and plenty of it. That's all he needs.' He put his bag down on the table. 'I really am of the opinion that it was pretty unwise of Mr Hartson to take on this film job of his, especially in light of the fact that he's not been used to doing such work for the past twenty years or so.'

'Whit's the matter wi' him?' T.K. asked, a worried frown on his face.

'Mr Hartson, I'm afraid, has quite a serious heart problem. He has been taking all the correct medication, which has worked well in controlling his condition up until now, but the extra physical effort and the undoubted mental strain of making this film has certainly exacerbated it.'

'Are ye saying he's gotta stop makin' the film?' T.K. exclaimed in disbelief.

'I don't think whatever I have to suggest will stop him from doing that. The making of this particular film obviously means a great deal to him, but nevertheless, my advice would be that he should take a couple of days off, just so he can recharge his batteries a bit.' He pulled back a tweedy sleeve and glanced at his watch. 'Now, I must be getting off,' he said, picking up his bag. 'I was given rather short shift by my receptionist this morning for taking on a house call.' He studied Jamie's face. 'You look as if you've been in the wars, lad. That's a nasty-looking bruise on your cheek.'

Jamie smiled at the old man. 'I'm fine, honestly.'

'Right, well, in that case, all I'd advise you to do is to take a couple of arnica pills.'

'I'll get some. Thanks.'

While Jamie showed the doctor out of the flat, T.K. walked along the hall and gently pushed open the door to his and Leonard's bedroom. The old cameraman was sitting fully dressed on the edge of his bed, leaning over with effort to tie up his shoelaces.

'Whit are ye daen', Leonard?' T.K. asked as he entered the room.

Leonard looked up. 'Oh, hullo, T.K.'

'Ah said whit are ye daen'?'

'Getting ready to go out, of course.'

'But, Leonard, the doctor said—'

The cameraman cut him short with a dismissive wave of his hand. 'Oh, the doctor says! I know exactly what I can do and what I can't. I've had this condition for the best part of five years, T.K., and I know exactly what my limitations are.' He pushed himself to his feet. 'Anyway, we simply cannot afford the time for me to be languishing in my bed,' he said as he approached his assistant, giving him a light pat on the arm, 'so let's get on with the work.'

As the cameraman opened the door of the bedroom, T.K. did not move, but stood with a worried expression on his face. 'Leonard?'

'Yes?'

'This is no' a good idea.'

Leonard turned and smiled reassuringly at the boy. 'I really am all right, T.K. Anyway, I decided myself last night that, due to present circumstances, I should try to take things a little easier, and for that reason, my plan for today is that you should take over the role of camera operator.'

For a moment, T.K. stared open-mouthed at Leonard, not quite believing what he had just heard. 'D'ye mean that?'

'Well, I've thrown you in at the deep end all the way through this shoot, so I don't see why we should stop now. It'll mean I can concentrate on the lighting.'

'In that case, what are we waiting for?' T.K. said excitedly as he bounded towards the door.

As his young assistant left the room and headed off down the corridor, Leonard shook his head. 'I think it was for you, my boy,' he laughed, closing the door behind him.

The lights shimmered and flared on the garishly bright silk kimonos of the Japanese performers as they dipped and turned and rolled with liquid precision through the ancient ritual of their dance. The shadows cast out by their bodies crossed over and merged together on the stage, arms and hands weaving like the high branches of a tree caught in the wind. The dancers, however, were not Leonard's focus of attention. He sat in the canvas-backed chair watching every move that T.K. made with the camera as he followed the action exactly as he had been directed. From what he witnessed, there was no doubt in Leonard's mind that the boy had the knack, using the top of his right arm to operate the panning handle of the tripod so that he could release his right hand to operate the automatic zoom. At every moment that Leonard thought the camera should pan or tilt, T.K. would carry it out, moving smoothly through the syncopated motions of the six dancers.

Oh, to be able to get the chance to live my life again, Leonard thought to himself as he slipped a hand inside his jacket to press against the pain that was once more building in his side. Why did I ever conceive the idea of giving up this kind of work? It was always my passion, my calling in life. Why did I allow myself to be cast out into the wilderness for all those years, to turn my back on so many potential opportunities to make films such as this? Yes, it had come about eventually, but only through a quirk of fate, and maybe, in the end, it was all going to be too late.

He took a neatly folded handkerchief from the top pocket of his jacket and dabbed at his watering eyes as he turned his attention to the lighting stage. He smiled sadly to himself as he glanced from one light to the other, following their perfectly balanced beams down on to the dancers on the stage. Maybe Nick Springer was right. Maybe now he should start admitting to himself that he was, indeed, still one of the best directors of photography in the business.

'Shall ah stop rolling, Leonard?' T.K. asked, taking his eye away from the viewfinder of the camera.

'Are you quite happy with it?'

'Ah think so.'

'Good lad. In that case, cut it.'

Forty-Six

The battered white van was sitting so low on its tired suspension, due to the weighty human load it was carrying, that Terry Crosland could hear the new exhaust he had had fitted before leaving Hartlepool scrape the ground at every bump as he drove up into Edinburgh via London Road. The journey had taken a good hour longer than he had envisaged, due to the heavy volume of weekend traffic on the A1 and the half-hourly pit stops requested by the committee members of Andersons Westbourne Social Club, who proved incapable of synchronising their interminable needs to relieve themselves. Much against Terry's expectations, it was the two youngest members of the rear-seated party, Robbie and Karen Brownlow, who had endured the six hours of bum-numbing discomfort the best, hardly opening their mouths as they sat on the makeshift seats, passing the time by listening to music on their MP3 players.

'Where do we go from 'ere?' Terry asked as he approached the roundabout on Leith Walk.

Gary Brownlow studied the Edinburgh Streetfinder they had bought at a filling station near Berwick-upon-Tweed. 'Left and then straight on at the next roundabout.'

Terry did as he was instructed and was immediately confronted by a long line of stationary traffic. He glanced at his wristwatch. 'We're cutting it fine, you know,' he murmured to Gary.

A head appeared between their seats. 'I told you we'd 'ave been better staying on the City Bypass and coming in on the Dalkeith Road,' Stan Morris said.

Gary turned and looked aggravatedly at the man's ruddy face. 'Oh, aye, and 'ave ye got some built-in bloody radar that tells ye traffic was running smoothly there or summat?'

'I'll 'ave ye know that when I served in the Royal Signals—'

Terry pressed his foot down on the accelerator, seeing an opening on the inside lane. The sudden forward motion made Stan disappear into the back and a gonglike sound resonated round the van as he hit his head on the roof before being returned to his seat with a forceful thump.

''Ave a care, Terry!' his voice moaned from the rear of the vehicle.

Terry caught Gary's eye and gave him a wink and both men bit on their bottom lips to stop themselves from laughing out loud.

'How far now?' Terry asked as he turned the van left at the traffic lights on to North Bridge.

Gary turned the map round and counted off the roads with his finger. 'West Richmond Street is about fifth on the left.'

'Bloody marvellous!' He glanced round at the seven other occupants of the van. 'Panic over. I reckon we'll make it by a good ten minutes.'

Stan Morris walked quickly to the front of the party as they hurried down the pavement towards the Corinthian Bar, eager that he should resume his role as spokesman once more. He pushed open the heavy glass door, letting it swing back on Terry's face, and approached the tall blonde girl in the black T-shirt who stood behind the ticket-office desk.

'Good evening, lass,' he said importantly, leaning an elbow on the desk. 'Would ye be so kind as to supply us with eight tickets for tonight's performance, please?'

Without even a welcoming smile, the girl began to rip off the tickets out of a book.

'And I don't suppose,' Stan continued, giving her the benefit of his most persuasive smile, 'that ye might see fit to give a reduction for juniors?'

The girl glared at him, a deep frown on her face. 'Juniors? What age are they?'

Stan turned and pointed at Gary's children in turn. 'That there is Robbie and he's ten and his sister, Karen is . . . how old are ye, lass?'

'Eight,' Karen breathed out, embarrassed.

Stan turned back to the girl, who was staring concernedly at the two children. 'There y'are. Ten and eight.'

The girl cleared her throat. 'Are you sure you want to take them to this show?'

Stan laughed. 'Of course we do, lass! It's their mother who's performing. They especially want to see her!'

The girl looked even more bemused, her mouth dropping open as she glanced back and forth between Stan and the children. Eventually, she shook her head. 'Well, if you insist,' she said, continuing to tear the tickets out of the book, 'and seeing it's the last night of the show, I'll let them in for free.'

Stan turned and smiled smugly at the group, feeling justly proud of his negotiating skills.

'There you are,' the girl said, handing him the tickets. 'Just go down the stairs behind you and the theatre's on the right.'

There were only seven other people in the dark little basement theatre, all occupying tables that were grouped around the small curtain-shrouded stage. Stan Morris stood with his hands on his hips, contemplating which of the remaining tables would offer the best view, but the rest of the party pushed past him and proceeded to group themselves around the three nearest the back of the theatre.

Stan let out a resigned sigh as he went over to join them. 'I wouldn't have chosen these meself. I think . . .'

'Aye, and we're getting tired of what you think,' replied sombre Derek Marsham, who had sat himself next to the diminutive Skittle. 'The place is no bigger than a public convenience, any road, so what the 'ell does it matter where we sit?'

'Aye, just take that chair there,' added Skittle, as he polished his thick-lensed spectacles on a grubby handkerchief, readying himself for the show.

'Well, I 'ave to say—'

'Just sit down!' the five voices of the senior party commanded him.

As Stan moodily rested his cavalry-twilled bottom on the hard wooden seat, the lights dimmed and a voice boomed out from the loudspeakers set up in opposite corners of the confined space. 'Ladies and gentlemen, welcome to tonight's performance of the Fruit Sundaes. We all know that an apple a day keeps the doctor away, but on this occasion, a word of warning: DON'T EAT THE FRUIT!'

'What's all this about?' Gary whispered to Terry, a look of incomprehension lining his face.

'No idea, lad. Maybe she's changed her act.'

Loud music now blared from the speakers and the curtains drew back to reveal a pair of identical female twins, quite obviously past their prime, standing centre-stage, the lumpy contours of their bodies swathed in voluminous aquamarine silk dressing gowns. Their arms were outstretched, and in each hand they bore a small wicker basket laden with a variety of fruit – tangerines and bananas and plums and grapes. As the party from Hartlepool cast querying glances at one another, a camp little dwarf of a man, dressed in a minute tuxedo, pranced on to the stage, and with a muselike flourish took

357

the baskets from the women. And then, stretching their deep-red-lipsticked mouths into wide teasing smiles, they undid the ties on their dressing gowns and simultaneously allowed them to drop to the ground.

'What the *'ell* . . . ?' Gary exclaimed, desperately trying to put his hands in front of his children's eyes.

'You've got me,' Terry replied, a look of revulsion on his face. 'What's she going to do with that banan— oh, God, no!'

'I'm getting the kids out of 'ere,' Gary said, grabbing the hands of both his children and heaving them to their feet, causing a chair to crash backwards to the floor.

As he hurried them off towards the door, with Terry in close pursuit, the committee members of Andersons Westbourne Social Club rose slowly to their feet and began shuffling their way between the tables, never diverting their eyes from the act. All, that is, except Skittle, who had not witnessed his associates move away from him. He got up from his chair and walked a couple of paces towards the front of the theatre, holding up a hand to cut out the blinding light that shone out from the stage, and squinting through his spectacles. 'Is that you, Rene? My, you've lost a lot of weight, lass.'

A hand reached out and grabbed the sleeve of his raincoat, giving him a heave that nearly took him off his feet.

'What the bloody 'ell's going on down there?' Gary angrily asked the girl behind the ticket desk.

'I'm sorry?'

'That act. That wasn't what we came to see.'

'I'm sorry, sir,' she said, displaying little interest in his complaint as she continued to tidy up the desk. 'That's the spirit of the Fringe, I'm afraid. Anything goes.'

Gary felt the rest of the committee pressing up behind him, eager to hear her explanation. 'But what 'appened to Rene Brownlow?' he asked. 'She was meant to be on 'ere.'

The girl slapped her hand to her mouth. 'But the gentleman didn't say,' she exclaimed, looking directly at Stan Morris, whose face coloured red when he felt the accusing eyes of the party upon him. 'Rene Brownlow isn't on here any more. She moved venues.'

'Where's she on, then?' Gary demanded.

'At the Underbelly.' She bent down and rummaged behind her desk, coming up with a bulky programme. 'Hang on a minute,' she said, flicking through it. 'She swapped venues with the Fruit Sundaes, so I should be able to find it.' She drew a red-nailed finger down a page. 'Here we are. She's on at the Belly Laugh, and there's a show at eight o'clock.'

Terry looked at his watch. They had twenty minutes before it began.

'I don't know if you'll get in, though,' the girl continued. 'Her new show's been a sell-out for the last week.'

'Is that right?' Gary asked with astonishment.

For the first time, the girl's face creased into a smile. 'She's been the talk of the town.'

Gary looked down at his children and gave them a proud wink. 'D'ye 'ear that, kids? Yer mam's the talk of the town.'

'Come on, lads, we'd better get going,' Terry said, pulling open the entrance door and ushering the party out into the street.

'Hang on a minute!' the girl cried out after them, pulling open the cash drawer and quickly counting out some money. She handed Terry a wad of notes. 'I think you deserve a refund. I'm sorry about the mix-up. If the gentleman had just said . . .'

'Don't worry,' Terry said, giving her friendly flick of the head. He held up the money in his hand. 'And thanks for this, love. Much appreciated.'

He went out of the door and then immediately opened it again. 'No idea where this place is, do you?' he asked the girl.

'Turn right out of this road, head back into town for about four hundred metres and then take a left on Chambers Street. Go to the end and turn right and you'll find the Underbelly about a hundred metres on the left.' She glanced up at the clock on the wall behind her. 'Have you got transport?'

'Aye, I 'ave.'

'Then I'd suggest you drive it, if you want to get there in time.'

Terry gave her the thumbs-up and ran out into the street.

The numbed silence in the van as they drove back towards town was broken by the quiet voice of timid Norman Brown, who had hardly opened his mouth since they departed from Hartlepool. 'They were very entertaining, those girls.'

Every head, including Terry's, turned to look at the mouse of a man.

'I think we'll draw a veil over that memory, thank you, Norman,' Stan Morris said prudishly.

'I reckon two large paper sacks would be more fitting,' Gary murmured in the front of the van, without lifting his eyes from the map.

A damned sheepdog, that's what we need 'ere, Terry thought to himself as he stood outside the ticket office in the cobbled courtyard of the Underbelly. Gary Brownlow and his two kids were the only members of the party in sight, standing at a fast-food stall where they were consuming hot dogs and Coke. Stan Morris and Derek Marsham had inevitably headed off to find a gents', and he had no idea where Norman Brown and Skittle had got to. Probably trampled underfoot in the crowd that was trying to get down the spiral staircase. With a shake of his head he turned and walked into the ticket office, digging into the pockets of his jeans for the wad of money.

'Can you give me eight tickets for Rene Brownlow's show?' he asked the red-T-shirted boy behind the counter.

'I'm sorry. That show's a sell-out. Has been for the past week.'

'Oh, 'ell, no!' Terry exclaimed, running an exasperated hand over his quiff of hair. 'Are ye saying there's no chance at all of seeing it?'

'I'm afraid not.'

'But it's 'er last show.'

'I realise that, sir.'

'But we've come all the way up from 'Artlepool to see 'er. We've got 'er 'usband and kids with us an' all!'

The boy did not reply for a moment. 'Hang on a minute,' he said, getting to his feet and grabbing the arm of a woman who was hurrying past him. They talked together in low voices before the woman nodded and then approached Terry.

'We can let you all in, but I'm afraid you'll just have to stand at the back of the auditorium.'

'Aye, that'll do us fine,' Terry said as he began to count out the money.

'Don't worry about that, sir,' the woman said with a smile. 'Seeing you're all from Rene's home town, I think we can let you in for free.'

'Thanks, lass,' Terry replied, pocketing the money. 'That's really good of ye.'

'You'd better hurry, though. It's just about to start.'

Terry ran back out into the courtyard where he found, to his relief, that the committee members had reunited and Gary and the kids had finished satisfying their appetites.

''Ave ye got the tickets?' Gary asked.

'None available,' Terry replied as he hurriedly led the way to the entrance of the Belly Laugh venue. 'The show's been a sell-out, so we're standing at the back.'

Arriving at the door, Terry gave it a push, but felt a pressure holding it closed.

'Come on, Terry,' Stan Morris called out impatiently from the back of the group. 'What are ye waiting for?'

''Old yer 'orses.'

The door was opened by a girl who pressed a finger to her lips. 'Are you the party from Hartlepool?' she whispered.

Terry nodded.

'Right, follow me, but be very quiet. The show's started.'

The auditorium was already echoing with laughter as the girl led them along the back aisle, the committee members of Andersons Westbourne Social Club jostling and bumping into one another in the dark, their eyes fixed on the stage. Rene stood close to one of the side wings with a white rose fixed behind her left ear, while on the opposite side a woman with a ruddy freckled complexion was passing comment on the red rose she wore in her wild entanglement of carrot-coloured hair.

Karen Brownlow tugged on her father's jacket sleeve and Gary bent down so that she could whisper something in his ear. Gary nodded and straightened up and leaned close to Terry. 'Kids can't see. Can you stick Karen on yer shoulders and I'll take Robbie?'

Terry gave the young Brownlow boy a hand to clamber on to his dad's shoulders before hefting up Karen on to his own. 'Who's the other woman with Rene?' he said to Gary.

'No idea. I've never seen 'er before in me life.'

'They seem to work well together.'

'Aye, they do.'

As they spoke, Rene walked across the stage and put a hand on the redhead's arm, cutting her off in mid-sentence. Rene turned, narrowing her eyes in the glare of stage lights, and looked up into the obscurity of the auditorium, directly to where Gary and Terry and the rest of the Hartlepool crew were standing.

'I've got great 'earing, you know,' she called out. 'Matti and me are dying for a rest, so seeing as you lot at the back seem to be in a talkative mood, we'd much appreciate it if you came down 'ere and did the show for us, so's we can get off to our beds.'

The audience tittered, and to a man turned round and looked towards the back of the auditorium, an action that made the committee members of Andersons Westbourne Social Club cast embarrassed glances from one to the other.

'Oh, shurrup, girl, and just get on with it,' Gary called out at the top of his voice.

Rene's mouth fell open in amazement and she walked to the front of the stage, shielding her eyes with her hand as she sought out the location of the heckler. 'Gary?' she said in a querying voice.

Terry took over the shout. 'Aye, get on with the show, lass. You just show 'em 'ow it's meant to be done.'

On hearing those all-too-familiar words, Rene started to laugh. 'You 'n all, Terry?'

The red-haired girl put her hands on her hips and scowled impatiently at her partner. 'Here, Yorkie, are you just going to gawp at the audience all night, or shall we continue? They've all paid good money, you know.'

'Oh, keep yer 'air on,' Rene replied as she returned to stand beside her fellow comedienne. She put a hand to her chin as she pensively scrutinised the untidy mass of red curls that tumbled around Matti's moonlike face. 'On second thought . . .'

And with that they slipped back into their routine, the initial slanging match between them turning, as it had done over the past eighteen shows, into a hilarious and warm-hearted ad-lib session that had both performers and audience alike falling over one another in laughter. An hour and a half later, after Rene and Matti had taken at least three more curtain calls than at any of their previous performances, the lights in the auditorium brightened and the audience rose from their seats in a hum of excitement and good humour.

'That was bloody marvellous!' Terry said, lifting Karen from his shoulders and putting her down on the floor. 'What d'ye think of yer mam, lass?'

'Can we go and see 'er now?' was all that Karen had to say in reply.

Terry rubbed a hand gently on her head. 'Aye, I'm sure we can.'

The girl who had shown them in led the Hartlepool party round the back of the stage to the small dressing room where Rene and Matti sat, slumped and exhausted, on a couple of wooden chairs.

'Oh, my Go-o-o-od!' Rene cried out, jumping to her feet when Robbie and Karen rushed towards her. She put her arms around them both and held them tight against her, raining kisses on their heads. 'Oh, 'ow I've missed you lot.'

'My word, Rene, you've got a real fan club here, haven't you?' Matti remarked as she surveyed the six faces peering round the doorway at differing heights.

Rene raised her eyes from her children's heads and glanced towards the door. 'Oh, for goodness' sakes, you're all 'ere,' she laughed, letting go of her children and hurrying over to the door, giving each of the committee members a kiss on the cheek. 'How wonderful ye've all come. Whose bright idea was this?'

'Gary's,' Terry replied. ''E thought you needed some moral support, but obviously 'e got the wrong end of the stick.'

Rene grinned at her husband. 'Oh, you beauty, come 'ere,' she said, grabbing hold of his hand and dragging him round the side wing and out on to the stage. She reached up and pulled his face down to hers and gave him a long, smacking kiss on the lips. 'Ye're a great man, Gary Brownlow, so y'are.'

'Not 'alf as great as you. That was a bloody fantastic show.'

'D'ye really think so?'

Gary clenched his fist. 'Just the best, lass, just the best.'

Rene gave him another long kiss before letting go his face and taking hold of his hand once more. 'So tell me, 'ow's it been?'

'No problems. We managed fine, but we 'aven't 'alf missed ye.'

Rene squeezed his hand. 'And I've missed you lot so much as well. Dare I ask 'ow the job 'unting's going?'

Gary smiled and gave her a wink. 'Don't let's talk about that. Tonight's your night,' he said, leading her back to the edge of the stage, 'so let's get celebrating.'

As they squeezed back into the changing room, Matti popped the cork on the second of the two bottles of Cava she and Rene had bought to celebrate their last night. 'You're the only two without,' she said, pouring the frothing liquid into two paper cups and handing them to Gary and Rene.

'Gary, this is Matti,' Rene said, grinning at the redhead. 'She's my new partner.'

Gary leaned towards her and gave her a kiss on the cheek.

'Please to meet you, lass. I was just saying to Rene you two were just tops tonight.'

Matti raised her eyebrows in appreciation of the compliment, and without taking her eyes off Gary, she gave Rene a nudge on the arm. 'Oh, I like him, girl. Has he got a brother?'

'If I could 'ave yer attention for a moment, please,' Stan Morris called out above the laughter that ensued, 'I would like ye all to raise yer glasses and drink a toast to the future success of these two girls, and I am pleased that it was due to my efforts – and of course, the other committee members of Andersons Westbourne Social Club – that talent such as Rene's has had a chance to be aired at a time when—'

'Oh, do shut up, Stan,' Terry cut in with a laugh, holding his paper mug in the air. ''Ere's to ye both. Ye really showed them out there tonight.'

'I couldn't agree more,' a softly spoken American voice interjected. Everyone turned, their cups halfway to their mouths, as they stared at the smartly dressed woman with coiffeured hair and glistening diamond studs in her ears who stood leaning against the doorpost. 'I apologise. I didn't mean to interrupt.'

'Not at all. Come in and join us,' Rene said, picking up a spare cup of sparkling wine from the dressing table and carrying it over to her. The woman took the cup and held out her hand to Rene.

'It's Rene, isn't it?'

Rene nodded as she shook her hand.

'My name's Mary Steinhouse. I've been in the audience for the last three nights, and I just wanted to say how much I've enjoyed your show. You and Matti have one of the most refreshingly original acts I've seen for a long time.'

'Thanks for that,' Rene replied, glancing round at Matti and shooting her a wink.

'And I'm sorry that I had to come round here and cut in on your celebrations,' the woman continued, 'only I'm heading back to the States first thing tomorrow morning, and I really wanted to see you both before leaving.'

'Oh aye?' Rene said, a questioning frown on her face.

'You see, my husband and I sponsor a large cultural festival held annually in Boston, and it just happens that it goes back-to-back with the one here in Edinburgh. I come over each year and seek out the best acts on the Fringe and invite them over to the States to take part in our festival, and I was very much hoping you and Matti might consider coming.'

Rene's jaw dropped. 'Are ye being serious?' She turned to Matti, seeing her face register similar disbelief. 'When would this be?'

'The week after next. I'm returning here for the Saturday-night Fireworks Concert, which I adore, and then those acts I have chosen to take part in our festival will fly back with me on the Sunday.' She paused, tilting her head to the side. 'That is why, I'm afraid, I need an answer as soon as possible.'

Gary cleared his throat self-consciously. 'I can't speak for Matti, but as far as Rene is concerned, she can do it.'

Rene looked at her husband, her heart missing a beat and emotion pricking her eyes at the support he was continuing to show for her. 'Gary?' she said quietly.

'What about it, Matti?' Gary said, pressing her for an answer.

'Oh, God, yes!' Matti exclaimed, coming over to Rene and throwing her arms around her. 'Yes, yes, yes!'

'I'm so glad,' Mary said with a clap of her hands. 'So, if we could meet up next Saturday afternoon at the Balmoral Hotel in Princes Street. I have half a dozen rooms booked, so you are invited to stay with me there. We'll have an early evening reception, during which I will brief all those who are coming as to what will be happening during the following week, and then afterwards we can all go out to watch the fireworks together. How does that sound?'

Rene uncoupled Matti's arms from around her neck and drew a hand across her damp cheeks. 'I can't go.'

Her remark caused a rumble of concern to sweep around the room.

'You can't?' Mary queried.

'No . . . not without my family, that is. I've been away from them for three weeks and I need to spend some time with them.'

Gary came forward and put a hand on his wife's shoulder. 'Come on, Rene, we'll be—'

'No, Gary,' she cut in, shrugging his hand away. 'I've made up me mind.' She smiled apologetically at the American woman. 'I can only go if me family comes too.'

Mary glanced at the strange little group in the room. 'What, *all* of them?' she asked in a surprised voice.

Rene spluttered out a laugh. 'No, just me husband and the kids.'

Mary shrugged resignedly. 'All right, I don't see why not. I'm sure we can find somewhere for you all to stay.'

Rene grinned at her. 'In that case, ye're on. America, 'ere we come.'

'Wonderful,' Mary said, pushing herself away from the doorpost. 'Until next Saturday, then, and enjoy your celebrations. You really deserve it, both of you.'

After she had left there was a momentary silence in the room before Matti let out a whoop of joy, and grabbing hold of the first person she could lay her hands on, who just happened to be sombre Derek Marsham, she began dancing around the room with him. Rene put her arms around her husband's waist and pulled herself against him, leaning her head against his chest. 'I think you'd better pinch me 'ard,' she said quietly.

'What?'

'Is this really all 'appening?'

Gary gave his wife a kiss on the top of the head. 'Aye, I think it is, lass.'

Having almost danced Derek Marsham off his feet, Matti sat him down on one of the two chairs to catch his breath. 'So, what d'you suppose we should do now?' she asked, turning to Rene. 'We can't stay up here for a whole week.'

'If I might be allowed to make a suggestion,' Stan Morris said quietly, already anticipating the usual cry of disapproval. When none came and everyone turned to hear what he had to say, he was, for a moment, too surprised to continue. 'Right, well, I was thinking about all this before that lady turned up, and what I'm going to suggest is that I ring up Harold Prendergast at Andy's and say to 'im that we are very lucky to have available for us one of the star turns of the Festival Fringe – that, of course, being Rene and Matti – and that they would be willing to come to our social club for a five-night run before taking their act over to the United States of America. Understandably, the performance fees would be greater than 'e would ever have considered previously, but I'm sure that a quick call to the newsroom of the *'Artlepool Mail* would 'ave everyone in the borough clamouring at the door for tickets.'

This was greeted with a complete hush as all those in the room contemplated his suggestion. 'Well, it was only a thought,' Stan mumbled dejectedly.

'Aye, and a damned good one at that,' Terry said, giving him a congratulatory thump on the shoulder. 'You always were the right man for the job, weren't ye, Stan. Spokesman extraordinaire.' He turned to the assembled company. 'Now before there 'appens to be any more interruptions, ladies and gentlemen, let's get back to unfinished business.' He raised his glass. ''Ere's to you two girls. Ye're both on the way to the top, ye are.'

Forty-Seven

The rain eventually came to Edinburgh on the Wednesday evening, more than eight hours later than had been predicted by the weather forecasters. However, it was as if the darkened clouds that had been rolling across the city since the early morning had held hard to their load until then, because the torrential downpour that ensued had every street awash with water, every gutter flowing like a river in spate. Yet the energy and enthusiasm of the festival continued unabated, the post-Fringe straggle of street performers in the High Street pressing on regardless with their shows, sheltering in the lea of buildings or the high-columned entrances to churches, while the tourists and punters and office workers still filled the streets under a seething mass of umbrellas, walking to their next point of interest, or to yet another venue, or to the peaceful sanctuary of their homes.

High on the castle battlements, where the wind caught the rain and threw it in violent blasts against the pitted, uneven walls, just as it had done over the past nine hundred years, Roger Dent held hard to the hood of his waterproof jacket as he raced across the courtyard to the steps leading down to the store, jumping over lines of multicore cabling already connected up to the forty-odd slave units that would power the explosions on the night. Hurrying down the steps, he threw open the door and entered into the fuggy interior of the small vaulted room.

'Bloody hell!' he exclaimed, shaking the water from his arms. 'That is just filthy out there.'

His crew looked up from the various maintenance jobs they were doing and laughed at his appearance.

'Jeez, mate, you look like a drowned rat,' Phil Kenyon said, getting up from the table and taking a pair of earphones off his head. 'How's about a cup of coffee?'

'Not just yet,' he replied, hanging his sodden jacket on the back of a chair. 'I'd rather find out what stage we're all at. How did you get on with Helen?'

'Really good. The score's written up with all the cues and the back-timings. We met up with good old Sir Raymond today and went through the whole piece with him, and he seems happy enough with it all.'

'Did you tell him to watch the speed when he's conducting?'

'Yeah, he listened to the recording we used to set up the programme, and he reckons he'll be able to stick quite close to that.'

Roger let out a nervous sigh. 'Well, as long as he doesn't tense up on the night and rockets through the whole thing. We just don't have the leeway for it to underrun.'

'I wouldn't worry too much about that. The old boy seems pretty laid-back about everything.'

Roger nodded and turned his attention to the small bespectacled figure of Graham Slattery, the computer programmer from IBM. 'Gray, what's the story with the bell wire?'

'Annie and I have got about six hundred metres of the stuff laid out. The tunnel, the gardens and the ground under the gun are all wired, which just leaves the rock face to be done.'

Roger stared at the man, a look of thunder on his face, his eyes burning with anger. 'What the *hell* do you mean, the rock face has to be done? The riggers were supposed to have that completed today.'

Graham's face coloured when the rest of the crew turned to look at him. 'It started to rain, Rog. They said it was too dangerous.'

'Jesus, that's what I pay them for, to risk their sodding necks. What happens if it rains tomorrow? Are they expecting to sit around drinking tea all bloody day?'

Graham cleared his throat, summing up courage to continue. 'They don't like the idea of doing the rock face, Rog. It's never been done before, and they just reckon it's not on.'

'I couldn't give a damn what they think. This is my final show and it's bloody well going to be done.'

'Don't get yourself all stressed up, mate,' Phil cut in, realising Graham was in need of some moral support. 'We'll get it done tomorrow.'

'We don't have time tomorrow, Phil,' Roger exclaimed, grabbing a web harness and karabiner off a hook on the wall. 'We're behind schedule as it is. If this isn't done tonight, there's no hope of us being ready on time.'

'Hell, Rog, you're not thinking of doing it now?'

Roger bent down and picked up a coil of thick climbing rope off the floor. 'Too right I am.'

'But it's bloody near dark! You'll kill yourself.'

Roger threw him the rope. 'Not as long as you're holding on to the other end of this.' Taking his jacket down from the wall, he pulled it on and picked up a large drum of bell wire from the corner of the store. 'Right, are you coming?'

Phil glanced at the concerned faces of the crew and shook his head slowly as he picked up his jacket. 'You're mad as a bull with ticks, mate.'

Roger beamed a smile around the room. 'Of course I am. That's why I'm in this business.'

Fifteen metres below the parapet of the castle, Roger flattened himself against the rock face as the wind tore the jacket hood off his head, the incessant rain soaking his hair even before he had managed to search out his next handhold on the slippery surface of the rock. He was getting into a routine now. Handhold first, then foothold, then uncoil the bell wire from the drum suspended from his waist. It was all right as long as he didn't look down. Whatever happened, he didn't want to look down. He was working so fast he felt the rope above him go slack and he realised Phil wasn't keeping up with him.

'Phil?' he yelled out as loud as he could.

'You all right, mate?' he heard Phil's faint voice shout out from above.

'Keep the rope taut.'

'Sorry, will do.'

Roger felt the rope once more reassuringly take his weight.

'How many of you have got hold of it?' he called up.

'All of us,' came the reply.

Roger smiled to himself as he put out his hand and felt for the next cleft in the rock. Only a few metres more and then he could start making his way back up to the safety of the terrace. Not before time, either. His hands were beginning to cramp up and the muscles in his arms were exhausted. He pushed his fingers deep into a crevice and swung his leg out, but as he did so his hand went numb and he lost his grip. He let out a cry as he dropped away and spun around in open air before the rope jerked taut, pulling the harness deep into his groin. His back slammed painfully against the solid wall and he swung, unsupported and spreadeagled against the rock face, looking down the sixty-metre drop to Princes Street Gardens below.

'Shit!' he murmured as he gulped in air.

'Rog?' Phil's worried voice yelled out from above. 'What's happened? You all right, mate?'

Roger took in a deep steadying breath. 'Yeah, I'm fine. I lost my grip.' He let out a laugh of relief. 'I think my balls have shot up into my throat, though.'

Phil laughed. 'Well, you're not sounding like a choirboy, so your manhood's obviously still intact.'

'Thanks for that,' Roger replied, not bothering if his colleague heard him or not. He closed his eyes and laid his head back against the rock. 'Phil?' he called back.

'Yeah?'

'Is the rope safe?'

'As houses. We've wound it round one of the bollards.'

'I need a couple of minutes to recover.'

'No worries. Take your time.'

Roger relaxed his body and stretched his arms out to the side to relieve his knotted muscles as he looked out across the glistening lights of Princes Street and over the roofs of the New Town, and it suddenly dawned on him that, as he hung there, high and isolated above the streets of Edinburgh, he felt strangely like the statue of Christ the Redeemer on the pinnacle of Corcovado above the city of Rio de Janeiro, enfolding its inhabitants in the benevolent protection of his arms. And in that moment he felt neither sacrilegious nor irreverent to think such a thing, and he wondered to himself if fate had not brought him to this. Because, for twenty-three years, this had been his city, and those diminutive forms far below him crowding on to buses and driving their cars and walking the streets were his followers, each year thronging to watch the spectacle that he himself conjured up for them from his exalted position high up on the castle walls. He felt a sense of well-being and peace come over him and a sudden overwhelming burst of love for those people radiated through the cold and fatigue in his body. 'Bless you all,' he murmured to himself, 'and thank you for those years, and when that final starburst lights up the sky, may your paths run true and your lives be filled with peace from then on.'

He broke away from his solitary meditation, feeling a hand along the rock face to find a new hold and heaving himself round so that he was once more facing the wall, and as he began to climb slowly back up towards the parapet, he let out an embarassed laugh. That really was a bit of a weird thing to go and say, he thought to himself. And anyway, what difference would the idiotic pseudo-religious rantings of an ageing old hippie make to anyone's life?

'Phil?' he called out.

'Yeah, mate,' came the distant reply.

'Take the strain again, will you? I'm on my way back up.'

Forty-Eight

Leonard Hartson stood on top of the small stepladder adjusting the spotlight so that it fell on to the face of the solitary female dancer he had called to the location that afternoon. There were only a couple of small insert shots to do, so he had decided not to involve either the director of the dance company or his young female interpreter. After three weeks of arduous and energy-sapping work, there were two things now prevalent in Leonard's mind: first, that what he had just completed was indeed his masterpiece; and second, that it had come at a drastic cost to his own health.

He glanced across to the other side of the lighting stage, where T.K. was shifting the camera to its new position, levelling the tripod head with an experienced hand. When he was sure the lad wasn't watching him, he climbed slowly down the ladder, clutching hard at the lighting stand for support, and then dragged his feet back to the canvas chair, grimacing with pain, and sat down heavily upon it. As T.K. left the camera and came towards him, Leonard forced an excited smile on to his face, taking in a deep breath before speaking, hoping to make his voice sound as normal as possible.

'We've just about done it, T.K.,' he said.

His assistant smiled at him. 'Aye, looks like you and I are goin' tae get tae see the fireworks this evening, efter a'.'

'You could well be right,' Leonard replied, clandestinely slipping a hand inside his tweed jacket as he felt the tightness in his ribcage building. 'Are you ready to shoot?'

T.K. picked up the clapperboard from beside Leonard's chair and scribbled a new scene number on it with a piece of chalk. He handed it to Leonard. 'Could ye mark it, then?'

The clapperboard felt a dead weight in his hand and he let it fall on to his lap. 'Let's not bother with that,' he said with a shake of his head. 'It's only an insert, so just roll the camera when you're ready.'

Leonard watched as T.K. walked out on to the stage and held Leonard's own trusty Weston light meter up to the face of the young dancer to check the skin-tone exposure. He returned to the camera, set the aperture on the lens and then unlocked the pan and tilt levers on the tripod. He checked his focus at the long end of the zoom lens before locking off the tripod once more. 'Right, Leonard,' he called out.

'In your own time, my boy, in your own time.'

T.K. turned on the camera and watched the flickering image of the girl's motionless face through the viewfinder. He pressed the zoom, bringing out the frame to head and shoulders, and let the camera run for a further fifteen seconds. 'I've got it, Leonard,' he called out. 'D'ye want me tae cut?'

The camera ran on as T.K. waited for a reply, never taking his eye away from the viewfinder. 'Leonard? Shall ah cut it?' he said again.

The sound of the clapperboard clattering to the ground made T.K. slip a hand over the eyepiece and glance round at the old cameraman, and he knew the moment he laid eyes on him that something was dreadfully wrong. Leonard lay slumped to one side of his chair, his head lolling awkwardly against his shoulder and his right arm dangling down towards the ground.

'Leonard!' T.K. cried out, quickly turning off the camera and running across to his mentor. He gently pulled Leonard upright and placed a hand either side of the cameraman's ashen cheeks. There seemed to be no sign of life in him. T.K. heard a gasp and glanced round to find the young Japanese dancer standing beside him, her tiny hands clasped to her mouth. He stood back, clapping his hands to his head. 'Jesus, whit d'we dae? Whit d'we have tae dae?' he yelled out in a panicked voice.

The young girl held out her hands in a hopeless gesture, not being able to understand one word that was being said to her. T.K. pushed roughly past her and grabbed his jacket from where it lay on one of the lighting boxes. He rummaged in the pocket for the mobile phone he had made Leonard buy so that they could be in constant touch with Springtime Productions in London, and with shaking hands pressed in the number for the emergency services.

'I need an ambulance doon at Leith Docks right now,' he yelled urgently into the phone. 'Where d'ye think it is? It's in Edinburgh . . . address? There isna one!' He scratched impatiently at the back of his head. 'In that case, jist get the ambulance doon tae Commercial Street and ah'll stand and wait fer it.' He glanced over at Leonard. 'Ah don' know. Ah think it could be his hert.' He stood listening for a moment longer before ending the call and then walked slowly back to Leonard's side. He reached over and pressed his fingers against the cameraman's neck, feeling for a pulse as he had been instructed. There seemed only the faintest sign of life.

'Leonard, ah'm jist goin' tae get the ambulance,' he said quietly, tears beginning to blur his eyes as he covered the old man with the jacket that had been bought for him, tucking it in carefully around his still body. 'Ye'll be all right, Leonard, I know ye will. Just sit nice and easy, mon, an' ah'll be back wi' lads who can help ye. Jist haud on, Leonard. Please, jist haud on.'

He turned to the young dancer to ask her to look after Leonard, but then realised it was a hopeless cause. 'I'm sorry, but ye have to stay here,' he said to her, pressing his hands down towards the ground, his speech slow and distinct in the hope she would be able to understand him. 'Just stay here.'

He ran across the warehouse floor and opened the fire door and stood there a moment, bathed in a watery beam of sunlight.

'I'm no' going far, Leonard,' he called back to the unconscious figure in the chair. 'I promise ah'll be back with ye in no time.'

Forty-Nine

When Tess Goodwin entered through one of the back doors of the Usher Hall, the high curving passage was already resounding to a cacophony of instruments warming up for the concert. She slipped off her coat as she followed the passage round, stopping outside a large dark-panelled door on which a small brass slide bore the name of Angélique Pascal. She stood listening for a moment, hearing the strains of a single violin going through a fast and complicated scale, before she knocked. The sound ceased immediately and a voice called out for her to enter.

Angélique was standing in the centre of the room, dressed in the same figure-hugging black dress she had worn for the opening-night concert, her violin and bow held loosely in her hands. Her face lit up when she saw Tess and she hurried over to give her a kiss on either cheek.

'How are you feeling?' Tess asked, placing her coat on a chair.

Angélique blew out a long breath. 'Rather nervous, actually. It has been quite a long time since I have done this.'

Tess folded her arms. 'I still feel bad about you having to perform at this final concert, but there was such a response to the announcement of your return we felt we couldn't just schedule one of the "lates" for you.'

Angélique shook her head. 'You must not worry. I have a feeling it will go very well. I have always loved the Brahms concerto, so all I have to do now is to play it properly.' She laid her violin and bow down carefully on the chaise longue that sat against the wall. 'How is Allan today?'

Tess laughed. 'Not feeling too good. He was called in early to the office this morning for some reason, so he decided to walk it, just to clear his head.'

'That was good fun last night,' Angélique said with a grin. 'I have not danced like that for so long.' She picked up a lipstick from the dressing table and applied it lightly to her mouth in the mirror. 'By the way, have you seen Jamie this evening?'

'Yes, I saw him in the foyer – oh, and he asked me to give you a message. He's going to be sitting in the third row back in the central block and he wants you to look out for him when you get up on the stage.'

Angélique turned to Tess with a quizzical frown on her face. 'For what reason?'

'I can't tell you. It's a surprise.'

'Ah, so you know what it is?'

Tess laughed. 'I said I can't tell you.'

Angélique approached her friend, her eyes wide with intent and her fists clenched. 'Tess, I am going to make you tell me, or I promise I will . . . play all the wrong notes and you will get the sack from your job for being the one who arranged this concert.'

'Well, that's just tough luck,' Tess said with a hardened glare, 'because you're not going to get anything out of me.'

At that moment there was a knock on the door. Angélique called out for the person to enter and an elderly woman put her head round the door.

'Mademoiselle Pascal, the orchestra is ready.'

'Thank you,' Angélique replied, turning to pick up her violin from the chaise longue. She walked towards the door and stopped by Tess, taking in a deep steadying breath. 'Well, this is it, then.'

Tess put an arm around her shoulders and gave her a hug. 'Believe me, you're going to have a wonderful time. Just enjoy every moment of it.'

As Angélique walked out on to the stage the orchestra rose to its feet along with every member of the audience, and the huge domed building rang with the sound of spontaneous applause. Angélique walked over to the conductor, and, as had been her custom at every concert at which she had played, she beckoned for him to lower his head towards her so that she could plant a kiss on both his cheeks. The applause increased in volume, the audience charmed by the gesture, as she moved to her position on the stage. She bowed first to the side galleries and then to the front, at the same time scanning the nearest rows for Jamie. She caught sight of him and gave him a broad smile, and then noticed that Harry Wills, the reporter, was beside him. She watched as Harry turned to his left and her eyes followed, and there, sitting next to him in a wheelchair in the aisle, was a tall, upright, old lady with white hair, her hands clasped together in her lap, her pale-blue eyes transfixed on where Angélique stood on the stage.

'Oh, *mon Dieu! Mon Dieu!*' Angélique murmured, clasping a hand to her mouth. She moved back towards the conductor's plinth, never taking her eyes off the old lady, until she bumped into the brass rail that surrounded it. 'Please,' she said, turning to the conductor, 'can we wait for a moment? I have to see someone. It is very important.'

The conductor beamed her a smile and reached down to take the violin and bow from her. 'Of course, my dear. You take your time. I had a warning this might happen.'

As Angélique quickly walked over to the side of the stage and descended the steps, the audience went so quiet that her foot-steps echoed around the concert hall. She approached the old lady, her hands cupped over her face as tears streamed down her cheeks. '*Oh, je ne le crois pas!*' She got down on her knees and gently took hold of the limp wrinkled hands. 'Madame Lafitte, you are here! You are truly here!' She kissed the hands and held them against her hot wet cheeks, looking up into the woman's kind smiling face.

'I . . . have . . . been brought . . . to hear you play,' Madame Lafitte said in a weak faltering voice.

'But who brought you?' Angélique asked breathlessly.

Madame Lafitte turned her head slowly to look at the man seated beside her. 'Mr . . . Wills here.'

'Oh, that is so wonderful!' Angélique got to her feet and flung her arms around Harry's neck. 'Thank you, Harry, thank you so much.'

'Not my idea, I'm afraid,' he replied, his face pumping with embarrassment. 'Jamie thought that seeing I was going to Paris, I might do a bit of a detour via Clermont Ferrand on the way home.'

For a moment Angélique stared open-mouthed at Jamie before she pushed past Harry's legs and sat herself down heavily in Jamie's lap. She took his face in her hands and pressed her lips against his for so long that by the time she broke away from the embrace he was left gasping for air. The audience loved it, Angélique's spontaneous action breaking through their customary staid demeanour, and reacted with wolf whistles and loud yells of approval. One man, high up in the gallery and still dressed in the suit he had worn to his law firm that day, even stood up to applause, his claps resounding around the auditorium, before he was pulled back to his seat by the red-faced lady sitting next to him.

Leaving Jamie with a whispered message in his ear, Angélique got up and edged past Harry, and stood once more beside Madame Lafitte, looking down into her tired smiling eyes. 'I shall play for you now,' she said, brushing the back of her hand gently against the old lady's cheek.

'I . . . have waited . . . too long . . . for this moment,' she replied.

Angélique bent down and kissed her lightly on the forehead. 'And you will wait no longer.'

And as she walked back on to the stage the conductor raised

his hands in the air to bring the orchestra once more to its feet to greet the second entrance of the young French maestra.

Every day since Angélique Pascal had left the Conservatoire in Paris, Lillian Lafitte had listened to her young protégée play, her music filling the large sitting room of the house in the rue Blatin in Clermont Ferrand. But never before had she heard her play as she did this evening. There was a powerful intensity, a newly discovered emotion present in her delivery, every note striking at her own inner being, making her feel that her passing years had been scrolled back in time, and she had the image of herself as a young girl once more, walking amidst a carpet of spring flowers in a mountain meadow high in the Massif Central, clutching hard to the hand of her companion, the dashing Dr Jean-Pierre Laffite. And then, breaking from her reverie, she realised what it was that made Angélique play in such a way. The girl had found love. It was the missing part of the jigsaw, completing her full understanding of the music she was playing, a part that could never be taught, but could only be found through the explosion of longing, and then belonging, in the heart. She turned her head slowly and looked along the row to the powerfully built young man with the blond hair who sat next to her chaperone. He was watching Angélique with a fascination, a boundlessness that would make it seem that he was the only person sitting in this vast concert hall. Lillian smiled to herself. She doubted very much he was listening to one note she was playing. How wonderful it is, she thought to herself, that in this modern day, when there seemed such reticence in the young to commit to love, the feeling between these two should be so entirely mutual.

She looked down into her lap and slowly interlocked the quivering fingers that Angélique herself had separated. Age has struck your body, Lillian, but your mind is still as sharp as a razor, so now use it, for Angélique's sake, while you still have the time.

She raised her head to watch the small delicate fingers dance across the strings of the violin, exactly as they had done so many years before in the sitting room in her house in Clermont Ferrand.

So, the young man is moving to London . . .

Fifty

Roger Dent pulled back the sleeve of the new jacket that his wife, Cathy, had had made up for him for the final show, a blousy black windcheater with the ESC logo embroidered on the back in gold thread and studded with sparkling diamante buttons. His watch read ten to nine. Ten minutes more and the display would begin. There was nothing more he could do now. Every connection, every cable, every slave unit and every shell rack had been checked a hundred times. Preparation was complete, and it now just remained for Phil to call the show.

He walked quickly across the courtyard to the firing position under the one-o'clock gun. Annie Beardsley gave the thumbs-up when she saw him and slipped her earphones on to her head. Returning the gesture, Roger ran off to do a last check with Dave Panton and Graham Slattery, who were manning the other two firing positions in the tunnel and in the gardens. Five minutes later he entered the small glass-fronted box where Phil Kenyon and Helen, his score reader, sat next to each other, looking down on to the huge white-shrouded stage set up in Princes Street Gardens where members of the Scottish Chamber Orchestra were readying themselves for the concert.

'Are we ready to go, Phil?'

The Australian leaned back in his chair and turned to him with a broad grin on his face. 'Yeah, mate, we're just about to hit it.'

Roger simply nodded in reply, letting out a long nervous breath.

Phil laughed. 'Jeez, Rog, don't get so uptight. It's going to be fine.' He pulled out the chair next to his. 'Come and sit down and enjoy your finest hour.'

Roger shook his head. 'Not this time.'

Phil looked at him quizzically. 'What d'you mean? You always sit here.'

Roger flicked a thumb towards the door. 'I'm going to be out there. I want to stand on the castle walls and watch the people in Princes Street. I want to watch those hundred thousand faces look up and marvel at what we've created for them.' He shot his colleague a knowing wink. 'Because that's what it's all about, Phil. Sheer, unadulterated entertainment.'

Phil grunted sardonically and shook his head. 'Go on, get outta here. I think you've finally flipped.'

A loud roar went up from the crowds below and Phil turned to look down on to the stage. 'That's our conductor on,' he said, taking the earphones from around his neck and putting them on his head, 'so let's get ready to roll.'

Four hundred miles to the south, in a tall office block overlooking Victoria Station in London, Nick Springer sat with his feet up on his desk, flicking through the remote control as he reran the video that had been delivered to his office late that afternoon. Stretching his arms above his head, he let out a long contented yawn before pulling back the cuff of his Turnbull and Asser shirt and looking at his watch. It was nearly bang on nine o'clock. Definitely time to call it a day.

He swung his feet off the desk and got up and took his jacket from the back of the chair. Pulling it on, he walked across to the television and switched it off and made his way over to the door. As he opened it, the telephone on his desk began to ring. He stared at it for a moment, thinking about just letting it go on to the answerphone, but then returned to pick it up.

'Nick Springer . . . oh, hi, T.K., how're things going? I've just been watching the footage you sent down yesterday. It really is quite fantastic. Leonard and you have done a hell of a job . . .

I'm sorry, T.K., I was talking over you. What did you just say?'

As he listened the colour drained from his face and he sat down heavily on the side of his desk.

'When did this happen?' he asked in a quavering voice, pressing his hand to his forehead. 'Oh, my God! And where is he now?'

He wound the telephone cord so tight around his fingers that he could feel their tips go numb. 'And were you with him?'

He felt his eyes prick with tears of emotion as the boy talked on. 'Oh, T.K., I know exactly what you mean. If it's any comfort, I think he saw you a bit like a grandson as well . . . yes, I know, lad . . . no, don't you worry yourself about that. I'll drive straight down to Kingston and break the news to her.' He took in a deep sad breath. 'So where are you now? Are you still in the hospital? . . . Why on earth have you gone back to the warehouse? . . . Have you really? . . . Well, you're a great lad, T.K., Leonard would be really proud of you. I'll see if I can fly up tomorrow with Grace and I'll arrange for someone to pick up all the equipment. You say the remainder of the exposed stock is in the camera case? . . . Right, and will the place be locked?' He turned and picked up a pen from his desk and began scribbling on a pad of paper. 'Under the brick below the rubbish skip outside the door. OK, I've got that, T.K., and you have the mobile if I need to get in touch with you . . . T.K.? . . . T.K., I'm sorry I didn't understand what you just said. Your voice sounds a bit slurred . . . T.K., are you there, lad?'

Nick hung up the telephone and put his hands to his face, pressing his fingers hard against his eyes. 'Oh my God, what I have done?' he murmured to himself. 'What the hell have I done?' He pulled his hands down the sides of his face. 'And how on earth am I ever going to tell Grace?'

T.K. sat in pitch darkness in the centre of the empty warehouse, the packed camera and lighting cases clustered about him. He pushed the mobile phone into the pocket of his jacket and bent down and picked up the half-empty bottle of vodka from the cold concrete floor. He took an enormous swig, coughing involuntarily as the neat alcohol ran down the back of his throat, burning his gullet. He got to his feet and began to stagger unsteadily towards the door. He stopped and then turned to walk back to pick up something that lay on top of the camera case. He cradled Leonard's Weston light meter in the palm of his hand, and for a few brief seconds, brought it up to his nose to inhale the smell of its old time-worn leather case before putting it into the pocket of his jacket alongside the mobile phone. He walked aimlessly across the warehouse floor for the last time and opened the door, seeing the dark night sky above the buildings opposite light up in blues and greens. The fireworks had started.

He turned the key in the heavy padlock and then placed it under the brick next to the rubbish skip. He straightened up and took another swig from the vodka bottle and then realised that the street, usually empty save for the film company van, was now lined with cars. He nodded his head in comprehension. The fireworks. People would have had to park this far away and walk uptown.

He began to make his way along the street, and then stopped, casting an admiring eye over the brand-new BMW parked there, its dark gleaming body reflecting the light of yet another firework that hit the night sky. He stood weaving back and forth as he eyed its plush cream-tan interior and leather-covered steering wheel. He let out a drunken laugh and walked back to the rubbish skip, and ten seconds later returned to the car with a heavy metal rod he had found buried in it. T.K., the master car thief, he thought to himself. That's all that's left for ye now. No broken windaes to attract attention, 'cos you know exactly how tae handle this joab.

Walking round to the front of the BMW, he raised the metal rod and brought it crashing down against the front bumper, caving it in. The effect was immediate. The airbags ballooned out from the steering wheel and the dashboard in front of the passenger seat, the locks clicked and the doors sprang open. Approaching the driver's door, T.K. placed the metal bar against the side of the car and took a last long swig from the vodka bottle before shattering it against the wall of the warehouse. He pulled open the door, and leaning in, slashed at the airbags with the broken glass. The interior was showered with white powder, settling itself on every square inch of the car's leather upholstery. T.K. clambered into the driver's seat, not caring about the powder now covering his clothes, and threw the broken bottle out on to the pavement. He reached for the metal rod and wedged it between the spokes of the steering wheel, and using every bit of his strength, he yanked it downwards until the steering lock gave way. He freed the rod, jammed it into the plastic covering below the steering wheel and removed it with a simple turn of his wrist, exposing the multi-coloured wiring. He dropped the iron rod into the gutter and rubbed his hands hard on the legs of his jeans. Right, T.K., he thought to himself, this is where the fun starts. If ye can get past the immobiliser on this beast withoot haein' tae use a laptop computer tae break the code, then ye truly are a bloody master at yer craft.

Lillian Lafitte sat in her wheelchair at one side of the crowded lobby of the Caledonian Hotel, listening to the thunderous booms of the fireworks exploding and the appreciative roar of the crowd outside in Princes Street. She lifted her hand with immense effort and brought it down on top of Angélique's.

'Now . . . you must . . . go . . . to watch . . . them,' she said, smiling at the girl.

Angélique glanced across to Jamie, who sat, cross-legged and relaxed, in an armchair next to the old lady. 'We do not need to see them, do we?'

Jamie shook his head. 'No, I've seen them often enough before.'

'I would prefer to stay here and talk to you,' Angélique said, rubbing her hand gently against Madame Lafitte's arm.

'No . . . I insist,' the old lady continued, 'but first . . . I tell you something.' She looked sternly at Angélique. 'You are twenty-one . . . years old now and you can handle . . . your own affairs. I am therefore . . . instructing my lawyers . . . to buy you a house . . . in London. It will be . . . a good place . . . for you . . . to base yourself.'

Angélique clasped her hands to her mouth in amazement. 'Oh, Madame Lafitte, that is . . . that is what I've always wanted!' She jumped to her feet and made to put her arms around the old lady's neck, but again Madame Lafitte raised her hand a fraction to stop her.

'And I have also . . . spoken to someone . . . who I hope will become your . . . new manager . . . and you will travel together . . . to your concerts.'

'Who is this person?' Angélique asked.

'I cannot say yet . . . because the . . . answer will be given . . . tomorrow.' She let out a tired sigh. 'Now . . . I cannot talk more . . . so please . . . go!'

Madame Lafitte visibly slumped in her wheelchair at the sheer effort of speaking. Angélique leaned over her and gave her a kiss on either cheek. 'I love you so much, Madame,' she said quietly to her. 'You have been so good to me.'

The old lady raised her eyebrows. 'Go . . . Angélique.'

Taking this as the definite cue to leave, Jamie got to his feet and took hold of Angélique's hand and began to pull her towards the entrance door of the hotel. 'Come on, those were our marching orders.'

'You will still be here when it is finished,' Angélique called back as Jamie hurriedly dragged her away.

Lillian Lafitte smiled her reply and watched as they entwined their arms around each other and left the hotel, talking excitedly together.

Five hundred metres along Princes Street from the Caledonian Hotel, high above the mass of spectators, Gavin and Jenny

Mackintosh stood on the balcony of the New Club, gazing up at the streams of light that showered down upon the castle. He waited with anticipation, slipping a hand around her waist, as the orchestra in the gardens below built up to a crescendo, and then, at the precise moment when the kettle drums pounded and the cymbals crashed, the whole of the rock face below the castle exploded into colour, cascading downwards, never losing its blazing flare until it hit the ground sixty metres below.

'Oh, my word,' Gavin murmured in astonishment. 'I don't think I've ever seen that done before.'

Jenny turned and smiled at him. 'When was the last time you ever saw the fireworks display?'

Gavin laughed and gave her a squeeze. 'True, very true.'

'Well, you certainly got yourself involved this year, didn't you?' she said, leaning her head against his shoulder.

'Yes, I can quite honestly say that, for myself, it's been a very satisfactory three weeks' – he let out a relieved sigh – 'but I am extremely glad it's all over.'

Jenny looked up at him, her eyebrows raised questioningly. 'No misgivings, then? You won't go pining after your young girl too much?'

Gavin leaned over and gave her a kiss on the top of the head. 'My dear, there's only one young girl in my life and she's standing right next to me.'

Across the roofs of Waverley Station, in a building adjacent to the North Bridge, Harry Wills sat in his office, oblivious to the noise and celebration that was taking place outside his window, as he typed away on the keyboard of his computer. He watched the final word of the article come up on his screen and then thumped the full-stop button with a flourish. Blowing out a satisfied breath, he scrolled back to the beginning of the document and began to read it through. It was headed 'The Inquisitive Little Girl Who Became a Worldwide Star' and opened with the line *'Once, long ago, in the darkened drawing room of a house in Clermont Ferrand . . .'*

It had been Madame Lafitte's suggestion that they should wait until they were on the plane before he started to ask her questions about Angélique, so as soon as they were airborne and climbing high above the jutting peaks of the Massif Central, Harry had taken his tape recorder from his briefcase and switched it on. Due to Madame Lafitte's faltering speech and her constant need to rest, the story was not finished being told until they finally touched down in Edinburgh. But during the course of the two-hour flight he gleaned from the old lady every bit of information he had been seeking over the past three years.

He saved the document and then selected the 'send e-mail' icon at the top of his computer screen, and as the flash of a firework lit the dingy interior of his office he pressed the button on his mouse, sending the article off for inclusion in the next day's edition of the *Sunday Times*.

Tess Goodwin climbed the final staircase of the tall Georgian block in Dundas Street and blew out a long breath, the result of both exhaustion and trepidation, before putting the key in the front door of her flat and opening it.

'Allan?' she called out when she saw the lights in the hall were on.

'Yup,' she heard his voice reply.

'Where are you?' she asked, taking off her coat and lazily dropping it on the chair along with her laptop case.

'In the sitting room.'

She made her way along the stone-flagged passage and pushed open the door. Allan was standing to the side of one of the large windows, looking out at an angle.

'I thought you might have gone to the fireworks,' she said, walking over to him and slipping herself under his arm.

'No, I didn't feel like facing the crush in Princes Street,' he replied. 'I thought I'd just watch the high ones go off from here.' He gave her a kiss on the top of the head. 'What about you? Why aren't you there?'

Tess shook her head. 'I had to meet up with Lewis Jones from the Fringe office for our customary end-of-festival drink, and then I just felt like getting back here.'

'You'll be quite relieved it's all over.'

'Yes, I am.' She smiled up at her husband. 'I'm glad everything's over, and I'm just longing for our honeymoon.'

He looked at her thoughtfully. 'Yeah, roll on the honeymoon,' he replied with little enthusiasm.

'What's the matter?' Tess queried, pulling herself away from his arm. 'You don't sound too keen all of a sudden.'

Sticking his hands in the pockets of his trousers, Allan looked down at the ground and began dragging the leather sole of a shoe back and forth across the stripped-pine floor. 'Tess, listen, you know I had to be in the office early this morning.'

'Yes,' Tess replied, her face frowned with worry.

He looked up at her. 'Well, I've been offered a new job in London.'

Tess stared at him, stunned. 'I don't believe this.'

'It's a hell of an opportunity, Tess,' Allan continued immediately, wanting to get out the explanation he had been conjuring up for her all day. 'The salary is twice what I'm getting up here, so it means we can sell this flat and buy a bigger house, which will be great when we come to have kids – which, OK, won't be for a bit, because this job at the outset involves a fair amount of overseas travel, and, well . . .' He ground slowly to a halt and studied her closely for her reaction. 'What d'you think?'

With a laugh, Tess reached up and kissed him on the cheek. 'I think it's a wonderful idea, and I'm very proud of you.'

'Really? You mean, you'd be happy to move down to London?'

'Yes, I think it's exactly what we both need, a new beginning to our lives. We can just leave all the old baggage back here in Edinburgh and start all over again.'

Allan shook his head in disbelief. 'Wow, that's weird! Those

were exactly my thoughts too. It's almost as if you'd been considering it as well.'

'Oh, I have.'

'For any particular reason?'

'A very good one. I've been offered a job too – in London.'

Allan stared at her, aghast. 'You're kidding me.'

Tess laughed. 'No, I'm not.'

'What is the job?'

'Working for Angélique Pascal as her new manager and
chaperone.'

'You never are!'

'I am.' She let out a relieved breath and shook her head. 'And
to think I've been trying to work out how to break the news
to you.' She reached up and brushed a kiss on to his lips. 'So
now we both seem to have got our lives in order, why don't
you fetch that bottle of champagne out of the fridge and we'll
go celebrate this all in style?'

Allan laughed and looked at his watch. 'Let's give it ten
minutes.'

'Why ten minutes?' she asked, looking amazed at his reaction
to her blatant call for seduction.

'You obviously haven't been reading your *Scotsman*.'

'Yes, I have, actually. What have I missed?'

'Only that it's the last show this fireworks chap is going to
be doing.' He positioned Tess in front of him, put his arms around
her waist and gazed out the window. 'He's decided to hang up
his Catherine wheels, so the finale's expected to be pretty
awesome.'

Tess disappointedly folded her arms and in protest at his
untimely rebuff looked down at the ground, where her eye was
caught by something that had been dislodged from between the
floorboards by Allan's foot. Bending down, she picked it up and
held it in the palm of her hand. 'Hey, d'you think we should
take this to Barbados with us?'

Allan held her hand up to his face and studied the one tiny
pink shred of confetti lying in the centre of her palm. 'Yeah,

why not?' he laughed, giving her a kiss on the ear that made goose bumps rise on her arms. 'I love you, Mrs Goodwin.'

'Woooooo,' said WPC Heather Lennox as she leaned her head out the window of the unmarked Vauxhall police car to watch a trailing meteor arc its way down from the sky.

'Whit wis that?' her young male colleague asked through a mouthful of egg roll.

'I jist said "woooo" at that firework,' she replied, still craning her neck out of the window.

'Ah, right.' He swallowed the remainder of his roll and wiped his hands on the legs of his trousers. 'Here, d'ya think we should get on the move?'

Heather brought her head inside the car. 'Why? Have we had a call-out?'

'No, but we're meant tae be driving aroond, no' just sitting here at the side o' the road.'

'Och, dinnae bother yersel',' Heather replied, knowing that his keenness came from his recent qualification as a police driver. 'Just relax and watch the show.' She looked up as yet another firework hit the sky. 'Onyway, there has tae be some compensation for being seconded tae traffic division for the night,' she murmured.

With a sigh, the police constable slumped back in his seat and crossed his arms and turned to look at the queue of traffic forming at the red lights at the top of Leith Walk. He followed each car down, glancing at the number plates, and then turned to the dark-coloured BMW next to him. 'Nice car, that,' he mumbled.

'Whit're ye saying now?' Heather asked.

'Nothin',' he replied morosely. He glanced across at the driver of the BMW. 'Here, d'ya fancy nicking a driver wha's no' wearing a seat belt *and* using a mobile phone on the move?'

Heather turned to him, a scowl on her face. 'Whit is it with you tonight?'

The police constable jabbed a finger in the direction of the BMW. 'Look for yerself. That lad there, a' dressed in white. No seat belt, mobile phone.'

Heather leaned forward to look past him. 'Jeez, Willie,' she said, pulling the radio handset out of its holder. 'That lad's no' dressed in white. He's got powder a' over his face and hands. We've got oorselves a ghost runner.'

'Eh?'

Heather strained her eyes as she peered through the window of the BMW just as it was taking off. 'Oh, for heaven's sakes, I know exactly who that is. Get after that car, Willie, and don't let him know ye're following him.'

As the Vauxhall powered away from the kerb, Heather called in to the control room to report their involvement in the pursuit of a stolen car.

'OK, can ye tell me now?' the police constable asked, as Heather replaced the handset in its holder. 'Whit's a ghost runner?'

'It's someone wha's broken intae a car by activating the airbags. The doors automatically spring open when that happens. Trouble is ye canna get behind the wheel unless ye burst the bags and they're filled wi' white powder, so that's why that lad's covered wi' the stuff.'

The police constable powered the car into the central lane of Queen Street to overtake a slow-moving vehicle, desperate to keep the BMW only two cars in front of him. 'But he's drivin' wan o' thae new BMWs. How the hell did he get past the immobiliser?'

Heather shook her head. 'If anyone's going tae dae it, he is.' She slammed her fist against the dashboard, just as another burst of fireworks flooded the night sky. 'Dammit, I thocht he wis going straight. His solicitor rang me up the ither day to tell me a' aboot him working wi' some film company.' She clicked her fingers as the police constable took the orange lights on the junction with Hanover Street at speed. She took her mobile phone from her pocket and started to press buttons.

'Whit are ye dain'?' the police constable asked.

'I'll hae his number here in "received calls". Aye, here it is, and it's a mobile number tae.' She punched the button and held the phone to her ear. 'Hullo, Mr Mackintosh. This is WPC Lennox here from Gayfield Police Station. Mr Mackintosh, I'm presently in pursuit of a stolen vehicle being driven by one Thomas Keene junior. Do you know whit . . . ?' She stopped speaking when the solicitor cut into her question, and for the next minute she listened intently to every word he said, every now and again grimacing at what she was hearing. Eventually, she took the phone from her ear and pressed the 'end' button, letting out a long sigh. 'All right, you can tak' it easy now, Willie. We know where he's goin'.'

'Whit d'ya mean?' the police constable asked, making no apparent effort to lessen his speed.

'The lad must have been on the phone to his solicitor at those traffic lights back there. Mr Mackintosh has arranged to meet him at his house in Ravelston Road in half an hour. He's on his way back from Princes Street right now.'

The police constable shook his head. 'Whit the hell's going on?'

Heather turned to him. 'It seems the old cameraman Keene wis working fer died this efternoon in the Royal, and the lad's real cut up about it. Mr Mackintosh reckons he's in a pretty fragile mood, no' helped by the fact that he's been drinking to drown his sorrows.'

'He's drunk!' the police constable exclaimed as he swung the Vauxhall into Randolph Crescent. 'Had we no' better tak' him, then?'

Heather glanced at the clock on the dashboard. It was twenty-six minutes past nine. 'No, just let's leave him be. He's no' driving dangerously. We'll have him in aboot five minutes.'

The police constable turned through the traffic lights into Queensferry Street and saw the BMW accelerate to take the next set of lights on orange. He gunned the engine of the Vauxhall to keep up and, on total instinct, reached down to his right and flicked on the switches for the siren and the row of blue lights set into the grille of the car.

'For Chrissakes, Willie, whit the *hell* are ye daen'!' Heather screamed at him.

'He's gettin' awa!' he yelled back.

'But we know where he's goin', ye daft bastard! Turn the bloody things aff!'

The noise of the siren broke through the hopeless mist of T.K.'s drunken misery. He glanced in the rear-view mirror with tear-filled eyes, seeing the blurry outline of the blue lights veering round a car that had pulled over to the side of the road. 'Oh, *shit*!' he yelled out, pressing his foot down on the accelerator, feeling the power of the car press his back into the soft leather upholstery.

'Oh, no, that's it. He's bloody well seen us now,' Heather moaned as she suddenly saw the gap between the two cars increase significantly.

The police constable pressed his foot down to the floor and the tuned engine of the Vauxhall roared. 'Dinnae worry, I'll keep up wi' him.'

'Hold on! It's against regulations tae give chase now.'

'I'm no' gi'in' chase! I'm jist keepin' him in front o' me.'

As T.K. drove fast along Queensferry Road, he glanced up into the mirror and saw that the police car was gaining on him. There were no blue lights now, only headlights fast approaching. This was all a completely new experience to him. He had stolen cars, but he had never been chased before, and a sudden terror gripped at his stomach, panic boiling up its sour taste into his mouth. Seventy yards in front of him, he saw the lights at the top of Orchard Brae change to orange and he pushed the accelerator to the floor, glancing down at the speedometer to see the needle move smoothly, effortlessly, through the hundred-miles-per-hour mark. He closed his eyes and braced his body for impact as he approached the red lights and then opened them as he heard the screech of a crossing vehicle being left far behind. He looked in the mirror. The headlights that were following him disappeared for a second, then reappeared from the wrong side of the road and continued the chase.

T.K. wasn't the only one who was frightened. Heather glanced across at the police constable and saw the determined set to his jaw, the steely intent burning in his eyes, his resolve being to capture at any cost. Red–mist syndrome, they called it in the police force. She had witnessed the results of it before. Three young lads, none of them more than fourteen years old, their decimated bodies being cut from the crushed mass of metal that once was a car, hounded to their deaths by an overzealous police driver. That had been the main reason for her requesting a transfer away from traffic division a year before.

She reached across and thumped the police driver on the arm. 'If ye dinnae pull over right this minute, Constable, I'm goin' tae put ye on report.'

But the driver was in no mood to reply to her, nor was he for stopping. He saw the BMW rock over on to its springs as it took a hard left at the roundabout on Queensferry Terrace, and ten seconds later he was actioning the same maneouvre.

'The little bastard's skidded,' the driver said in a controlled voice, his mouth showing a hostile smile. 'We're right up on him now.'

'Oh, God, this is a' wrong,' Heather said with a shake of her head, knowing now that she was unable to control events. 'This is goin' tae end in disaster.'

As the BMW slid broadside across the road, T.K. spun the wheel as fast as he could to the right to correct the skid, glancing over to his left through the rear passenger-seat window to see the police car turn the corner at the roundabout. He pressed his foot down to the floor once more, and with a squeal of rubber took off, looking in the mirror to see the full beams of the police car no more than twenty yards behind him. The powerful BMW almost left the road as it hit the crest of the hill and he accelerated down Belford Road towards the sharp left-hand bend at the bottom.

'Oh, no. Please, God, no,' Heather murmured as she saw the

BMW go straight across the corner and head down a narrow lane. 'Stop the car, Willie. For Chrissakes, stop the bloody car!' she screamed, as she watched the BMW career down the lane with no sign of its brake lights coming on.

'Whit the hell's up wi' you?' the police constable exclaimed, bringing the car to a juddering halt.

'He's jist gone down a cul-de-sac,' Heather cried out, her eyes wide with horror, 'and he's no' got any airbags or seat belt!' She shut her eyes tight and covered her ears with her hands, anticipating the appalling sound of the impact.

The muffled explosion was so powerful that the police car shook, and for a second, it seemed to suck the air from inside it. Heather opened her eyes, immediately having to shield them with a hand against the blinding glare of light blazing in the sky, so powerful that it was as if night had turned to day. The craggy outline of the houses and buildings in Edinburgh stood out, solid and erect, unperturbed by the constant shower of colour that appeared to be raining down upon their roofs. Open-mouthed with shock and amazement, she turned and looked towards the narrow lane down which the BMW had disappeared, and in the brief seconds of flickering darkness between the starbursts that lit up the street, she saw that all was quiet, all was safe.

'Oh, thank God! Thank God!' she cried out with relief as she undid her seat belt and threw open the door of the car. She got out and began to run as fast as her stocky little legs would take her down the road.

T.K. never lessened the power of the car as he drove at break-neck speed down the lane, his hands clutching hard at the wheel as he steered it through the narrow gap between the parked vehicles on either side of him. He had no knowledge of this part of the city and he had no idea where this was going to take him. A resounding bang made him jerk his body away towards the gear shift and he glanced at the dangling wing mirror, taking his eyes momentarily away from the direction in which he was travelling. And then suddenly, a dazzling flash of light fell upon the street, making him turn to see, in its glaring brilliance, the wall that was looming up in front of him at the end of the lane. He let out a scream of panic, bracing his arms against the steering wheel as he transferred his foot to the brake pedal and slammed it to the floor. The car screeched angrily at the sudden transference of command, its sophisticated anti-lock brake system keeping it to a straight path through the parked vehicles, and it came to a tyre-burning halt no more that three feet away from the end of the cul-de-sac.

T.K. sat shaking as he stared wide-eyed at the solid stone wall in front of him, catching his breath in great gulps of fear and relief, wondering what kind of extraordinary phenomenon had just occurred to save his life. And then it dawned on him that it could only be that someone didn't want this to happen, someone who really cared for him was watching over him, and he bent forward, resting his head on the steering wheel, and began to cry once more. Another blaze of light shone out and he looked up, knowing now that it was a sign from Leonard, calling out to him. He opened the door and staggered out and leaned on the car roof, tears streaming down his face, as he stared up at the gigantic starburst that exploded high in the night sky, stretching its flaming tentacles up towards heaven and, as only he knew, carrying with it the spirit of the man he had come to admire and to love.

He raised up a hand. 'See ya, Leonard,' he murmured. 'See ya, mon.'

He turned and began to walk away from the car, his body now shaking both with grief and adrenalin, and then he saw the figure, wearing a luminous yellow vest, run down the lane towards him. The woman police constable slowed to a walk the moment she caught sight of him. T.K. focused his bleary vision on the uniform and, in that moment, he was hit by the forgotten reality of his situation. He looked around desperately, trying to find some way to escape.

'It's a' right, Thomas,' Heather called out. 'It's me, Constable Lennox. I know aboot Mr Hartson, Thomas, I know aboot every-thing that's happened.' She held out her arms to the side, only to show she had no means of restraint about her person. 'Come on here, lad, ye'll be a' right.'

She saw him start to run towards her, and as he got nearer she saw the wild, seething anger in his eyes and she took a couple of steps back, bracing herself to stop him from pushing her off her feet in his attempt to make a getaway. She opened her mouth to yell out for support from her colleague, but her breath was forced from her body when T.K. flung himself into her arms, clutching tight to her as he sobbed inconsolably on her shoulder.

She stood there until she could no longer support the full, sad weight of his body against hers. 'Come on, Thomas,' she said quietly, giving him a pat on the back. 'Let's get you away from here.'

And linking a steadying arm through his, Heather Lennox began walking him back up the lane.

Two miles away, in one of the west-facing bedrooms in the Balmoral Hotel, Gary and Rene Brownlow lay in bed in the darkness, propped up against soft down pillows and gazing out of the open window at the fireworks display as they sipped their glasses of champagne.

'I bet the kids are enjoying all this,' Rene said as she cuddled herself in against her husband's naked body.

'Aye, I bet they are,' Gary replied, too mesmerised by what was going on outside even to look at his wife. 'It was good of Matti to take them.'

Rene sniggered as she traced a finger down the centre of her husband's chest. 'What do kids of that age think when their parents say they're going to bed at nine o'clock in the evening?'

'No idea,' Gary replied, taking a drink from his glass. He turned to her briefly. 'Ye 'aven't told them, 'ave ye?'

'Told them what?' Rene said with a smile.

'About, you know, the birds-and-bees stuff.'

'No, don't worry. I 'aven't said a thing.'

'Good,' Gary said with a nod and continued to look out of the window.

Rene let out a contented sigh. 'America tomorrow.'

'Aye.'

'Are ye looking forward to it?'

'Bloody 'ell!' Gary exclaimed as a blinding incandescence of light filled the room like an atomic explosion. He threw back the duvet and ran over to stand at the window.

'Gary!' Rene screamed in hilarity. 'Get away from there! Ye're stark-bollock naked!'

'Don't be stupid! No one's remotely interested in seeing me tadger,' he said as a second explosion lit up the outline of his lean body. 'They're all looking up at the castle, any road.'

A sudden roar rose up from the crowd in the street and Gary pressed his hands against the windowpane to see if he could work out what had caused it. He looked back towards the castle and immediately saw the reason for the cry.

'My God, Rene!' He turned and beckoned urgently to his wife. 'Come over 'ere quick, lass. You've got to see this.'

'I can see more than enough from 'ere,' Rene replied, leaning on an elbow as she studied with satisfaction her husband's neat rounded buttocks.

'No, come quick! Now!'

Clambering out of bed, Rene grabbed a towel off a chair and wrapped it around her as she walked towards the window.

'Look up there on the battlements of the castle,' he said, putting an arm around her shoulders and guiding her line of sight with an outstretched hand.

Rene followed his direction, and beneath the giant palm-tree spread of shimmering light she saw the tiny figure standing high up on the castle wall like the cross of St Andrew, his legs apart and his arms raised towards the sky as if commanding the multicoloured tempest taking place in the firmament above to cease.

'What d'ye suppose 'e's doing?' Rene asked.

'No idea. It's a powerful sight though.'

'It's a bit creepy, in't it?'

Gary shook his head. 'No, I think it's quite . . . well, biblical, like.'

Rene crossed her arms and looked disappointedly at her husband. ''Ere, I thought we were meant to be doing something during all this?'

Gary glanced round at her and gave his chin a thoughtful rub. 'Aye, ye're right, we were.' He flicked a thumb towards the window. 'D'ye want me to go and ask them to do it over?'

'No, don't bother,' she laughed, her attention suddenly caught by the largest starburst of all, exploding high above the city, illuminating the thousands of people who lined the length of Princes Street and showering its trailing beams down upon them. She put her hands up to her towel and let it fall to the ground. 'But the show's not over yet, you know.'

Gary smiled at her, his eyes twinkling. 'No, it's not, is it!'

And, together, they ran across the room and dived on to the bed.

Epilogue

It was mid-November the following year, when another festival had come and gone, and already the ticket hall at Waverley Station was being decked out for Christmas. A large tinsel-covered tree brightened up the starkness of the seating area while paper streamers were jauntily looped along the full length of the glass-fronted ticket desk. Gavin Mackintosh took off his leather gloves and undid the buttons of his overcoat as he approached one of the two clerks manning the desk, the place being considerably warmer than outside, where a freezing mist hung over the city, settling its thick rimey blanket on the sparsely populated platforms of the station. He purchased a return ticket to London King's Cross, only because it was better value than buying a single, but there was no doubt in his mind that the return leg would never be used. Slipping his credit card back into his wallet, he took out two twenty-pound notes before returning it to the inside pocket of his suit jacket. He turned to the young man who stood behind him carrying a large rucksack on his back, the straps cutting deep into the brown Timberland jacket he wore, along with a woolly hat pulled down over his ears to cover his shaven head.

'There you are, Thomas,' he said, handing the ticket to T.K. before glancing up at the departures monitor on the wall. 'Your train is the ten-thirty from platform one, but it looks to be running about five minutes late.' He looked at the lad. 'Once you're on it, you don't have to think about changing or anything like that. If you have any worries, just ask someone. Do you know what you're doing when you get to London?'

'Aye,' T.K. replied, putting his hand in the pocket of his jacket and pulling out a well-thumbed letter and handing it to Gavin. 'Mr Springer's written it a' doon there.'

Gavin opened the letter and read quickly through it, the offer of a job at Springtime Productions, the plans made for T.K. at Christmas, and the directions he was to give the taxi driver on his arrival in London. Gavin refolded the letter and handed it back to him.

'I see you're going down to Kingston for Christmas.'

T.K. nodded. 'Aye, ah'm spending it wi' Grace.'

'Well, that'll be good for you both. No doubt you'll be looking forward to seeing this great award Leonard's film received at this year's Film Festival.'

'Ah've seen it, 'cos Grace sent me a photo of it. She'd written on the back, "This is yours as well".'

Gavin smiled. 'Nothing could be truer, T.K. Leonard couldn't have made that film without you.' He reached out for T.K.'s hand and pressed the two twenty-pound notes into his palm. 'This is just to wish you on your way.'

T.K. glanced down at his hand, opening it a fraction to see what was there. 'Cheers, Mr Mackintosh,' he said, without lifting his head.

'Best of luck with your future, Thomas,' Gavin said, giving the lad a pat on the shoulder. 'You've served your time, so now you can just put all that behind you.' He laughed briefly. 'And for goodness' sakes, don't go driving any cars unless they belong to you, is that understood?'

T.K. looked up with an embarrassed smirk on his face and glanced across at the woman police constable who stood next to them.

Gavin consulted his wristwatch. 'Well, I must be getting back to the office,' he said, holding a hand out to T.K. 'Keep in touch now.'

'Aye, ah will,' T.K. replied, shaking his hand.

When their goodbyes were finished, Heather Lennox to gave T.K. a brief hug. 'Cheerio, Thomas. Look after yersel'.'

'Aye, and thanks for pickin' us up this mornin'.'

Heather smiled, raising a stern finger to him. 'Well, you mak' sure that's the last time *you* ever get tae ride in a police car again, right?'

She gave a short wave of farewell and turned and walked with Gavin towards the doors of the ticket office, leaving T.K. with a broad grin on his face.

'Well, Constable Lennox,' Gavin said as he stood on the pavement doing up his overcoat, 'it looks like things have turned out all right for that young man.'

Heather rubbed her hands together to stave off the morning chill. 'Aye. He's the lucky one.'

'Very true,' Gavin replied, 'and consequently I doubt very much this will be the last time you and *I* will be meeting up.'

He left her with a smile and crossed over the taxi sweep and, setting a brisk pace, began making his way back up the ramp towards Princes Street.

AN OCEAN APART
Robin Pilcher

When his wife dies of cancer, David's life falls apart. Unable to pick up the pieces, he withdraws from his children, his parents and his work, devoting all efforts to restoring a garden – and, in doing so, cultivates an order and beauty he is denied elsewhere.

Forced into a business trip in America, he hits rock bottom and then, through his friendship with an unhappy young boy, finds the strength to recover and regain a longing for home.

'Perfectly constructed'
The Times

'An ideal read for a lazy winter weekend'
Woman and Home

'A captivating yarn . . . a total tear-jerker'
Woman's Journal

978-0-7515-2389-8

A RISK WORTH TAKING

Robin Pilcher

Dan Porter thought he had his life sorted: a high-flying job in the City, a beautiful wife and three wonderful children. But when his struggling new firm makes him redundant, Dan's life – and his marriage – begins to fall apart.

But then he sees an article in a magazine about Vagabonds, a small company up for sale in Scotland with massive potential for expansion. With his wife away on yet another business trip, Dan casts fate to the wind and heads north. What he discovers isn't at all what he expects, but it's certainly about to change his life . . .

978-0-7515-3090-2

Now you can order superb titles directly from Sphere

☐ An Ocean Apart	Robin Pilcher	£7.99
☐ A Risk Worth Taking	Robin Pilcher	£7.99
☐ Starting Over	Robin Pilcher	£7.99

The prices shown above are correct at time of going to press. However, the publishers reserve the right to increase prices on covers from those previously advertised, without further notice.

———————— sphere ————————

SPHERE
PO Box 121, Kettering, Northants, NN14 4ZQ
Tel: 01832 737525, Fax: 01832 733076
Email: aspenhouse@FSBDial.co.uk

POST AND PACKING:
Payments can be made as follows: cheque, postal order (payable to Sphere), credit card or Maestro Card. Do not send cash or currency.

All UK Orders	**FREE OF CHARGE**
EC & Overseas	25% of order value

Name (BLOCK LETTERS) . . . .

Address . . . .

. . . .

Post/zip code: . . . .

☐ Please keep me in touch with future Sphere publications

☐ I enclose my remittance £ . . . .

☐ I wish to pay by Visa/Mastercard/Eurocard/Maestro

Card Expiry Date ☐☐☐☐   Maestro Issue No. ☐☐